The Immortal Woman

The Immortal Woman

by
Pierre-Alexis Ponson du Terrail

translated, annotated and introduced by
Brian Stableford

A Black Coat Press Book

Visit our website at www.blackcoatpress.com

ISBN 978-1-61227-175-0. First Printing. May 2013. Published by Black Coat Press, an imprint of Hollywood Comics.com, LLC, P.O. Box 17270, Encino, CA 91416. All rights reserved. Except for review purposes, no part of this book may be reproduced or transmitted in any form or by any means, electronic or mechanical, including photocopying, recording, or by any information storage and retrieval system, without permission in writing from the publisher. The stories and characters depicted in this novel are entirely fictional. Printed in the United States of America.

Introduction

La Femme immortelle by Pierre-Alexis Ponson du Terrail, here translated as *The Immortal Woman*, was first published in book form by Librairie Internationale in 1869, having previously appeared as a feuilleton serial in *La Petite Presse*. It was one of numerous works written in between episodes of the long-running adventures of Ponson's most famous hero, Rocambole, whose final exploits ended up in the same periodical. The latter series had moved so far into the realms of the flamboyantly implausible as eventually to occasion the coining of the adjective "Rocambolesque," and, by 1869, when Ponson was nearing the end of his career and his life, the Rocambolesque had become his principal stock-in-trade. *La Femme immortelle* was undoubtedly conceived as a bold exercise of that stripe, but it did not enjoy the same success or retain the same celebrity, and fell into long neglect until a new edition was released in 2006 by Éditions de l'aube, shortly after the text was made available on-line and as a print-on-demand text by Ebooks gratuits.

Ponson was famous by the time he wrote *La Femme immortelle* for his ability to write as many as five daily serials simultaneously, although he boasted that he only wrote in the mornings, preferring to keep his afternoons and evenings free for physical exercise, including fencing, and hanging out in cafés. He also bragged that he marketed his wares by telling editors that if they would commission three episodes of a serial from him, he would spin it out indefinitely if it succeeded in hooking their readers, and bring it to a prompt conclusion if it did not.

It is probably unnecessary to take those boasts too seriously, as Ponson, like many of his characters, might well have been prone to exaggerate more than a little, but they do reflect certain aspects of the reality of his situation. He really did write in a tearing hurry, juggling four or five stories simultaneously, and, whether he always got the work done by lunchtime or not, he certainly did not linger over it. Even though he was presumably using a primitive steel-nibbed pen, little better than a tradition goose-quill, there is nothing so very remarkable about being able to write between five and ten thousand words a day, six days a week, provided that one's mind is sufficiently fertile to feed one's hand with sufficient imaginative fuel, and that one has mastered all the tricks of the serial writer's trade, especially the extensive use of clipped dialogue.

As for the ability to spin out a story indefinitely, change its direction to order or end it at a moment's notice, those were the conditions under which all feuilletonists worked, and whose effects on narrative technique can still be seen, brought to a curious level of perfection, in today's television series, specially "soap operas," whose potentially-eternal spinning out eventually builds up such an enormous burden of contrivance that they inevitably end up in the realms of the absurd. Ponson was one of the writers who invented, pioneered and developed the methods by which that labor is nowadays routinely carried out; although his work in that vein is understandably primitive, it is nevertheless prescient, and his endeavors certainly did not go to waste. Although one can clearly see the influences upon which he drew himself—Alexandre Dumas, Eugène Sue and Paul Féval principal among them—one can also see, by the merest glance at 20th century pulp fiction and popular TV, the echoes of his achievements.

It is not uncommon nowadays, as it was in Ponson's day, for writers producing long-running serials to find, when they have been focusing all their attention for years on spinning them out, that they have reached a level of labyrinthine complication that makes any kind of rational denouement out of the question, thus forcing their writers to reach beyond conventional limits of contrivance. Ponson, like Dumas, Sue and Féval, arrived at that sort of pass over and over again, and coped with it as best he could. If some of the devices he used seem silly or direly disappointing—as the one employed in *La Femme immortelle* will undoubtedly seem to some—they have nevertheless been echoed many times since, and we have surely have not seen the last of them.

The tricks that Ponson used in the attempt to maintain dramatic tension, in all the phases of his narratives, worked well enough when the stories were serialized, but not so well when they were reprinted in book form. The endless series of narrative hooks dangled at the end of every episode still kept the pages turning, but a book always has a back cover literally in sight, even if not until the end of a second or third volume, and it always functions as a seeming measure of the text and as a climatic objective for the reader, although there was no such measure in use or objective in sight for the writer during the bulk of his work of composition. It is not surprising, therefore, that Ponson, who was enormously successful in his own day, could not sustain that appeal and that fame once he was dead and condemned to languish exclusively in book form. Even so, there are still rewards to be obtained from reading him—and perhaps particular rewards for those connoisseurs who understand his mode of production.

La Femme immortelle has a particular appeal to modern readers because of its flirtations with the supernatural, although the text is careful to offer that apparatus in the form of secondary narratives whose reliability is immediately called into question, thus creating an enduring uncertainty as to what exactly might be going on behind the conspiracy that lies immediately behind the superficial narratives. The story was composed in an era when editors of feuilletons were very nervous of the supernatural, because they suspected that a substantial fraction of their readers were averse to it, although they had no objection at all—quite the reverse—to the use of seemingly-supernatural appearances that would ultimately be explained in a supposedly-naturalistic manner. Authors, however, routinely thought differently, often being much more interested in spreading their imaginative wings and always being much more conscious that the supposed boundaries of possibility are utterly irrelevant to the ambitions of storytelling, so Ponson—like Dumas and Féval—often seems to be battling in his narratives between the desire to follow his own inclinations and his consciousness of the narrow-minded demands of his paymasters.

Ponson had always been attracted by the more fanciful aspects of traditional story-telling, and by such relatively recent refashionings and supplementations of those materials as Antoine Galland's *Les Mille-et-une nuits*. In such early botched attempts at feuilleton writing as *Le Castel du diable* (1853; tr. as "The Devil's Manse" in *The Chambrion and Other Stories*), he had exhibited his fondness for sumptuous Gallandesque appearances that might be bizarre impostures, and he recapitulated that kind of insensate ambiguity repeatedly. *La Femme immortelle* is his most sustained exercise in that vein, and might have been his most successful had he been able—or perhaps allowed—to follow it through to the conclusion for which it seemed to be aiming before he decided, or was compelled, to bring the curtain down with an abrupt crash. In the story's early stages, he does a fine job of scene-setting, albeit one that suffers from over-explanation while he was presumably working out the basic schema in his own mind, and in its extended middle phase he shows off his ability to improvise in no uncertain terms—and there are very few *romans feuilletons* that can reasonably be expected to deliver more than that, even when under the control of a master like Dumas.

It is worth noting that *La Femme Immortelle* is slightly constrained by the fact that its episodes are only a thousand words long, at maximum, and often less—standard for *La Petite Press* but somewhat shorter than the typical episodes the Ponson was writing in parallel with it for *La Patrie, Le Petit Journal* and various other periodicals. For that reason, its narrative style is even more streamlined than that of most *romans feuilletons*, and its narrative pace even more exaggerated. It is, therefore, one of the most extreme examples of feuilleton methodology, and that does add a certain zest to its innate charm as an item of proto-pulp fiction.

The historical setting of the story is the Regency that followed the death of Louis XIV—a period that always seemed uniquely Romantic to writers of French popular fiction because of the supposed extreme of its decadence and debauchery. As in many of Ponson's novels of the period, real historical individuals play a significant part in the background schema, and their real situations and fates help to orchestrate the plot, but again, *La Femme immortelle* provides one of the more extreme examples of that stratagem, in giving the Regent himself a significant role to play in the *mise-en-scène*. For that reason, it is worth making a few preliminary observations here with regard to facts that would have been at least vaguely familiar to Ponson's readers, even a century-and-a-half after the events in question.

When the aged "Sun King" Louis XIV died in 1715, his great-grandson and heir apparent, Louis XV, was only five, numerous previous heirs apparent having died one after another. The situation was complicated by the fact that Louis' morganatic wife, the Marquise de Maintenon, had persuaded him to elevate children born outside his marriage to Marie-Thérèse of Spain to the rank of "Princes of the Blood," thus making them potential heirs if the primary bloodline became extinct—as, indeed, it had threatened to do—and also making them rival candidates for the Regency. Although the king had earlier appointed Philippe II, Duc d'Orléans as future Regent, he had also saddled him with Regency Council bound to be deeply divided, and while he was on his deathbed he added a codicil to his will naming Madame de Montespan's son Louis-Auguste de Bourbon, Duc du Maine instead. The Grand-Chambre du Parlement (a Supreme Court rather than a Parliament) set aside the codicil and confirmed the Duc d'Orléans as Regent, but his grip on power was always precarious, and he had very obvious and very jealous rivals, not merely in the Duc du Maine and his brother the Comte de Toulouse, but in Philip IV of Spain, who had been Madame de Maintenon's first choice as Regent, and in favor of whom the famous Cellamare conspiracy was formed in 1718.

From the inevitably liberalized-viewpoint of subsequent history, the Duc d'Orléans did a good job politically, and was therefore ripe for the heroic status that Ponson and some other feuilletonists routinely awarded him—a status not at all compromised, in their view, by his reputation as a *bon viveur*, lover of the arts and enthusiastic debauchee (quite the reverse, in fact). He was assisted in his progressive political maneuvers by his former tutor, Guillaume Dubois, who became his chief minister; it was Dubois who undid the Cellamare conspiracy. Dubois' appointment as a Cardinal was a purely political move, the title being bought from the Vatican in order that Dubois could follow in the hallowed footsteps of Cardinals Richelieu and Mazarin, and his reputation for debauchery matched that of the Duc's.

That the Duc d'Orléans had favorite companions such as those credited to him by Ponson in *La Femme Immortelle* is certain, and Charles de Nocé, Seigneur de Fontenay was one of them, although Ponson seems to have invented some of the others he cited in his various novels. There would certainly have been a member of the Provençal Simiane family at court at the time, but he has left little imprint on history, leaving a useful blank space for Ponson to improvise a character of that name—on that he found sufficiently useful to locate in the background of several novels of the period. Significantly, from the viewpoint of the present story, one of the Simiane family's other titles was that of Marquis d'Esparron, and that presumably prompted the naming of the hero of *La Femme immortelle*.

Various other aspects of the story are also based in reality, including all of its Parisian locations. The Rue de l'Hirondelle still exists, although it had already been cut short when the novel was written by the creation of the Place Saint-Michel in 1855. How well Ponson knew the street is unclear, but it is not improbable that he had visited the Cabaret de Bolée, still widely reputed in 1869 as a literary rendezvous, although he is unlikely to have done so in the days when Charles Baudelaire used to hang out there with Jeanne Duval. The Rue Saint-Honoré remains a landmark, of course, and Ponson could not have known that the corner of the Rue des Bons-Enfants, where he located the Margrave's temporary residence, would one day be one of the principal sites of the Ministry of Culture.

There is no principality in Germany called "Lansbourg-Nassau" (I have retained Ponson's spelling in the text), but he presumable had the district of Landsberg in Saxony in mind, which had been a Margraviate of the Holy Roman Empire in the thirteenth century, as well as the famous aristocratic House of Nassau, which took its name from a castle in the Rhineland. The founder of the House of Nassau was Dudo-Heinrich von Laurenburg, and the similarity of that name to Landsberg might have prompted the fictitious fusion.

Similarly, there is no Norman Château de la Roche-Maubert, although there a Normandy cheese called Brie Le Maubert and there is more than one Roche Maubert known to rock-climbers in other French regions. A more like prompt for the invention of the character in the novel, however, might have been provided by Paris's Place Maubert, where public executions were once carried out, including the burning of the sixteenth-century humanist Étienne Dolet.

"President Boisfleury" is also completely fictitious, although it is possible that Ponson borrowed the name from Eugène Boisfleury, whose doctoral thesis on the authority of French judges in civil cases was submitted to the Faculté de Droit in Rennes in 1851 and subsequently published—a rather unkind appropriation, if so. The surname was associated with other notable Bretons, including one involved in the abortive Vendean revolt of 1832 against Louis-Philippe, which also features in several of Ponson's historical fictions.

A few other references to real people and places included in the text are best left to footnotes.

This translation has been made from the London Library's copy of the Librairie Internationale edition of 1869.

Brian Stableford

PROLOGUE
The Enchanted House

I

Just as midnight chimed, the double doors of the dining-room opened and a chamberlain announced to the few select guests of His Royal Highness, Monseigneur le Duc Philippe d'Orléans, Regent of France, that supper was served.

Madame de Sabran, His Highness's mistress, did the honors. Monsieur de Nocé and Monsieur de Simiane, the two favorites par excellence, had been responsible for the invitations, and Cardinal Dubois had asked them to send one to a relative of his, a provincial gentleman who had not come to Paris for forty years, but whom Monseigneur Gaston d'Orléans, the brother of the late king and father of His Royal Highness, had had in his service.

On seeing that name, the Regent, to whom the list had been submitted, had exclaimed: "But my friend, what do you expect us to do with that sexagenarian?"

"He's very good company," Dubois had replied, "and he knows a great many anecdotes about the old court."

"And you say that he was in my father's service?"

"In the capacity of *valet de chambre*."

"Forty years ago?"

"Perhaps forty-five, Monseigneur."

The Regent had not persisted.

So, at midnight, they sat down at table.

Two places, however, remained empty, and Madame de Sabran observed that there were two settings too many.

"No, my dear," Philippe d'Orléans replied. "One of those places is intended for a relative of Dubois and the other is for the poor Chevalier d'Esparron."

That name, pronounced in a melancholy fashion by the Regent, spread a vague sadness among the guests.

"Poor d'Esparron!" said Madame de Sabran. "Such a cheerful companion; such a witty fellow!"

"That's why, my friends, he shall have his place-setting here for six months, even though we are all resigned to never seeing him again."

"Alas, Monseigneur," said the Cardinal, "Your Royal Highness though it a nice gesture, in the beginning, to maintain the Chevalier's place-setting; it was even thought that he could not fail to return to take his place some day…but after the police report that I received three days ago, I believe that the setting can be removed, and that the only and last service that can be rendered to the Chevalier is that of having a mass said for him."

"Truly, Cardinal," said the Marquise de Sabran, "you believe that the Chevalier is dead?"

"A man of the court does not disappear, Madame," replied Dubois. "He is murdered."

"But by whom?"

"That is what our bloodhounds are trying in vain to discover."

The Regent sighed. "It's four months since d'Esparron left us one evening, and we never saw him again. Where is he? What has become of him? By my ancestor the Béarnais,[1] it's a strange thing, in truth, that a man that I, the regent, honored with my friendship could be made to disappear in the heart of Paris."

"But after all," said Monsieur de Nocé, who had not thus far unclenched his teeth, "what do you know, exactly, Cardinal?"

"What I have already said, and nothing more," Dubois replied.

"Excuse me," Simiane observed, "I've just arrived from the depths of my estates, and I know absolutely nothing."

---

[1] Henri IV.

The door opened at that moment, and the guest invited at Dubois' request appeared on the threshold.

Dubois went to take him by the hand and introduced him to His Highness, saying: "Monsieur le Marquis de la Roche-Maubert."

He was a man of tall stature, but a trifle stooped, his hair entirely white but his face still young, his eyes keen, his lips sensual, with a perfect distinction of manners.

For a man who had been living in the provinces for forty years, in an old manor house in Normandy, the Marquis was certainly neither ridiculous nor ill-at-ease. His clothes were fashionable and he bowed to the ladies had loved a great deal, and perhaps still did.

"Pardieu!" said the Regent. "Your name had slipped my memory, Marquis, but not your person. I recognize you now—you were in my father's household."

"Yes, Monseigneur."

"And it was you that he addressed informally as Maubertin?"

"Precisely, Monseigneur."

The Marquis having taken his place at table, Monsieur de Simiane repeated his question: "Tell me, then, how the Chevalier disappeared?"

"Well," said Dubois, "the Chevalier d'Esparron arrived here one evening in an even more cheerful mood than usual."

"Aha!"

"He showed us a note he had received that morning. The note, perfumed with ambergris and written in a woman's hand, but bearing no signature, invited him to a rendezvous on the edge of the river, in a well-known tavern on the location of the ancient Tour de Nesle. The rendezvous was for two o'clock in the morning."

"And he went?"

"Yes. We were expecting him the following day. We were curious to know whether the lady belonged to the court or the city, and we had even placed a number of wagers on that question. But d'Esparron did not come back the next day, nor in the days that followed. Then Monseigneur became worried and asked me to set in the police in action."

"And the police have found nothing?"

"They have not found d'Esparron, but they were able to follow his tracks for forty-eight hours."

"How?"

"The tavern where the rendezvous was arranged is called the Pomme d'Or; it's kept by a woman nicknamed La Niolle."[2]

"An odd name," observed Madame de Sabran.

"Our bloodhounds went to the Pomme d'Or and threatened La Niolle with imprisonment if she didn't tell them where the Chevalier d'Esparron had gone. La Niolle told them—and all the people in her service supported her story—that the Chevalier had arrived first, and that a woman wearing a black velvet mask over her face but who appeared to be very beautiful arrived a quarter of an hour later in a boat rowed by two mariners, similarly masked, which remained moored beneath the windows of the tavern. The Chevalier and the lady had supped in a private room. At daybreak, the woman in the mask had emerged from the room alone, gave La Niolle and handful of gold and said: 'He's asleep; don't wake him. I'll come back tonight.'"

Dubois paused, and then went on: "When half the day had gone by without the slightest sound being heard in the Chevalier's room, La Niolle finally went in. The Chevalier was asleep, with his shirt open, and La Niolle noticed that he had something like a pinprick on his neck..."

As the Cardinal revealed this detail the Marquis de la Roche-Maubert started abruptly in his chair.

"What's the matter?" his neighbor asked him.

---

[2] Niolle is an argot term for an old hat in poor condition. The Tour de Nesle was the site of an alleged series of murders credited by legend to a fourteenth century queen, the fame of which was renewed by an enormously successful melodrama co-authored by Alexandre Dumas in 1832.

"Oh, nothing...a memory," stammered the old man. "Excuse me."

The incident passed unperceived, however, so interesting was Dubois' story.

"He was sleeping so soundly," the Cardinal continued, "that La Niolle went out on tiptoe. That evening, the lady came back with her two boatmen, masked as she was herself. La Niolle served a second supper, which was prolonged well into the night; then the lady left the tavern, this time taking the Chevalier d'Esparron with her. He was very pale, but his eyes were sparkling like a madman's. The Chevalier took his place beside her in the boat—and since then, has not been seen again.

"I had La Niolle threatened with being put to the question, or being brought before a criminal judge, in order to try to extract a confession, but he hasn't said anything more, for the excellent reason that she doesn't know any more."

"And the woman didn't take off her mask before her or anyone else in the tavern?" asked the Marquis de la Roche-Maubert, with increased emotion.

"No one saw her face."

Then the old gentleman addressed the Regent. "Monseigneur," he said, "forty-five years ago, a similar adventure happened to me."

"But not with the same woman, I imagine?" said the Regent.

"Who knows?" said the old gentleman. "It wouldn't astonish me if it were the same one."

This time, some of the guests protested, while others, including the Regent, looked at the Marquis with an astonishment that might have been translated as: *Are we dealing with a lunatic?*

"I can see that you don't believe me," said the old man, gravely, "but if Monseigneur will permit, I'll tell you a very strange story, and you shall see that the vampire woman is not a fable."

"What! She was a vampire?"

"She nourished herself on my blood for three months."

"Speak, then, Marquis," said the Regent, seized by curiosity.

And the guests hung, breathlessly, on the lips of the old Marquis de la Roche-Maubert.

II

The white hair and grave visage of the Marquis de la Roche-Maubert set aside any thought of a practical joke. It was evident that what he was about to relate was true.

"Monseigneur," he said, still addressing the Regent, "I beg Your Royal Highness, however extraordinary my story might seem, to deign to listen to it until the end."

"Go on, Marquis," said the Regent.

The old man began as follows.

"It was at the end of the summer of the year 1675,[3] and I was then a page to Monseigneur Gaston d'Orléans, Your Highness' father.

"I was nineteen years old, but I was tall and strong and seemed three or four years older.

"One evening, when I was roaming the streets of Paris in search of adventure, I went passed a litter whose curtains were hermetically sealed. I heard a voice that said: 'Oh, what a handsome young gentleman!'

"Intrigued, I tried to look through the curtains, but it was impossible for me to see the person who had made that flattering remark. Then I followed the litter.

"It went along the Rue Saint-Honoré, and I kept a respectful distance, hoping that it would stop at the door of some noble house and that the person inside would emerge—but the litter went along the entire length of the street, went past the charnel-house of Les Innocents into the Place du Châtelet, and thus reached the river-bank.

"It was getting dark; the sun had disappeared some time before and a light mist was covering the river.

---

[3] If the Marquis really is remembering events forty years earlier, this would imply a date for the contemporary story of 1715—the year of Louis XIV's death—while his earlier suggestion that it was "perhaps forty-five" might shift the action as far forward as 1720.

"The porters stopped about a hundred paces from the Pont au Change. Then I heard a shrill sound, which resembled a whistle-blast.

"Immediately, a boat left the opposite bank and came straight across the river. Then the litter's curtains parted, one of the doors opened, and I saw a woman of medium height, with the figure of an enchantress, get down.

"She was masked, but her abundant black hair, the dark eyes sparkling behind the mask and the whiteness of her swan-like neck suggested that he was young and beautiful.

"She leapt briskly into the boat and the two boatmen, who were also masked, immediately pushed off into open water.

"I was standing still, dazzled and fascinated, following the boat with my gaze. It drew away, traveling upstream, and ended to disappearing behind the terrace of Notre-Dame. It was only then that I thought about going back to the Place du Châtelet. The litter and the porters had gone without my paying any heed to them.

"As I was going back along the Rue Saint-Honoré in order to go back to the Palais-Royal, however, a hand fell on my shoulder. I turned round, and thought I recognized one of the two porters.

"'Sire,' he said, 'if you care to tell me your name and the address of your lodgings, I can promise you that you won't regret it.'

"'My name is Paul de la Roche-Maubert,' I replied, a trifle excited, 'and I'm resident at the Palais-Royal, where I'm in the service of His Highness the Duc d'Orléans.'

"The man went away.

"That same evening, an unknown hand deposited a note in my little bedroom, which said: *You are handsome and I love you. Are you discreet? Are you a true gentleman? Burn this letter and be downstream of the Pont au Change at nightfall tomorrow.*

"I could not doubt for an instant that the note had been sent to me by the masked woman. Who has ever hesitated, at nineteen, when he is invited to an amorous rendezvous?

"I was discreet; I did not tell a living soul about my adventure, and awaited the following evening impatiently. At the designated time I was on the bank; a minute afterwards, a boat cleaved through the water and I recognized my two masked boatmen—but the lady was not in the boat.

"I thought that she had sent them to fetch me, and I embarked boldly. Then one of the boatmen said: 'Sire, it's necessary that you allow your eyes to be blindfolded.'

"That mysterious condition completely turned my head. I was doubtless dealing with some great lady jealous of her reputation. It was not a blindfold that was put on me but a kind of hood that descended to my shoulders and plunged me into complete darkness. Then the boat drew away.

"It traveled for a good hour. Where were they taking me? I had no idea—but in order to see the beautiful unknown woman again, I would have gone to the Devil.

"Finally, I felt the boat stop. One of the boatmen put his arm around me, and lifted me on to the bank.

"Then a small, dainty hand took hold of mine, and a woman's voice said: 'Follow me; my mistress is waiting for you.'

"At the same time, I heard the sound of oars falling back into the water, and inferred that the boat was leaving.

"The hand that was drawing me along made me walk for a few minutes on sand, and then I heard the noise of a door opening, and felt the tiles of a corridor beneath my feet.

"A little later, another door opened, and I was enveloped by a warm and perfumed atmosphere. At the same time, the voice of my guide said: 'Now take off the hood you have over your eyes.'

"You can imagine that I didn't have to be asked twice, and I immediately found myself in a pretty boudoir hung with brightly-colored silken fabrics, lit by spherical alabaster lamps, and I saw the masked woman sitting beside me.

"She took my hands and said: 'So your name is Paul? That's a very pretty name, you know.'

"At the same time, her mask came off.

"I uttered a cry of admiration, she was so beautiful.

"How many hours—days, perhaps, went by? Only God and the Devil know—but I had gone to sleep drunk on heady wines, perfumes and sensuality.

"A slight pain woke me up—something like a pin-prick.

"I opened my eyes. I was in the unknown woman's eyes, and she said to me, delightedly: 'I love you—oh, I love you!'

"However, I had raised my hand to the place where I had just felt a pain—which is to say, my neck—and I brought it away stained by a drop of blood.

"As I went pale, she said: 'It's one of my hairpins that has scratched you.'

"The explanation was so natural that no other came to mind.

"The following night, however, I felt the same pain, and, waking up with a start, I felt the lips of my adorable unknown pressed to my neck. I pushed her away, saw blood on my hand again, and uttered a cry.

"Then she knelt down and said to me: 'Forgive me, but your blood is so pink and so fresh that I wanted to taste it.'

"An unspeakable horror took possession of me. I was in love with a vampire!"

With these final words, the Marquis de la Roche-Maubert stopped once again.

The Regent's guests were no longer eating or drinking, and were looking at one another in amazement.

"But this is a fairy tale that you're telling us, Marquis," said the Prince.

"A tale to give one nightmares," added the beautiful Madame de Sabran.

"Madame," the Marquis replied, "all that is nothing, yet. You are about to see where the marvelous and the implausible begin, but I swear to you, nevertheless, that what I am telling you is scrupulously true."

"By all the devils, Monseigneur!" cried Cardinal Dubois, "La Roche Maubert is my relative, but, at the risk of falling out with him, I will say to him that we already have enough trouble believing in Heaven without needing that of adding faith to his nonsense!"

The Marquis looked at Dubois disapprovingly, but the Regent said to him: "Continue, Marquis; we believe you."

And the Marquis resumed the strange story of the masked vampire woman.

III

"All of you who are listening to me now know how harsh and savage the language of passion is. One loves because one loves, and love has no excuse, since it has no remedy.

"I loved a vampire, that was certain—and yet I did not race to my sword, which I had placed on a side-table within arm's reach.

"What happened between her and me. God knows—but when daybreak came, I was at her knees, pleading, weeping and begging, and she was looking at me tenderly.

"'You love me,' she said, 'and yet I inspire you with horror. Of, if you only knew!'

"Then, as I was holding her hands in mine, raising them to my lips with a furious frenzy, she told me the following tale. I listened, my ecstasy increasing as she progressed.

"'I'm nearly a hundred years old, and yet you find me beautiful, and on seeing me, people think that I am no older than twenty. Do you know that I once knew King Henri IV, and was born during his reign? Would you like to know my story? You will then understand why I have drunk a drop of your blood, my darling, whom I adore.

"'I'm Italian by origin. My mother came to France with Queen Marie de Medici, and was the favorite of Maréchal d'Ancre.[4]

---

[4] The Florentine nobleman Concino Concini (1575-1617) came to France with Maria de Medici, who married Henri IV. He married the queen's lady-in-waiting Leonora Dori, nicknamed Galigai (after a Florentine tower), and eventually rose to become a Maréchal de France and Chief Minister, purchasing the Marquisate of Ancre to strengthen his ties with the nation; he introduced Cardinal Richelieu to the political sphere. He was, however, hated by many French noblemen, and Louis XIII was persuaded to have him arrested: he was killed on the Louvre bridge, on the (false) pretext of having resisted the arrest. His wife was imprisoned, condemned to

"'When Leonora Galigai was murdered, my poor mother shared her fate, and I do not believe, my darling, that politics and the fury of the people had anything to do with those terrible murders. No—but my mother had disdained the love of a gentleman, the Chevalier de Flavicourt, and the Chevalier took his revenge. He it was who guided the murderers.

"'I was ten years old then, but I can still see him exciting the wretches and rejoicing in the sight of my poor mother's corpse. As she died, my mother pronounced the words: "You will avenge me!"

"'When I became a woman, I remembered the order my mother had given me."

"'The murderer had changed his name; he had made an immense fortune at court and the King had made him a Duc. My vengeance pursued him in the shadows however. For five years an invisible hand struck him in his fortune, his affections and his amours. One night, the Chevalier, crazed by despair and not knowing whence all those terrible blows came, became disgusted with life and killed himself.

"'Anyone else might have thought her task complete, but the shade of my mother pursued me, and I went to find a necromancer from my homeland who was reputed to be able to summon the dead from the depths of their tombs.

"'The man in question, who lived in a hovel in the Rue de l'Arbre-Sec, accepted the money I offered him, drew magic circles on the floor of his room, and pronounced mysterious words—and I suddenly found myself plunged into profound darkness.

"'Then my mother appeared to me.

"'She was just as I had seen her on the day of her death, clad in a white dress with its breast bloodstained. "I am not avenged," she said to me.

---

death on a trumped-up charge of sorcery, and burned in the Place de Grève in 1617—an obvious inspiration for the protagonist of Ponson's novel, although a character in the novel gives a different account of her death.

"'And as I bowed before that redoubtable and venerate shade, she said to me: "In order for my household gods to be satisfied and for me to enjoy eternal rest, it is necessary that you can strike down the great-grandson of my murderer, who will be born in a hundred years."

"""But Mother," I cried, "in a hundred years, I'll have been dead for a long time."

"""No," she told me, "for I've brought you the secret of living, if not forever, at least until the day when you have carried out my task."

"'I listened to her in amazement. She went on: "Not only will you live, but you shall be as young and beautiful as you are at present, and this is the means of conserving your beauty: every ten years, you will seek out a young and handsome man and you will make love to him; then, at night, when he is asleep, you will prick his neck slightly with a pin and suck a few drops of his blood. You will do it again for ten nights in succession, and you will thus be able, at the price of half a pint of blood taken from a man who adores you, to begin a new life for ten more years."

"""But if I must wait for more than a hundred years to avenge you, Mother, how shall I find the descendant of the murderer, of whom you speak?'

"""When the time comes," she told me, "I will appear to you one night, while you are asleep, and I will tell you what you must do."

"'That is my secret, O my adored darling. I have now been alive for nearly a hundred years, and in that time I have had ten lovers, who have all accepted the sacrifice of nourishing me with their blood for ten nights. I did not love them, however—but you I love, and if you wish, I shall die without having completed my task. I am rich, I have great treasures buried in a corner of the globe that only I know, and which I will indicate to you. Tell me, would you like me to go one living, or would you prefer that I die?'

"And she offered me her breast, saying: 'Strike!'

"You can guess the consequence, can you not? I knelt down, glad that my blood could eternalize her youth.

"What, in any case, were a few drops per night?

"On the tenth day, I woke up prey to an ardent fever and an extreme weakness. I was no longer a man; I was a walking cadaver.

"Where was I? I did not know, at first.

"That mysterious room, full of perfumes, in which she had made love to me, no longer surrounded me with its decorated walls reflecting a voluptuous light. I was lying on a meager bed in a fisherman's hut on the bank of the Seine near Saint-Cloud.

"When I was able to ask where I was and what had happened to me, the coarse folk who surrounded me replied that they had found me in a boat that was adrift, borne by the current, devoid of oarsmen.

"For six months I was suspended between life and death. Finally, life triumphed—but my ardent love had been succeeded by a violent hatred for the vampire, and I had resolved to avenge myself."

"Aha!" said the Regent.

"Monsieur le Marquis," said the beautiful Madame de Sabran, "I shall have nightmares, thanks to you! But I want to know everything..."

"Alas, Madame," the Marquis replied, "I have no intention of hiding anything from you, but what I have just told you is noting by comparison with what I have still to relate."

And the Marquis emptied his glass in a melancholy fashion.

IV

The tone of authority, with which the Marquis de la Roche-Maubert had spoken had ended up overwhelming the guests, and the most skeptical among them were beginning to listen with religious attention.

He continued: "Hatred is merely the consequence of love, when it is not love itself.

"I hated the vampire.

"But why?

"Was it for those few drops of blood, provoked with the aid of a golden pin, which her lips had drunk?

"No.

"I hated her because she had imposed a limit on the harsh and deliriant love with which she drank from me. I hated her because she had expelled me from that mysterious dwelling to which I had been taken and whose inexpressible delights I had known.

"I had gone to sleep in her arms and had woken up in a fisherman's hut.

"I left the latter dwelling with rage in my heart, having sworn an oath to avenge myself at any price.

"But how? I was not only unaware of the name of my mistress, but that of the street to which I had been taken with my eyes blindfolded.

"Having returned to the Palais-Royal after an absence of several days, however, I went to find the Captain of Pages and told him what had happened. He listened to me with his brows furrowed.

"'What you have just told me,' he replied, 'is most extraordinary. However, I'm tempted to believe you...'

"As I looked at him, seeking to divine on what he might be basing his confidence, he continued: 'Do you know Raoul de Berny?'

"'My fellow page?'

"'Yes.'

"'Of course, since he's my intimate friend.'

"'Well, Raoul has disappeared, as you did.'

"'When?'

"'Ten days ago, and, less discreet than you, he related his adventure before going to the rendezvous, and must have been taken away in the same manner as you.'

"'Oh!' I said, keenly curious.

"'That being the case,' the Captain of Pages went on, 'I shall make my report to the King. Give me the most minute details, in writing.'

"I obeyed, and wrote four long pages, in which I recounted everything that had happened to me.

"The police were alerted, and went into action—but found nothing.

"A week went by.

"Suddenly, Raoul reappeared. Like me, he had woken up far from the lady in the mask, for, like me, he had had proofs of his love. Like me, he had a pin-prick in his neck, evident proof that the vampire had drunk his blood in a similar manner. Unlike me, however, he was completely mad.

"Then a form of irresistible jealousy took hold of me.

"My hatred was, at bottom, merely love, and the woman was all the more guilty, in my eyes, because she had deceived me.

"I would have liked to kill Raoul.

"The police embarked on a further search, in which I took a great personal interest, but they found absolutely nothing, while hazard favored me.

"It was a full months since I had left the fisherman's hut, and I had recovered all my strength and energy.

"One evening, I left the Palais-Royal and I was heading toward the Place des Victoires, where Monsieur le Duc de La Feuillade[5] had just had a magnificent town-house built, when I crossed the path of a man who was taking long strides.

---

[5] François de la Feuillade, Vicomte d'Aubusson (1631-1691) demolished the old private mansions in the Place des Victoires in order to make room for an equestrian monument to Louis

"On seeing me, the man attempted to flee, but I ran after him, seized him by the cellar and called for help to two guardsmen who were passing by.

"The man was none other than one of the litter-bearers—the same one who had brought me the unsigned note and arranged the rendezvous on the bank of the Seine, downstream of the Pont au Change.

"The man, arrested on my insistence, was taken to the Châtelet. There, he was interrogated by a criminal judge—but he claimed that I was mistaken, that he was not the man of whom I spoke, and that he had never seen me before.

"Then he was put to torture.

"Without weakness, he endured the torture of the boot; then he allowed the flesh of his arms and legs to be torn with pincers—but his courage failed during the water torture. As his belly swelled up and the executioner was getting ready to pour a further pitcher of walker down his throat, he begged for mercy and promised to reveal all.

"He said that the masked woman who had a young and handsome gentleman taken away from time to time to a mysterious retreat was not a vampire but a woman in search of the philosopher's stone. The proof, he said, was that while she was drinking a few mouthfuls of her lovers' blood, she had herself bled in her turn by a surgeon, who was her accomplice, and that the blood taken from her was used in scientific experiments, the objective of which was to find a means of making gold.

"The litter-bearer even alleged that she had found it."

"Did he give you her address?" asked the Regent.

"Yes, Monseigneur."

"Was she found, then?"

XIV but the rebuilding project was taken over by the royal architect Jules Mansart in 1685. It is not clear how this can be accommodated to the earlier date of 1675 cited by the Marquis.

"She lived in the Rue de l'Hirondelle, which opens into the Rue Gît-le-Coeur, on the other side of the Seine, in a house situated at the back of a garden. That house was raided by the police that same evening."

"And they found her?"

"Yes, Monseigneur. She was busy bringing to the boil a mixture of blood and medicinal drugs in a silver dish, in a room situated under the roof of her house, which was full of retorts, alembics, crucibles and other implements of chemistry and sorcery. Taken to the Châtelet and brought before the great criminal tribunal, she refused to vouchsafe any revelations. She was put to the torture, but in vain. Then she was condemned by the court to be burned alive."

"And did her execution take place?"

"Yes, Monseigneur. I witnessed it. As she was going up on to the pyre she spotted me in the crowd and shouted: 'But you know very well that I'm immortal!'

"An immense remorse took hold of me. At that moment, I would have given all my blood to save her, but it was too late...

"The executioner lit the pyre and the flames swirled around her, projecting light through a dense could of smoke..."

The Marquis de la Roche-Maubert concluded: "And hour later, nothing remained of the vampire than a pile of smoking ashes—and yet the woman was not dead..."

The Marquis covered his face with both hands, and tears were seen flowing through his thin fingers...

V

The Marquis de la Roche-Maubert's audience was by no means composed of credulous individuals. The very existence of God had been debated at that table, and the old provincial, who had just told those roués of the court that a woman burned alive and reduced to ashes was still not dead, bore a striking resemblance in their eyes to a madman or a trickster.

No one protested, however; no one accused the old man of lying. Curiosity—a curiosity mingled with terror—caused all of them to keep quiet.

They were waiting for the story to continue.

"Pardon me," said the Marquis, wiping away his tears, "But at a distance of forty years, I still experience the same emotion."

Then he continued: "The Rue de l'Hirondelle, as you know, is one of the narrowest streets in Paris; to the west, it opens into the Rue Gît-le-Coeur, and to the east, extends all the way to the Pont Saint-Michel.

"It was in the very middle of that street that the house stood in which the masked woman had devoted herself to her strange and mysterious commerce in sorcery. Bizarrely enough, the common people of the quarter had barely heard mention of her. She rarely went out, and almost always at night, in a litter. When the archers of the watch had come to arrest her, there was a considerable commotion among those worthy people, the majority of whom had never set eyes on her.

"On the evening of her execution, however, something very extraordinary occurred in the Rue de l'Hirondelle, as you shall see.

"It was summer, in the middle of June, and the inhabitants of the street spent the evening on their doorsteps, seeking a little fresh air before the time came to cover their fires.

"On the night of the day when the vampire had gone up on to the pyre, therefore, her name was on all lips, and the privileged individuals who had been fortunate enough to get close to the fire were obligingly giving all the rest the details of the execution.

"Now, the witch's house had been sealed on the day of her arrest, and the doors and windows had remained shut ever since. Well, as night was falling, an old woman was seen to turn into the street from the Rue Gît-le-Coeur. In one hand she was carrying a little bag that seemed to be full of ashes, while the other was leading a large black billy-goat on the end of a tether, whose eyes were so bright that they might have been thought to be hot coals.

"The old woman had a evil smile on her thin lips, and when she came into the Rue de l'Hirondelle some people shivered as they looked at her, while others were unable to tolerate the goat's bright eyes—and all of them avoided her with a superstitious terror.

"Where was the woman, whom they were seeing for the first time, going?

"She went as far as the house of the executed woman. There, the astonishment increased when she was seen to take a key out of her pocket and open the door.

"When the door was open the goat went in first; then the old woman followed it—and both remained in the house. Lights were then seen moving behind the windows, and interlaced shadows passing by. Melodious sounds were heard, and everyone ran away, for the rumor went around that Satan had come to take possession of the house and was giving a ball for the notabilities of Hell.

"One man, however, braver and more curious than the rest, resolved to discover exactly what was happening in the house. He was an old soldier known as Pivoine, who would have taken the Devil by the horns if he had ever encountered him. He therefore knocked boldly on the door, which opened to him. At the same moment, the music and dancing stopped and the illuminated windows went dark again.

"Pivoine did not reappear that night. He was not seen again until the following day, at dawn, when the night-watchman found him sitting on a boundary-marker about a hundred meters from the mysterious house His hair had turned white and there as an idiotic smile on his lips. For more than a week he was prey to a fearful delirium, and no one could get anything out of him.

"Finally, he appeared to recover his reason, and recounted that when he had knocked on the door, it had opened. Then a flood of light had dazzled him, and he had felt himself drawn by a mysterious force into a large room in which there were about thirty people. The people were dancing but not talking, and Pivoine had noticed, with terror, that they were as transparent as glass. They were not human beings but phantoms.

"The men each had a little red mark on the neck, like a pin-prick, and Pivoine, who had followed the arguments in the trial of the female vampire, thought that all of them were her victims.

"The mysterious force that had drawn him into the room constrained him to sit down in a corner. Suddenly, a metallic noise, like that of a bell struck by a clapper, resounded. Then the doors at the back of the room opened, and Pivoine saw the old woman come in, leading her goat and carrying her gray canvas bag.

"The dancing stopped.

"The old woman advanced into the middle of the room, opened the bag and poured the contents on to the floor. It was a quantity of ashes.

"'There!' she said. 'All that remains of the woman you have loved.'

"Then she took a staff and began to trace magic circles and bizarre lines all around; then she made a sign to the black goat—and the latter, standing up on its hind feet, began sketching out a kind of saraband around the heap of ashes.

"Then, suddenly, the metallic stroke was heard again and darkness fell.

"When Pivoine, who had fallen over backwards, got up again, rubbed his eyes and tried to understand what had happened, he found that he was sitting on an ottoman next to a beautiful young woman, whom he recognized as the same one that had climbed on to the pyre.

"'I've just been reborn from my ashes,' she said, 'and if you want to make love to me, I'll make you the happiest of men...'"

The Marquis de la Roche-Maubert had reached that point in his story when the sound of a bell reached the ears of the guests.

Now, that bell only rang to announce a late guest—someone who had been invited but was not in the Palais-Royal when everyone sat down at table.

The Regent, looking at Simiane, said to him: "Who are we expecting, then?"

"No one, Monseigneur—unless it's poor d'Esparron."

"He's dead," said Dubois.

"Or married to the female vampire," said someone else.

"Neither dead nor married," replied a sonorous and joyful voice from the threshold of the room—and the guests, increasingly astonished, saw the very same Chevalier d'Esparron whose disappearance had been worrying the court and the city for weeks.

Monsieur de la Roche-Maubert looked at him with an ardent and inquisitive expression.

VI

The appearance of the Chevalier d'Esparron was a surprise even greater than La Roche-Maubert's fantastic nights, all the more so because the young gentleman had not entered in the fashion of ghosts or phantoms, which glide soundlessly over the floor and whose bodies are as transparent as glass.

The Chevalier was definitely a man of flesh and bone, perfectly alive, whose red heels sounded on the parquet and who threw his frost-covered cloak—proof that he had been outdoors—on to an armchair.

The Regent had risen to his feet, and, with the entirely spontaneous bonhomie and affectionate affability characteristic of that Prince, had stepped forward to meet the Chevalier and hug him in his arms.

"Morbleu, Messieurs!" he said. "I swear to you that he's not diaphanous, and that it's no vain shade that I've just embraced." Then, looking at the young man, he said: "But where have you been, my dear boy? We've been mourning you for three months."

"I've been in love, Monseigneur," the Chevalier replied his tone full of enthusiasm. "Or, rather, I still am, for I'm in love with a divine woman."

The Chevalier d'Esparron was a handsome and charming fellow of twenty-eight, of medium height and well-built, with dark eyes, chestnut-brown hair, dazzling teeth, red lips, a slightly hooked nose and small hands and feet, who summarized very well the type of southern good looks that characterize the Frenchified Latin race, of which the Provençal aristocracy is the purest specimen.

The peers of England extract vanity from their Norman origins, but the nobles of Provence, the land that Louis XII described as a "perfumed beggar," say with pride: *we are the sons of Caesar's soldiers, and the Franks were still barbarians feeding on raw meat when we had been the masters, carousers and philosophers of the world for a long time.*

Being handsome, the twenty-eight-year-old d'Esparron had the harmonious and seductive traits that have passed from the Italian and the Roman into the Frenchmen of Provence. Women were crazy about him; men treated him as a friend and held him in high esteem because he was brave.

His disappearance, as one can imagine, had been a great loss the court. His return occasioned an explosion of joy. After Monseigneur Philippe d'Orléans, everyone else wanted to embrace him and press him to their hearts, and if the Regent had not been the most indulgent and philosophical of princes, he might perhaps have frowned on seeing the Marquise de Sabran subject to the general impulse.

Then there was an avalanche of questions.

"Do you still have any blood?" asked some.

"Has the vampire spared you?" asked others.

Only one man did not speak, and held back. That was the old Marquis de la Roche-Maubert.

As for the Chevalier, he seemed bewildered by that avalanche of questions, of which he did not appear to understand a single one. And as the means of regulating that discussion, of brining a bit of order into the conversation, was for him to address himself to the Regent, he said to him: "Monseigneur, I have absolutely no understanding of what people are saying to me, and I implore Your Highness to give me an explanation."

Philippe d'Orléans made a gesture, and silence was reestablished. "My friend," he said then, "We thought you were dead."

"Really?"

"Dubois has even pronounced your funeral oration."

The Chevalier d'Esparron bowed to the cardinal.

"But Monsieur le Marquis de la Roche-Maubert, who is here, has taken care to reassure us."

The Chevalier d'Esparron looked at the Marquis with the indifference that indicates that one is seeing someone for the first time. "Do I have the honor of being known to Monsieur le Marquis?" he asked.

"No," replied the Regent, "but Monsieur le Marquis has affirmed, in accordance with the information supplied by the police, that you were in love with an immortal woman."

The Chevalier uttered one of those fine sighs, full of melancholy, which are the pure gold of passion. "Ah," he said, "I would dearly like the woman I love to be immortal, and that she might share her immortality with me, for a happiness like mine should never come to an end."

"Peste!" said the Regent.

"But damn it," said Dubois, "for a man from whom a pint of blood is drawn every night, you don't seem too exhausted, Chevalier."

"Monseigneur," said the Chevalier, "the enigmas are commencing again. If Your Highness still honors me with the slightest amity, I beg him to put an end to this confusion."

"Let's see if we can," said the Regent. "When did you leave us?"

"Three months ago."

"To go to an amorous rendezvous?"

"Yes, of course."

"At La Niolle's Pomme d'Or?"

"Precisely."

"A masked woman came to join you there?"

"A woman came to join me, Monseigneur, yes—but she was not masked."

"She came in a boat?"

"No, in a carriage."

"You ate supper?"

"Yes, Monseigneur."

"You fell asleep?"

"Not so far as I know. After supper, I climbed into her carriage, and she took me away."

"To the Rue de l'Hirondelle?"

"No, to her château, near Sceaux."

"Were your eyes blindfolded?"

"Why would they be, Monseigneur?"

"Finally, during the night you woke up under the impression of a slight pin-prick and discovered the vampire..."

"What vampire?"

"The woman in question, if you please, drinking your blood."

"Monseigneur," said the Chevalier d'Esparron, I believe I am listening to one of the fairy tales of the architect Monsieur Perrault. And if Your Highness will permit me to tell him about my adventure, he will think, I'm sure, that Monsieur le Cardinal here, and Monsieur le Marquis, whom I do not have the honor of knowing, have taken the liberty of playing a joke on the greatest person in the realm after the King."

The Chevalier was speaking coolly, with a strong tone of sincerity, and the Regent, looking angrily at Dubois, exclaimed: "Friend, here's an enigma that is becoming complicated, but beware! If it's explained to your disadvantage, I'll break my cane over your singular eminence's backside."

The Regent's anger infected Dubois, who showed his fist unceremoniously to the old Marquis de la Roche-Maubert—but the latter was not disconcerted. "Monseigneur," he said to the Regent, "I have hair as white as snow, and my father's son has never lied!"

As the Regent had said, the enigma was becoming complicated.

VII

When women are not playing the role of Discord, they always want to play that of Conciliation. It was Madame de Sabran who reestablished peace, by saying to the Chevalier: "Continue, then, my dear d'Esparron; we're all ears."

The Chevalier resumed: "There is nothing mysterious about the woman I love. She is young, beautiful and rich. She's a widow, and we're going to be married. Perhaps she has steeped her lips from time to time in a glass of Aï wine, but she has never drunk human blood."

"So," said the Regent, "you didn't fall asleep in La Niolle's establishment?"

"No, Monsieur."

"Why, then, did La Niolle, when put to the question, say the opposite?"

"That I don't know."

"And why, for three months, haven't you given us any sign of life?"

"Because the amorous lose their heads; because three months have passed like three days; because I haven't even thought about leaving her for an hour, and it was not until this morning that I finally remembered that people were eating supper every night at the Palais-Royal and that no one had seen me there for three months."

"In truth," said the Regent, "I can only see one way of getting out of this."

"What's that, Monseigneur?"

"For the Marquis to tell you what he was telling us just now."

"Gladly," said the Marquis. And in a tone no less laden with sincerity, he repeated the same tale that the Regent's guests had already heard.

Several times, the Chevalier started laughing and murmured: "Absurd! Absurd!"

Then, when the Marquis had finished, Monsieur d'Esparron replied: "Monsieur le Marquis, I don't mind at all that you're superstitious, and I'll even go further and grant that your story is true in every detail. But what does it prove? One thing: that the police report given to Monsieur le Cardinal Dubois is the departure-point of your error. You have been told that I was taken away in a boat by a masked woman, and you concluded that the woman was the vampire who was the apple of your eye. That's quite natural, and I don't hold it against you, but..." Here the Chevalier paused momentarily and looked at the cardinal. Then he continued: "But Monsieur the Cardinal, have you thought that your police might have made a mistake?"

"I don't believe so," said Dubois, angrily.

"Or that Your Eminence might have been misled by rogues who wanted to obtain favor and an advantage from the tale they told you?"

"But Le Niolle was put to torture," said the Regent.

"La Niolle is a rogue who reached an understanding with the tricksters."

That last reply had a certain logic, which struck Dubois. After all, he only knew what the police had told him. "Thunder!" he said, thumping the table. "I'll send someone to fetch La Niolle."

"That's how it's necessary to begin," said the Regent. "And while we're waiting for her to come, let's eat."

The Chevalier d'Esparron sat down at the table, and found himself beside the Marquis. The latter showed perfect courtesy toward him throughout the meal. He continually filled his glass, and the Chevalier, who was a hearty companion, reckoned with it every time.

In the meantime, a captain of the guard was sent to the Pomme d'Or with orders to bring La Niolle back, whether she liked it or not.

An hour went by. The captain of the guard came back. "La Niolle's here," he said.

"Where is she?"

"In the antechamber."

"Send her in," said the Regent.

41

"Oh yes, send her in!" stammered the Chevalier, in a tipsy voice—and so saying, he slumped back in his chair.

"Shh!" said the Marquis, immediately—and the old man pointed to the Chevalier, who had just closed his eyes. "He's gone to sleep," he whispered."

"He's drunk," said the Regent.

"And I've hastened his drunkenness," added the Marquis. At the same time, he placed his left hand on the table, the ring-finger of which was ornamented by a large ring. "Just now," he said, "I let three grains of opium enclosed in the bezel of this ring fall into his glass."

The Regent made a gesture of surprise.

"He's asleep," the old man went on, in a tone of authority that impressed everyone. "You can bring in La Niolle later, Monseigneur."

"Why not now?"

"Because I don't need her to prove to you that I've told the truth."

"How?"

"The Chevalier is in love with the vampire woman."

"Oh, of course!"

"And I'll prove it here and now."

The Marquis stood up then; he pushed back the armchair in which the Chevalier d'Esparron was asleep. Then, to everyone's great amazement, he set about untying the young man's lace collar.

Suddenly, the guests uttered a cry.

The Chevalier had an enormous scar on his neck, still bloody—something like a large puncture-wound—and the Marquis said, triumphantly: "There are the traces of the vampire. Do you doubt me now?"

VIII

It is difficult to describe the amazement of the Regent's guests at the sight of the scar that the Chevalier d'Esparron bore on his neck, and which the Marquis de la Roche-Maubert had just uncovered.

So the Marquis had told the truth! There was a female vampire, a frightful ghoul who nourished herself on human blood! And the Chevalier d'Esparron was in love with that woman, and was her victim and accomplice, since he had denied everything from the start.

The old Marquis was triumphant—but that triumph was not sufficient for him yet; it was not complete, in his view. Addressing himself to the Regent, who did not believe in anything, he said: "Monseigneur, if the woman who has bitten him on the neck really is the same one who nourished herself on my blood, we shall know it very soon."

"How?" said the Regent.

"While unfastening the Chevalier's collar," Monsieur de la Roche-Maubert went on, "my hand encountered a hard object on his breast which I believe to be a medallion."

"Her portrait?"

"Yes, the portrait of the vampire."

"Let's see it," said the Regent.

The Marquis shook his head. "Not yet," he said.

"Why not?"

"First, I would like Your Highness to grant me a word in private."

"Very well," said the Prince. Addressing Madame de Sabran, he said: "The coffee has been served in your boudoir, has it not. Marquise? Would you care to take these gentlemen there."

The Marquise left the table, and everyone followed her. No one remained in the supper-room except the Regent, the old gentleman and the sleeping Chevalier d'Esparron.

"Let's have a look at the medallion," said the Regent.

Monsieur de la Roche-Maubert slipped his fleshless hand between d'Esparron's shirt and breast, and pulled out a medallion suspended around his neck by a silken cord. The Marquis was trembling, and he turned his head away, as if he feared that his gaze might be burned by contact with the portrait.

"Look, Monseigneur," he said.

The Regent took possession of it, approached a candelabrum with three candles—and a cry of admiration escaped him. "Oh, Marquis!" he said. "If this ravishing young woman is a ghoul, I'll consent to be vampirized myself."

Indeed, the Regent had before his eyes a miniature representing a blonde woman who appeared to be about nineteen or twenty years of age, and whose beauty had something ingenuous and veritable celestial about it. It was the head of an angel on a virgin body.

The Regent's exclamation forced the Marquis to look in his turn. "Yes," he said, with a somber energy, "it's really her!"

"Get away!"

"On my honor, Monseigneur."

"But can't you see that she's a child."

"Since she's immortal, and doesn't age."

The Regent looked alternately at the sleeping Chevalier, whose parted lips were smiling, the old Marquis de la Roche-Maubert, and the medallion.

The woman's portrait and the young man with the charming face formed a singular contrast with the old man, whose forehead had suddenly darkened, whose lips were imperceptible flecked by foam, and whose eyes had a wild gleam.

Without the little red mark that the Chevalier had on his neck, the Regent would not have hesitated to believe that the old Marquis was mad.

In fact, since the other guests had left, the Marquis was no longer the same man. His former calmness had given way to an almost furious agitation, and he suddenly exclaimed: "Oh, Monseigneur, Monseigneur, what use are the white hair and frosts of age? It was sufficient for me to see that portrait for my heart to wake up and beat as it did at twenty!"

"What!" said the Regent, amazed. "Even admitting that this woman is the one you know forty years ago, do you love her still?"

"Yes, Monsieur."

"But if she's a ghoul?"

"So be it."

"A vampire—it's you who said it."

"What does it matter?"

"Then why hold d'Esparron to account for having obeyed the same sentiment of admiration?" said the Regent, with a hint of irony.

The Marquis made no reply, but he looked at the sleeping young man with an expression of furious jealousy.

Philippe d'Orléans had suddenly become serious, and his face had taken on a severe aspect. "Marquis," he said, "everything you've just told me has interested me to the highest degree, but at the same time, as I have a keen affection for the Chevalier d'Esparron, whom you have put to sleep a trifle treacherously, you will permit me to ask you to swear an oath."

"What oath, Monseigneur?"

"That you will not breathe a word of this to a living soul before I have enlightened myself with regard to this tenebrous affair."

"But Monseigneur," said the Marquis, "all the people who were here jut now..."

"I'm sure of their discretion. Where are you staying, Marquis?"

"At the Croix-Jaune in the Rue des Nonnains d'Hyères, Monseigneur."

"Well then, go home, Marquis, and don't budge until I give you the word." So saying, the Regent lifted up a tapestry masking a door, which he opened. The door led to a hidden stairway. "You'll find the inner courtyard at the end," he said. "Go, Marquis, and await my orders."

The old gentleman bowed and left without saying a word.

Then the Regent put the medallion around the sleeping Chevalier's neck and refastened the collar, taking care to retie the silken ribbon sown over it. Then he pickled up the hand-bell that was on the table and shook it. In response to the sound the guests came back in, seemingly a trifle astonished to find that the Marquis had disappeared.

"My friends," said the Regent, "I believe that Monsieur de la Roche-Maubert is not entirely in his right mind."

"I think so too," said Cardinal Dubois.

"But after all," the Regent continued, "this is certainly an adventure that has its merits from the viewpoint of strangeness, and I think that it would be impolite not to show our appreciation of it. How many are we here?"

"Eleven," said Dubois, "including the Chevalier."

"Let's stick at ten," Philippe d'Orléans continued. "Well, we're going to swear an oath."

Everyone waited for the Regent to explain.

"An oath to say nothing to d'Esparron about what we have seen," the Prince concluded.

"Why?" asked the Cardinal.

"Because, my friend, if d'Esparron permits himself to love a ghoul, he must have his reasons."

"Good!"

"And from now on, he'll take precautions to deflect all our investigations," the Regent continued. "Now, we amuse ourselves every day, you must agree, and perhaps this is the first serious occasion that has presented itself. Since Esparron has come back, it's because he wants to be one of us again, while conserving his amours. If he's suspicious, we won't discover anything, and I want to know..."

"Me too," murmured the Marquise de Sabran—curious, like all women.

And everyone swore the oath demanded by Monseigneur Philippe d'Orléans.

Then the latter added: "Now let's allow him to sleep." And at a sign from the Regent, Simiane and Monsieur de Nocé put their arms around the Chevalier and carried him to an ottoman, where they laid him down at full length.

The Chevalier was still asleep.

IX

The Chevalier d'Esparron's slumber did not last long. Either because the narcotic employed by the old Marquis de la Roche-Maubert was almost inoffensive, or because the calm and the silence suddenly succeeding the noisy laughter and conversations surrounding him had a direct effect on his nervous system, the Chevalier had not been alone for an hour when he woke up.

He did not wake up in the fashion of someone who has had a nightmare, rubbing his eyes, wondering where he was, his thoughts only disengaging themselves with difficult from the fog of sleep, slowly and gradually recovering his lucidity, but all at once, instantaneously, without astonishment or fatigue.

The Regent and his guests had gone, but the table, still set, bore the remains of the supper. Spherical frosted-glass lamps spread a gentle and mysterious light around. A profound silence reigned.

To begin with, the Chevalier went toward the table, took a glass and poured himself a drink. Then he went to look at the clock on the mantelpiece.

It was three o'clock in the morning.

A smile, the significance of which it would have been hard, if not impossible, to determine then glided over his lips. "I have time," he murmured.

He went to a mirror and cast a glance at his costume. The knots of his ribbons were a trifle crumpled, but that was not what he was checking. What he was examining with scrupulous attention was his collar and the sky-blue ribbon worn outside it by way of a cravat.

"Ah!" he said.

It was evident to him that the knot had been undone—for it was not tied in the same manner—and that his collar had been opened…and that the little puncture-wound he had on his neck had certainly been shown o the Regent and his guests.

Another smile played upon his lips. "Perfect!" he said, between his teeth. And he looked for the cloak that he had thrown on to a chair when he arrived. He readjusted the belt of the small court épée that he was wearing tidied his hair slightly—for he wore it long and unpowdered—put his tricorn hat under his arm and murmured again: "Now let's go. Unless there have been great changes at the Palais-Royal and all the doors are now locked at night instead of being left discreetly open for all the lovers who need a little fresh air. I'll be in the Rue Saint-Honoré in ten minutes, and they'll have lost track of me again."

Having said that, the Chevalier d'Esparron took a step toward the same door by means of which the Regent had enabled the Marquis to leave—but a gesture of impatience escaped him, for the door was locked.

"Fortunately," he said then, "everyone must be asleep or in the arms of beauty, and no one's thinking about me any longer." He headed for another door, which opened into an antechamber leading to a large staircase. That door was not locked, and it yielded to the Chevalier's hand.

As he was about to cross the threshold, however, he found himself face to face with Monseigneur Philippe d'Orléans in person.

"Well," said the Regent, "did you sleep well, my boy?" Then, instead of stepping aside to let the Chevalier pass, he pushed him gently back into the supper-room. "Where the Devil are you going like that, my friend?"

"But Monseigneur..."

"You might be thinking," said the Regent, amicably, "that as no one has seen you for three months, it's quite possible that your lodgings have been let, and if you're going out to look..."

"Not exactly, Monseigneur."

"Where are you going, then?"

"Why," said d'Esparron naively, "I'm going home."

"Where is that?"

"To the house of the woman I love."

"Oh yes—the Rue de l'Hirondelle."

The Chevalier started laughing. "Your Highness believes that, it seems."

"To the Rue de l'Hirondelle?"

"Yes, and the vampire." And the Chevalier continued laughing.

This time, a furrow formed in Philippe d'Orléans' broad forehead. He directed a clear, cold, almost severe gaze at the young man. "Chevalier," he said, "Would you please have a chat with me for a moment?"

"Monseigneur..." said the young man, bowing

"Listen to me," the Regent went on. "You know that I've always treated you with amity."

"Oh, Monseigneur, your generosity heaps me with pride and confusion."

"Do I then, have a right, if any such right exists, to your frankness?"

"Yes, certainly, Monseigneur, and Your Highness has only to give me a sign for me to obey."

"Good," said the Regent. "This evening, you told us that you were in love with a woman who wanted to marry you."

"Yes, Monseigneur."

"And when the Marquis de la Roche-Maubert affirmed that the woman in question was a witch, an abominable creature, you protested very loudly."

"It's the truth, Monseigneur."

"Chevalier," said the Regent severely, "have you not lied to someone tonight?"

"Yes, Monseigneur."

"And to whom have you lied?"

"To the Marquis de la Roche-Maubert."

The Regent made a gesture of impatience. "To him alone?" he said.

"Yes, Monseigneur."

"And not to me?"

"I have not lied to Your Highness."

"Be careful, Chevalier!"

"Oh, I'm not afraid, Monseigneur," the young man said, calmly. And as the Regent's face became increasingly severe, a smiled slid over d'Esparron's lips. "While I was asleep, Monseigneur," he said, "or, rather, while I was feigning sleep, for I heard everything..."

The Regent made a new gesture of surprise.

"My collar was opened," the Chevalier continued, "and the triumphant Marquis showed you the pin-prick that I have on my neck." D'Esparron opened his collar for a second time, and the puncture-mark reappeared to the Regent.

"You can see," the latter cried, "that you lied!"

"Not to you, Monseigneur."

"To whom then?"

"I repeat to Your Highness that I lied to the Marquis de la Roche-Maubert."

This time, the Regent looked at the Chevalier d'Esparron with a mixture of amazement and anger. "I believe you're mocking me!" he said.

"No, Monsieur, and if Your Highness will deign to listen to me..."

"Speak!" said the Regent, who saw the enigma becoming even more complicated.

X

Still calm and impassive, the Chevalier d'Esparron took a small instrument from his waistcoat pocket, which he showed to Philippe d'Orléans, and which the latter recognized as a surgeon's lancet.

"What are you going to do with that?" said the Prince.

"Prove to Your Highness that I lied to the Marquis de la Roche-Maubert."

"How?"

"Your Highness is convinced, are you not, that I have the bite of a vampire on my neck?"

"Indeed!"

"Who has been drinking my blood for three months,"

"Probably."

D'Esparron went to stand in front of a mirror, opened the lancet, put it to his neck and caused a drop of blood to emerge, which he wiped away with his finger. Then he returned to the Regent.

"Now, Monseigneur," he said, "let Your Highness decide which of these two marks is the first."

Indeed, the one that had just been made with the lancet was beside the other, and both had the same depth, the same form and the same appearance.

The Regent let out an exclamation.

"You can see, Monseigneur," said the Chevalier, who had lost nothing of his calmness, "that I simply had in my pocket, in the form of this little instrument, the vampire whose extraordinary story Monsieur de la Roche-Maubert has told you."

Philippe d'Orléans shook his head. "I understand less and less," he said.

"It is, however, simple, Monseigneur."

"Ah! Truly?"

"It was me who made the first puncture, as I have just made the second, in the presence of Your Highness."

"But...with what objective?" The Regent was still looking at d'Esparron with a severe expression.

"Monseigneur," the latter replied, "I knew that the Marquis de la Roche-Maubert would be present at Your Royal Highness' supper."

"And that is why...?"

"That is why I came, Monseigneur."

The Chevalier's tone had suddenly become solemn, and the Regent was impressed. "You knew the Marquis, then?"

"Yes, Monseigneur."

"But..."

"But he was seeing me for the first time. However..." The Chevalier d'Esparron paused again. Then he pulled out the medallion that the Regent had already examined. "However, this woman knew him," he concluded.

"So you agree that what he said was true?"

"Yes and no, Monseigneur."

The Regent shook his head again. "Explain yourself, Chevalier," he said.

"Monseigneur," d'Esparron replied, "the woman I love is twenty years old."

"But the Marquis recognized her.. "

"Possibly."

"And it was really her that made love to him, bit him in the neck and drank his blood more than forty years ago?"

"Yes and no, Monseigneur."

"You're talking like the ancient sphinx, Chevalier."

"That's because I can't explain any further, Monseigneur."

"Even if I demand it?"

An expression of melancholy sadness spread over the Chevalier's face. "Monseigneur," he said, "I'm a poor youth from Provence, who has only become something by virtue of the benevolence and noble protection of Your Highness, but I will have the courage to repeat: *I can't explain any further today.*"

"Ah! Today?"

"Yes, Monseigneur."

"But…tomorrow…?"

"Tomorrow, perhaps," the Chevalier went on, "if I appeal to the justice of the Regent of France, Your Highness will not refuse it to me."

"Someone owes you justice, then?"

"Not me, Monsieur."

"Who, then?"

"The woman whose portrait Your Highness has seen."

"Against whom?"

"Against an old man of respectable appearance, with hair as white as snow, Monseigneur."

"The Marquis de la Roche-Maubert?"

"Yes, Monseigneur."

"Damn," said the Regent. "But do you know, Chevalier…?"

"What?"

"That he's a relative of Dubois."

"I knew that, Monseigneur."

"And if you cause me to quarrel with my friend, you'll cause me a great deal of trouble."

"So, Monseigneur, I shall not ask Your Highness to strike him…"

"Ah!"

"But to refrain from punishing those who do strike him."

"But Chevalier…"

"Monseigneur," said the young man, then, "Your Highness has more than once, in my company and that of Messieurs Simiane and de Nocé, roamed the streets of Paris by night with your face hidden by your cloak."

"Yes, certainly, Chevalier," said the Regent, "and we have often amused ourselves."

"Well, Monseigneur, what if I were to ask Your Highness to take your cloak…?"

"Good!"

"To raise a flap over his face, and to follow me."

"Where will you take me?"

"During my pretended sleep, did not Your Highness say that you wanted, at any price, to know where I was going"

"Yes."

"Well, Your Highness shall know."

"And I shall see the vampire...pardon me...the woman you love?"

"Yes, Monseigneur."

"Good!" said the Regent. "That suits me. The Marquise has a headache tonight; she will dispense with my visit. Come this way."

The Regent, suddenly entering into the boyish joy, went into the next room, where he picked up his épée and cloak. "Come on," he said to the Chevalier, taking the key to the hidden door from his pocket.

Ten minutes later, the Chevalier d'Esparron was leading Philippe d'Orléans along the Rue Saint-Honoré to the Place du Châtelet. Then he took him down to the river bank, downstream of the Pont au Change.

Putting two fingers in his mouth, he whistled.

Immediately, a boat hidden under one of the arches of the bridge came forward rapidly. Two men were rowing it; both men were masked.

"You see!" exclaimed the Regent. "They're the two boatmen of whom the Marquis spoke."

"Possibly," d'Esparron replied. "But of Your Highness still wants to follow me, he shall see many others."

"I'd follow you to the Devil," replied Philippe d'Orléans. And he leapt nimbly into the boat.

XI

It required at the adventurous spirit of Monseigneur Philippe d'Orléans, Regent of France, for him to embark thus, at the mercy of two masked men, in the company of a single gentleman—whom he had honored with his friendship, it is true, but whom he had not seen for three months and might easily have gone over to the enemy.

Now, the Regent's enemy was, first of all, Spain; then the Duc and Duchesse du Maine, who were conspiring night and day; and then all the other legitimate or legitimated princes who had also dreamed of the Regency.

The Cellamare conspiracy, thwarted at the last moment, was of recent date, and it might easily have been the case that the Chevalier d'Esparron was audacious enough to want to abduct the Duc d'Orléans.

That idea occurred to the latter, who said: "Tell me, d'Esparron, at least, that you haven't been received into the Ordre de la Mouche à Miel?"[6]

"Of whom the Duchesse du Maine is the grand-mistress?"

---

[6] L'Ordre de la Mouche à Miel [The Order of the Honey-Bee] was a mock-chivalric order created by the Duchesse du Maine in 1703, the petite duchesse having long preferred that nickname to the one attributed to her by her enemies ("la poupée du sang" [the bloody doll]). Although the Order was a joke, a social and literary *salon*—its oaths referred to the Duchesse's Château de Sceaux as "an enchanted castle" and demanded a fervent commitment to dancing—it inevitably became a focal point of opposition to the Duc d'Orléans during the Regency; its membership included numerous important intellectuals, including, Voltaire, d'Alembert, Montesquieu and Fontenelle. The Duchesse was the former Mademoiselle d'Enghien, the grand-daughter of "the Great Condé," and was universally reckoned to be much more forceful and ambitious than her ineffectual husband.

"Precisely."

"No, Monseigneur."

"You have no Spanish gold in your pocket?"

"No, Monseigneur."

"You're still devoted to me, then?"

"All my blood is at Your Highness' disposal."

The frankness of the Chevalier's tone caused the suspicion that had momentarily crossed Philipp d'Orléans' mind to vanish."

The Prince and the Chevalier sat down at the rear of the boat. The two mariners began rowing vigorously.

"To *her* house!"

"Indeed! Where are you taking me?" asked the Regent. Is it far?"

"No, Monseigneur—but you will be the first man who has entered it with open eyes."

"Bah!"

"My own eyes were blindfolded."

"You can see that the old Marquis de la Roche-Maubert's stories had some truth in them."

"Yes and no, Monseigneur."

"A singular reply!"

"Monseigneur," replied the Chevalier d'Esparron, gravely, "if you tell me that the woman of whom I speak surrounds herself with mystery, marvels, and the apparatus of magic and witchcraft, I shall reply to Your Highness that he is right."

"Ah! You agree?"

"But if Your Highness believed the Marquis de la Roche-Maubert when he told you that the woman in question is a ghoul and that she drinks human blood, Your Highness is mistaken."

"But after all, my fine friend," the Regent said, "the Marquis was bled while in his youth."

"Pooh!" said d'Esparron.

"And you have on your neck..."

The young Provençal gentleman was bold enough to interrupt to Regent. "Monseigneur," he said, "I am bound by an oath; I cannot say anything to Your Highness, but *she*—the woman we are going to see—will tell you everything, and then Your Highness will understand a great many things that are incomprehensible at present, but will become as clear and limpid as crystal."

The Regent was too fond of the marvelous not to accept that response for the time being. "So be it," he said. "I'll wait."

"Monseigneur," d'Esparron went on, "she and I have such a blind faith in Your Highness that I have not even asked you for an oath."

"What oath?"

"That of not revealing to anyone the route that we are taking at present."

"In order that it should not worry you, I swear that I shall not say anything about it, my dear boy."

The boat was, in fact, making rapid progress—but it was not assisted by the current; on the contrary, it was heading upstream, and, after having passed under the Pont au Change it was now going alongside the Île de la Cité, leaving the towers of Notre-Dame behind on the right.

The night was foggy, however; there were neither stars nor a moon in the sky, and a lantern placed in the bow of the boat enclosed the Regent in a circle of light beyond which all was darkness—which did not permit him to see exactly what route he was following.

The boat went around the eastern extremity of the Cité—"the terrace," as it is called—in that fashion and went into the smaller arm of the Seine. By means of a skillful and rapid maneuver, the boatmen came about so suddenly that the Regent did not notice it. Instead of continuing upstream, the boat was now traveling downstream with vertiginous rapidity. The edifices of the Cité, the gigantic towers of Notre-Dame were now on the left, but the Regent did not take account of the change of direction.

D'Esparron went on: "Until now, Monseigneur, our voyage has been very similar, has it not, to that of the old Marquis de la Roche-Maubert?"

"Indeed," said the Regent. "The mysterious boat, the masked boatmen—it's all here."

"But Your Highness will soon notice a slight difference."

"Ah!"

"Previously, the boatmen leapt on to the bank, moored their boat, the person they were bringing with blindfolded eyes set foot on the shore, and was taken by the hand..."

"And that won't happen this time?"

"No, Monseigneur."

"What will happen, then?"

"Your Highness will arrive in the house in the boat."

"How's that?"

"Your Highness will see..."

The boat had passed under the Pont Saint-Michel, skirted the Place Maubert and was now heading toward the Pont Neuf.

Suddenly, it came close to a smoke-blackened house whose foundations plunged into the water. Then one of the boatmen stood up, and took hold of a chain that was hanging on the wall; the boat stopped instantly. At the same time, the lantern went out.

Then it seemed to the Regent that a whirlpool was hollowed out beneath him; the boat turned round, plunged, the sky disappeared—and Monseigneur Philippe d'Orléans felt himself drawn with vertiginous rapidity into a subterranean channel through opaque darkness.

"Ah! Is it to Hell that you're leading me?" exclaimed the Regent.

"Perhaps," replied d'Esparron, laughing.

And the boat continued its strange voyage through the unknown abyss that had just opened up in front of it.

XII

The boat continued to whirl, and was carried away with a vertiginous speed. Darkness enveloped the Regent, and, brave as he was, he might have been genuinely fearful if the Chevalier d'Esparron had not taken care to explain to him how that fantastic voyage was being effected.

"Have no fear, Monseigneur," he said, taking the Regent by the hand. "We're in a channel hollowed out beneath the river, which ends at the house where we're going. We'll stop soon, for the channel will make an abrupt turn and then return to the river."

"But will we at least be able to see?" asked the Regent.

"Soon."

"Why was the lantern extinguished?"

"It's the air-current that blew it out, Monseigneur." As he said that, the boat received a sudden shock. "Keep hold of my hand, Monseigneur," the Chevalier continued.

The shock had been so violent that the Regent, although seated, had nearly been thrown out of the boat—but when equilibrium was restored, the Chevalier added: "Lift your leg slightly, Monseigneur. We're at the first step of a staircase."

Indeed, the Regent, stepping over the side, suddenly felt firm ground beneath his foot. D'Esparron was still holding him by the hand.

The Regent climbed some thirty steps, still drawn by the Chevalier. Then the latter halted.

The Prince heard the sound of a key in a lock; then, a door having suddenly opened, the darkness enveloping him was suddenly succeeded by a bright light, and Monseigneur Philippe d'Orléans found himself on the threshold of a long corridor, at the end of which a lamp was shining.

"Monseigneur," said the Chevalier, "We're on the threshold of the enchanted house."

"*Enchanted* is the right word," the Regent replied, "for one gets into it in a singular fashion."

A smile came to d'Esparron's lips. "Your Highness has seen nothing yet," he said.

At the end of the corridor there was a second door. The Chevalier did not open it, as he had the first, but knocked on it with the hilt of his épée.

The door opened, and this time, the Regent stepped back, dazzled, so sparkling was the beam of light that struck his face.

Oriental tales only give an imperfect idea of the place in which Monseigneur Philippe d'Orléans, Regent of France, then found himself.

There was no drawing-room in the Palais-Royal, nor at Versailles, even on the day of a gala, that could rival for luxury, elegance and originality the boudoir into which the Chevalier introduced the Prince.

At first glance, one might have thought it a virgin forest of the New World. The walls disappeared behind flowers and foliage, and lamps with alabaster globes, suspended from the ceiling at intervals imitated the light of the sun filtered through great trees in a woodland clearing, closely enough to be mistaken for it. The air as laden with mysterious perfumes; unknown flowers overflowed vast boxes; there was fine soft sand underfoot by way of a carpet.

Instead of chairs one saw hammocks suspended from the artificial forest, every tree of which bore marvelous fruits.

"Monseigneur," said the Chevalier, smiling, "we're no longer in Paris; we're in India."

"Are you sure that we're not dreaming, and that we haven't slipped under the table after drinking too much?" said Philippe d'Orléans.

"Your Highness is wide awake," said the Chevalier.

"And what do you call this room?"

"It's the Nymphs' Grotto, Monseigneur."

"Where are the Nymphs?"

"Here's one—look."

The Regent turned round and took another step backwards. The foliage had just parted, and an ideal, celestial creature appeared to the Prince's fascinated gaze.

It was the woman depicted in the medallion, but a hundred times more beautiful, as if the painter had found himself impotent in the presence of such a model.

Even more bizarre, however, was the fact that, although there were the same features and the same facial expression, the woman of the medallion had blonde hair, while this one had hair as black as a raven's wing.[7]

Her costume justified the Chevalier's words: *we're no longer in Paris, we're in India.*

Indeed, she was clad in an Asiatic robe in harmonious colors, shod in little slippers devoid of heels; her beautiful bare arms were laden with bracelets and she had a triple necklace of pearls as large as hazelnuts, each of which represented, beyond a doubt, the life of a poor Indian diver.

The Regent contemplated her, and wondered whether he might be in the presence of the daughter of some Nabob or the King of Bengal.

She came toward him, however, and made a curtsey as correct as any lady of the court could have done, and said to the Prince, smiling: "Thank you for coming, Monseigneur. The Chevalier promised me that you would, it's true, but I dared not believe him." And she held out her lovely hand to the Regent, which he kissed gallantly.

---

[7] This detail, which Ponson sets up but then does not utilize in the plot as it actually develops, is reminiscent of Paul Féval's *La Vampire* (1856; tr. as *The Vampire Countess*, Black Coat Press, ISBN 978-0-9740711-5-2), in which the eponymous character sometimes appears with blonde hair and sometimes with dark, and pretends that she is actually two different people. That novel presumably played some part in inspiring the present one, which might have been vaguely intended to resemble it more closely before Ponson changed its direction in mid-stream.

Then she drew him on to a carpet of moss spread out around the trunk of one of those exotic trees which seemed to have been transported by a magic wand.

"Since you have been kind enough to come, Monseigneur," she said, "I shall tell you my strange story, and you will see that I do not drink human blood, as the Marquis de la Roche-Maubert claims."

She spoke in a soft and harmonious voice—but it suddenly hardened when she pronounced the Marquis' name.

The Regent was still contemplating her, and had not noticed that d'Esparron was no longer there, and that he was alone with the queen of that marvelous palace.

XIII

What happened then between the Regent and that woman, who was so marvelously beautiful?

That is what no one would be able to say, for they remained alone for nearly an hour, talking in low voices. It was certainly not a matter of making love, however, and the well-known gallantry of Monseigneur Philippe d'Orléans had no role to play in the conversation.

The Chevalier d'Esparron had removed himself, as we have said, but he was undoubtedly not far away, for when the Regent called out to him he reappeared immediately.

The Prince was pale, and his whole face betrayed a violent emotion. He was holding the immortal woman's hand in his own, and gazing at her affectionately.

What would the Marquis de la Roche-Maubert thought?

"Come here," he said to the Chevalier—and took his hand too, and placed it in the young woman's. Then, in a sad and grave voice, he said: "Now that I know everything, listen to me, my children."

They huddled around him as if he were really their father.

"I'm not vindictive," said the Regent. "I'm even too ready to forgive. However, I confess that if I were in your shoes, I would think as you do and I would pursue the objective that you have given yourselves, as the holiest of duties. Unfortunately, my children, above the human heart there is human reason, and humans, in reasoning, have made laws to restrain their passions. If the truth came to light tomorrow, your vengeance having been accomplished, you would be arrested and taken before a tribunal assembled in the criminal court. The judges might absolve you in the depths of their conscience, but they would surely condemn you. You would be burned as a witch, my poor child, and you too, my good friend."

They made no reply, but their silence testified to an unbreakable resolution.

The Regent was still looking at them. "However," he said, "but for the heritage of hatred that has been transmitted to you, you might be so happy, my children! You are young, you are beautiful, you love one another..."

"Oh yes," said the mysterious creature, putting her arms around the Chevalier's neck.

"To live and die together—that is happiness," added the Chevalier.

"Listen to me," said Philippe d'Orléans again. "I'm the Regent. For a few years yet, I have supreme power—but the king will reach his majority and I shall no longer be anything, and if your work is not complete by then, I shall no longer be able to save you. Make haste, then, and pray to God that he will conserve me, for if I were to die tomorrow my heritage might well fall to that austere priest who goes by the name of Monsieur de Fréjus,[8] and has only shown less pity for witches because he does not believe in witchcraft.

"Make haste, then—and when your work is done, leave Paris, flee the kingdom and go to some corner of the world where you can live happily ever after."

As he pronounced these final words, the Regent kissed the hand of the strange woman. Then he supported himself on the Chevalier d'Esparron's shoulder in order to stand up—and when he was upright, he said: "Adieu, my children—and may God protect you!"

"Monseigneur," said the Chevalier, then. "I'll take you back."

"By the same route?"

---

[8] André de Fleury, Bishop of Fréjus, was appointed as tutor to Louis XV shortly before the death of Louis XIV, became the power behind the throne after the Regent's death, when he was elevated to the rank of Cardinal, completing the set of four great political cardinals begun by Richelieu, Mazarin and Dubois. He was elected to the Academy as "Monsieur de Fréjus," hence this reference.

"Oh no! Now that Your Highness knows everything, what point is there in the marvelous? Come."

"Adieu, Monseigneur," said the young woman, who took the Regent's hand and kissed it in her urn.

Then the Chevalier parted a curtain of foliage and the Prince found himself on the threshold of another room, with a completely different decoration that had nothing Oriental about it.

The Chevalier took the Regent through that room, then along a corridor, and then up a staircase, and they finally arrived in a comber vestibule with old wood paneling. At the far end of the vestibule d'Esparron opened a door.

A gust of cold fresh air struck the Regent in the face, and he found himself in the street: a narrow street, bordered by tall dark houses.

"Aha!" he said. "Is this, by any chance, the Rue de l'Hirondelle?"

"Yes, Monseigneur."

"And the house from which we're emerging...?"

"Is the one," the Chevalier said, smiling, "into which the old woman and the billy-goat were seen entering, on the evening of the execution."

"And you dare to stay here?"

"Monseigneur," said the Chevalier, coldly, "if all of the police employed by Your Highness' friend Cardinal Dubois were to search this house from top to bottom, they would not find anything."

"Not even the Nymphs' Grotto?"

"Not even the grotto of the subterranean channel by which we came."

"I hope so, for your sake," said the Regent. He uttered a sigh, then wrapped himself in his cloak, and they both headed for the Rue Gît-le-Coeur, which descended toward the river, as did the Rue de l'Hirondelle.

Early the next morning, Cardinal Dubois came into the Regent's study.

The Regent who had been up for a long time, was at work.

"Ah! You're here, my friend?"

"Yes, Monseigneur—has Your Highness had a nightmare?"

"None, my friend."

"The story told by my relative, however..."

The Regent frowned. "Listen, Dubois," he said. "Would you like me to give you some good advice?"

"Speak, Monseigneur."

"Your relative is lodging in the Rue de l'Arbre-Sec, is he not?"[9]

"Yes."

"Go see him."

"Very well."

"Put him in a post-chaise."

"And then?"

"And send him back to his estates."

"But Monseigneur..."

"Telling him that if he wants his old age to be protracted, the country air will be better for him than that of Paris. That's all I can tell you." And the Regent dismissed Dubois with a gesture that said: *You won't get anything else.*

---

[9] The author appears to have forgotten where the Marquis reported that he was lodging a few chapters ago—the first of many lapses of memory to which the story is subject.

XIV

Let us go back a little way now, and follow the Marquis de la Roche-Maubert on leaving the Palais-Royal.

In the same way that there are volcanoes crowned with snow, there are old men who have retained beneath their white hair all the ardor and impetuosity of youth. The Marquis de la Roche-Maubert was one of them.

After a stormy youth spent at the court of the great King, the Marquis had retired to the provinces. A young woman that he had loved very much and a large fortune had made him forget Paris and Versailles for a while.

One morning, however, the patriarch had woken up to find himself a widower, with his married sons living far away. Then the young man had reappeared in the old, and had said to him: "My sons have no need of me; I'm still sturdy; I have at least another twenty years of life; let's go amuse ourselves a little at court."

How did Dubois, that lackey risen to the rank of Cardinal, come to be the relative of the noble Marquis de La Roche-Maubert? It was incomprehensible at first sight, but on looking harder, one found that the father of the said Dubois had married a demoiselle as poor as she was noble, who was the Marquis' cousin. The latter, who had long ago dispensed with such a relationship, had remembered it again on the occasion of that unexpected return of youth.

Dubois was a cardinal, the first minister, the Regent's friend, and the Marquis had said to himself: *There's a man who seems expressly made to call me his cousin."*

So the Marquis had come to Paris; he had seen Dubois; he had opened his purse to him—and Dubois, who was always in debt, had accepted without a scruple.

That is how the Marquis de la Roche-Maubert had come to be one of the Regent's guests that evening. The rest of the adventure is known. The Marquis had got drunk on his own memories and then, with the self-regard that old men have in common with children, he had set out to prove to the Regent that everything he had said was perfectly true and that the Chevalier d'Esparron was the lover of a vampire woman—a ghoul, as people said in those days. For in that epoch, vampirism had already played a considerable role.

The people who drank human blood were not beings of pure invention, if one could believe all the gossip of the city and the court, and the example was even offered of a Prince of the Blood who only owed his beauty and his vigor to warm baths mixed with bull's blood and human blood.

The princes also played a role, in spite of the skepticism that ruled at court. There was not a quarter of Paris that did not play host to two or three alchemists trying to make gold, and at least one sibyl who could see the future through a carafe or in the residues of a coffee-cup.

That explains the success that the Marquis' story had had—a success further augmented by the arrival of the Chevalier d'Esparron. But that very triumph had had deadly consequences for the old man.

After having put the Chevalier to sleep, having laid his neck bare and displayed the vampire's puncture-wound, the Marquis had taken the medallion and showed it to the Regent.

That medallion represented the creature of ideal beauty that the Marquis accused of having drunk human blood, who had been burned forty years before, and who, resuscitated nevertheless from her ashes, was still young and still beautiful.

And the Marquis, in contemplating that medallion, had sensed a kind of tempest of love rising in his heart and his brain, and he had said to himself as he went down the narrow staircase into which Monseigneur Philippe d'Orléans had pushed him: "I have to find her; I have to see her again…and if she wants, I'll marry her."

So he had set forth, his head burning, his eyes aflame, his old heart hammering in his breast, and while going along the Rue de Saint-Honoré he had said to himself: "I can see why the Regent has ordered me to remain tranquil and not to budge from my hostelry. The Regent is smitten with the portrait, and as he's the most important person in the realm, and nothing can stand in his way, he'll find a way to send the Chevalier to the Bastille, as he's already enjoined me not to emerge from the hostelry of the Pomme d'Or.[10] But, we shall see..."

And the old man, who was far from having the wisdom of a Nestor, who was proceeding at a brisk and jaunty step, with his face concealed by his cloak and his hat pulled down, made the steel sheath of his épée rattle against the walls.

At such a nocturnal hour the streets were deserted—including the Rue Saint-Honoré, where the Marquis did not encounter so much as a cat.

As he turned the corner of the Rue de l'Arbre-Sec, however, he stopped, a trifle astonished, forced to interrupt his dream of love momentarily.

The street was noisy and animated; the populace, who ought to have been in bed a long time ago, were pressing curiously at the door of the Pomme d'Or, the hostelry at which the Marquis was staying, which was literally besieged by an urgent and inquisitive crowd.

What did all that signify?

The Pomme d'Or only accommodated provincial lords and gentlemen, ordinarily worthy men who came to solicit favors, spent their days at Versailles, return exhausted and went to bed early. When the curfew rang, it was rare to find lights still on in the Pomme d'Or—and yet, tonight, the windows of the hostelry were alight; the stoves were lit, the spit

---

[10] The author also seems to have forgotten that the Pomme d'Or was the name of La Niolle's tavern on the site of the Tour de Nesle; he must have liked the name, because he subsequently attributes it to a third establishment unrelated to the others. The lapse seems to be related to the fact that the story changes direction abruptly in this chapter; thus far, d'Eparron's actions only make sense if it is the Marquis who is the target of the alleged witch's vengeance, but Ponson obviously changed his mind at this point, perhaps because the editor of *La Petite Presse* did not like the idea of a noble Norman villain, and demanded the substitution of a foreigner.

was turning, and an army of scullions were going back and forth among them. César le Borgne—as the hotelier was named—was giving orders with the calm and dignity of a senior general on the battlefield.

"What the devil's all this?" exclaimed the marquis, increasingly surprised.

He made way for himself, distributing a few blows with the flat of his sword, shouting and using his elbows, cleared a path and finally got into the hostelry.

Then he saw, sitting on a stool by the fireside, a man of about fifty, wearing rich scarlet livery, who appeared to be watching all the preparations attentively,

César le Borgne said to him: "Excuse me, Monsieur le Marquis, but I fear that you won't sleep well tonight. You can see that everything is in turmoil."

"What's going on?" asked the Marquis.

"That gentleman," said the hotelier, pointing at the man in scarlet livery, "is the steward of the Margrave Prince of Lansbourg-Nassau."

"Ah!" said the Marquis.

"And his noble master, whom he is preceding by a few hours, will arrive very soon, and will do me the signal honor of staying here. He's coming, it's said, to get married."

"Is he a young man, then?"

"No, he's seventy years old," replied the steward, silent until then.

Good! thought the Marquis. *I'm not the only old fool of that age, then!* And he looked at the steward curiously.

XV

The individual at whom the Marquis was looking was, after all, well worthy of attention.

He was a short man with an angular profile, a clean-shaven face, yellow teeth, and gray eyes sparkling with malice. His thin lips were armed with a mocking and sardonic smile.

"Ha ha!" he said, looking at the Marquis. "It astonishes you, doesn't it, that my noble master wants to get married at seventy? It will astonish you even more when you've seen him. He's puny and stooped, he can scarcely stand on his legs, and he doesn't go out when the wind is blowing for fear of being bowled over."

There's an excellent servant, the Marquis thought, *who sings the praises of his master's physique so well.*

"But he's so rich, the Margrave Prince," the short man continued, "that marriageable girls will latch on to him...you'll see..."

"What?" said the Marquis. "Your master isn't coming to marry a woman chosen in advance, then?"

"Not at all!" the steward replied. "My master wants to choose. He wants to get a feel of the goods. The youngest and most beautiful will carry him off. A fine stake, believe me!"

The little man laughed so wholeheartedly that the Marquis said: "Do you joke so cheerfully in your master's presence?"

"Oh, my God, yes!" replied the little man. "He's never annoyed with me, and I can say anything to him. Anyway, he only does what I want..."

"You're a fortunate steward," said the Marquis, with a smile.

"It's me who advised him to marry."

"You?"

"Of course. What do you expect him to do on his own? Besides which, he has no heir."

"And he probably won't have one, if he's as decrepit as you say."

"Bah! Who can tell?" said the little man, sarcastically. "You know the proverb, Monsieur: God is great." And he started laughing even more loudly.

"Wait a moment," said the Marquis, whose memory was singularly refreshed tonight. "It seems to me that I was once acquainted with your Margrave Prince."

"That's quite possible."

"He has spent time at the French court?"

"Oh, only a year."

"In what epoch?"

"It was so many years ago that I can't tell you exactly, but it was when a witch was burned in the Place de Grève, who, it was said, nourished herself on human blood."

The Marquis shivered again, and his memories became gradually clearer.

The steward, the little man in scarlet livery, was still smiling, and looking at the Marquis as if to say: *I'll tell you something else, if you want...*

That gaze was doubtless understood by the Marquis, for he did something unusual in those times. He fetched a chair and came to sit down—him, a gentleman, a man of good family—beside the lackey.

"Yes, yes," he went on, in a tone that he would have employed with an equal. "I remember perfectly now. The Margrave Prince of Lansbourg-Nassau! But that's all I know."

"That's quite possible," repeated the little man.

"And were you in his service then?"

"Me, no—I wasn't ten years old...but my father..."

"Ah! He was a friend of the Comte d'Auvergne, wasn't he?"[11]

"Yes, certainly."

---

[11] Godefroy de la Tour d'Auvergne was the Grand Chambellan of France from 1658-1715.

"And of the Baron de V*** —a very important person in those days."

"Exactly."

"And you say that your master is rich?"

"Fabulously rich."

"That's odd," murmured the Marquis.

The little man was still smiling. "Ah," he said. "I know what you're going to say. At the time of which we're speaking, the Margrave had absolutely nothing except debts."

"At least, so people said..."

"The Principality of Lansbourg is the size of a hand, and although my master was related on the distaff side to the noble House of Nassau, he was then a very petty lord."

"That was what I was about to tell you," said the Marquis.

"I've heard my father say," the steward continued, in a low voice "that the Margrave had found a means of making gold."

"Really?"

"But shh!" said the steward, "one can't speak of such things here."

"However," said the Marquis, with a casual familiarity that manifestly flattered the steward, "I'd like to hear about them."

"Are you staying here?"

"As you can see."

"Where's your room?"

"On the second floor—number three."

"Well," said the little man, "my noble master can't be long delayed in arriving now. When he's come, had supper and I've put him to bed, I'll come to say goodnight to you."

"And you'll tell me...?"

"Anything you wish to know."

The Marquis had no time to reply, for there was a loud noise in the Rue de l'Arbre-Sec." Rifle shots were heard, the ringing of noisy bells, the hoofbeats of several horses resonating on the roadway and a continuous rattle of wheels. It was the Margrave Prince of Lansbourg-Nassau.

"My word!" said the Marquis. "I'm not usually curious, but I want to see this individual." And he hastened to the threshold of the hostelry.

The landlord and his scullions, armed with torches, surrounded the Margrave's post-chaise.

A man got down.

He was tall, but so stooped that he seemed short. His face was clean-shaven, as yellow as a sheet of parchment, but his eyes were still flashing and had a kind of fateful expression. The Marquis met his gaze, and, brave and stout-hearted as he was, felt a chill in his heart.

"That's a demon in the decrepit body of a centenarian," he murmured—and he immediately experienced a sentiment of violent hatred for the man, who already seemed to have one foot in the grave.

XVI

The Margrave Prince of Lansberg-Nassau was followed by a veritable miniature court—fifteen people, at least, were accompanying him: pages, grooms and petty German gentlemen, and a woman by the name of Edwige.

The woman was a strongly-built matron with a highly-colored complexion and masculine good looks, about forty years of age. She had white, pointed teeth like a carnivorous animal, fleshy and sensual lips, and a robust but attractive figure.

Was she a cook or a noblewoman?

Neither.

Madame Edwige, as she was addressed, was the wife of the little man in red and gold livery who bore the title of steward. However, the pages, valets and gentlemen of various rank who formed the Margrave's retinue treated her with a servile respect that seemed to establish, at the very least, a mysterious relationship between her and the wealthy prince, if not some terrible secret on which her authority was founded.

The Margrave went into the inn, like a man used to trampling everything underfoot.

At first he had only seen the hotelier and his scullions, and had allowed to weigh upon the crowd of curiosity-seekers assembled at the door one of those indifferent and scornful glances which the great bestow upon the petty. The old Marquis de la Roche-Maubert returned to sit down tranquilly by the fire, and, as he was somewhat in the shadows, the Margrave did not perceive him there to begin with.

Even Madame Edwige, who went over to the steward and asked him whether everything was ready for the reception of their lord and master, did not look at the Marquis attentively.

The Marquis had sacrificed all his gentlemanly pride to his curiosity. Instead of asking curtly to be taken to his room, he remained where he was for nearly an hour, mingled with the people of the Prince's retinue. The latter sat down at table.

In that epoch, the kitchen had not yet abdicated its importance to the dining-room in hostelries. The latter did not exist yet. It was in the kitchen, next to the fiery stoves. Opposite the fireplace with the large mantelpiece, beneath which a Homeric spit was turning, that the tables had been set for the feast.

That night, César le Borgne, the man in who supervised the arrangements in the Pomme d'Or, had set two tables. One, the higher, laden with silverware and crystal, was reserved for the Margrave and only had one place-setting. The other was reserved for the members of his retinue.

The Margrave sat down, therefore, and only then did he perceive the Marquis de la Roche-Maubert, who had not budged from the fireside. He fixed his little diabolical eyes upon him; his thin lips were pinched by a nuance of disdain and he called for César le Borgne.

The hotelier came running.

"Who is that seigneur?" the Margrave asked, in a quavering voice.

The Marquis hear the question and took responsibility for answering it. "I am, Monsieur," he said, "Marquis Paul de la Roche-Maubert, a Norman gentleman and former page of the Duc d'Orléans."

At the mention of that name, the Margrave could not suppress a start of surprise. Evidently, the Marquis was not unknown to him.

"Truly, Monsieur?" he said to him. "You were the Duc's page?"

"Yes, Monsieur."

"Just a moment..."

The Margrave looked at the Marquis avidly. The latter had advanced, obligingly, and was now fully illuminated. The Margrave continued staring at him. He was obviously trying to rediscover the features of the page beneath the old man's white hair.

"Yes, yes," he said, finally. "It must be you. I recognize your gaze, which has remained young."

"Did you see much of me, then, in days gone by?" said the Marquis.

"Oh, more than you think."

"Ah!"

"But it was a long time ago..."

"Indeed," said the Marquis. "I, too, remember having seen you, in the company of the Comte d'Auvergne."

"Ah!" said the Margrave, in his tone—and his eyes too on a fierce gleam, while a malevolent smile played upon his lips."

"You were then, Monsieur, a very handsome cavalier, dark-haired, tall and slim—and the women were crazy for you."

"Ha ha!" laughed the Prince. "I was thirty; I'm seventy now, so it was forty years ago." Then he nodded to the Marquis again. "Have some supper with me, Monsieur," he said. "It would give me great pleasure."

"And that pleasure would certainly be shared," replied the Marquis, courteously. "Unfortunately. I've already had supper."

"Really?"

"With Monseigneur le Régent," added Monsieur de La Roche-Maubert.

"Will you at least do me the honor of drinking a glass of malmsey with me?"

"Oh, gladly." And the Marquis, who thought the Margrave well enough born, in spite of his principality, sat down facing him and accepted the glass that was offered to him."

The Margrave was doubtless traveling with his own wines, for as soon as the supper began, an immense basket filled with bottles and pitchers of various forms had been removed from the vast flanks of his post-chaise. At a sign from him the red-clad steward, who was constantly posted behind his armchair, took the stopper from a stone jug as stout as a monk, from which a few cobwebs were hanging. Then he poured out a wine, more yellow than amber, first for the Margrave and then for the Marquis.

In accordance with the old custom, the Margrave drank the first mouthful, then clinked glasses with his guest. "In truth," he said, "I'm very glad to have run into you, Marquis."

"As am I, Prince," replied Monsieur de la Roche-Maubert.

"Ha ha!" the Margrave continued. "I owe you more than you think, you know."

"Me?"

"You."

"What is this enigma, Prince?"

The Margrave had his glass filled again and emptied it in a single draught. "In the epoch when we saw one another at Versailles," he said, "I wasn't rich."

"Ah!"

"Today, I have enough gold to buy Paris and the rest of the kingdom."

"Really?"

"Really—and I owe that to you."

"You're joking, Prince."

"No...no..." the Margrave sniggered. "Only I can't explain...but believe me, it's the truth."

As he said that, Madame Edwige, silent until then, got up from the other table and came to stand in front of the Margrave, and said to him: "You're going to do yourself harm, Monseigneur, by talking so much."

The Margrave lowered his eyes before the gaze of the Megaera, and stammered a few words that were unintelligible to the Marquis.

XVII

Everything that had happened in the hostelry of the Pomme d'Or for an hour—everything he had seen and heard, from the promise of confidences that the steward had made him, to the Margrave's confession that he owed his immense fortune to him—had surprised the Marquis de la Roche-Maubert so much that he had almost forgotten the medallion, the Chevalier d'Esparron and the vampire woman.

But his astonishments were not yet at an end.

Madame Edwige made a sign to the steward, her husband.

The steward, who seemed as meek before her as the Margrave, hastened to the basket of wine. He took out a small bottle of Bohemian glass with a carved gold stopper, and handed it to Madame Edwige.

The Margrave looked up at the Megaera timidly. "Already?" he said.

"Yes," she replied. "You've been traveling for most of the day, and you're wearier than usual."

"No," stammered the old man, "I'm not as tired as you think, my good Edwige, and I'll even tell you that the sight of Monsieur le Marquis has strangely rejuvenated me."

"Then you're doubtless renouncing getting married?" said Madame Edwige, dryly.

"No...no...that's true..." And the cruel smile that the Marquis had already noticed returned to his lips. Then he turned to Monsieur de la Roche-Maubert. "Yes, yes," he said. "I've come to Paris to get married again."

"Really!"

"I'm looking for a young woman, beautiful and good."

"And you'll certainly find her," replied the Marquis, with a hint of irony.

"When one is as rich as I am, one can find anything one wants," said the Margrave.

"Even youth," said Madame Edwige. "Come on, Monsieur—hold out your glass."

"Adieu, Marquis," said the old man. "Bonsoir…we'll see one another again tomorrow."

Before Monsieur de la Roche-Maubert had had time to ask for an explanation of those bizarre words, the Margrave had held out his goblet to Madame Edwige. The latter emptied the contents of the Bohemian glass bottle into it.

Then the Marquis had the explanation of the adieu that the Margrave had just bid him, for scarcely had the latter emptied his glass than he slumped backwards abruptly. His eyes closed and his entire body took on the immobility of death.

As the Marquis let out an exclamation of astonishment, the Megaera said to him: "That surprises you, doesn't it?"

"Indeed," said the Marquis.

"Oh well, listen and you'll understand! That man is worn out, completely worn out; his life is hanging by a threat, and the physicians who are for him in his principality have only succeeded in keeping him alive by plunging him into long lethargies. He'll now sleep for two successive days and nights. When he wakes up, you'll no longer recognize him, for he'll have recovered a false youth for a few hours."

With these words, Madame Edwige made another sign, not to her husband the steward, this time, but to two young pages, who immediately got up from the table and came to pick up the Margrave bodily.

César le Borgne, who had doubtless been warned about all these singularities, took a torch and headed toward the staircase that led from the back of the room to the upper floors.

The pages followed him, carrying their sleeping master. Madame Edwige brought up the rear—but first she leaned over and whispered a few words in German into her husband's ear.

Thos words made the Marquis de la Roche-Maubert tremble, for he had once served in the army that Prince

Eugène[12] had held in check for such a long time, and he understood German perfectly.

What Madame Edwige had said to her husband was: "Now, Conrad, you can go to the Rue de l'Hirondelle."

And the Marquis felt new light dawning in his mind; a final veil that had darkened his mind as ripped away, and he remember that, on the day when the witch of the Rue de l'Hirondelle had been burned, there had been a man in the front row of the spectators surrounding the pyre. That man he now remembered perfectly. It was the Margrave de Lansbourg-Nassau.

There had been another man with him—a man already old, but whose face had had a strangely malevolent expression. As she had gone up on to the pyre, the witch had looked at them with an expression of scorn and anger. She would certainly have shaken her fist at them had her arms not been bound to the sinister stake that the flames were beginning to surround.

And the Marquis also remembered that those two men had stayed there until the witch was no more than a heap of ashes. Then the Margrave and his companion had gone away, and the former had murmured: "Now we can rest easy—the future and the world are ours."

The Marquis de la Roche-Maubert remained absorbed by those bizarre memories for such a long time that he did not notice that everyone had gone to bed, with the exception of the steward Conrad.

The latter had gone out silently

---

[12] Prince Eugène of Savoy grew up in Louis XIV's court but was rejected for service in the French army and entered the service of the Hapsburgs of the Holy Roman Empire, becoming one of its most successful military leaders. The Marquis was presumably fighting against his forces in the early 1700s during the War of the Spanish Succession.

He promised to tell me things, the Marquis thought. *I'll wait for him...*

Then he went up to his room.

Instead of going to bed, however, he opened his window and leaned on the sill, in order to watch for the return of the steward, whom Madame Edwige had charged with a mysterious message for the Rue de l'Hirondelle.

XVIII

More than an hour went by.

The Marquis de la Roche-Maubert was still waiting, leaning out of his window, his eyes fixed on the Rue de l'Arbre-Sec.

The street was now deserted. When they had seen the lights go out one by one in the inn, the worthy bourgeois whom curiosity had initially crowded around the door had gone away, one by one. The police sergeants making their rounds had swept away the laggards.

So, the street was deserted and silent, and the old Marquis de la Roche-Maubert was waiting for the steward to return—and while he waited, the old gentleman was pensive.

His head was fresh and his brain clear, in spite of the snow that covered it. The name of the Rue de l'Hirondelle had plunged the Marquis into the vast domain of suppositions, and his jealous imagination soon carried him away to fantastic realms.

To begin with, he revisited his dream of love—which is to say, the woman who triumphed over death, who was resurrected in the midst of the ashes of a pyre, and, younger and more beautiful than ever, had turned the head of the Chevalier d'Esparron.

But that dream, which made him forget the Margrave momentarily, was suddenly complicated by that new individual—which is to say that, having heard Madame Edwige tell her husband to go to the Rue de l'Hirondelle, the Marquis did not doubt for a moment that it was at the immortal woman's house, and nowhere else, that the red-clad steward had a mission to fulfill.

What could that mission be?

The Marquis had guessed—or thought he had guessed.

The Margrave had come to Paris in order to get married. In the Rue de l'Hirondelle there was a marvelously beautiful woman, and she was the one who was being considered. The matter even seemed so simple to Monsieur de la Roche-

Maubert that, to begin with, he thought of putting his épée under his arm, going down to the next floor, going into the Margrave's room, and killing him without further ado.

However, a glimmer of reason traversed his brain just in time to prevent him from putting that insane plan into action.

He remembered that the Margrave had witnessed the execution of the immortal woman, and had appeared to rejoice in it. In consequence, even admitting that he might have maintained communications with the creature that laughed at flames and death, there was no evidence that he loved her and wanted to marry her.

So, the Marquis de la Roche-Maubert put his épée back under his bolster and went back to the window to wait for the steward again.

Soon, the sound of footsteps became audible in the street, coming from the direction of the river. The night was dark, and the Marquis initially had difficulty recognizing the man who was coming forward, hiding his face in his cloak—but there were two lanterns lighting the street, and when the man had passed under one of them he was in no further doubt.

It was indeed the steward.

As long as he hasn't forgotten that he promised to meet me, thought the Marquis, seething with impatience.

He closed the window, and waited. A few more minutes went by; then there were two discreet raps on the door.

Monsieur de la Roche-Maubert hastened to open it.

"Is it you?" he said, in a low voice.

"It's me," said the steward.

"Wait while I light a candle."

"Oh, no, there's no need," said the other, in a low voice. "Edwige thinks I'm out, and I came up very softly."

The Marquis concluded from these words that the steward was as fearful of the terrible Madame Edwige as the Margrave was. "As you wish," he said. He brought a chair forward for the steward, and sat down himself on the foot of the bed. There was a question burning his throat. He had a strong desire to ask the steward why he had gone to the Rue de l'Hirondelle, but a sentiment of vulgar prudence prevented him.

Let's find out first what he promised to tell me, he thought. *Then we'll see.*

Overcoming his jealous emotion, rendering his voice as calm as his age warranted, he said to the steward: "Oh, my dear Monsieur Conrad, you have curious things to tell me?"

"Very curious, Monsieur le Marquis."

"Regarding your master the Margrave?"

"Naturally," said Conrad, lowering his voice "but I would perhaps have hesitated to do so, in spite of my promise, if I had not seen Monseigneur recognize Monsieur le Marquis."

"Ah!"

"And if I had not heard him say that he owes his fortune to you."

"That's true," said the Marquis. "He did say that."

"He certainly did."

"Is the Margrave mad, or was he making fun of me?"

"Neither."

"What?"

"Monseigneur was telling the exact truth."

"Oh! Indeed?"

"As I have the honor of telling you."

"But..."

"It's impossible," Conrad continued, "that Monsieur the Marquis has forgotten a certain witch that was burned in the Place de Grève?"

"Certainly not. I haven't forgotten her."

"Well, it's because the witch was burned that my master is so rich."

"Really?"

"And as it was on Monsieur le Marquis' denunciation that the witch was burned..."

A cloud passed over the Marquis' face. "Oh, you know that too!" he said.

"Of course," the steward replied. "Otherwise, would I be telling Monsieur le Marquis about my petty affairs?"

"Well, go on—I'm listening."

The Marquis wiped a few beads of sweat from his forehead.

XIX

Darkness, as we have said, reigned in the room where the Marquis de la Roche-Maubert and the steward were sitting. From the latter's sarcastic tone, however, one could deduce that his face must have an infernal expression.

"Monsieur le Marquis," he said, "it isn't commonplace, is it, for a servant to talk about his master as irreverently as me?"

"Indeed," said the Marquis, "it's not very frequent—but continue, if you please, my dear Monsieur Conrad."

"I don't want you to think ill of me, though, Monsieur, and that's why I shall tell you right away that I got the story I'm about to tell you from my father."

"Ah!"

"My father was in the Margrave's service, as I am, and he left me memoirs."

"Well," said the Marquis, impatiently, "Let's hear your father's memoirs."

"I'll begin, then. My father and the Marquis were almost the same age. They arrived in Paris together, and as the Margrave was as poor as Job, servant as he was, my father was almost his friend.

"The Prince came to Paris to claim a certain indemnity that was due to the family as a consequence of the Thirty Years' War, but which had never been paid; my father attached himself to the ill-fortune of that sovereign without a sovereignty, hoping for better days.

"After six months of taking all possible steps, the Margrave Prince of Lansbourg-Nassau still had not obtained anything. He had seen ministers, who had sent him to the king, who had sent him to his ministers. He had hardly a penny in his purse, and the day when it would be completely empty was fast approaching.

"One morning, however, the Prince, who had gone out very early, came back to the wretched inn where he was staying, and where he had been given to understand that he could no longer stay, radiant with joy and hope. He slapped my father on the shoulder and said: 'We're going to be rich.'

"My father thought that the famous indemnity was about to be paid, but he didn't ask. He did well to refrain, in fact.

"However, the Prince took a pile of gold coins out of his money-bag and paid the innkeeper what he owed, to the latter's great joy and brief shame at having refused him credit. Then he ordered my father to gather up their clothes, pack their suitcases and get ready to leave.

"My father asked whether they were leaving Paris, but the Margrave made no reply. The waited for nightfall.

"When the curfew had sounded, they both left the hostelry on foot. My father was carrying the suitcases on his back, and the Prince did not disdain to carry a few small parcels. They went down to the river bank. There, the Prince stuck two fingers in his mouth and emitted a loud whistle.

"Then a boat left the opposite bank, slowly crossed the river and came to touch the shore at their feet. The boat was rowed by two men whose faces were covered by black velvet masks. They had undoubtedly been waiting for the Prince and his companion, for they did not say a word, and pushed off as soon as the latter had embarked.

"My father tried once again to ask where they were going, but the Prince imposed silence upon him and the boat headed downstream.

"Half an hour later, they passed under the Pont Saint-Michael and came to skim the gray walls of a old house whose foundations plunged into the water. Then they stopped. At the same time, a window that was almost at water level opened. The Prince stepped through the window-frame and my father followed him.

"They found themselves in profound darkness, but my father heard whispering. He thought he could make out a woman's voice, and understood that the Prince was being led by the hand.

"Then a door opened in front of them. Light succeeded the darkness, and my father stopped in astonishment.

"He was on the threshold of a room of ordinary dimensions, but entirely round and vaulted. One might have thought that he was under the cupola of some vast edifice. The walls were devoid of windows. A lamp hanging from the vault projected a dim light around it. By that light, however, my father could see the surrounding objects. He saw retorts, alembics, a live sheep attached to the wall by a chain, a table laden with old books and parchments, and, in a corner, another table on which there was another sheep. That one had had its throat cut, and its blood was dripping into a silver basin placed underneath it.

"As soon as they had gone in, a woman appeared. She was young, to judge by her gait and her figure. She was beautiful, to judge by the luxuriant curls of blonde hair that fell confusedly on to her semi-naked shoulders—but it was impossible to see her face, which was covered by a mask through which two shiny black eyes were visible.

"She greeted the Prince with a gesture; then she looked at my father.

"'He's the servant I mentioned,' he said.

"The masked woman nodded her head.

"Then the Margrave turned to my father. 'Hermann,' he said, 'We've entered into the temple of Fortune. We'll leave here as rich as we wish, but we're risking our lives...'

"'Ah! said my father, indifferently.

"'We shall be kings of the world, or burned alive as sorcerers,' the Prince added. 'If you're afraid, say so, and leave.'

"'No,' my father replied. And he stayed."

"And then?" said the old Marquis de la Roche-Maubert, intrigued by the story, in which interested him to the highest degree.

XX

Monsieur de la Roche-Maubert was listening avidly to Master Conrad's story. The latter continued.

"Now, Monsieur le Marquis, I'll tell you in a few words who that woman was and what the bizarre objects and bloody things surrounding her signified. My father had entered, in the Margrave's wake, into an alchemist's laboratory. The woman had found the means of making gold."

"Indeed," the Marquis put in, "I remember that when the woman was condemned as a vampire, she protested with all her might and claimed that she had never abused human blood for anything other than her mysterious preparations."

"And she was telling the truth, Monsieur le Marquis."

"Is it possible?"

"I could tell you in a few words," Conrad continued, "what was really happening in the house in the Rue de l'Hirondelle, but allow me to begin at the beginning—which is to say, to tell you how the Prince and the woman had met."

"I'm listening," said the Marquis.

"Two days earlier, the Margrave Prince, prey to a somber sadness, which had no other cause than the lack of success of the steps he had taken and his almost absolute destitution, after walking for a long time at random, had chanced to enter a low tavern, over the door of which hung a sprig of holly. The tavern, which was on the river bank, was almost deserted when the Prince went in, and it was gloomy inside.

"The landlord brought wine in a pewter jug to the client he was seeing for the first time, and then went back to his counter.

"Two coarse fellows, doubtless mariners, were talking in low voices at the table next to the Prince's. One of them said: 'It's a long time since the masked woman has come.'

"'That's true,' the other replied.

"'Work's in short supply on the river,' said the first, 'and I wouldn't be sorry if she came. Two pistoles are always good to have.'

"'Damn right!' said the other. 'Even if we have to give a pint of blood to get the pistoles.'

"'That's true—but when one's as robust as we are...'

"That strange conversation had an impact on the Margrave Prince and, noble lord as he was, he didn't disdain to approach the men and question them. They made no great mystery of it.

"'Monseigneur,' said the first—for, poor and threadbare as he was, the Prince had an aristocratic bearing—'what you want to know is quite simple. From time to time, a woman comes here whose face we have never seen, but who is sent by a physician. That physician does experiments, it seems, and for that he needs human blood. He's searching, she's told us, for a remedy for a disease thus far considered to be fatal.'

"'And he needs human blood for that?'

"'So it seems. So, poor people like us, who can barely make a living, consent, for two pistoles—sometimes three—to hold out our arms. The woman takes a lancet and a little silver ewer from her pocket, makes a little incision on our forearm, draws off a little blood, which falls into the ewer, and leaves, after having paid us.'

"'And you let her do it?' asked the Prince.

"'One must live,' said the other man of the people.

"'Is such a thing permitted, then?' asked the Margrave.

"'I don't know—but we can't see any harm in it, ourselves.'

"'But such bleedings must weaken you enormously?'

"'Pooh! As you can see, we're robust. For more than a year she's bled us once a fortnight, and we're not dead.'

"The other sighed, and added: 'We've been waiting for her for three evenings running now, but she hasn't come yet.'

"'I'm afraid so,' said the first. 'Come on—we'll come back tomorrow.'

"And they both got up.

"'You're leaving?' said the Prince.

"They nodded their heads, and as the landlord approached, the one who had replied to the Prince initially said to him: 'Comrade, we don't have a penny, and we can't pay you today. We'll settle up tomorrow.'

"'Go on,' said the tavern-keeper, like a man who has confidence in his actions.

"The Prince remained alone. A keen curiosity took hold of him. He wanted to see the woman who traded in human blood for ready money.

"His desire was to be satisfied, Less than a quarter of an hour had gone by since the two men of the people had left when the door of the tavern opened and the masked woman came in.

"She was enveloped in an ample cloak, which entirely hid the elegance of her figure, and the mask she wore entirely covered her face.

"Seeing that the men of whom she was doubtless in search were no longer in the tavern, she was about to withdrew when the Prince, having risen to his feet, blocked her way.

"'Pardon me,' he said, 'but I'd like to talk to you for a minute.'

"She shivered, looked at the man she was seeing for the first time, uttered a little cry, tried to get out, but was nailed to the ground by an irresistible force.

"The Prince was then a man of about thirty. He was very handsome, with the fatal beauty that dominates and fascinates. He suddenly exerted upon the masked woman an absolute magnetic power, and the fluid that sprang from his eyes penetrated her completely.

"'What do you want?' she stammered, trembling all over.

"'To talk to you,' he said. 'But in private, all alone.' And he took her by the arm and drew her outside. She went with him, without offering any resistance.

"Outside, there was the river bank and pitch darkness. There was a tremulous light on the water, however, and the Margrave recognized the light of a boat—undoubtedly the boat that had brought the masked woman.

"'What do you want with me?' she said, still trembling.

"'My name,' he said, 'is Otho, Margrave Prince of Lansbourg-Nassau; I'm poorer than the men you were looking for, and if you want to take two pistoles-worth of blood from me, I'm at your disposal.'

"The masked woman uttered a cry, and sought to read in the Prince's eyes, which were sparkling in the darkness, whether he was mocking her, or setting a trap for her."

XXI

"Between the moment when the Margrave Prince had offered his blood to the masked woman for money and the one when my father saw them together in the alchemy laboratory, he did not know for sure what had happened—but he was able to guess subsequently.

"The Prince had suddenly exerted a mysterious fascination on the woman. Had it carried her away? Probably. When the Prince and my father came to take up residence in the Rue de l'Hirondelle she was already passionately, madly in love with him, and had associated him with her fortune.

"Now, that fortune consisted of the secret that the singular creature possessed of making gold—a true, pure gold of the finest quality, which any goldsmith in Paris would have certified without hesitation.

"She had not, however, revealed her secret in its entirety.

"The Prince knew that it required copper, lead and tin, and that to those three metals, melted in a crucible, a mysterious powder was added that served to bind them together, but he did not know either the name of that powder or the means of procuring it. After thirty-six hours of fusion, the three metals, in combination, became a single unified block, brown—almost black—in appearance; it was then a matter of its clarification. For that, it was thrown, red hot, into a bath of sheep's blood or bull's blood, which had been mixed with human blood in a proportion of approximately one tenth.

"Save for the secret of the mysterious powder, the daughter of alchemy had surrendered all her other secrets to the Prince, for whom her love had arrived at the paroxysm of folly and delirium. Thus, after a week, the Prince knew that the woman, to whom he gave the name of Janine, was pursuing a nobler aim than that of having gold. She needed a great deal of it, and wanted to possess immense treasures—but why?

"To avenge her race, persecuted and proscribed for a century, and to strike powerful enemies.

"The Prince also knew that, in order to procure human blood, Janine often had to struggle against exceptional difficulties. It was not always possible to find men who would sell her their blood voluntarily.

"Until the day when she met the Prince, Janine had made that trade honestly, and the idea of crime had never entered her head—but the Prince, as I've told you, exercised an irresistible power over her, a domination so fatal that she obeyed him blindly.

"Until then, she had manufactured some five or six thousand livres of gold per month. When that gold was fabricated she divided it into two parts; one went to increase the mass of the mysterious treasure that she was amassing for the purpose of her vengeance. The other served for the Prince's prodigalities.

"For don't imagine, Monsieur le Marquis, that the Prince buried himself alive in Janine's laboratory. For a year, the Prince, who had suddenly become rich, dazzled Paris and Versailles with his luxury, was linked with the Baron de V   and the Comte d'Auvergne—two bad lots—and, while Janine worked for him, he delivered himself to all pleasures.

"Janine, as I've told you, loved him madly.

"One day, the Prince said to her: 'I need gold—much more gold than you're giving me.'

"'But I can only make a certain quantity of it,' she replied.

"'Why?'

"'Because of the lack of human blood.'

"'Is that all?' said the Prince, laughing.

"From that day on, horrible things happened in the house in the Rue de l'Hirondelle. Muted rumors were heard in Paris; there was talk of people disappearing, children abducted, cadavers found in the nets of Saint-Cloud which appeared to have been bled like pigs.

"The King received complaints, and ordered investigations, but the police didn't find anything. The Comte d'Auvergne, who was a Prince of the Blood, was covertly protecting the murderers.

"And Janine made gold: a great deal of gold.

"Then the Prince, who no longer loved her, said to her: 'When one is as beautiful as you are, one can have as much gold as one wants.'

"And from then on, Janine played the role of ghoul and vampire, as obedient as a slave to the will of the man who took her gold from her and forced her to sell her honor.

"In the midst of that folly, however, Janine conserved a glimmer of reason.

"She did not want to surrender the secret of the mysterious powder that operated upon the mixture of metals when dissolved in the crucible, and transformed them into gold.

"'That secret is not mine,' she said. 'It was transmitted to me and I must transmit it faithfully to a person who is not in Paris, whom I have never even seen, but who is of the same blood as me, and who will continue my work if I suffer misfortune some day.'

"Nor did Janine want to surrender to the Prince the key that she wore around her neck day and night. The key was that of a steel chest of colossal proportions, which was buried in the cellars of the house in the Rue de l'Hirondelle. It was filled with the gold that Janine had accumulated for her work of vengeance.

"'No,' she said. 'Take what I give you, but let me pursue my work.'

"The Prince had employed threats and pleas in vain. Janine remained unshakable.

"One day, the Prince said to my father: 'If we had the contents of the steel chest we could go back to Germany. I could redeem my principality and you could be my Prime Minister.'"

At this point the narrator interrupted himself again.

"A thousand pardons, Monsieur le Marquis," he said, for having given you so many details, but it's necessary for you to know how the Margrave Prince owes you, in reality, his immense fortune."

"Continue," said the Marquis de la Roche-Maubert, who was listening to the steward's story avidly.

Conrad went on.

XXII

"My father was devoted to the Prince in spite of his crimes and his evil nature. Besides which, he had become his accomplice in the mysterious existence that they had been leading for nearly two years. In consequence, he was not at all repelled by the idea that his master suggested of returning to Germany, redeeming the principality of Lansbourg-Nassau and seeing himself raised to the dignity of Prime Minister.

"However, he permitted himself a few objections.

"The first one was that the steel chest was sealed in the wall, and it would have required several people with the appropriate tools to remove it.

"The second was no less important. The triple lock of the chest had been forged in Milan at the beginning of the last century, and it was not only impossible to force it, but even to open it with the key, because it was provided with a secret that only Janine knew.

"The Prince was not embarrassed by so little, however.

"'Have no fear,' he said to my father. 'I shall be able to force Janine to give me the secret.'

"My father shook his head. 'Has she ever surrendered that of the mysterious powder to you?' he said.

"The Prince became furious.

"'We shall see,' he said. 'I shall have both of them. It's a matter of patience, that's all.'

"And in speaking thus, the Prince had a plan, as you shall see.

"Janine was Italian in origin; she had blood that was burning in her veins, and the frenetic passion that the Margrave had inspired in her was the proof of it. However, Janine no longer loved the man who had forced her to commit crimes—but she was subject to his terrible and fatal influence, giving him as much gold as he desired, and submitting like a slave to his strangest whims.

"He had demanded that she make use of her beauty to attract victims to her house, and she had obeyed again. That, perhaps was the secret of the lassitude full of disgust that had replaced, in her heart, the ardent love that she had experienced in the beginning.

"She had resisted his pleas and threats, however, and all the means of violence or seduction that he had employed in order to obtain her double secret.

"'No,' she always replied, 'those two secrets are not mine. Kill me, if you wish, but you won't know anything.'

"Several months had already passed since the Margrave had confided his hopes to my father, and he was no further forward than on the first day—but he wasn't discouraged. Like a tiger lying in wait for its prey, he waited.

"What was he waiting for?

"You shall see.

"From time to time, when they needed human blood for their infernal crucible, Janine lured to her den some petty gentleman newly arrived from the provinces and still unknown in Paris, or some page, soldier or clerk from the Latin country. The unfortunates went to sleep, drunk on all intoxications, and did not wake up again.

"The blood collected the cadaver went to rejoin the other cadavers in the Seine.

"One day, however, Janine rebelled. Her heart, mute since she no longer loved the Margrave, suddenly spoke, beat faster, and she fell in love with a young and handsome gentleman whom she had, like the others, treacherously lured to her home.

"When at the end of an orgiastic night, the unfortunate man fell asleep, my father and the Prince came in, as usual, one armed with a cutlass with which he cut their victims' throats, the other with the silver bowl destined to receive his blood, Janine uttered a scream. She fell at the Prince's knees; she wept and begged, pleading for mercy for the sleeping gentleman.

"The Prince laughed like a demon.

"Janine covered the gentleman with her body, tore out her hair, and wrung her hands. When her despair reached its paroxysm, the Prince said to her: 'If you want me to show him mercy, tell me your secret.'

"Janine was vanquished.

"In order to save the gentleman, she would have consented to be torn to shreds with red hot pincers."

"And so," the Marquis de la Roche-Maubert interjected, wiping away the cold sweat that moistened his brow from time to time, "Janine surrendered the secret of the steel chest?"

"Yes, Monsieur."

"And that of the brown powder?"

"Similarly."

"And the gentleman lived?"

"Undoubtedly."

The Marquis was speaking with a profound emotion.

"Wait, though," Conrad went on. "I haven't finished. When Janine had surrendered her secret, the Prince said to her: 'That's good. You've given me a mark of confidence that I shall not abuse.' He resumed his customary life of debauchery and pleasures, and no longer said anything to my father about returning to Germany and taking Janine's gold with him.

"In the meantime, she loved her petty gentleman, and neglected to make gold.

"Then, one day, the petty gentleman disappeared.

"Then the Prince said to my father, coldly: 'I thought at first about killing Janine, but there's no need.'

"'Why?'

"'She has killed herself.'

"'What do you mean?'

"'By loving the man who will doom her.'"

Conrad sniggered, as he concluded his story. "Indeed, Monsieur—Janine was to be arrested, condemned and burned alive, on the denunciation of the man she had saved from death…for that man, as you cannot have any doubt, was you!"

The Marquis de la Roche-Maubert uttered a cry, hid his face in his hands—and tears oozed through his fingers.

Conrad laughed—a curt, mocking laugh—and said: "Poor Janine! She had no luck at all!"

XXIII

"I haven't finished yet, Monsieur le Marquis," Conrad went on. "Permit me to continue."

"Speak," replied the Marquis, in a muted voice.

"The witch was burned as a consequence of your denunciation," Conrad continued. "The Margrave and my father stayed in the Place de Grève until the execution was concluded.

"The poor woman had boasted of being immortal, but the flames surrounded her and she uttered screams of agony; then the smoke rose up, swirling, and enveloped her entirely. Her screams could still be heard...

"Then the screams ceased...and when the flame overcame the smoke, there was no more to be seen but a charred body.

"Janine was finished.

"Then the Margrave said to my father: 'The gold is ours, and the secret too.' And they slipped away from the square, and headed for the Rue de l'Hirondelle.

"It's necessary to tell you that when Janine was arrested, numerous and minute searches had been carried out in the house, but the police hadn't found anything, for the simple reason that they hadn't been able to discover a mysterious door whose existence was only known to her and the Margrave.

"That door, which was at the back of the laboratory, hidden in the wood paneling, gave access, when it was opened, to a staircase and a subterranean corridor. At the end of the corridor was a second laboratory, and in that subterranean room, fixed into the wall, was the famous steel coffer, to which the Margrave now had the key.

"Having found nothing, the police had abandoned the house.

"They waited for nightfall to go to the Rue de l'Hirondelle.

"At nine o'clock, when the curfew had rung and the bourgeois has gone home, my father and the Prince went to the house.

"At the corner of the Rue Gît-le-Coeur, the Margrave suddenly stopped.

"'What is it?' asked my father.

"'Look.'

"And he pointed at a widow, behind which a light was flickering.

"'It's doubtless the police making a final visit,' my father replied.

"They stayed at the street-corner for a few minutes more. Then the light went out.

"The Margrave set off again. He had kept a key to the house, and they went in. No sound could be heard inside, and the vestibule was plunged in darkness. As the two of them moved quietly through the darkness, however, a strong odor of sulfur gripped them by the throat. At the same time, two shadows glided toward them, and the Prince felt his hair standing on end.

"One of the two shadows appeared to be that of a human body, but the other was that of a quadruped.

"They reached the door that the Prince and his companion had left open, and when they were in the street they took flight.

"The Prince retraced his steps as far as the threshold. The two shadows passed under the lantern that lit the street as best it could, and the Prince saw distinctly, for the duration of a second, an old woman running away as fast as her legs could carry her, dragging a goat that she held on a leash.

"Who was that old woman?

"The Prince subsequently found out.

"She was a kind of witch, a fortune-teller to whom Janine had once given a mission. That mission consisted of getting into the house, if anything bad ever happened to her, and taking possession of a little ebony box that contained important papers.

"To whom was the witch to give that box?

"A mystery!

"The first moment of emotion, almost of terror, having passed, the Margrave said to my father: 'Now let's get busy making gold ourselves.'

"They opened the secret door, went down into the laboratory that the police had been unable to discover, and set to work.

"Poor Janine had—or, at least, the Prince was certain of it—surrendered the recipe of the mysterious powder, and during the unfortunate woman's trial the Prince had manufactured that powder in his lodgings in the Rue Saint-Honoré.

"They spent the entire night devoted to that work.

"The three metals were seething in the white-hot crucible.

"As they had no human blood that night, my father had pledged his own, and had placed his arm over the ewer. The Prince had opened a vein, and my father's blood had flowed.

"When the three metals had melted, the Prince threw the powder into the crucible.

"As usual, the crucible crackled. The three metals combined, and the prince drew out a brown ingot, which he plunged into the ewer full of blood, with the conviction that the ingot would be clarified and turn to gold.

"But what a disappointment! The ingot remained black.

"Furious, the Prince waited until it had cooled down, then took a heavy hammer and broke it. He obtained a mixture of copper and tin, but no gold.

"Janine had only surrendered half of her secret, and Janine was dead.

"Then, drunk with rage, the Margrave raced to the steel chest and opened it.

"This time, there was no disappointment. The chest was full of gold, and there was an enormous sum—a sum so considerable, Monsieur le Marquis, that the Margrave Prince redeemed his principality, and no longer knew the exact figure of his fortune."

"But he has never been able to make gold?" asked the Marquis de la Roche-Maubert.

"Never."

"And you believe that Janine is dead?"

"Of course!"

"Then," said the Marquis, suddenly standing up, "what were you doing this evening in the Rue de l'Hirondelle?"

At that abrupt question Conrad uttered an exclamation. "Ah!" he said. "You know that? So you understand German?"

There was a sudden note of threat in his voice, as he added: "You've made a mistake, Monsieur le Marquis, in knowing German!"

The Marquis then experienced a sentiment of indefinable terror.

XXIV

There was a moment of silence between Conrad the steward and the Marquis de la Roche-Maubert.

The Marquis was afraid.

Afraid of what?

He certainly could not have said—but he experienced the vague fear that takes possession of the bravest of men at certain times.

Finally, Conrad resumed speaking, his time with a tone of authority, and intonation mingling scorn and mockery. One might have thought it one of those strange scenes in which a valet suddenly dominates his master.

"My dear Marquis," he said, employing—him, a man dressed in livery—that familiar mode of addressing a gentleman. "why have you come to Paris? You're old, you're rich, you could live happily in your province. What fly has stung you and brought you here? You've supped with Monseigneur le Régent tonight? So what? You wanted to know the Margrave's story, and I've related it to you. Well, now what? Would you like some good advice—and believe me, I never give any to anyone else. Would you?"

"Well?" said the Marquis, cut to the quick by the tone of that strange familiarity.

"My dear Marquis," Conrad went on, "sleep well; get up tomorrow morning at your usual time, settle your bill here, ask for a good traveling coach and post-horses, and go away!"

The Marquis was gripped with a mad rage. "I won't go!" he cried.

"You're mistaken."

"Mistaken?"

"Yes." Conrad stated laughing.

"Wretch!" howled the Marquis, rushing to his épée. "You'll still tell me, before I go, what you went to do in the Rue de l'Hirondelle."

"I won't tell you anything at all, my dear Marquis."

"Oh! You think so!"

"It's none of your business."

They had no light, but a vague glow coming from outside and entering through the window permitted Monsieur de la Roche-Maubert to see Conrad. He lunged toward him, sword raised. "Speak, or I'll nail you to the wall," he said.

Conrad sniggered.

Then the Marquis stretched out his arm. His épée hit the wall, and snapped into two pieces. The steward had nimbly stepped aside, and the Marquis' weapon had run into the wall instead of his body.

Conrad precipitated himself toward the door, opened it and disappeared.

Monsieur de la Roche-Maubert found himself alone.

For a moment, blinded by anger, he thought about pursuing the steward, catching up with him and plunging the stump of his épée into his breast—but the corridor and the staircase were plunged in the most complete darkness, and anger cannot hold up against darkness for long.

Conrad having disappeared, the Marquis went back inside.

He threw himself on his bed and murmured: "I know perfectly well what he went to do in the Rue de l'Hirondelle. The immortal woman is still there; she was resurrected from her ashes like the phoenix, and the old Margrave wants to marry her. But I lover he too, and I shall marry her!"

As is evident, the Marquis was still a very young man in spite of his white hair.

He spent the rest of the night prey to an indescribable agitation, but with the first rays of dawn his nerves calmed down and a kind of mental and physical prostration took possession of him. Then he threw himself on to his bed, fully dressed, and a heavy sleep succeeded that tempest of fury and love.

How long did that sleep last?

A long time, no doubt, for the last rays of the setting sun were brushing the surrounding roofs when two abrupt raps on the Marquis' door woke him up.

He leapt out of bed, rubbing his eyes, and went to open the door.

Imagine his surprise on finding himself face to face with Monsieur de Simiane, one of the favorites of His Royal Highness Monseigneur le Régent.

"Bonjour, Marquis," said Monsieur de Simiane, in a detached tone. He came in and closed the door.

"Monsieur," stammered Monsieur de la Roche-Maubert, stupefied. "I really have no idea to what I might owe the honor of your visit."

"I've come on behalf of His Highness."

"The Regent?"

"Exactly."

"Ah!" said the Marquis—and waited.

"My dear Marquis," Monsieur de Simiane continued, "how long have you been in Paris?"

"Two days."

"Then you don't know?"

"Know what?"

"There is an epidemic raging in Paris."

"Bah!"

"It attacks, in particular, men of a certain age."

"Really?"

"And the Regent is very fond of you..."

The Marquis inclined his head.

"The Regent," Monsieur de Simiane continued, "asked me to come to warn you."

"I'm confused by such generosity."

"He has even asked me to tell you that you would do well to return to your estates in Normandy, and to send him, as soon as you arrive, news of your health, in which he is enormously interested."

And Monsieur de Simiane bowed, pirouetted on his left heel, and headed for the door.—but before crossing the threshold, he turned round.

"Oh, pardon me," he said, "I forgot..."

"What?" asked the Marquis.

"His Eminence Cardinal Dubois adds his voice to that of Monseigneur le Régent in giving you the same advice."

This time, Monsieur de Simiane went out.

Then the Marquis, who felt his anger of the previous night returning, murmured in a stifled voice: "They all want me to go—but I shall stay! Yes, I shall stay!"

XXV

Monsieur de la Roche-Maubert was, in spite of his white hair, mad with love—which is, in an old man, the most terrible madness of all—but he had in his intelligence the rigorous logic that maniacs apply to the pursuit of their obsessions.

When Monsieur de Simiane had gone, after having cried that although everyone wanted him to leave, he would not go, the old Marquis began to reflect.

He knew that, no matter how great a lord one might be, and however rich one might be, one could not openly resist either Monseigneur the Regent or His Eminence Cardinal Dubois.

They want me to go, he said to himself—*well then, I shall go, but only to return.*

Then Monsieur de la Roche-Maubert announced that he was leaving Paris. He sent for César le Borgne, the proprietor of the Pomme d'Or, and asked him to find him post-horses.

The Marquis had come to Paris in an old family carriage that had served for his father's marriage. He had brought a servant with him, both secretary and *valet de chambre*, who had gone to bed a long time ago the previous evening, when he had come back from the Palais-Royal.

Monsieur de la Roche-Maubert sent for the valet, whose name was Jonquille, sand said to him: "Go to the Cardinal's house and tell him that, being on the point of leaving Paris, I beg the favor of taking leave of His Eminence."

While Master Jonquille went out to carry out this instruction, the Marquis had his baggage loaded on to the carriage, put on traveling costume, settled his bill at the Pomme d'Or and made sufficient noise and fuss for the entire quarter to be aware that he was returning to his estates.

Jonquille came back and told him that the Cardinal would be happy to shake his hand before his departure.

The Marquis therefore climbed into his carriage; the postillions took their seats, cracked their whips, and the Marquis set out noisily for the Palais-Royal.

In the middle of the Rue Saint-Honoré, however, he called a momentary halt at Buffalo's door.

Who was Buffalo?

An enchanter, a sorcerer, whom no one thought of burning.

Buffalo had a beautiful boutique which bore the sign: *À la Fontaine de Jouvence.*[13]

Buffalo was an Italian by birth and a perfumer by profession. He sold exquisite odors to the petty mistresses of the court, rare and precious cosmetics, marvelous waters that restored the original colors to white hairs, soaps that made the skin supple and ointments that made wrinkles disappear.

One went into Buffalo's establishment old, and one reemerged young.

Nevertheless, the Marquis did not undergo to any metamorphosis there. He limited himself to buying a case of little phials, soaps, ointments and cosmetics, put all of it in his carriage, and continued on his way to the Palais-Royal.

Dubois was waiting for him.

"My dear relative," he said, "I can only congratulate you on having followed Monseigneur le Régent's advice."

"In truth!" said the Marquis, with a smile.

"Believe us," Dubois went on, "life in Paris is no good at a certain age. You're robust; you have eyes full of youth, and you have every chance of living to be a hundred if you stay in your beautiful Château de la Roche-Maubert, which is situated in the very best air and in the richest and most charming country one can see."

Then, having made this little speech, that strange Cardinal, whom the Regent considered to be a rogue and who did not believe in God, shook the Marquis' hand and escorted him back to his carriage."

"The road to Normandy!" cried Monsieur de la Roche-Maubert to the postillions.

---

[13] At the Fountain of Youth

The road to Normandy was then what it is today. One left Paris, going through the village of Chaillot, then passed over the Seine at Courbevoie; from Courbevoie one headed toward Bezons and from Bezons one went to Mantes, leaving Saint-Germain to the left.

It was almost nightfall when the Marquis had left Paris; it was two o'clock in the morning when his carriage, drawn by post-horses, stopped at the door of the hostelry of the Singe Vert.

The Singe Vert was the finest inn in Mantes, and that inn was kept by a worthy Norman born on the Marquis' estates, whose name was Blaisotin.

The Marquis told Blaisotin, who had got out of bed in haste to welcome him, that he would sleep in his inn after having eaten supper, and asked him for the best saddle-horse in his stables—for Blaisotin was a post-master as well as an innkeeper.

What did he want with a saddle-horse, since he was traveling in a carriage?

That was what Blaisotin could not work out.

The Marquis allowed Jonquille, his *valet de chambre*, the honor of being admitted to his table; he ate with a hearty appetite; then, having instructed Blaisotin to have the post-horses and the saddle-horse ready, he retired to the room that had been prepared for him in haste.

Jonquille went with him, to undress him—but the valet was astonished when he saw his master, instead of getting ready for bed, set out on a table to cosmetics and bottles bought from Buffalo's. His astonishment became amazement when, with the aid of those mysterious preparations, the Marquis set about dyeing his hair and moustache a beautiful ebony black, putting a layer of vermilion on his lips, and applying a nacreous paste to his leathery forehead with a silver-bladed knife, which caused his wrinkles to disappear.

When it was done, the Marquis said to Jonquille: "Go down to the stables."

Jonquille bowed.

"Saddle the horse that Blaisotin promised me."

"And mount up?" asked the valet.

"No, it's for me."

"What! Monsieur the Marquis isn't going to bed?"

"No, I'm going back to Paris."

"Alone?"

"And you're going to return to Normandy."

Jonquille was bewildered, but he carried out the orders he had been given.

An hour later, the carriage—whose leather curtains had been carefully drawn—emerged from the courtyard of the Singe Vert as noisily as it had arrived.

The Marquis, whose metamorphosis was complete, and whom no one recognized, was riding alongside it.

The carriage went through the entirety of Mantes, and then the Marquis turned his bridle and took the road to Paris at the gallop, murmuring: "It's the immortal woman I need now!"

XXVI

The Marquis de la Roche-Maubert galloped for the remainder of the night. At daybreak, he reentered Paris by the same route he had followed when he left.

As he had dyed the moustache and white hair black, and had made his wrinkles disappear beneath Buffalo's marvelous pastes, buckled his slightly corpulent figure in a corset, and had adopted an entirely youthful appearance, he could easily have returned to the vicinity of the Palais-Royal, found himself face to face with the Regent or Dubois, without either of them being able to recognize him—any more than César le Borne, proprietor of the Pomme d'Or, would have done.

Even so, the prudent Marquis—for he was prudent, although mad—instead of taking the road to the Rue de l'Arbre-Sec, went over the Seine and into the Latin Quarter.

In the Latin Quarter, in the Rue Saint-Jacques, there was a hostelry well worthy of its reputation. It dated from nearly two hundred years before, and had been famous in the days of the Valois for a siege it had sustained on Saint Bartholomew's Eve; it bore the sign: *Au Cheval Roan.*

Good King Henri IV had been placed astride the said horse as an afterthought, in such a way as to establish a second historic memory. The Béarnais had lodged there while he was still King of Navarre.

It was, therefore, toward the Cheval Rouan that the Marquis de la Roche-Maubert headed. He dismounted there, introducing himself as a Beauceron gentleman who had come to Paris on important business, and carefully concealed his name.

Then, as, in spite of the youthful appearance he had adopted, he began to feel the weight of the years and had lost the habit of violent exercise, and had, in addition, passed a sleepless night, he felt sufficiently tired to ask for a bed right away.

In any case, the Marquis, having returned to Paris with the sole aim of finding the immortal woman, knew full well that he could not carry out his search in broad daylight without exposing himself to a host of petty dangers and obstacles.

I'll start tonight, he said to himself.

In consequence, he slept all morning and part of the afternoon.

He woke up at about three o'clock, with a hearty appetite. Before summoning the landlord or the serving-girls, however, he did a little face-painting. He had taken care not to forget the perfumer Buffalo's little jars and bottles, which he had put in one of the bags attached to his saddle.

Having thus repaired his artificial youth, the Marquis went down to the hostelry's common room and had dinner served to him.

He ate and drank like the robust Norman he was, waited patiently for dusk, and went out, having warned the hotelier that he would undoubtedly be late returning.

From the Rue Saint-Jacques to the Rue de l'Hirondelle is only a short journey.

Let's reconnoiter the position, the Marquis set to himself. And he went forth at a deliberate pace, with a triumphant air, his face hidden by his cloak and his hat pulled down, his épée beating his calves with a victorious click.

When he reached the Rue Gît-le-Coeur, however, his memories of forty years ago took him by the throat, and he could not prevent his heart from racing violently. He slowed down, and even stopped several times, requiring considerable will-power to go on.

The Rue de l'Hirondelle, narrow and dark—the same, in sum, as forty years before—was as silent and placid as ever.

Two children were playing on one doorstep, a draper was sitting on his own, and that was all. There was still no light anywhere; the crepuscular gloom known as "between dog and wolf" was sufficient for the good folk of the quarter.

The Marquis was emotional, but his memories were coming back to him, one by one, with perfect clarity. He had often come, at the time of Jeanne's trial, to look at the exterior of the vampire woman's house, which had then been sealed by the police. The house was situated on the left, in the middle of the street.

The Marquis recognized it.

There was, however, nothing mysterious about its appearance. The windows were open and the door ajar.

A young woman was sitting on the doorstep, knitting a white stocking, taking advantage of the last glimmers of twilight.

The young woman was neither beautiful nor ugly, and was dressed as a maidservant. With the best will in the world, it was impossible to see her as the slightest instrument of Satan, or the house whose entrance she was guarding as anything but the dwelling of some peaceful bourgeois.

I'm not mistaken, though, the Marquis de la Roche-Maubert said to himself. *That's definitely the one...*

He went back and forth in front of the house a couple of times, as if he hoped to grasp some mysterious clue, see some fugitive gleam wandering behind the windows, or hear some unusual noise appropriate to the house of a witch or sorcerer.

Nothing at all!

Then the Marquis decided to approach the young woman, who looked up at him with large astonished eyes.

"My lovely child," he said, "to whom does this house belong?"

"To my master, Monsieur," she replied.

"And what is your master's name?"

"Guillaume Laurent."

"What is his profession?"

"He was a mercer in the Rue Saint-Denis, but he's made enough to live on and no longer does anything."

"Has he lived in the house for a long time?"

"Oh yes, Monsieur."

The Marquis had an inspiration. "Yes, yes, my lovely child," he said. "Guillaume Laurent, that's the name I was looking for."

"You know my master?"

"No, but I've been asked to give a message to him."

The Marquis wanted to get into the house, at any cost, and that was why he told that petty lie. At the same time, he stepped over the threshold.

"But Monsieur," said the red-haired young woman, rising to her feet. "My master isn't at home."

"Where is he, then?"

"Every evening, after supper, he goes over the river and walks to the Place du Châtelet, where there's an inn in which he meets old friends."

"Well," said the Marquis, insistent on entering, "I'll wait for him."

"In fact, Monsieur," said the maidservant, "you won't have to wait long, for here he is."

Indeed, a fat man marching with a heavy tread appeared at the corner of the street at that very moment.

XXVII

The bourgeois who was walking with a heavy tread stopped ten paces away, doubtless astonished to see a man with his maidservant.

On seeing that, the Marquis bowed.

Then the bourgeois came forward again, and recognized that he was dealing with a gentleman, for the Marquis' épée was causing his cloak to bulge slightly.

"Monsieur Guillaume?" said the Marquis, in a courteous tone.

"Yes, Monseigneur," the bourgeois replied, bowing almost as far as the ground. He was a man of middle age, obese and graying, with a thick and jovial face and a low brow devoid of intelligence.

"Monsieur Guillaume," the Marquis went on, "a thousand pardons for coming so late, but it's absolutely imperative that I talk to you for a few minutes."

Drunk with pride, the bourgeois bowed again and stood aside from his door to leave the entrance wide open.

"I'm entirely at your service, Monseigneur," he said. Then, addressing the maidservant, he said, abruptly: "Make up the fire in the drawing-room, Suzon, and light the candles." Turning back to the Marquis, he said: "Please come in, Monseigneur."

This is quite bizarre, thought the Marquis—and he went in.

The bourgeois Guillaume did not even try to guess what this unknown individual might want with him. He was a gentleman, a man with an épée, who was doing a bourgeois the honor of visiting him. That was sufficient.

Suzon, the red-haired maidservant, hastened to light the fire in the large room that followed the vestibule. At the same time, Guillaume lit the candles and placed them on the mantelpiece.

By their light, Monsieur de la Roche-Maubert took exact stock of his surroundings.

Certainly, nothing was less mysterious than the large room with bare walls and vulgar furniture in which he found himself. And the blissful face of the bourgeois! One could have sworn, at a glance, that he was neither the confidant nor the servant of the immortal woman.

When the fire was lit, Master Guillaume dismissed Suzon with an imperious gesture, after which he brought out a chair for the Marquis—and, standing respectfully before him, he said: "Monseigneur, I am at your orders."

"Sit down, Monsieur Guillaume," said the Marquis, with the politeness of a true nobleman.

"In truth, I hardly dare," stammered the bourgeois.

"But I can hardly converse with a man who is standing up," said Monsieur de la Roche-Maubert.

Guillaume was vanquished. He bowed again and sat down on the edge of a chair.

Then the Marquis said: "So you're retired from business, Monsieur Guillaume?"

The bourgeois seemed flattered by the question. "Yes, Monseigneur," he replied.

"And you've made a petty fortune?"

"I have enough to live," Guillaume replied, modestly.

"Don't be astonished, Monsieur Guillaume," the Marquis went on, "by the questions I'm asking you. I've been asked to see you by a nobleman of the Court, who is your friend and in greatly interested in you."

"In truth!" exclaimed the bourgeois, increasingly flattered, and repeated: "I'm at your orders, Monseigneur."

"So," Monsieur de la Roche-Maubert went on, continuing to parade an investigative gaze around him, "Having made your fortune, you've left the Rue Saint-Denis?"

"Yes, Monsieur."

"And you've rented this house?"

"No, it's mine."

"For a long time?"

"For more than twenty years, Monseigneur."

"And you bought it without any reluctance?"

"Well," said the bourgeois, naively, "the street is tranquil, inhabited by worthy people, and the house is large, well-built and well-ventilated."

"It had a bad reputation, though..."

"This house?"

"Yes. Didn't you know?"

Master Guillaume, amazed, stared at the Marquis.

"Forty years ago," the Marquis went on, "it belonged to a witch."

"I never heard mention of that."

"A witch who was burned..."

Monsieur Guillaume shivered.

"I wouldn't be surprised," Monsieur de La Roche-Maubert continued, "if you sometimes heard strange noises at night."

"I've never heard anything, Monseigneur." Master Guillaume manifested a vague anxiety as he said that.

"It's even said," the Marquis continued, "that even though the witch was burned, she isn't dead."

"Oh! Really?"

This time, Master Guillaume laughed out loud.

"At any rate, from whom did you buy the house?"

"From an old draper who died the same year that he sold it to me."

"And he didn't mention the witch to you?"

"Never."

"You must, however, have discovered secret doors, subterranean passages..."

"Absolutely none."

"That," said the Marquis, his conviction becoming increasingly deep-rooted, "is because you haven't searched very hard, my dear Monsieur Guillaume."

"Do you know, Monsieur," said the other, "that what you're saying is frightening me."

"Indeed!"

"And that tomorrow, I'll mount a search from the attic to the cellars."

"Why not right away?"

Guillaume shivered again. "In the middle of the night!" he said.

"Are you afraid, then?"

"No...but...however..."

The Marquis opened his cloak and displayed the hilt of his épée. "With Finette," he said, "I'm not afraid of anything myself—and if you wish, we can go fathom the mysteries of your house."

"As you please," said Master Guillaume, who seemed slightly reassured.

"Send your maidservant to bed," the Marquis went on. "For one thing, we have no need of her...and for another, there's no need to frighten the poor girl."

"Oh, undoubtedly," murmured Guillaume, whose teeth were chattering with terror.

The Marquis made a sign bidding him to pick up a candle. "Where shall we begin?" he said.

"Wherever you wish, Monseigneur." Guillaume's legs were trembling.

"Let's go down into the cellars first, then," said the Marquis.

Monsieur de la Roche-Maubert remembered that the steward Conrad had said that Janine's secret laboratory was under ground, and said to himself: *I'll wager that the subterranean chamber still exists and that Janine is there, since the Margrave's steward came to the Rue de l'Hirondelle two days ago.*

And Monsieur de la Roche-Maubert, who would have gone to the ends of the earth to find the immortal woman again, headed bravely for the door of the room, followed by the bourgeois Guillaume, who looked more dead than alive.

XXVIII

The maidservant, the red-haired girl whom Guillaume had addressed as Suzon, was in the vestibule when the Marquis and the bourgeois came out.

"You can go to your room and go to bed, Suzon," Guillaume said to her.

The maidservant bowed and headed toward the immense well of the staircase leading to the upper floors. It was underneath the same stairway that the door to the cellars was located—or, rather, the cellar, for Master Guillaume said, as he opened the door for the Marquis: "Our visit won't take long, Monseigneur; the cellar is neither large nor deep.

The sight of his maidservant seemed to have calmed Master Guillaume's fear somewhat. His tread was almost firm as he took the lead in going down the damp and slippery steps.

He raised the candle above his head, and Monsieur de La Roche-Maubert walked behind him unhesitatingly.

On the thirtieth strep, Guillaume turned round. "We're here," he said.

The Marquis saw a vaulted subterranean room, which appeared to be as wide as the house it supported, and around which barrels were arranged, the majority of them full.

"Damn," said the Marquis. "This is a fine cellar, and well-furnished, Monsieur Guillaume."

The bourgeois inclined his head.

"Let's see the others," the Marquis went on.

"What others, Monseigneur?"

"The other cellars, of course."

"There are no others—at least, I don't know of any."

"Of course!"

Monsieur de La Roche-Maubert was a conscientious man. Sustained by the double conviction that Janine's laboratory was underground, and that the immortal woman was living somewhere in the house, unknown to the bourgeois, he armed himself with a cooper's hammer that he found on a barrel.

122

"What are you going to do?" asked Guillaume.

"Search for blocked-up doors."

He took a candle then, holding it in one hand while the other held the hammer, and he started tapping the walls of the cellar at intervals, sometimes high up and sometimes low down. The Marquis knew perfectly well that a door, even one that is walled up, always renders a sound less full than an ordinary wall. In any case, he was convinced that the iron door that Conrad had mentioned still existed, but had disappeared under a layer of plaster, for the walls seemed to have been resurfaced only a few years earlier.

The Marquis' efforts went to waste. The walls returned the same sound everywhere.

Then, as one of the ends was pointed, intended to be slid if necessary between the staves of a barrel, Monsieur de la Roche-Maubert, who was not discouraged, began digging in the floor here and there.

The hammer sank into moist and porous earth, encountering no resistance anywhere.

"This is bizarre!" he murmured, finally. "There must, however, be another vault or floor somewhere beneath our feet."

"I don't think so," murmured Guillaume.

The Marquis went back to work. After an hour, he was no further forward.

"I must be mistaken," he muttered, finally, "and the door, the exit I'm searching for, must be somewhere else."

Monsieur Guillaume seemed perfectly content. The Marquis wanted to go back up to the ground floor. Guillaume followed him again.

The Marquis had kept the hammer. He began sounding the walls again on the ground floor, and then the upper floors, but without any result.

Nothing was less mysterious than that house, and it really was the residence of a peaceful bourgeois living on his petty income.

"You see, Monseigneur," said Guillaume, "there are no hollow walls, no secret doors, no subterranean passages. I've never heard it said that this house was once inhabited by sorcerers, and I think you've been wrongly informed." He said that with perfect candor—so perfect that a suspicion crossed the Marquis' mind.

I might have mistaken the house, he said to himself.

Then he made a thousand apologies to Master Guillaume, told him that he would or be long delayed in bringing him news of the nobleman, his friend, who was interested in him, and ended up leaving without giving him any further explanation.

Once in the street however, the Marquis would not consider himself beaten. It was, indeed, possible that he had mistaken Guillaume's house for that of the immortal woman; but he was, after all, in the Rue de l'Hirondelle, there was no doubt about that, and it was definitely in the Rue de l'Hirondelle that Janine had once lived.

While the Marquis had been with Master Guillaume the moon had risen, and its rays were streaming into the street, reflected from the pointed gables of the houses. The Marquis set about examining all the house on the left-hand side, one by one, for he remembered clearly that it was on the left and not on the right that the person he sought had lived.

The more conscientious his examination was, however, the stronger his conviction became. Janine's house really was the one from which he had emerged, the house of the good-for-nothing Guillaume.

Even if I have to stay here all night, the stubborn old man said to himself, *I'll find something.*

Directly opposite that house was another, whose porch was steeped in shadow. The Marquis went to station himself there and remained there, with his eyes fixed on the house, only one window of which was illuminated—that of the bedroom of the bourgeois, who was doubtless going to bed.

The Marquis waited for about an hour. The light went out. Guillaume was asleep, or going to sleep.

The Marquis, however, did not budge. Something told him that he was about to witness something unexpected, if not extraordinary.

Indeed, as midnight chimed in the distance at Saint-Germain l'Auxerrois, a man's footsteps, accompanied by the click of an épée on the pavement, became audible.

In the moonlight, the Marquis saw a man marching briskly, his face hidden by a turned-up flap of his cloak. It might well have been a passer-by, but the Marquis felt a quickening of his heartbeat that was soon justified, for the man in the cloak stopped at Master Guillaume's door.

Then the Marquis crossed the street and came to stand before him.

The unknown man started in surprise, and Monsieur de La Roche-Maubert saw that his face was masked.

"My dear sir," said the Marquis, "Permit me to ask you where you're going?"

"Home," replied the man in the cloak.

"This house is yours?"

"Undoubtedly." And by way of proof, he took a key out of his pocket, which he inserted in the lock.

"This is too much!" the Marquis exclaimed—and he placed himself in front of the door, adding: "You shan't go in until you've given me an explanation." At the same time, he drew his sword.

The man in the cloak did likewise, and the Marquis heard him snigger through his mask.

XXIX

Monsieur de la Roche-Maubert had, therefore, placed himself in front of the door, his blade in the air, determined not to let the unknown man enter until the latter had given him an explanation.

The unknown man laughed through his mask. "You'll let me go into my own house, I suppose," he said.

"Not before we've had a little chat," said the obstinate Marquis.

"I don't know you, Monsieur," said the unknown man, courteously.

"Nor I you, Monsieur."

"What can we have to say to one another, then?" said the unknown man, haughtily.

"Monsieur," said the Marquis, "you want to go into this house."

"Of course."

"And you claim to be going into your home?"

"Indeed. The proof is that this is a key that will turn in the lock."

"I, Monsieur, have come out of this same house."

"Ah!" And through the holes in the mask, the unknown man's eyes were shining life fireflies.

"I found a worthy man therein named Guillaume Laurent."

"Really?"

"Who affirmed to me that the house was his."

"Ah!"

"Now," said the Marquis, with increasingly severe logic, "if the house is Guillaume's, it isn't yours; if it's yours, it isn't Guillaume's."

"And what can that have to do with you, for God's sake?"

"It intrigues me."

"My dear sir," said the masked man coldly, "curiosity is unhealthy on certain moonlit nights."

"Really?" sniggered the Marquis.

"I therefore advise you to go to bed quietly at your hostelry, for you appear to me to be a provincial gentleman," said the masked man, ironically.

"Whether I'm from the provinces or not, I'm not going anywhere," said the Marquis, obstinately.

"My dear Monsieur," said the unknown man, who had lost none of his calmness, "if you did not have a black moustache I would swear that it was an old madman that I was dealing with, so much does your voice resemble his. Are you not, by chance, the Marquis de la Roche-Maubert, an old Master who has plunged into some bath prepared by Buffalo?"

The Marquis shuddered. He too thought that he had heard the voice that was resonating in his ears before. Abruptly, he said in his turn: "And I recognize you, in spite of your mask."

"Aha!"

"You're the Chevalier d'Esparron."

"So you *are* the Marquis de la Roche-Maubert."

"Perhaps..."

"Marquis," said the masked man, coldly, "I thought that you had left Paris."

"I did leave, in fact—but I've come back."

"To get mixed up in things that don't concern you."

"Perhaps."

"You're making a mistake, Marquis."

"*I want to see her!*" said the old man.

"Who?"

"Her! The witch! The immortal woman who lives in this house—for, at present, I can no longer doubt it."

"Bah!"

"Since you're here..."

"I swear to you, Marquis, that It's good advice that I'm giving you in inviting you to go to bed. You're staying in the Rue de l'Arbre-Sec, aren't you?"

"No, not any more—in the Rue Saint-Jacques, at the Cheval Rouan.

"That's nearer. *Bonsoir*, Marquis." And the masked man tried to move the Marquis aside—but the rejuvenated old man raised the point of his épée to his face.

"Come on," said the man in the mask. "I agree with Monseigneur le Régent—you're the most obstinate man in France and Navarre." And as he, too, had his sword in his hand, he placed himself *en garde*.

The street was deserted; all the bourgeois were asleep. Even if they had not been asleep, however, they would have refrained, on hearing the clash of swords, from going to their windows. The Parisians of the lower orders have long acquired the habit of never getting mixed up in the quarrels of men of quality.

The Marquis and his adversary were free to go at it wholeheartedly. Their blades touched, therefore, and the man in the mask murmured, in a mocking tone: "You'll grant me this justice, Monsieur, that I tried to talk sense into you."

But the Marquis did not want to hear anything. He had been very fond of the blade in his time—and his adversary sensed at the first pass that he was dealing with a rude épée.

"So much the worse," he said. "Come what may."

For ten minutes, a furious clicking was heard; the two épées were engaged to the hilt; iron clashed with iron; and the old man and the young one struggled with a terrible equality of strength, suppleness and courage.

A spectator, however, if the combat had had one, would have seen that the man in the mask was defending rather than attacking, and conserving all his strength, while the Marquis was beginning to tire.

"Marquis," he said, suddenly, "Believe me, there's still time: follow my advice, go back to your inn, and tomorrow, take the road back to your château in Normandy."

"I'd rather die," replied the Marquis, who seemed to acquire a new vigor.

And the combat recommenced, more ardent than ever.

XXX

Terrible as the clash of arms was, however, it did not prevent the two adversaries from exchanging a few words.

"You've recognized me," said the Marquis, "but I've also recognized you. You're the Chevalier d'Esparron, the lover of the witch, the vampire, who makes gold with human blood."

"In truth," sniggered the man in the mask, "you know too much, Marquis."

"Oh, you think so!"

"It's said that precocious children don't live long," the masked man continued, "but old men with too much memory finish badly."

"We'll see about that," said the Marquis, furiously—and his épée writhed and hissed like a viper, still seeking the way to his adversary's breast and incessantly encountering iron.

"I'm not astonished," the latter said, "That you've conserved the passions of a young man, Marquis. My God, you have a rude blade!"

"I certainly hope to kill you," said Monsieur de la Roche-Maubert, completely losing his self-composure.

"Good! Let's talk..."

"And when I've killed you..."

"Ah! Yes, when you've killed me, what will you do?"

"I shall go into that house."

"And then?"

"And then I shall put my sword, still streaming with blood, to the throat of the man I was chatting to a little while ago, and he'll have to talk."

"What do you want him to say to you?"

"I want him to show me the subterranean passage that leads to Janine's residence."

"The immortal woman?"

"Yes."

"You believe that, then?"

"Do I believe it! But you believe it too!"

"Perhaps..."

"Since you're her lover."

The Marquis' adversary continued to snigger through his mask. "But what do you want with that woman?"

"I want to see her."

"Why?"

"I love her."

"Still?"

"And I want to marry her."

"Marquis, you're mad!"

"What does it matter to you?" And Monsieur de la Roche-Maubert pressed his adversary even harder—but the latter continued to parry and seemed to be invulnerable.

"Marquis," he said, again, "at your age, this really is pure folly. You're no longer twenty years old, as in the days when you denounced the poor witch you loved and sent her to the pyre. Believe me, between the woman for whom you're looking and the one whose death you caused, there is no connection."

"She's the same!" howled the Marquis.

"All right, let's admit that—but then, the woman no longer loves you."

"Oh!"

"She hates you, in fact."

"However," Monsieur de la Roche-Maubert went on, "I'm not the most guilty."

These words brought an exclamation of astonishment from the man in the mask. "Really?" he said.

"No—the man who really domed Janine is the Margrave Prince of Lansbourg-Nassau."

"You know that?"

"Yes."

"Aha! You do know many things."

"I also know that the Prince is in Paris."

The man in the mask shivered again.

"And that his people, if not him, have renewed communications with the Rue de l'Hirondelle," the Marquis finished.

"Ah! This time, you really do know too much," said the man in the mask, suddenly changing tactics; abandoning defense for attack, he suddenly started pressing the Marquis, forcing him to break and thus driving him back against the wall. "So much the worse for you," he said. And he stretched out his arm, feinted, and thrust.

A cry escaped the Marquis; his hand opened, and dropped the épée. Then he collapsed, coughing up blood.

"I believe I've settled my account," he said. Then his eyes closed, and he lay on the ground, bloodied and motionless.

"Hot-head!" murmured the man in the mask. At the same time, he took out a little silver whistle that was suspended around his neck and put it to his lips.

In response to the noise, the door of the house opened and three men came out. Two were dressed as lackeys; the third was none other than the worthy Guillaume Laurent.

The latter made a gesture of dolorous astonishment on seeing the Marquis bathed in blood. "What!" he said. "The old fool stayed here, then?"

"Yes—and I'm very much afraid that I've killed him. Look."

The bourgeois bent down over the unconscious Marquis, unfastened his doublet, opened his chemise and set about examining the wound by moonlight.

"Is he dead?" asked the man in the mask.

"No."

"Is his wound mortal?"

"I don't think so."

"Too bad! Better for him to pass from life to death in that fashion."

Then the man in the mask turned to the two lackeys. "Pick him up, you two," he told them, "and carry him."

"Where to?" asked one of the lackeys.

"Rue Saint-Jacques—the Cheval Rouan."

"What shall we say?"

"Nothing. Leave him at the door."

The two men drew away, carrying the unconscious Marquis in their arms—but not before Guillaume Laurent, tearing up his handkerchief, had put a preliminary dressing in order to stop the blood-flow.

Then the man in the mask opened the door, and the two of them disappeared into the depths of the mysterious house.

XXXI

Guillaume Laurent, the bourgeois who had seemed to the Marquis to be an imbecile, was not mistaken about the Marquis' wound in saying that it was not mortal.

The valets had undoubtedly carried out the masked man's orders faithfully too, for, when he came round and became master of his reason for the first time, the Marquis found himself in the room that he had previously occupied in the hostelry of the Cheval Rouan.

At first, he had some difficulty in reassembling his memories. Then, having shifted in his bed, he experienced a sharp pain caused by his wound, to which he swiftly raised his hand.

Then he remembered the man in the mask.

At the same time, a little man clad in black, already old, came in.

"Who are you?" asked the Marquis.

"I'm your physician," the little man replied.

"Ah!"

"You've been very dangerously ill, Monsieur le Marquis," the man added.

"In truth!"

"But I've been without anxiety for two days."

"For two days?"

"Yes. For four others, however, I wouldn't have given a pistole for your life."

"What!" the Marquis exclaimed. "Four more days?"

"Yes, certainly."

"How long have I been here, then?"

"Ten days."

"A thousand thunders!" exclaimed the Marquis. "It's ten days since I fought the Chevalier?"

"I don't know with whom you fought, Monsieur le Marquis," the little man said. "All that I know is that you were found one morning at the door of the hostelry, covered in blood and unconscious."

"Aha!" sniggered Monsieur de La Roche-Maubert. "He had the courtesy to have me brought to my door. But we shall see one another again—my God, we shall see one another again!" He looked at the physician. "So," he said, "I'm out of danger?"

"Entirely."

"My wound..."

"Your wound is almost healed."

"I can get up, then?"

"Oh, not yet...but in three or four days..."

"That's good." And the Marquis swore a silent oath to find the man in the mask again—who could be none other than the Chevalier d'Esparron—and to return the sword-thrust he had received with interest.

"Can I, at least, get out of bed?" he asked.

"On condition that you don't leave your room."

"So be it!" said the old man, with a sigh.

A mirror placed opposite his bed had just made him a sad revelation. During his illness his hair and beard had lost their beautiful dark color and had become white again.

As Monsieur de la Roche-Maubert was sighing, the door opened again; this time it was the hotelier who came in.

"Ah, Monseigneur!" he said. "You've had a narrow escape—but as Monsieur the surgeon predicted, you're out of danger now."

"Really?" said the Marquis. "I was as ill as that?"

"You were delirious for three days and three nights, Monseigneur."

"Really?"

"But you're out of danger now, and I can announce His Eminence's principal *valet de chambre*."

"What?" said the Marquis. "What Eminence are you talking about?"

"Monseigneur le Cardinal Dubois, your relative, Monseigneur."

"The Cardinal knows that I'm here?"

"He has sent for news of you twice a day, and His Royal Highness the Regent once every morning."

"What! The Regent too?"

"Yes, Monseigneur."

"That wretched Chevalier!" muttered the Marquis, not doubting that his adversary must have hastened to inform the gentlemen of the court of his presence in Paris."

"And I've also been asked to give you a letter," the hotelier added.

"A letter from whom?"

"I don't know. It was brought this morning. Here it is." And the hotelier held out a sealed letter to Monsieur de la Roche-Maubert, who opened it immediately and, before reading it, skipped to the signature.

But there was no signature.

Then the Marquis, biting his lips with chagrin, read:

My dear relative,

My charitable advice, and that of a highly-placed person you know very well have had no success with you. With a stubbornness for which I am far from congratulating you, you have absolutely insisted on returning to Paris, and have deceived both of us.

You have been promptly punished, and I hope that you will profit from the lesson. According to the surgeon's reports, you can be in a fit state to travel by carriage in four or five days. We therefore hope that you will leave Paris, and no longer expose yourself to dangers that we are powerless to prevent.

One whom you know well,
and who has the interests of a relative.

The letter had evidently been dictated by Dubois to some secretary, and the prudent minister had not signed it.

Monsieur de la Roche-Maubert crumpled it angrily. "Four or five days," he muttered, between his teeth. "They're giving me four or five days. That's more than I need, and with God's help, I'll be on my feet well before then."

And the Marquis stirred in his bed, in order to take account of his strength.

XXXII

Monsieur de la Roche-Maubert reasoned as follows:

The surgeon has said that I can't get up for four or five days; the Cardinal and the Regent share that opinion. In consequence, they won't be keeping watch on me here, and I can make arrangements to go back to the Rue de l'Hirondelle before then.

After the surgeon and the hotelier had brought him up to date with what had happened, the Marquis only had one idea in his head: to be alone for a moment.

The surgeon dressed his wound.

The old fool who was known as the Marquis de la Roche-Maubert had been a man of war in his youth, and he had received more than one cut, either on the field of battle or in single combat. Thus, he knew something about wounds, bruises and other inconveniences of the profession of arms.

Having seen his wound, he said to himself: *It's three-quarters healed; in two days, there'll be no more evidence of it.*

The surgeon left, and then the hotelier, leaving the Marquis alone momentarily.

He did not waste a minute, and leapt out of bed. Then he set about walking back and forth in his chemise, agitating his arms and legs, and bending his knees—in sum, taking account of the strength that remained to him.

His épée was in a corner. He picked it up and thrust two or three times at the wall.

"Come on, come on!" he murmured. "I'm not as low as they think. We'll see tomorrow."

He went back to bed, and spent the rest of the day there, and the night that followed.

The surgeon came early the following day, still accompanied by the hotelier, who assisted with the dressing.

"Wretched barber," said the Marquis to the surgeon, "are you going to keep me on a diet? I'm dying of hunger this morning."

"Monseigneur can eat a chicken-wing and drink a few mouthfuls of old wine," the little man replied.

"I'm hungry, and profoundly bored," said the Marquis.

"You're bored, Monseigneur?" said the hotelier.

"Mortally."

The hotelier scratched his ear. "I don't really know what to say to Your Lordship," he said, "but..."

"But what?"

"Perhaps I can propose a distraction to Monseigneur."

"What's that?"

"There's a young man from Gascony staying here, who's very witty."

"He's staying here?"

"Yes—he's come to Paris to seek favor," said the hotelier. "When he heard that the Regent and the Cardinal send for news of Your Lordship every day, he was keenly interested."

"Naturally," said Monsieur de la Roche-Maubert, smiling.

"So," the hotelier went on, "He'd be only too happy, Monseigneur, to pay you a visit."

"What's his name?"

"The Chevalier de Castirac."

"Very good. How old is he?"

"About thirty."

"Good company?"

"And mettlesome, Monseigneur."

"Can he play chess?"

"Certainly."

"Well, ask him if he wants to give me a game."

And when the hotelier went out, along with the surgeon, who had finished the dressing, Monsieur de la Roche-Maubert said to himself: *A boy who's come to seek favor and believes in high influence might have need of a useful auxiliary.*

The Chevalier de Castirac arrived. He was a tall young man with long legs and a big nose.[14] He was very ugly, but full of wit; in addition, he had a very resolute manner and his rapier, which slapped his calves, had a conquering ring to it.

He's ugly enough for me not to fear a rival in him, thought Monsieur de la Roche-Maubert, *and given that his purse is flat and his épée bold, I can use him.*

The Chevalier de Castirac was infinitely grateful for the favor that Monsieur de la Roche-Maubert was doing him in accepting him as a partner in a game of chess. The marquis having invited him to dinner, he accepted with alacrity, and after an hour they were the best of friends.

Then the marquis said to him: "You've come to Paris to seek favor?"

"Like all Gascons, since King Henri," replied the Chevalier, smiling.

"What do you want?"

"A musketeer's uniform."

"Do you have any money?"

"I only have ten pistoles left."

"My young friend," said the Marquis, "do you think that a man like you can get into the musketeers in a week and that you'll be given two hundred pistoles right away?"

Gascon as he was, the Chevalier de Castirac was abashed, and looked at the Marquis. "Why are you mocking me, Monsieur?" he asked.

---

[14] Although this detail is subsequently forgotten, its initial citation was surely calculated to remind readers of another Gascon, Cyrano de Bergerac, who was a legendary figure in the heyday of the *roman feuilleton*, although his character and reputation had not yet been given final literary form by Edmond Rostand. In 1869, Alphonse Daudet had not yet provided the other great literary archetype of Southern braggadocio, Tartarin of Tarascon, whose character Castirac foreshadows.

"I'm not mocking you," the Marquis replied, "and the two hundred pistoles will be yours whenever you wish."

"The Devil's horns!" exclaimed the Chevalier. "Are you Satan, then, Monsieur le Marquis, and do you want to buy my soul?"

"No," replied the Marquis, "but I have need of you."

"Ah!"

"And your épée."

"It's a fine fellow, for sure!" said the Gascon, slapping the hilt of his rapier. What's it about?"

"Such as you see me," said the Marquis, "I'm in love."

"Really!"

"And it was in going in conquest of my mistress that I received the sword-thrust that is keeping me abed."

"Right!"

"But I won't give up, and I want to set out on campaign," said Monsieur de la Roche-Maubert.

"When?"

"This very evening. Would you like to accompany me?"

"I'm your man," said the Gascon.

"Then the two hundred pistoles are yours—but listen to me carefully."

"Speak."

"I wouldn't be astonished if I were being watched here, and that they'll try to prevent me from going out."

"Aha! Well, we'll see about that—you can rely on me."

And the Gascon, full of conceit, drank a large glass of Medoc and slapped the hilt of his sword again, adding: "Mamzelle Finette, I think there's going to be work for you to do."

XXXIII

A fortnight had passed since the Gascon, the Chevalier de Castirac, had arrived at the Cheval Rouan. In consequence, he knew its customs and habits, and he informed Monsieur de la Roche-Maubert with regard to whom, he was convinced, the Regent or Dubois must have given some mysterious order.

Every evening, in fact, the Chevalier, whose room was on the same floor but at the other end of the corridor, had noticed a sturdy fellow, who was a groom in the stables, setting up a camp bed in front of the Marquis' door and lying down there.

Now, the hostelry was not sufficiently crowded with visitors at that moment for the table-hand to have nowhere else to sleep. The Chevalier had, therefore, remarked on that to Monsieur de la Roche-Maubert.

"I would have bet on it!" he latter had said. "I'm being watched." Then he experienced a surge of anger. "I'll pass my épée through the fellow's body," he muttered.

The Gascon started laughing. "There's no need," he said. "I have a simpler means of getting rid of him."

"What?"

"Every evening, I spend some time in the kitchen, drinking a few mouthfuls from a flagon of Jurançon wine. The landlord and his wife go to bed, and I sometimes remain alone with the stable-hand. He's from my part of the world, and although I'm a gentleman and a little proud, like all gentleman without a sou to their name, I don't disdain to have a drink with him."

Monsieur de la Roche-Maubert started to smile.

"Until now," the Gascon went on, "I've only offered him a glass of wine; this evening, I'll make him drink a bottle and get him drunk."

"Good."

"Then I'll come to fetch you."

"Perfect."

Monsieur de la Roche-Maubert, as is evident, had found an auxiliary.

Things happened as the Chevalier de Castirac had anticipated. The Marquis, moreover, took the precaution of pretending to be weaker and in greater pain than the previous day; he told the surgeon who came to dress his wound that he was afraid of being unable to sleep. The surgeon prepared him a calming potion, which the Marquis pretended to drink, but which he discarded on the other side of the bed.

The landlord came, as usual, to help with the dressing, and wished Monsieur de la Roche-Maubert goodnight. He went out with the surgeon, and the Marquis heard him say: "He won't be giving us any trouble today."

An hour later, another sound, to which he had never paid attention before, reached his ears, and he recognized that the stable-lad was doubtless setting up his bed in the corridor. Finally, not long after, he heard sonorous snoring. His jailer was asleep.

Then the Marquis slipped silently out of bd.

The moon was shining and the nocturnal star's light was entering the room profusely. Monsieur de la Roche-Maubert had no need to light a lamp.

Thanks to the moonlight he got dressed, opened his little pots and bottles, and set about tinting his hair and beard, and covering his face with an ointment intended to make wrinkles vanish. Then he made sure that his épée moved easily in its scabbard and loaded two pistols, which he placed in his belt—after which he waited.

About an hour went by.

The snores of the stable-hand could still be heard, and the other noises of the house died away one by one.

Finally, someone knocked softly on the door.

The Marquis opened it.

"Oof!" said the Gascon, coming in, "I thought the landlord wasn't going to bed tonight. He was chattering like a one-eyed magpie. Are you ready?"

"Yes."

"Come on, then."

"What about the stable-lad?"

"He's as drunk as a Swiss, and we can take the key to the stables from around his neck—we'll go out that way; the landlord sleeps too close to the other door."

"As you please," said the Marquis.

The Chevalier, who knew the lie of the land, took him by the hand and they went into the corridor. The stable-lad's bed had been set across the door, but the Gascon had moved it side without difficulty. With no less audacity, he turned back the blanket in which the fellow had wrapped himself, and took possession of the key he wore around his neck.

The stable had a door that opened into a back street, and that was the door whose key the Gascon had taken from the valet. A few minutes later, the two fugitives were out of the hostelry, and a quarter of an hour after that, they went into the Rue Gît-le-Coeur.

It was then nearly midnight, and the peaceful quarter was deserted.

At the corner of the Rue de l'Hirondelle, however, a human form was stirring on a boundary-marker on which it was seated.

The Marquis de la Roche-Maubert stopped.

The human form stood up and extended a hand.

"Charity, if you please," it said.

Reassured, the Marquis drew nearer and saw an old beggar-woman. "Charity," the latter repeated, "in exchange for good advice."

"What is it?" asked the Marquis. And he placed a pistole in the old woman's hand.

"You're generous," she replied, "and ought not to suffer misfortune."

"What misfortune are you talking about, you old witch?"

"Don't go to the Rue de l'Hirondelle," the beggar-woman replied—and took flight.

XXXIV

Something akin to glimmer of light dawned in Monsieur de la Roche-Maubert's brain—but a glimmer of common sense.

The old woman who had been seen, forty years before, going into Janine's house on the night of the execution, holding a billy-goat on a leash, suddenly returned to his memory. Perhaps the beggar-woman to whom he had just given alms was the same old woman.

Since his amorous folly had gripped him, the Marquis had not experienced a single moment of dread. He had one now, and perhaps he would even have beaten a retreat had he been alone—but the Gascon was with him: the Gascon who wanted to earn his two hundred pistoles, and who burst out laughing.

The Gascon's laughter made the Marquis shiver; he was ashamed of his hesitation. "Let's go," he said. "Forward ho!"

"That's my opinion," replied the Chevalier de Castirac.

They lengthened their stride and went into the Rue de l'Hirondelle—but the Marquis had taken his young companion's arm and he said to him: "It's necessary, though, that I bring you up to date with the situation."

"Very well—I'm listening."

"It's not yesterday," the Marquis went on, "that I fell in love."

"Ah!"

The Marquis dared not admit, however, that his amour dated back forty years. The Chevalier might well have laughed out loud, as he had at the beggar-woman.

"So, my love isn't recent," the old fool continued, "but the woman I love is perhaps the purest and most beautiful in the world."

"I can well believe it, Monsieur," put in the Chevalier de Castirac, a flatterer and courtier, as any man must be who lodges the Devil in his purse.

"Look—that's the house where she is," the Marquis added.

"Good."

"It's a matter of laying siege to it."

"And of killing a lover or a jealous husband, no doubt."

"No, it's not that..."

"What, then?" And the Chevalier looked in turn at Marquis, whose face reddened, and at the house, which was silent and seemed deserted.

"That house is full of mysteries, like the woman I love," Monsieur de la Roche-Maubert went on.

"Really?"

"Between ourselves, that creature of idea beauty is a trifle bizarre, a trifle...extraordinary. She's occupied with science."

"What do you mean?"

"Chemistry and alchemy," said the Marquis, judging it unnecessary to tell the Chevalier everything, but needing nevertheless to make him understand certain things in order to utilize the assistance of his épée when the time came.

"So she does chemistry and alchemy? What is she looking for?"

"The philosopher's stone."

"Which is to say, a means of making gold?"

"Precisely."

"And...has she found it?"

"Perhaps...I don't know, exactly. But what I do know is that this house is double."

"What do you mean?"

"It has a subterranean section in which the object of my amour lives—a lamplit palace into which daylight never penetrates."

"So?" said the Gascon, intrigued.

"The upper part of the house—which is today, the one we can see—is inhabited by a bourgeois simpleton named Guillaume Laurent, but it's necessary not to be deceived by his stupidity and placidity, which are only apparent; the man is like the Cerberus of the subterranean palace, the entrance to which I don't know."

"Very well," said the Gascon, coldly. "I'll put my sword to his throat and he'll have to show us where it is, this entrance."

"That's not all," said the Marquis.

"Ah!"

"The beauty has a lover..."

"Oho!"

"And it's with him that it will be necessary to come to blows, if we reach the subterranean part of which I speak."

"I'll make short work of him," said the Gascon, who was not from the banks of the Garonne for nothing.

"So this," Monsieur de la Roche-Maubert, went on, "is the best plan to follow, in my opinion..."

"Go on."

"You're going to knock at the door."

"And?"

"It's probable that only a spy-hole will open, and someone will ask you what you want, calling at such an hour."

"What do I reply?"

"I've come from the Place du Châtelet, Monsieur Guillaume, and I have a message for you."

The Gascon nodded.

"It's probable that the bourgeois will let you in."

"I get it—in which case, I shove him inside and you come in behind me."

"That's it, exactly."

"The rest will go like clockwork," added the Gascon. "Hide behind me."

The Marquis flattened himself against the wall.

Then the Chevalier de Castirac lifted the heavy door-knocker, which awoke the sleeping echoes in the house when it fell back.

A few seconds went by; then heavy footfalls were heard inside, and then, as the Marquis had foreseen, a spy-hole opened in the middle of the door and a voice he recognized as that of the bourgeois Guillaume said: "What the devil do you want with me at such an hour?"

A ray of light passing through the spy-hole attested that the fellow was carrying a lamp.

"I've come from the Place du Châtelet and I have a message for you," replied the Chevalier.

The bourgeois replied: "Come in, then." And he opened the door.

Suddenly, the Chevalier seized him by the throat and shoved him to the back of the vestibule.

At the same time, the Marquis came in and closed the door. "This time, my good man," he said, "you'll have to talk..."

And he raised the point of his sword to his face.

XXXV

Master Guillaume Laurent, the placid bourgeois, had recoiled precipitately, but he had not dropped the candlestick that he was carrying in his hand and he did not utter any exclamation.

"Ah, rogue!" said the Marquis. "This time, you'll talk."

Guillaume was still moving backwards, and thus arrived in the room where he had received the visit of the amorous Marquis a few days earlier.

"Marquis, Marquis," said the Chevalier de Castirac then, "I can see that the fellow doesn't want to offer us the slightest resistance. In consequence, I think that we can sheath our blades."

"Yes, but the fellow will talk!" the Marquis repeated.

Guillaume, out of breath, with sweat on his brow, had backed up against the wall, having placed his candlestick on the mantelpiece.

The Marquis sheathed his épée, and closed the door at the same time. Then he planted himself in front of the bourgeois. "Now, fellow," he said, "let's have a little chat. You told me that this house belongs to you?"

"Yes, Monsieur."

"For more than twenty years?"

"Yes, Monsieur."

"You were playing the simpleton with me, and pretending that you had no landlord."

Guillaume made no reply.

"You even had such an air of honesty, when we visited the cellars, that I was persuaded that you knew absolutely nothing."

A smile played upon Guillaume's lips then; he seemed to have recovered from his initial moment for fright.

"However," the Marquis continued, "instead of going away, I stayed in the street and kept watch on your house. Shortly thereafter, a gentleman appeared, put a key in the lock, and..."

"Monseigneur," said Guillaume, then, "there's no need to go on. I know the rest."

"Good," said the Marquis. "You know everything, then."

"Absolutely everything."

"And you'll talk?"

"Guillaume looked at the Chevalier de Castirac. "This young man is doubtless your friend," he said.

"I have that honor," said the Gascon.

"I can talk in front of him, then?"

"Of course."

The bourgeois suddenly seemed transfigured. The glimmer of a smile came to his lips, and his simpleton's face lit up with an expression of cunning; at the same time he took a chair and straddled it, with no further respect for the man upon whom he had, until then, lavished *Monseigneurs*."

The Marquis, however, seemed to be so avid for information that he overlooked the lack of courtesy.

"Monsieur le Marquis," Guillaume went on, "a provincial gentleman as rich as you must be a hunter."

"So what?" said the Marquis.

"To say hunter implies familiarity with poaching, and Your Lordship must know how one sets snares for hares and rabbits."

"Of course I know that—but what are you getting at?"

"The hare and the rabbit run head down," Guillaume continued. "The woodcock, more circumspect, raises her head from time to time, and if she sees a little piece of white paper attached to a stick, she retraces her steps."

"What are you trying to say, clown?"

"Wait a moment, Monseigneur. The piece of paper I mentioned has been placed there by a poacher who is warning off the woodcock and doesn't want her to be caught in the snare he's set for a hare."

"Have you finished talking nonsense!" exclaimed the Marquis, impatiently.

"I've finished," said Guillaume. "This house resembles a snare, Monseigneur."

"Good!"

"And I'm the piece of white paper."

"Which means?"

"That the trap isn't intended for you."

"Really!"

"The snare is for someone else, and that's why I'm telling you what others have already said to you, Monseigneur—if you're wise, you'll go away."

"Clown!" exclaimed the Marquis. "I swear to you that if you don't show me right away the passage that leads to the underground part of the house, I'll plant my épée in your throat."

Guillaume let out a sigh. "In truth," he said, "there are people to whom one shouts in vain: *Look out!*"

"Possibly."

"Then you insist?"

"I insist."

"Well, so be it."

Guillaume left the place where he was and went to the fireplace, in which there was no fire. Then the Chevalier de Castirac and the Marquis, amazed, saw him take one of the andirons and rap three times on the back of the fireplace.

About a minute went by; then the back of the fireplace turned on invisible hinges, like a door, and the Marquis and his young companion saw a kind of black gaping hole appear.

The Marquis uttered a cry of triumph. He picked up the candlestick and approached the mysterious corridor.

"I can see a staircase," he said.

"A staircase that will take you where you want to go," said Guillaume.

"I certainly hope so."

"But from which you won't come back," sniggered Guillaume.

"You think so?"

"I'm sure of it."

"Well, personally, I'm sure of the contrary."

"Ah!"

"Chevalier," the Marquis said, taking out his watch. "It's one o'clock in the morning. You're going to stay here, with Master Guillaume."

"Very well," said the Chevalier.

"If, at three o'clock, I haven't come back..."

"I'll lodge my rapier in the fellow's breast, no?" said the Chevalier, coldly.

"Precisely," said the Marquis.

Then he took the candlestick and, sword in hand, ventured into the mysterious stairway.

XXXVI

When the Marquis de la Roche-Maubert had stepped into the mysterious passage and the noise of his footsteps, resounding at first on the steps of the staircase, had died away in the distance, the bourgeois Guillaume Laurent suddenly changed his attitude to the Chevalier de Castirac.

"Monsieur," he said to him, "we might chat for a while, if you like."

"Gladly," the Chevalier replied, sitting astride a chair and putting his naked blade between his legs.

"Are you the son, the nephew or simply a friend of the Marquis?" Guillaume went on.

"I'm simply his friend."

"For a long time?"

"Since this morning."

"So much the better," said the bourgeois. "A friendship of such recent provenance isn't dangerous."

"What do you mean?"

"One can console oneself for the loss of a friend of twenty-four hours," Guillaume continued, phlegmatically.

"Are you mocking me, Bumpkin!"

"God forbid, Sir!" But Guillaume's voice, in making that humble reply, was no longer the same. It had taken on a hint of irony, mingled with a tone of authority."

"I certainly hope," the Chevalier said, "not to have to mourn the Marquis."

"Pooh! Who knows?"

"And in any case," the Gascon went on, "you know what I've promised him..."

"No, I don't know," said Guillaume.

"I've promised him that if the Marquis doesn't come back in two hours, I'll run you through," said the Gascon.

"Oh, that's true—I wasn't thinking about that."

"You have a very bold attitude now, Clown!"

"Would you like me to weep?"

"No, but I want you to adopt the attitude with me that a bourgeois ought to have with regard to a gentleman."

"Excuse me," said Guillaume, "I'm unfamiliar with fine manners—but we have two hours before us, haven't we?"

"Two hours of life for you—for if the Marquis doesn't come back..."

"God—I understand. But what are we going to two for those two hours? Are you thirsty?"

"Ho ho!" said the Gascon, clicking his tongue.

"In that dresser you can see there," Guillaume went on, "I have two or three bottles of old wine."

"Well, let's see them..."

"Do you like card games?" Guillaume said, then.

"Of course."

"*Bête ombrée*, for instance?"[15]

"It's my favorite game."

"Well," said Guillaume, "it seems to me that we might amuse ourselves a little during those two hours."

He went to open the dresser, took out two venerable bottles covered with cobwebs and brought them, along with two goblets, to the table that was in the middle of the room. Having uncorked the bottles, he filled the goblets.

"Your health!" he said.

"To yours, rather," said the Gascon, "or, even better, to that of the Marquis."

The bourgeois shook his head, and made no reply.

"And where are the cards?" asked Castirac.

"In the next room, which serves as my bedroom."

"Go fetch them."

"Don't drink it all while I'm gone, at least," said Guillaume, smiling. And he went into the next room.

---

[15] The French card game known as *bête* [beast] was a primitive ancestor of whist and other trick-taking games. This version of it is presumable the one known in English as *ombre*, that name being a corruption of the Spanish *hombre* [man] rather than having anything to do with shadows.

He's a thoroughly good chap, said the Gascon to himself, *and I hope, in truth, that the Marquis comes back safe and sound from his adventurous expedition, for I'd be reluctant to kill him.*

Two minutes went by. The door to the room that Guillaume had entered reopened.

The Chevalier could not suppress a gesture and an exclamation of surprise.

Guillaume was no longer Guillaume—or, rather, he was Guillaume metamorphosed from head to toe. He had taken off his cinnamon-colored smock, his otter-fur cap, his chestnut slippers and his black woolen socks. He was clad in a fine doublet of thick cloth, shod in funnel-shaped boots, coiffed in a plumed hat tilted over his left ear, had a mantle over his shoulder and a rapier sat his side. His boots were also fitted with spurs, which rattled on the floor-tiles.

No less surprisingly, Guillaume's face had lost its expression of amiable simplicity, to assume and audacious expression that advertised a swordsman.

Advancing toward the stupefied Gascon, he said: "There—with what game would you like to start, my man?"

"But..." the Gascon stammered. "I find this masquerade pleasant, amusing..."

"Where do you see a masquerade?"

"Well...those clothes..."

"Are mine."

"That épée…"

"Will make the acquaintance of yours, my petty Monsieur."

"Bumpkin!" said the Gascon. "A gentleman like me..."

"Can fight with another."

"You're a gentleman?"

"At your service."

"You're not a mercer, then?"

"No more than you are."

"Then what are you doing here?"

"I'm helping friends who have need of me."

"In truth!"

"And sometimes, I give good advice to people I like, have nice faces and deserve it. You're one of them."

"And you have some advice to give me."

"Perhaps."

"In that case, let's have it."

"Put your rapier back in its sheath, your hat on your head, your cloak over your shoulders, drink a last glass with me, and leave."

Master Guillaume had pronounced these words coldly, in an authoritative tone.

"You're joking, Clown!" said the Gascon.

"No, I'm speaking in your own interest."

"And if I don't want to go?"

"It's my opinion that it will be a game very different from *bête ombrée* that we'll be playing, my little Gascon cadet.""

And with these words, Guillaume blithely drew his sword. Then he put himself *en garde*.

"The two of us, then!" he said.

XXXVII

The Chevalier de Castirac was brave—that is incontestable—but he was a Gascon, and the Gascon temperament exaggerates everything.

Now, ten minutes earlier, the Chevalier, thinking that he was dealing with a placid bourgeois, had been slapping the hilt of his rapier with a bravado to make one shiver. That rapier, one could have sworn, was fit to hollow out a breach like Roland's famous Durandal.

However, when the pretended bourgeois reappeared with a gentleman's costume and a sword in his hand, the Chevalier's rapier lost some of its prestige, and the Chevalier his self-assurance.

Nevertheless, as he placed himself *en garde*, he did not cease to protest.

"Clown!" he said. "I believe you're mocking me."

"Really!" Guillaume sniggered.

"You're no gentleman."

"Bah! You think not?"

"And since you dare to stand up to me..."

"I beg your pardon," said Guillaume. "I understand that a poor unarmed bourgeois, trembling and throwing himself at our knees, would suit you better—but after all, my petty Monsieur, one does what one can, and for want of lard, one makes do with butter."

"I can teach you a lesson!" howled the Gascon.

The two épées were engaged all the way to the hilt, and from the first second, the Chevalier sensed that he was dealing with a strong opponent. Guillaume thrust well, with great calm and a remarkable wrist-speed, in spite of his paunch and his heavy appearance.

"Teach me a lesson?" he said, laughing. "But you're not thinking straight, my young friend."

"Oh, you think so?"

"And look, at this moment, you have other things to do. You're only thinking of covering yourself, and you're right."

Indeed, the Chevalier was parrying as best he could, and had a great deal to do, for Guillaume was pushing him vigorously.

The Chevalier was not a Gascon for nothing, however. "Sandis!"[16] he cried. "This will end with your death, my poor friend."

"That's quite possible," Guillaume replied, "but then, it's necessary not to keep retreating eternally."

And Guillaume was right. The Chevalier was retreating, again and again, constantly, and Guillaume was pressing him so hard that he had already gone twice around the room—which did not prevent the Chevalier from crying: "I'll finish by nailing you to a all, Bumpkin!"

"I don't say no." Guillaume replied, still cal and full of irony. "Except..."

"Oh! You're asking for mercy?" But the Gascon was still retreating before Guillaume's terrible blade.

"I don't seem to be," said the latter, "but it's quite possible that you'll lodge your rapier in my body."

"You can count on it. Sandis!" Nevertheless, the Chevalier was still retreating.

"Except," Guillaume went on, "I think I'll have time to have a chat with you."

"Ah!"

"And make you a little proposition."

"Really!"

"Preceded by a question."

"What?"

"I'll let myself observe that you've only been the Marquis' friend since this morning."

"That's true—but there are wines strong enough for one to drink them from the vintage barrels. My friendship is like that."

"He's rich, the Marquis," Guillaume went on.

---

[16] This term, used by Castirac as an oath, is an Old French word for madder, and hence a euphemism for blood.

"The Chevalier shivered, made an error, left himself momentarily exposed, and Guillaume's épée brushed his breast.

"If I had wanted to, I would have killed you," the latter said calmly, "but let's keep talking. So, the Marquis is rich..."

"What's that to you?"

The Chevalier had foam on his mouth, and his forehead was bathed in sweat, while Guillaume appeared to be as calm as a fencing-master.

"I'd like to know what promise he made to stimulate your young friendship."

"Wretch!"

"Bah! Between ourselves, we can tell all...come on, was it a hundred, two hundred, three hundred pistols?"

The Chevalier uttered a cry of rage.

"If you want to go," Guillaume went on, "You'll have to swear to me to keep the secret of this adventure, and convince yourself that you have nothing now to gain from the commerce of the Marquis de la Roche-Maubert—who, in any case, you might never see again...but take care...that's the second time I've had your life in my hands... So, as I was saying, if you want to keep the secret and go, it's not two hundred pistoles but double that I'll offer you..."

The Chevalier was still retreating, and if he had not been a Gascon he would have shouted immediately that he accepted—but the diabolical blood of the banks of the Garonne was flowing in his veins...

"Scoundrel!" he said. "I believe you're insulting me."

"No," said Guillaume,

"Or mocking me?"

"Not at all."

"I'll have all your blood."

And the Chevalier, drunk with wrath, thrust with all his might. Guillaume parried the stroke, and countered—and the Chevalier, as he straightened up, felt the other's blade on his breast.

"Bah!" said Guillaume, "I'll have all the time in the world to kill you. Let's see if we can reach an understanding." And he put up his sword.

The Chevalier found himself, at that moment, driven into the corner of the doorway.

"Would you like four hundred pistoles?" repeated Guillaume.

"Never."

"Then let's get it over with."

Guillaume matched blades with the Gascon, made a vigorous whiplash movement—and the épée, escaping from the Gascon's hand, landed twenty paces away.

"This time, my young friend," said the pretended bourgeois, putting the point of his own weapon to the Gascon's throat, "it's necessary to choose…either pass on to the other world, with neither noise nor trumpet, or take my four hundred pistoles and go away."

"Oh! You've convinced me," murmured the Gascon.

"You accept?"

"Of course!"

"And you'll keep quiet?"

"As the tomb."

"Good! I knew that Gascons were intelligent men."

And Guillaume put his sword back in its sheath. Picking up the Chevalier's, he held on to it, to remove any temptation from his vanquished adversary to continue an obviously unequal contest.

XXXVIII

Now, let us see what has become of the Marquis de la Roche-Maubert.

There is nothing so tenacious, it is said, as the amorous fantasy of an old man. We have seen, by his conduct during the last week, that the Marquis had taken it upon himself to justify that assertion fully.

To rediscover Janine, the immortal woman, the witch who made gold, was henceforth the sole objective of his life.

He had, therefore, ventured bravely, candlestick in hand, into the stairway that the mobile slab of the fireplace had just unmasked.

Where did that stairway lead?

To the laboratory, for sure, the Marquis told himself.

And, with the candlestick in one hand and his naked sword in the other, the Marquis continued downwards.

The stairway wound around in the form of a spiral. Gusts of damp air rose from the depths, striking the Marquis in the face—but he kept going down.

At the fortieth step, or thereabouts, he heard a dull sound. He stopped, and cocked an ear. The sound was reminiscent of the distant rumble of thunder—but the Marquis soon recognized it for what it was. It was the splash of water against a rock that he could hear—and Monsieur de la Roche-Maubert understood that the stairway led down to the river.

Momentarily, he thought about retracing his steps and looking elsewhere for the route that led to the laboratory, but then he remembered that, during her trial, Janine had said to her judges: "One can reach my dwelling by water as well as by land."

The judges had undoubtedly not understood those words, since the investigations and searches ordered by the court in the house in the Rue de l'Hirondelle had not produced any result—but the Marquis, remembering that reply, was able to conclude that by descending further he would find some lateral corridor, or some door fitted into the stairwell, which would take him where he wanted to go.

He therefore set out again, still going downwards.

The sound became more distinct, the air damper.

However, the Marquis was not mistaken. At the sixtieth step, he found a recess. The stairwell broadened out and a tunnel opened to the left.

"That's my road," said the Marquis. And, leaving the stairway, he went into the tunnel.

He had scarcely taken twenty paces when the air became fresher and a gust of wind blew over his candle, putting it out.

Then the Marquis found himself plunged into intense darkness.

Anyone other than the stubborn old man would have lost his calmness at that moment, and all his presence of mind. Perhaps he would not have dared to budge—or, moving backwards, would have had only one objective: that of finding the stairway and returning to the surface of the living world.

At any rate, no one but the Marquis would have thought of going forward—but the Marquis did not hesitate for long.

He was in the dark, but what did that matter? So he resumed walking, extending his épée before him to sound for obstacles, murmuring: "Even if this were the road to Hell, I'd follow it to the end."

The tunnel was damp underfoot, a trifle muddy; it also followed an inclined plane, and the Marquis understood that he was still heading downwards. As it descended deeper underground, however, it also curved slightly, as Monsieur de la Roche-Maubert realized, for the darkness surrounding him became less dense, and something like the glimmer of a star half-lost in a cloud, or the tip of a firebrand covered in ashes, appeared in the distance.

"Aha!" he said, with an infantile joy—and he increased his pace.

As he advanced further, the luminous dot came closer, but did not increase in size.

When he was very close to it, the Marquis was able to take exact account of what he saw. The tunnel he had been following was closed by a door; in the middle of the door there was a little hole, and a ray of light as escaping through that hole.

The Marquis put his eye to the hole.

He perceived a further tunnel. This one was illuminated by a lamp suspended from the vault.

But how could he get into it? The door separating it from the first was locked, and seemed to be very thick. The Marquis rammed it with his shoulder, but only succeeded in bruising himself fruitlessly. The door held firm.

Then the old man started running his hand over it, from top to bottom and from side to side, and suddenly stifled a cry of joy. His hand had encountered a cord. He pulled that cord, and immediately, a bell began to ring.

"Good!" said the Marquis. "It's the visitors' bell!"

And he pulled the cord again.

Then he waited.

A few seconds went by.

The Marquis had applied his eye to the hole in the door again, and was exploring the lighted tunnel. Suddenly, the light became brighter, and a second light-source appeared in the distance. Then, behind that light, which was that of a candle, the Marquis perceived a man.

The man came forward, the candlestick in his left hand and a bunch of keys in the right..

He was draped in a capacious cloak—and when he came closer, the Marquis felt his blood flow away from his heart, and his lips crease with anger.

The man with the bunch of keys was masked.

The Marquis did not doubt for a single instant that it was his adversary, the man who had gallantly laid him out, with the thrust of an épée, in the gutter of the Rue de l'Hirondelle. And that adversary could not be anyone but the Chevalier d'Esparron, Janine's present lover.

162

"This time, I shall have my revenge!" the Marquis growled.

The masked man arrived at the door and said: "Who rang?"

"Me," said the Marquis, in a voice stifled by anger.

"What's your name?"

"La Roche-Maubert."

The man sniggered through his mask—but he inserted a key into the lock, and the door opened.

"I've been expecting you, Marquis," the masked man said, in a mocking tone.

At the same time, he put his hand on the hilt of his sword, which was lifting up a corner of his cloak.

XXXIX

The Marquis had his sword in his hand. When he found himself in the presence of the man in the mask, he uttered a kind of roar.

"You and me," he said.

The masked man left his sword in its sheath. "You want your revenge, then?" he said, calmly.

"Of course," said the Marquis, "and I'm astonished that you haven't drawn your weapon yet."

"That's because I didn't know you were in such a hurry."

"Really."

"And because I'm not, personally."

"You must, however, have expected find me on your trail," said the furious Marquis.

"Certainly—and the proof is that I've just opened the door to you."

"Ah! That's true," said the Marquis, struck by the logic of the reply.

"Now," the Chevalier went on, "if you care to listen to me for a second, you'll see..."

"Speak!"

"You came into the house up above..."

"Naturally."

"You were absolutely intent on seeing the immortal woman, as you call her," the man in the mask continued, "and all the good reasons that Master Guillaume could have given you must have seemed bad, since here you are."

"You knew that?"

"I imagine so, since Guillaume struck the block in the fireplace, behind which there's a bell connected to the place where I was—for which reason I came to meet you."

"Well, Monsieur," said the Marquis, "now that you're here, *en garde*, if you please."

"One more word, and I'm at your orders."

"All right, but hurry."

"It's quite evident," the man in the mask continued, "that you haven't come this far solely to fight with me again and get your revenge."

"No, I've come because I want to see her."

"Well, if we fight right away, and I kill you, you won't see her."

Once again, that was perfectly logical.

The Marquis made a disdainful gesture, however. "I believe you're afraid," he said, "and trying to get away from me."

"God forbid!" said the man in the mask, angrily. "Far from it, in fact. Given that you've come this far, we no longer have any reason to bar your way, and if you want to see the immortal woman, I'm ready to take you to her. After which, if your heart still drives you, I'll put myself at your disposal."

In all conscience, the Marquis de la Roche-Maubert no longer had any objection to raise.

"All right—so be it," he said. "Let's go."

"Follow me," replied the man in the mask. Then, lifting the candlestick above his head in order to light the way, he went on ahead.

The Marquis had sheathed his épée.

The corridor was long, and circled around like a broad stairway, following a rather steep slope; it reminded Monsieur de la Roche-Maubert of the eccentric path constructed by Louis VIII in one of the towers of the Château d'Amboise, which permitted the monarch to arrive in a litter, on horseback or in a carriage on the flat roof of the palace, which was more than a hundred feet above the level of the Loire.

"Does this corridor never end!" exclaimed the Marquis, losing patience.

The masked man turned round. "It will end too quickly for you," he said, in a voice imprinted with sad mockery.

"Oh yes," sniggered the Marquis, "you're doubtless going to speak to me in the same language as the Regent."

"The Regent is very fond of you, Marquis."

"He'll still be fond of me..."

"Or, at least, he'll miss you."

"What?"

The man in the mask had stopped. "Listen, Marquis," he said. "You're mad, but honor must still be dear to you, and I'm convinced that if you give me your word, you'll keep it."

"What do you mean?" aid the Marquis, arrogantly.

"That you're going, head down, to your death."

"Oh! Is it you who's going to kill me?"

"I can't say any more—except, please, listen to me. You've attacked Guillaume, you've found a road that no one wanted you to take, and you've got this far—that's all well and good. Consent to go back, give me your word as a gentleman that you'll return to your province, that you won't say anything to anyone about what you've seen, and that you won't pronounce the immortal woman's name again, and there's still time. I'll save you."

"Monsieur," said the Marquis, angrily. "I've accepted you as a guide, not as an adviser."

"You want to go on, then?"

"Damn it! Yes, I want to!"

"Well," said the man in the mask, sadly, "you'll get your way." And he resumed walking.

In addition to his épée, you will be remember, the Marquis was armed with his pistols.

"Good God!" he murmured, as he followed the man in the mask, who had lengthened his stride. "An army couldn't make me retreat now!"

The corridor made one last turn, and the Marquis found himself in the presence of another door.

"Listen," said the man in the mask again. "If you've reflected since a little while ago, there's still time to go back."

"Never!" cried the Marquis.

The man in the mask silently removed his hat.

"What are you doing?" demanded the Marquis, beside himself.

"I'm saluting someone who's about to die," he said. And he knocked on the door in front of him.

A woman's voice was heard behind the door, saying: "Who's there?"

"The Marquis de la Roche-Maubert," replied the man in the mask.

"You haven't been able to make him retrace his steps, then?"

"No."

"It's Janine's voice—I recognize it!" cried the Marquis. "I want to see her."

"Let the will of destiny be accomplished, then!" said the same voice.

At the same time, the door opened.

Then the Marquis, dazzled by a flood of light, found himself on the threshold of the Oriental room into which the Regent had penetrated a few nights before.

Janine was sitting on a pile of cushions, her intoxicating smile on her lips—and the Marquis, drunk with love, precipitated himself toward her and set himself at her knees.

"Oh yes—it's really you! You, whom I loved...you, whom I love still!"

And he took one of the immortal woman's hands in his and lifted it to his leathery lips.

The door through which he had just come had closed again, and the man in the mask had disappeared.

XL

"O Janine, I love you! Janine, I feel my reason abandoning me and my heart recovering its twenty-year old self, when I was at your feet, Janine. I want to repair my involuntary errors of old...I want to be your husband, Janine. You shall be the Marquise de la Roche-Maubert."

The amorous old man remained on his knees.

She was silent, and looked at him with a mixture of pity and hatred.

"Monsieur le Marquis," she said, finally, "you wanted to come here, even though you were told...that you have made a mistake..."

"I would have gone to Hell to search for you, Janine!"

"Perhaps you're there," she said—and smiled, enigmatically. Then she pulled away the hand that he was still covering with kisses. "Come on," she said, "look at me carefully. Do I look like a woman who can traverse the centuries without acquiring a wrinkle, conserving an eternal youth? Are you not mistaken, Marquis?"

"No, no," he said. "You're Janine!"

She shrugged her shoulders and said, sadly: "Janine is dead."

"Dead!"

"You saw her on her pyre. Can you doubt it?"

"Janine, it's you, and you're immortal!" said the obstinate old man.

"Janine had black hair."

"And you have blonde hair, don't you?"

"Indeed! As you can see..."

"Oh," said the Marquis, "what does that prove? Nothing. There are marvelous lotions for coloring hair."

"Marquis, you're insane."

"So be it—but I love you..."

"In that case," she said, coldly, "prove your love to me by your submission."

"What must I do?"

"Listen to me."

"Speak," he said, contemplating her ecstatically.

The smile had disappeared from her lips, and her gaze was now as steely as the blade of a dagger. "Since you've come here," she said, "I want to make one last effort to save you... for your life is hanging by a thread..."

He shrugged his shoulders in his turn, and smiled as if to say: *Death can do nothing to me.*

She went on: "Suppose for a moment that I am not Janine but her niece, and that I have inherited, along with her beauty and a striking resemblance to her, a legacy: her vengeance..."

"Oh, yes!" said the Marquis. "You said the same thing to me once before... on the night when you bit my neck."

"Will you listen to me!" she said.

"So be it—speak," said the Marquis, seemingly resigned.

"I have a mission to strike a man—or, rather, a monster. You have come, O white-haired scatterbrain, to plant yourself in my way, and you're hindering my plans..."

"I love you..."

"And I ought to hate you," she said, "because you betrayed Janine... but Janine, as she died, forgave you... or rather, she did not leave any instruction concerning you. Well, I shall, in my turn, make the plea that the Regent has made of you, that the man who is above you has also made, and which was repeated by the man who brought you here..."

The Marquis laughed ferociously. "You want me to go away?" he said.

"Yes."

"To return to my château in Normandy," he continued, sniggering, "and never speak about you to a living soul?"

"Oh!" she said. "No, it's too late."

"Aha!"

"From the moment you got in here," she went on, "you have been condemned..."

"To death?"

"To death," she said, coldly.

"And who will take charge of the execution of the sentence?" he said, standing up and placing his hand on the hilt of his sword.

"It doesn't matter!" she said. "Well, I'd like to commute your sentence."

"In truth?"

"Say the word," she continued, "and I'll give the order. You'll be brought a beverage that will plunge you into a lethargic sleep for several hours, or even days. When you come round, when you open your eyes again, you'll be traveling in a carriage in company with two men who will have orders not to leave you by day or by night, and to stab you to death at the first imprudent word that emerges from your mouth."

"Charming!" said the Marquis, sardonically.

"You will travel thus for days and weeks, and will not stop until you are in Italy, tin the city of Milan, where your guardians will take you to a palace that belongs to me, and where you will be kept prisoner until the work I have to do here is complete. Then, you will be set free, Marquis, and you will be able to return to Paris, and seek Janine, if that is what you want. Janine will have nothing more to fear from you."

The Marquis was still laughing. "It's you who are mad!" he said.

Then the amorous delirium that gripped him went to his head. "Ah!" he said. "You don't want to be my wife... Well, then..."

His eyes were on fire; he was furious and tremulous...

He wanted to hurl himself upon the immortal woman and seize her in his arms...but she leapt backwards, and, as rapid as lightning, took refuge at the other end of the Oriental room. Her hand took up a whistle that was hanging from her belt, and raised it to her lips.

The whistle uttered a shrill sound.

At that sound, two men came in. One might have thought that the wall of foliage had opened in front of them.

One of the two men was the same masked adversary with whom the Marquis had fought such a fine duel. The other was a hideous dwarf, a negro dressed in red, carrying a tray on which there was a silver goblet.

"Help me!" she said. And, looking at the Marquis with inflamed eyes, she said: "You have but one minute more. Drink the contents of that goblet, or you're dead!"

But the Marquis replied with an outburst of laughter. At the same time, he let his cloak fall, took his pistols from his belt, aimed them at the breast of the masked man and said: "You're mistaken, Madame. It's me who is the master of the situation!"

XLI

A thought, as rapid as a lightning-flash, had shot through the mind of the madman who was known as the Marquis de la Roche-Maubert.

The man in the mask, he had no doubt, was the Chevalier d'Esparron.

The Chevalier was the new lover of the woman he persisted in calling Janine, and she doubtless adored that lover.

Now, in directing one of his pistols at the Chevalier's breast, Monsieur de la Roche-Maubert had firmly believed that the immortal woman, terrified, would fall at his feet and beg for mercy.

On the contrary, she began to laugh, and then man in the mask said: "You can fire, Marquis..."

A cloud passed over Monsieur de la Roche-Maubert's face; his eyes became bloodshot, and his finger pressed the trigger feverishly.

The shot departed.

A further burst of laughter was heard, while a thick white smoke filled the room momentarily.

The Marquis, beside himself, fired a second shot—and another burst of laughter replied to him.

The smoke was so thick that he could not see anything at first, but that only lasted for a minute.

The smoke dissipated, and then the Marquis uttered a cry of amazement.

The immortal woman and the dwarf had disappeared. There was no longer anyone there but the man in the mask, who was still laughing.

The Marquis drew his sword and charged at him—but the man in the mask had also drawn his sword, and he found himself on the defensive.

"Ah! Wretch!" said the Marquis. "I'll have your blood, down to the last drop."

"And if you spill it, you know whence it came," his adversary replied, his mask dropping.

The Marquis had not been mistaken; it was indeed the Chevalier d'Esparron, with whom he had supped in the Regent's apartment, who was standing before him.

"So you want your revenge before dying?" said the Chevalier, still calm and mocking.

"It's you who'll die!" replied the Marquis—and he attacked his adversary furiously.

The two épées clashed, throwing off sparks, and clashed again—and the Chevalier, superbly self-composed, continued the conversation.

"In truth, Monsieur le Marquis," he said, "you couldn't be more unreasonable if you were still twenty years old! Let's see what you've done! One morning, in the depths of your manor, you were gripped by a desire to see Paris again; you got yourself invited to supper with the Regent; you told an absurd story there; you slandered a woman; you poured ridicule on a gallant man like me, who never asked for anything but to respect your white hair—but that wasn't enough for you. When you were advised to go home, to let your memories of youth rest, you were carried away by an imaginary love, you defied the Regent's orders, scorned the advice of your friends..."

"I'll kill you like a dog!" howled the Marquis. And he thrust at his adversary with all his might.

The Chevalier evaded the thrust, and the Marquis' épée, continuing in its trajectory and striking the wall violently, snapped into three pieces. And as the old man uttered a cry of rage, the Chevalier raised the point of his sword to his face to hold him at bay.

"One last time," he said, "let me give you some advice."

"Kill me, but don't mock me, bandit!" cried the Marquis.

"I'm not mocking you, Monsieur. Here—look at that side-table. The goblet containing the narcotic is still there. Take it and drink!"

"Never!"

"Drink!" said another voice, behind the Marquis.

He turned around abruptly, and perceived the immortal woman, who was on the threshold of a door that had just opened soundlessly.

The door opened into the corridor that the Marquis had already traveled. "Ah!" he said. "It's you! You!" And he launched himself toward her.

As nimble as a frightened hind, however, she had leapt backwards, and was now in the corridor.

The Marquis forgot his adversary; he forgot that he was disarmed; he forgot everything—and, rediscovering the legs he had had at twenty, he launched himself in pursuit of the immortal woman, who fled before him down that interminable corridor.

"Since you don't want to be my wife," he said, "you'll be mine nonetheless!" He increased his speed—and the moment when he would catch up with her was imminent.

Suddenly, she turned round

Her gaze was so flamboyant, so dominating, that he stopped abruptly, as if fascinated.

"Marquis," she said to him. "One last time—do you want to live?"

"I want to love you!" he said, furiously.

Something akin to a heart-rending sigh was heard, which lifted the strange woman's bosom.

"Well," she said, "May your will be done!" And she started fleeing again.

"Oh!" said the crazed old man, "I'll catch you in the end...and if you don't want to love me...well, I'll kill you!"

Suddenly, the immortal woman made one last leap. One might have thought that she was hurdling some mysterious object.

The Marquis took another step...

Then, suddenly, a terrible cry was hear—a scream of supreme agony—and then nothing.

A trap-door had just opened beneath the old man's feet, and the Marquis de la Roche-Maubert had been precipitated into the tenebrous depths of an unknown abyss.

Pale, quivering the immortal woman and the Chevalier d'Esparron stood face to face, looking at one another.

"Oh, it's frightful!" she murmured.

"He wanted it," replied the Chevalier, in a dull voice.

"Oh well," she murmured, while a dark gleam appeared in her large limpid eyes. "To work, now! It's the Margrave it's necessary to strike."

"To the Margrave," repeated the Chevalier—and he took the hand of the immortal woman and raised it respectfully to his lips.

PART ONE

I

The Rue Saint-Honoré was then a street of the finest quality. More than one great lord was proud to have his town house there, and litter's and beautiful carriages crossed paths there heading in all directions.

The late king had almost never left Versailles, but the Regent loved Paris.

Now, the Regent was then the power—which is to say, the Court—for a nine-year-old king hardly counts. High society had, therefore, fled Versailles for Paris, and the Rue Saint-Honoré was the most fashionable street of all.

No one was astonished, therefore, one morning, to learn that the exceedingly noble and exceedingly powerful lord, the Margrave Prince of Lansbourg-Nassau, having spent forty-eight hours in the Rue de l'Arbre-Sec, had taken up residence in a fine house in the Rue Saint-Honoré, on the corner of the Rue des Bons-Enfants.

The arrival of that noble individual had caused some noise in Paris. Marvelous things were said about him.

First of all, the Margrave was fabulously rich; secondly, he threw gold around recklessly; finally, he had come to Paris to get married.

Announce that a rich man wants to marry, and young women rain down.

The Margrave could have been a hundred and twenty years old and had the head of Medusa, and still he would have had plenty of choice.

The Court and the city were excited. In hr vicinity of the house where he was living, gossip as heap upon gossip. The good people of the quarter, scorning the curfew, gathered in the evenings on doorsteps and indulged in a thousand conjectures.

No one, however, had seen the Margrave.

He had moved into his new abode by night and had not shown himself thereafter.

Was he young? Was he old? That was a question no one was able to answer. All that anyone knew was that the Prince had let it be known in Paris that the prettiest young women could present themselves, and that he would make a choice, starting on the Monday after Pentecost—which was the very day on which this story recommences.

Directly opposite the house—and, in consequence, on the other side of the street, was Master Chaubourdin's boutique.

Chaubourdin was an apothecary.

Apothecaries, in general, have always played a role in the history of peoples, and Chaubourdin, even more than his colleagues, had the right to a certain consideration.

Chaubourdin was a short, middle-aged man who meddled in everything that did not concern him, and whose laboratory was open to anyone with news to spread or a story to tell. Chaubourdin's boutique was a veritable information bureau, to which everyone brought a little tale or the rumor of the day—but Chaubourdin was not content with the role of spectator. He searched for news, for his own part, with much more zeal than conscience, and when he had none, he invented it.

Chaubourdin had, therefore, put himself under arms as soon as the Margrave moved in, determined not to let the noble personage's slightest act or gesture pass unperceived.

On the first day, he struck up a conversation with a chatty little page, who had told him about his master's matrimonial projects. An hour later, he had made the acquaintance of Master Conrad, the scarlet-clad steward whom we have already seen making his confidences to the Marquis de la Roche-Maubert. By midday, Chaubourdin knew that the Margrave was old. By five o'clock in the evening he was able to affirm that the Margrave's fortune rendered the King of France jealous.

The following morning, as he was opening his shop, the door of the house similarly opened. A man came out. It was Conrad, the red-clad steward. On seeing him cross the street and come toward him, Chaubourdin thought that he was simply being polite, but Conrad filled him with joy by disillusioning him.

"I have need of you," he told him.

Chaubourdin, who was very short, suddenly felt himself grow a hundred feet.

Conrad said to him: "The Prince has a physician."

"Is he ill?"

"No."

"What's the point of the physician, then?" asked the apothecary, full of skepticism.

"To prevent him from becoming ill," Conrad replied-and stuck a prescription under the apothecary's nose.

Chaubourdin read it.

The prescription was so bizarre that the apothecary exclaimed: "Good God! But what's the purpose of all that?"

The steward started laughing. "Bah!" he said. "You seem to me to be a man of common sense..."

"I'd like to think so," said Chaubourdin, proudly.

"Discreet..."

"As the tomb."

"Then I can tell you something in confidence?"

"Speak..."

"The Prince is old."

"Ah!"

"So old that he wanted to be rejuvenated."

"That's difficult."

"The prescription I've brought you is from his physician. By following it, you'll concoct a beverage that will restore some strength to His Highness."

"Perfect."

"In addition to the beverage, the prescription specifies a certain ointment, doesn't it?"

"Yes."

179

"That ointment is intended to cover the Prince's wrinkles and make them disappear."

"Marvelous!"

"After that, there's a question of a cosmetic. I believe?"

"Yes, certainly."

"That cosmetic has the objective of tinting the Prince's white hair and beard brown."

"Better and better."

"Get to work, then."

"This very moment."

"And be discreet..."

"I swear it."

The steward had good reason to trust the discretion of Master Chaubourdin the apothecary. That same evening, the entire quarter knew that the Margrave Prince of Lansbourg-Nassau was employing beverages, ointments and cosmetics designed to rejuvenate him.

And everyone waited—for Chaubourdin had told them that a great event was in preparation...

II

The great event that was in preparation, as the steward had whispered to Chaubourdin, and Chaubourdin had said aloud to everyone, was the Prince's marriage.

The Prince had spent thirty-six hours in a dark room, wrapped in his sheets, covered in mysterious unguents. In a few more hours, he would have contrived a second youth.

On the evening that same day, the Monday after Pentecost, at eight o'clock, the competition would be opened—which is to say that any young woman who believed her beauty to be remarkable had the right to present herself at the house's spy-hole.

First, she would be received by the steward. If the steward thought her pretty enough to be subjected to an initial trial, she would cross the first threshold and would be introduced to the steward's wife, Madame Edwige.

Madame Edwige was the second judge. If Madame Edwige thought the young woman pretty, she would take her into the main hall of the house. There, she would doubtless encounter other young women admitted, like her, to the competition.

At a certain hour, the Prince would appear. He would examine the aspirants to the rank of princes one by one, chat with them, take notes, and tell them that he would reflect—unless, of course, he found among them some sovereign, ideal beauty who subjugated him and swept him off his feet.

That was what Master Chaubourdin recounted in his boutique that evening, as night fell. All the idlers in the quarter were gathered in his establishment. Everyone had even brought an acquaintance, a friend or a relative. Chaubourdin, sitting behind his counter, obligingly gave all the details, and they listened to him avidly.

A brave mercer whose sign read *A la Chemise de la Vierge* came in at that moment, followed by a man with an épée. A man with an épée always caused something of a sensation among the bourgeois.

The mercer, whose name was Rabuteau, combined with his primary industry that of landlord. He let out a furnished room in the house that stood at the corner of the Rue des Frondeurs and the Rue des Orties-Saint-Honoré. The man with the épée he had brought was none other than his tenant.

The tenant in question was a Gascon, the Chevalier de Castirac, who talked about his châteaux and his lands to all comers, and took his hand out of his pocket full of pistols.

You can guess where those pistoles came from, if you recall the Gascon's duel with Master Guillaume Laurent, the bourgeois gentleman of the Rue de l'Hirondelle—a duel that had terminated in a little arrangement.

So, the Chevalier de Castirac had accompanied the mercer Rabuteau who, the day before, had already heard mention of the Margrave Prince and who was coming to Chaubourdin's establishment with the certainty of leaning interesting things.

The apothecary began again, perhaps for the tenth time in an hour, the story that he had already told, regarding the Margrave who was seeking to rejuvenate himself.

As night fell, Chaubourdin's boutique became increasingly crowded. The time was not far off when the aspirants for the Margrave's hand were to present themselves.

Indeed, at half past seven, a carriage and two litters were seen arriving at almost the same time. The litters and the carriage went through the coaching entrance of a vast courtyard, which immediately closed again. Five minutes had not gone by, however, when the door reopened and the carriage and one of the litters came out precipitately.

"Damn!" murmured several voices. "That's two out of the competition already."

As the door of the boutique was half-open, Chaubourdin's guests had overflowed into the street and were darting avid glances through the curtains of the litter and the windows of the carriage.

Both contained exceedingly pretty women, and the Chevalier de Castirac exclaimed: "My word, the old fool's difficult to please!"

For two hours the scene was renewed.

Chaubourdin had illuminated his boutique and converted it into a mortuary chapel, with the sole aim of projecting the light a long way into the street, so that no detail of the nocturnal scene would be lost.

Litters, carriages, modest "chamber-pots"—little hired cabs then in fashion—succeeded one another, and the same scene was played out repeatedly.

"Sandis!" exclaimed the Chevalier. "He's damnably difficult, this Prince...those are the most beautiful women in France, who are being turned away without even crossing the first threshold."

Suddenly, however, something even more extraordinary occurred. A woman was seen arriving on foot, who also wanted to enter the competition. She was a beautiful young woman of nineteen, as dark as an Andalusian, her ebony locks imprisoned with difficulty in a red headscarf, and her opulent figure in a black velvet corsage set over a blue and white striped skirt. She walked along, insouciantly placing her little arched feet in the black mud of the street, her head held high, a smile on her lips, as befitted someone sure of victory.

The crowd that was thronging the street at the door of the house applauded.

"Sandis!" cried the Chevalier de Castirac. "My God, it's a Bayonnaise! It's a compatriot...and she's fit to become a princess, for she's more beautiful than all the rest!"

With these words, like a shrewd man who never lets an opportunity to make his way escape, the Gascon headed straight for the young woman, bowed gallantly, and offered her his services.

III

The Bayonnaise stopped and looked at the Chevalier curiously.

"What do you want with me?" she said, finally.

The Gascon replied to her, in the Basque language: "As I'm convinced that you're going to become a princess, I've come to offer you my services and ask for your protection."

The language of her native land suddenly ringing in her ears had made the young woman shiver; she looked at the Chevalier for a second time. There was a kind of exchange of electric fluid between them, and of magnetic gazes.

The two beings, who were seeing one another for the first time, divined that destiny had wanted them to meet, and that they were bound to one another—and to be sure, love was not irrelevant to those presentiments.

The young woman said to herself: *Here's the protector I need.*

The Gascon similarly said to himself: *I've come to Paris to seek my fortune, and it might be that I've found the instrument that will enable me to make it.*

He took her arm, and she did not pull away.

She had been marching resolutely toward the Margrave's door a little while before; he drew her to the other end of the street, and she did not resist.

The curiosity-seekers cluttering the vicinity of the house had time to see that maneuver. A few clapped their hands, saying: "The most beautiful girl won't be for the old man; it's that young man who's leading her away."

The Chevalier had taken the young woman to one side, saying to her: "You'll lost nothing by waiting. When you appear the Margrave will fall at your feet."

She did not doubt it for a moment, since she followed him without resistance.

There was a sort of tavern in the street, deserted at present The Chevalier pushed the Bayonnaise inside. "We'll have a little chat," he said, "and see how I might be useful to you."

A minute later, they were sitting at a table facing one another, and no one gave them another thought.

"Where are you from?" said the Chevalier de Castirac, continuing to gaze at the splendid young woman, whose close were faded, but who had a queenly air in spite of her poverty.

"You want to know my story?" she said.

"Yes."

"I'll tell you. It's brief, but not lacking in interest, as you'll see."

The Chevalier put his elbows on the table, still gazing at the Bayonnaise.

She went on: "My costume tells you my native land. My name is Jeanne, I'm from Bayonne. I'm nineteen. I came to Bordeaux two years ago to look for a situation here. I met a handsome sergeant in the Picardy regiment, which was garrisoned in Bordeaux, and I fell madly in love with him.

" The sergeant promised to marry me, and he would have kept his promise, I'm certain, if he hadn't had the unfortunate idea of showing me to his captain. The captain was smitten with me, and I was soon smitten myself, abandoning the sergeant.

"The Captain brought me to Paris. We stayed at the Croix du Trahoir in the Rue de l'Arbre-Sec,[17] and lived together for a month. The captain as a cadet; he didn't have much money. He got into debt with me and abandoned me one morning, leaving me four pistoles. That happened last week. Since then, a host of plans have passed through my mind. I told myself at first that there couldn't be a woman at the Court as beautiful as me..."

"That's true," said the Chevalier.

---

[17] The Place de la Croix de Trahoir, at the intersection of the Rue de l'Arbre-Sec and the Rue Saint-Honoré, was one of the busiest crossroads in Paris at the time. It had accommodated a gallows not long before known as the Arbre-Sec, although that street-name had originally come from a mythical tree mentioned in Marco Polo's account of his travels.

"And that if I could get to the Regent, he'd lose his head as soon as he saw me."

"That's quite possible, in truth!"

"Then," Jeanne the Bayonnaise went on, "I heard that this old madman who has incalculable treasures was going to marry the most beautiful woman he could find, and I told myself that I ought to be the most beautiful of those he might see."

"You're right," said the Chevalier, who admired the young woman's robust faith in her beauty.

Jeanne continued: "My father and mother were wretched tavern-keepers who had an inn at the gate of Bayonne on the road to Spain. I was six years old when a gipsy woman to whom we had given hospitality told my fortune. She examined the lines on my hand and affirmed that I would be a princess. I have a profound faith in the gipsy's prediction; if it isn't this prince I'm to marry, it will be another—but I shall still find one. I'm at the end of my resources, however, and I don't have any time to lose."

The Chevalier smiled. Then he put his hand in his pocket and pulled it out full of gold. "Jeanne," he said, "I have as much faith as you now in the gipsy woman's prediction, and like her, I tell you that you will be a princess."

"Good," she said.

"In Paris, however, a woman on her own can do nothing; she needs a cavalier, a protector, a friend. Would you like me to be all of that?"

"I'd like nothing better," she replied.

"Would you like to associate our fortunes?"

"Yes, certainly."

"That's agreed, then." And he took the small hands of Jeanne the Bayonnaise in his own, adding: "Now we can go to the Margrave's house. Give me your arm."

He threw a copper coin on to the table of the tavern and went out, triumphantly leading the young woman who wanted to be a princess.

There was a new murmur of astonishment in the curious crowd stationed in front of the Margrave's house. People had applauded on seeing the Gascon take the pretty girl away, but when they saw them reappear, arm in arm, go into the court-yard and present themselves at the spy-hole where the first inspection—the steward's—took place, a few whistles were heard.

The Chevalier turned round.

"Imbeciles that you are," he said, "can't you see that she's my sister?" And he continued on his way with his head held high.

IV

Let us now penetrate, before the Chevalier de Castirac and his new ally Jeanne the Bayonnaise, into the Margrave's house, whose courtyard was lit up like a cathedral on a feast day.

Paris was then what it is today. The golden wand transformed everything in a matter of hours.

While the old German Prince, the former associate of Janine the gold-seeker, had spent two days at the hostelry in the Rue de l'Arbre-Sec, an army of upholsterers, masons and painters, under the orders of Master Conrad, the red-clad steward and the tremulous spouse of the terrible Madame Edwige, had invaded that old residential house and had converted it into a palace from the Thousand-and-One Nights.

The Margrave had arrived there two days earlier, at night, at a late enough hour for no one to see him. He had got down from his litter painfully, so old and infirm was he; then, leaning on the shoulders of one of his pages and giving his arm to Madame Edwige, he had dragged himself as far as the sumptuous bedroom that had been prepared for him.

There, Madame Edwige had confided him to his two physicians, one of whom was German and the other Hungarian.

For forty-eight hours, the old man had been plunged into various odorant baths, rubbed with oils and perfumes and smeared with mysterious ointments. Then he had been plunged, by means of a narcotic, into a profound sleep.

He went to sleep old and woke up young...at least for a few hours.

The moment of that resurrection having come, the Margrave, who had been remade by these metamorphoses, had opened his eyes and stretched his limbs, to which a temporary flexibility had been rendered. He had looked at himself in a small mirror that had been brought to him, and had seen himself young, his hair black and his forehead free of wrinkles.

At the same time, Madame Edwige had come in. "Well, Monseigneur," she had said, "do you still intend to hold an inspection of the most beautiful young women in Paris and marry the one who pleases you the most?"

"Yes, certainly," the Margrave had replied.

"I've had the news spread to the four corners of the city," Madame Edwige went on.

"Very good."

"And the street is already cluttered with litters and carriages. You have a choice, and it's possible that you'll be embarrassed."

"Bah!" said the Margrave. "I'm enough of a connoisseur to discern the most beautiful at the first glance."

"It's sufficient not to hurry," said Madame Edwige. Then she had gone out, and sent the Margrave two of his pages. The latter had proceeded to dress their lord and master.

Once that dressing was complete, none of those who had seen the old Margrave get down from his carriage at the door of the hostelry in the Rue de l'Arbre-Sec would have recognized him, so much had he changed. The old man was almost young, and was dressed with extreme elegance.

He started walking, head held high, stretching his legs, his hand, surrounded by lace, coquettishly placed on the hilt of his ceremonial épée.

"You're twenty years old," Madame Edwige said to him, when she reappeared, "and I don't feel sorry for the woman who'll have the pleasure of pleasing Your Highness."

"Where are they?" asked the Margrave.

"Oh," said Madame Edwige, smiling, "Your Highness is too impatient. More than a hundred have arrived so far, and Conrad and I have been obliged to devise a system of triage."

"How?"

"Conrad is in the courtyard."

"Good."

"If a woman's beauty is merely mediocre he asks her to climb back into her carriage or litter and tells her that she has no chance of pleasing Your Highness."

"Ah! That's very good," said the Margrave. "It's a means of simplifying things."

"Exactly," Madame Edwige continued. "As for the prettier women, they're introduced into a small reception-room. There are already half a dozen in there."

"I'll go there, then," said the Margrave.

"No," said Madame Edwige, "that's not how matters have been arranged. Take my hand, Monseigneur, and come with me..."

The Margrave always followed Madame Edwige's orders. He made no objection, and obeyed.

She took him into a room dimly lit by a frosted glass lamp, sat him down on a sofa and lifted a curtain.

"Now look," she said.

The curtain that she had just raised covered an unsilvered looking-glass. Through that glass once could see the little reception-room that Madame Edwige had mentioned, brightly illuminated, in which there were several young women.

The Margrave looked at them one by one.

"Pooh!" he said. "They're ugly."

"Very well," said Madame Edwige. "I'll send them away, then."

She left the Margrave, went into a corridor and entered the small reception-room by another door.

The Margrave could not hear what she said through the glass, but he saw the young women stand up one by one, go pale and blush in turn, and leave, one by one, in utter confusion.

In the meantime, Conrad came in.

"Is the Prince at his post?" he asked his terrible wife.

"Yes; he arrived a few minutes ago."

"Good. None of those pleased him?"

"You can imagine," Madame Edwige replied, smiling, "that the glass through which he's gazing, which enlarges the features, isn't calculated to embellish. We could pass all the women in Paris before his eyes in this fashion without a single one pleasing him."

"And that's what we want, isn't it?" murmured Conrad.

"Of course! In order for the one we obey to triumph, it's necessary. You can send in as many others as you wish."

Conrad went out.

From his hiding-place, the Prince then saw six more young women come in, one after another.

They were certainly as beautiful as one could wish, but the mirror whose secret Madame Edwige had betrayed did not display them to advantage.

The prince tapped on the glass twice.

Madame Edwige left the reception-room and went to re-join the bizarre individual.

"They're all ugly," he said, "and I don't see why I've been disturbed for so little."

Madame Edwige returned to the reception-room and sent the six young women away.

At that moment, the Chevalier de Castirac came through the courtyard, with Jeanne the Bayonnaise on his arm.

Conrad stopped him. "Where are you going?" he said.

"Mademoiselle is my sister," he said.

"So what?"

"She is beautiful enough, as you see, to have some hope of success."

"I don't deny it," said Conrad, "and if Mademoiselle would like to follow me..."

"No," said the Gascon. "I accompany her everywhere, and I want to go in with her."

"But that's impossible!"

"Get away!" said the Gascon, looking Conrad in the eyes. And he pushed the steward aside and went into the small reception-room where Madame Edwige was waiting.

Jeanne was triumphant, and said to herself: *The Margrave will fall at my feet and offer me his fortune and his hand!*

V

Until then, all the women who had presented themselves had come alone. The Chevalier de Castirac, in formulating the pretention of accompanying his sisters, as therefore inaugurating a new manner of introduction.

Master Conrad had tried to prevent him going any further, but the Gascon had an épée at his side, spoke loudly, and strutted like a warrior—and the poor steward was intimidated.

There's a fellow, he thought, *who might spit me like a pullet if I resist him.* And he had started to let him pass. Just as the Chevalier and his pretended sister were about to cross the threshold of the small reception-room from which all the aspirants had so far emerged disappointed, however, Conrad saw a phantom loom up before him.

That phantom was that of Madame Edwige—the terrible Madame Edwige who made the Margrave tremble, and undoubtedly made her husband tremble even more.

What would she say?

Conrad felt his legs go weak; a cloud passed before his eyes and he lost heart.

Fortunately, that general malaise was only momentary, and was followed by an inspiration.

"Monsieur," he said, taking the Chevalier by the arm. "A word—just one."

"So be it, my man," replied the Chevalier, "but be quick, for my sister is in haste to become a princess."

Conrad felt a flood of eloquence rising to his lips. "Sir," he said, "not only do I see no inconvenience in your accompanying Mademoiselle your sister..."

"Good!" said the Gascon.

"But I'm even persuaded that such a step might incline His Highness in your favor."

"I believe so," said the Gascon. "In our family, the demoiselles are well brought-up and never go out alone; one can have confidence in them."

"You're too much of a gentleman," Conrad went on, "not to grant me one minute—just one."

"In order to do what?"

"In order that I might alert His Highness."

"So be it," said the Chevalier, who saw no inconvenience in that.

"Wait for me here; I'll be back in a flash."

And Conrad slipped into the reception-room, leaving the Chevalier and Jeanne the Bayonnaise at the door.

At least there would be time to warn the terrible Madame Edwige.

The latter, on seeing him come in, guessed that something extraordinary had happened. Frowning, she came to meet him and said: "What is it?"

"A devil of a man, a Gascon with moustache like a yard-stick and a mile-long épée."

"What does he want?"

"He wants to come in."

"The Prince has no business with a man."

"He's accompanying his sister, and says that his sister can't come in without him."

"Well, then," said Madame Edwige, coldly, "sent them away!"

"You're crazy," said Conrad. "He'll smash everything up at run us through."

"What's his sister like?"

"Dazzling—and that's why I don't want the Prince to see her."

"You're an idiot," said Madame Edwige. "Are you forgetting that the disfiguring glass is still there?"

"No."

"Well then, let them in."

"What about the Prince?"

"I'll warn him."

And Madame Edwige lifted a curtain, opened a door and went into the large drawing-room, where the Margrave had not left his observation-post, and whom that conversation had intrigued considerably.

"What is it?" the Prince asked Madame Edwige.

"Monseigneur," she replied, "there's a gentleman who wants to come in with his sister, saying that she's a well-brought-up girl who can only go out alone when she's married."

"I like that," said the Prince. "It's always a guarantee."

"Pooh!" said Madame Edwige.

"He wants to come in with his sister?"

"Yes?"

"And how is the sister?"

"I haven't seen her, but Conrad says that she's neither beautiful nor ugly."

"Let's see her anyway," said the Prince, attracted by the family introduction.

Fortunately, thought Madame Edwige, *the glass is there...*

And she went back to the small reception-room.

In the meantime, Conrad went back to the Chevalier de Castirac and his pretended sister. Perhaps he had been wrong to leave them momentarily, however—and this is why.

The courtyard was crowded, and in the crowd there was a young woman who had just been sent away by Madame Edwige, and who was making a great fuss and a great deal of noise, shouting that it was all a great hoax.

As she was very beautiful, the Chevalier had approached her, saying: "In truth, you've been unceremoniously eliminated from the competition?"

"My God, yes!" she replied.

"The man is mad..."

"Or very difficult to please," said a local bourgeois who had slipped into the courtyard.

"But I haven't seen him!" the young woman added.

"You haven't seen the Prince?"

"No."

"Then who sent you away?"

"The steward's wife."

That's good to know, thought the Chevalier. *Either the Prince will come, or I'll smash things up.*

"I believe there's some trickery in this," the young woman said, again.

The word *trickery* caused the Chevalier to open an eye. He learned toward Jeanne the Bayonnaise and whispered to her: "Don't be astonished by anything, and let me act. We'll see."

It was at that moment that the steward Conrad returned.

"Would you care to follow me?" he said.

"Certainly," said the Gascon. And, still lending his arm to the Bayonnaise, he went into the reception-room where Madame Edwige was waiting.

"Well," he said. "Where's the Prince?"

"You won't see him," said Madame Edwige.

"What?"

"But he can see you..."

"Bah!"

"And Mademoiselle your sister."

"Madame," said the Chevalier, coldly, "as I don't like enigmas, people are always obliged to explain them to me."

And he stood before her, his fist on his hip, and resumed his attitude of a warrior—to the great displeasure of the terrible matron, whose only hope was the magic glass, because the Bayonnaise was incomparably beautiful.

Madame Edwige put on a brave face, however, in the presence of the blackguard who seemed ready to cut loose and smash everything up.

"My dear sir," she said, "the enigma is easy to decipher, I assure you."

"Well?"

"You see that mirror?"

"Of course."

"It has no silvering, and the Prince is behind it, in dim light—which permits him to see without being seen."

"Very well!"

"If the Prince does not appraise the marvelous beauty of your sister at its full value, he will rap three times on the glass."

"And then?"

"Then you will go away," said Madame Edwige, "escorted by me. If he only raps twice, you will go into another room, and then..."

While Madame Edwige was speaking, the Chevalier had approached the unsilvered mirror and was examining it curiously. At the same time, the Bayonnaise, sure of her beauty, had placed herself full in the light.

The Margrave was in no hurry to rap three times, and Madame Edwige was on tenterhooks. Had the magic glass lost its virtue?

Suddenly, she heard a small grating noise, followed by a crack. At the same time, a cry of admiration resounded from the other side of the partition.

The Chevalier had a diamond ring on his finger. With that diamond he had inscribed a circle on the mirror, as skillfully as a professional thief would have done—and the cut glass had suddenly come away; and immediately, the amazed Margrave had been able to see Jeanne the Bayonnaise, no longer disfigured but as she was, and it was him who had uttered that exclamation of naïve admiration.

"Monseigneur!" cried the Gascon, then, while Madame Edwige let a gesture of fury escape. "As you see, you've been deceived..."

The Margrave had opened the door behind the curtain and he came into the reception-room, murmuring: "Oh, how beautiful she is!"

"And virtuous," said the Chevalier, audaciously.

"Accursed Gascon!" exclaimed Madame Edwige.

The Chevalier was in a bold mood. He struck an arrogant and protective pose before Madame Edwige. "You can leave us now, respectable matron," he said. "Can't you see that the Prince desires to talk to us?"

But Madame Edwige did not budge. She had launched one of the stares at the Margrave that overwhelmed him.

"Let her stay, Monsieur," said the Margrave. "The good Edwige is my steward's wife, and I have no secrets from her."

"That's doubtless why she has deceived you," said the Chevalier.

The Margrave had no intention of getting angry. "But no...I don't know..." he stammered. "All that I can tell you is that Mademoiselle is very beautiful...more beautiful than any of the women I've seen..." He looked at the Gascon. "She's your sister?"

"My sister, Mademoiselle Jeanne de Castirac," said the Chevalier, with aplomb.

The Margrave enveloped the young woman with an avidly ardent gaze.

"Well," said Madame Edwige, who would not concede defeat, "I'll take Mademoiselle into the large drawing-room, and Monseigneur can then see the other young women..."

"No," said the Margrave, "there's no need. Mademoiselle is so beautiful...that she can have no rival..."

"So," said the Chevalier, who liked to get to work quickly, "you'll marry her?"

"I'll marry her," said the Margrave. "However..."

"Ah! Be careful!" said the Gascon, whose audacity was increasing. "The Castiracs are like the Rohans and the Crécys;

they do not deign to be Princes or Ducs, but they have been noble since Clovis, and to break one's word to them would be to offend God himself, who has always treated them as cousins."

This Gasconade brought a smile to the lips of the Margrave Prince.

"I beg your pardon," he said. "I never make a promise without keeping it religiously. However, I request twenty-four hours of reflection. During those twenty-four hours, however, you will remain here..."

"And?" said the Chevalier.

"...With Mademoiselle your sister, and you will be treated with distinction. I will even ask you the favor of eating at me table...and..."

"That is acceptable to us," said the Gascon, who had complete faith in the physical perfection of Jeanne the Bayonnaise.

"So, Monseigneur," said Madame Edwige, "there's no need for me to have anyone else come in?"

"No need whatsoever."

"In that case," said the terrible matron, "I'll tell Conrad to close the doors."

And Madame Edwige went out, furious.

Conrad, who was still at the door, deduced that something extraordinary must have happened in the small reception-room. When he saw Madame Edwige appear, pale with anger and her eyes inflamed, he had a strong desire to make himself scarce—but she came straight toward him.

"Announce," she said, "that the Prince has made his choice."

"It can't be!" murmured Conrad.

"It's the truth!" And Madame Edwige, speaking German in order that no one would understand, told him about the Gascon's unexpectedly audacious move and what had followed.

"All is lost, then," said the steward.

"I don't know..."

"And Janine..."

"Silence!"

The people crowding the courtyard passed on the news that the Prince had made his choice.

"It's that beautiful girl who went in with the Gascon," said Chaubourdin, who had quit his boutique for the courtyard.

"His mistress," said someone.

"His sister," said one of the local housewives.

"Oh don't make me laugh!" exclaimed a mocking masculine voice. A sergeant in the French guards who was twirling his moustache said: "Jeanne the Bayonnaise has no brother—she's a whore."

"How would you know?" asked Chaubourdin.

"Parbleu!" replied the sergeant. "I was her lover for three months...and I'm not the only one..."

At these words, which reached her ears, Madame Edwige uttered a cry of joy. Then she launched herself toward the sergeant like a shipwreck-victim heading for the rock that might be his salvation.

She took him by the arm and said: "Is that true, what you just said?"

"Of course it's true!"

"Can you prove it?"

"As easily as I can draw my sword from its scabbard."

"Well," said Madame Edwige, in a triumphant tone, "if that's the case, I swear to you that your fortune is made."

VII

Madame Edwige clung on to the sergeant like a sheet-anchor.

She had told him, excitedly, that if he could prove what he said, his fortune was made—but that was not sufficient for her. She slipped two pistoles into her hand, as a down payment on their future bargain, and said to him: "There must be an inn nearby?"

"There are fifty," the sergeant replied, who was hooked.

"Well, go and raise a glass to my health."

"Very well," said the sergeant, pocketing the two pistoles without further ado.

"Then," Madame Edwige went on, "wait for everyone that I'll clear out of the courtyard, who'll be cluttering up the street for a while yet, to disperse."

"And then?"

"Then come back to the house, where you'll find that little man dressed in red that you can see over there."

The sergeant looked at Master Conrad and nodded his head affirmatively.

"He'll tap you on the shoulder and give you a sign to follow him."

"Say no more," replied the sergeant, caressing the two coins in his pocket with his fingertips. And he left the courtyard,

The sergeant of the French Guards was none other than the former sergeant in the Picardy Regiment who had been Jeanne the Bayonnaise's first lover—except that he had changed his uniform and corps.

Perhaps, in other circumstances, he would not have had much faith in Madame Edwige's promises and would have gone to drink the two pistoles without any thought of returning, but one always becomes a little amorous again of a woman one has abandoned when one perceives that someone else holds her in high esteem.

The sergeant, whose name was Lafolie, was subject to that impression, and he left Madame Edwige fully intending to come back.

The timid bourgeois stepped aside respectfully before the man, who had a long sword beating his calves. He cut through the crowd without difficulty, therefore, and went straight across the street from the Margrave's house to sit down at a table in a tavern bearing the sign *Au fils de Mars*, next door to Chaubourdin's boutique, in which the soldiers serving at the Palais-Royal usually gathered.

Placed next to the door, he was able to watch, while swilling a bottle of old Burgundy, the Margrave's pages and valets clearing the bourgeois out of the courtyard with the flats of their swords. Then the people before whom the doors were closed formed a crowd in the street and the discussions continued their course.

It is quite probable that the crowd would not have dissipated so soon and that a few idlers would have spent all night under the Margrave's widows if the watchmen had not passed by. The curfew had fallen into a certain neglect, but the Lieutenant of Police,[18] although he did not care about what the Parisians might be doing in their homes, did not want the streets to be troubled. Thus, when the watchmen appeared, the bourgeois vanished.

Even Chaubourdin, the loquacious apothecary, closed his shop.

---

[18] *Lieutenant-générale de police* was a position created during the reign of Louis XIV, when it was realized that the bodies traditionally entrusted with maintaining order in Paris were no longer able to cope with the city's increasing population and increasing agitation. He was the senior magistrate with overall responsibility for the capital's policing. When the story is set the position was held by Nicolas d'Ombreval, but it is doubtful that Ponson had a particular individual in mind when giving the lieutenant a minor role in his plot.

Then the sergeant, who was on his second bottle, through a half-pistole on the table and left the tavern.

A man was walking up and down in front of the door of the house. Sergeant Lafolie recognized him immediately as Master Conrad.

Conrad had received instructions from Madame Edwige, his terrible spouse, and he came straight to the sergeant. "Was it you," he asked, "who was given two pistoles?"

"Yes," Lafolie replied.

"Follow me, then."

Instead of going back into the house by the main door, Conrad took the sergeant into the Rue des Bons-Enfants, opened a side-door by means of a key that he took from his pocket, and they both went into a dimly-lit corridor.

Madame Edwige was there, and seemed to be waiting for them impatiently.

Conrad said to her in German: "What do you want with this ruffian, my dear?"

"This ruffian is our salvation," Edwige replied. She took the sergeant by the hand and said to him: "Come—you're on the road to fortune." At the same time, she made an imperious sign to Conrad, who stayed in the corridor.

At the end of the corridor there was a narrow staircase. Madame Edwige, still holding the sergeant by the hand, made him climb some twenty steps, paused momentarily, opened a little door—and the sergeant found himself in a small room lit by a lamp suspended from the ceiling.

Madame Edwige closed the door and said: "Are you sure of what you said an hour ago?"

"Perfectly sure," said the sergeant.

"You saw the woman come in?"

"Of course! It's definitely Jeanne the Bayonnaise, my former lover."

"And her brother?"

"She has no brother. The man passing himself off as such must be something else."

"That's all right," said Madame Edwige. "Before putting the plan I have in mind into action, I want you to see her."

"Well, you'll see whether she dares to recognize me or not."

"You'll see her, but she won't see you."

So saying, Madame Edwige bent down in a corner of the room and lifted up the carpet that covered the floor.

The astonished sergeant was able to see that the floor as made of glass and that a bright light was passing through it. Beneath him there was a splendidly-lit room, a fully-laid table, and three guests around the table: the Margrave, the Chevalier de Castirac and the Bayonnaise. The woman was to the Prince's right, smiling as she listened to his tender words.

"Right!" said the sergeant. "It's definitely her. May I be changed into an apothecary on the spot if I'm mistaken!"

Madame Edwige let the carpet fall back. "Very well," she said. "Wait here...I'll come back soon and tell you what has to be done." At the same time, she pulled a bell-cord.

A valet appeared immediately. He was carrying a small table on which there were two bottles of old wine, a pâté and a fowl.

"You can have supper in peace," said Madame Edwige. "You have a good two hours before you."

And she left.

VIII

Let us leave Madame Edwige and Sergeant Lafolie for a while and see what was happening on the ground floor of the house, in the room where the Margrave, the Chevalier and the Bayonnaise were eating supper.

In less than an hour, the Chevalier de Castirac had taken a giant stride in the esteem and confidence of the aged Prince.

How had he worked that miracle? In the simplest possible fashion. The Chevalier was the first man who had stood up to Madame Edwige before the Margrave's eyes.

The Margrave was fabulously rich; he had a court, pages and gentlemen; in his principality, he rendered justice. None of that prevented him from being subject to Conrad's will and being Madame Edwige's slave. For twenty years that Megaera had made him tremble, and he had not found anyone around him who dared to take his side against the female demon.

Now, here was a foreigner, a Gascon, an adventurer, who had overwhelmed Madame Edwige at the first stroke, speaking to her almost as a master.

Examples are contagious. For an hour, the Margrave had become the master in his own home again. He had spoken in an imperious voice, given orders that people hastened to carry out.

And, aided by the Bayonnaise's beauty, the Margrave had said to himself: *I believe that I shall become the happiest of men. I shall have an exceedingly lovely wife, and her brother will rid me of those two wretches who have imposed their yoke upon me for such a long time.*

The Margrave had supper served.

As usual, Conrad had presented himself in his red coat, a napkin under his arm, ready to fulfill the functions of a butler—but the Prince had sent him away.

"I have no need of your services this evening," he had said. "Send me my pages."

Conrad had left, in consternation.

Madame Edwige had attempted to intervene in her turn, but the Gascon had said to her: "Sandis, my dear! You get on my nerves in a singular fashion, and I'll throw a bottle at your head if you don't get out!"

Madame Edwige had left without another word—but, as we have seen, she already had an auxiliary in hand, and promised herself that she would obtain a crushing revenge on the two adventurers.

The Gascon, whom we have previously seen less than brilliant in the presence of Master Guillaume the bourgeois suddenly transformed into a swordsman, was of the opinion that one must strike while the iron is hot, and that it was necessary to lay waste as soon as possible to the residuum of credit that the steward and his wife still had."

"My God, Prince!" he said, looking at the Margrave from the corner of his eye, "you have two great rogues in your service, and no mistake!"

"That's true," replied the Margrave.

"Have you understood the infernal trick of the mirror?"

"Well...not entirely...."

"What did you think of my sister, at first?"

"I confess," the Margrave replied, "that her beauty had no great immediate effect on me."

"The glass, my Prince—it was the glass!"

"What power did it have, then?"

"The glass was tinted, and gave faces a jaundiced appearance."

"Right!"

"And it also magnified and enlarged the features."

"Ah! I understand..." The Prince slapped his forehead. "But then," he said, "I undoubtedly sent away a host of lovely women."

"Undoubtedly," repeated the Chevalier, frowning slightly.

"Oh," said Jeanne, "if Your Highness wants to bring them back, I have no objection—I'm not afraid of the comparison."

"I'm convinced," said the Margrave, "and my choice is made."

"There!" said the triumphant Chevalier. "I was quite sure of it, Monseigneur. My sister is the most beautiful woman in the kingdom of France."

"And I shall marry her tomorrow," the Margrave added.

"You'll be right."

"But there's one thing I don't understand," said the Margrave.

"What?"

"What interest did those two wretches have in making me think that all the women they presented to me were ugly?"

The Chevalier winked. "Might one speak frankly to Your Highness?" he said.

"Certainly."

"Madame Edwige is no longer in the first flush of youth."

"No!" said he Margrave. "She might well be forty."

"But she was once young...and beautiful..."

"Aha!" said the Margrave.

"And Your Highness noticed that, I'm sure..."

"Hmm...perhaps..."

"And that explains the domination that she has exercised over Your Highness for a long time."

"So?" said the Margrave.

"Well, Madame Edwige wouldn't be sorry, while encouraging Your Highness to marry, if Your Highness didn't find any woman worthy of his love."

"Parbleu! Yes!" exclaimed the Margrave. "You're right—I understand everything now."

"Might I be permitted to give Your Highness some advice?"

"What?"

"Dismiss those two scoundrels."

"That's what I intend to do tomorrow. Isn't that so, my dear?" And, turning to the Bayonnaise, he attempted to steal a kiss—but the Chevalier grabbed his arm and stopped him.

"Forgive me!" he said. "You're going too quickly."

"What?" said the Margrave.

"You're going too quickly," the Gascon repeated, dryly.

"But since…I'm marrying…"

"When you're married…but not before." And the Gascon adopted a severe expression.

The Margrave, no longer watched over by Madame Edwige, had drunk more than usual that evening, and the first fumes of intoxication were beginning to go to his head.

"What if I want to embrace my wife!" he said, haughtily.

The Gascon stood up, drew his word and said: "Not before you have regulated our situation."

"What do you mean by that?" said the Margrave, sobered by the sight of the naked blade.

"It's not just a matter of marrying my sister."

"Oh?"

"It's necessary to conform to the wishes of her father and mine, the Marquis de Castirac," added the imperturbable Gascon. And he leaned on his sword, increasingly affecting the pose of a brave warrior.

A faithful and docile ally, Jeanne did not breathe a word—and the Margrave, somewhat intimidated, murmured: "Well, go on then. What are these wishes of which you speak?"

IX

The Chevalier was, as is evident, the master of the situation.

Jeanne, marveling at the initial results he had obtained, now had a blind faith in him, and had no intention of contradicting him.

As for the Margrave, old and fragile in spite of his unguents and cosmetics, he was full of respect for the rapier whose blade was sparkling in the candlelight.

Gascon verve then assumed all of its empire.

"Monseigneur," the Chevalier said, "the story I'm going to tell you is a little long, but it's necessary for you to know it in order to understand the position I'm in."

"Go on," sighed the Margrave.

"My father," the Chevalier continued, "was one of the richest lords in the land of Gascony. We had two dozen châteaux and hundreds of tenant farms on the banks of the Garonne, and a King of France, passing that way, once cried: 'I believe that I'd rather be Marquis de Castirac than king—the fellow is richer than I am.'"

The Margrave did not blink at the Gasconade, and the imperturbable Chevalier went on: "Unfortunately, my father had one great fault: he was a gambler. Every time he went to Bordeaux, he lost one of his châteaux and half a dozen farms. Our mother died of grief. My father continued gambling, and all our farms went the same way, then our châteaux—with the exception, however, of the manor of Castirac, which was built in the days of King Solomon by one of our ancestors."

"Damn!" said the Margrave, smiling. "You have a fine nobility."

The Chevalier coughed modestly. "I'll go on. My father, therefore, had gambled so much that nothing remained to us any longer but the manor of Castirac.

"We had a neighbor, whose property was located opposite Castirac on the other side of the Garonne, was very jealous of us, and rejoiced on learning of our ruin. One day, he met my father and said to him: 'Would you like to wager Castirac against my château?'

"'Never!' my father replied. Then he assumed a disdainful pose and said: 'Your château has only two towers, and mine has four.'

"'Don't let that stand in your way!' the neighbor replied. 'I'll wager my two towers against two of yours.'

"'What do you mean?' asked my father.

"'Listen carefully. If I lose, I'll raze my two towers.'

"'And if you win?'

"'You'll raze two of yours—the ones that overlook the Garonne.'

"'And which make you squint when you look at them,' my father sniggered.

"'Perhaps...and it's agreed that the loser can only buy back his two towers by paying a ransom of a hundred thousand livres.'

"'Agreed,' said my father.

"He always had a cup and dice in his pocket. He and the neighbor both sat down in the shadow of a hedge, used a stone for a table, and started the game; by the third throw, my father had lost."

"And you razed your two towers?"

"Naturally."

"And you've never reconstructed them?"

"Not yet...but wait..."

"Go on."

"There's a legend in our family."

"Does it go back to Solomon?"

"No, but to Saint Joseph, who was a great friend of one of my ancestors,[19] who was his contemporary."

"And?" said the Margrave.

---

[19] In Provence, Joseph of Arimathea was reputed to have brought the Holy Grail to that region, although Anglo-Norman romances transferred the legend to England after the Conquest.

"That legend claims that a woman of incomparable beauty will reconstruct the two towers of Castirac, and render that ancient house all its former splendor."

"That's no problem," said the Margrave. I promise to reconstruct your two towers."

"Yes," said the Gascon, "but it's necessary to pay the ransom—which is a hundred thousand livres."

"Oh!"

"I swore to my dying father that no one would embrace my sister until he had paid that sum in advance. Do you understand me now?"

"Perfectly," said the Margrave. "Well, I'll call Conrad and tell him to give you the money."

"Marvelous!" said the Chevalier, quivering with joy.

At that moment, however, the door opened and one of the pages serving at table came in. He was carrying a tray on which there was a bottle of Rhine wine and two goblets of Bohemian glass."

"Here's the betrothal wine," said the Margrave.

"I'll drink to the health of the towers of Castirac," said the Gascon.

"And I to the health of the future Princess of Lansbourg-Nassau," said the Margrave.

The page filled the goblets.

Then the Margrave and the Chevalier clinked glasses and bowed to Jeanne.

"This is a man's wine, which is forbidden to women by an edict of the Emperor Josef," said the Margrave. "Let's respect his will." And he emptied his glass.

The Chevalier did likewise, and licked his lips.

"Sandis!" he cried. "That's a fine wine, Brother-in-Law, and when you've paid me the hundred thousand livres..."

"Oh, that's true," said the Margrave,

"You can embrace my sister."

At these words, the Bayonnaise thought she ought to blush.

The Margrave spoke to the page, saying: "Child, go tell my steward to bring a hundred thousand livres here right away." Then, looking at the Gascon, he said: "How do you want the sun—in gold or banknotes?"

"Banknotes—that's more convenient."

The page went out.

Almost immediately, however, the Chevalier uttered an exclamation and raised his hand to his forehead. "Ah!" he said. "That's quite bizarre!"

"What is?" said the Margrave.

"That wine's having an effect on me…it seems to me that my head is being broken by a hammer…"

He tried to stand up, but fell back into his chair.

"Me too!" said the Margrave, who uttered a cry in his turn.

Both of them struggled momentarily against a sudden and overwhelming drunkenness.

Jeanne, frightened, looked at them both.

For a few minutes, they struggled convulsively; then their eyes closed, their groans died away, and they slid under the table like dead weights.

Then a door opened and Madame Edwige appeared.

X

The Bayonnaise was somewhat distressed.

The Chevalier de Castirac, her chance protector, was unconscious, and she could not expect any help from him. The Margrave, here future spouse, was in the same condition, and she was at the mercy of the terrible housekeeper.

Her first movement, therefore, as one of dread—but then she experienced an instinctive need to defend herself, and a knife that she grabbed from the table became a weapon in her hand.

Madame Edwige had a smile on her lips, however, which excluded any idea of violence, and Jeanne suddenly felt reassured.

The Megaera approached her with a respectful, almost timid expression, and said: "Don't be frightened, my dear demoiselle, by what has just happened. The Margrave, in a fit of bad temper, refused the services of his steward, and it's the page who has done the harm. Fortunately, the harm isn't great."

Jeanne looked, alternately, at the two bodies snoring under the table.

Madame Edwige went on: "The Margrave, who is going to marry you, is very old, and you'll soon be a widow. He has only conserved an appearance of youth on condition of taking a glass of the wine he's just drunk every evening, which plunges him into a profound sleep that sometimes lasts for twenty-four hours. The page, whom the steward Conrad didn't warn, brought the usual beverage, of whose effect he was unaware. The Margrave drank it, not knowing that the wine was mixed with a narcotic—and that explains the misadventure that has overtaken Monsieur le Chevalier, your brother, which has knocked him out. You understand now, don't you?" Madame Edwige smiled as she concluded.

Nevertheless, the Bayonnaise's suspicion was not disarmed.

"Oh," said Madame Edwige, divining her thought., "I know that you don't trust me, and in that you're quite right, at least apparently, for I've tried to harm you—but I'll tell you why."

With these words, she took the Bayonnaise by the hand, and continued: "I have a protégée, a very beautiful girl—not as beautiful as you, however—who aspired to be a princess. That's why I contrived the uglifying mirror, and I hoped that my protégée, who will only arrive in Paris tomorrow, would get here in time to take possession of my master's heart." Madame Edwige winked. "It must he admitted," she added, "that my protection wasn't disinterested. It was agreed that if my protégée became a princess, she would give my husband and me a hundred thousand livres, with which we could both live contentedly in our homeland. Would you care to promise me that some, in order that I could be entirely devoted to you?"

Madame Edwige's proposition seemed so perfectly frank that Jeanne allowed herself to be taken in by it.

"All right," she said. "I promise you that if I marry the Margrave, you'll have your hundred thousand livres."

"You'll marry him," said Madame Edwige. And, kissing the Bayonnaise's hand, she added: "Now I'm your ally, and you recognize me as your mistress."

With these words, she moved toward a bell-cord and shook it.

Immediately, a door opened and two women appeared: two maidservants, lively, brisk and spirited.

"Here are your chambermaids," said Madame Edwige. "They'll take you to your apartment."

The Bayonnaise wondered whether she might not be the victim of some dream, and whether all this was real.

She followed the two chambermaids.

They opened another door, and Jeanne found herself alone in a veritable miniature palace—or, rather, a bedroom that seemed to have been arranged for a queen.

Rich garments were laid out on the bed. A perfumed bath was waiting for her.

Jeanne was one of those women who, though born on a dung-heap, seem made for grandeur. She allowed herself to be bathed, perfumed and clad in sumptuous night-attire, and lay down on a soft ottoman—after which, she sent her soubrettes away, instructing them to come and wake her early in the morning, and to bring her brother, the Chevalier de Castirac, to her as soon as he had recovered from his stupor.

She had not wanted to go to bed right away. She felt a need to reflect for a while, to recover all her self-composure, all her presence of mind—and also to enjoy, with her gaze, all the luxury that surrounded her.

Evidently, she said to herself, *I've been brought to the bridal chamber, the one that the future wife of the Margrave will occupy. Now, since I already have the room, it will be difficult to dispossess me of it—unless I become stupid, ugly and hunchbacked in a matter of minutes, which could only happen by a miracle—and that miracle, I'm sure, won't occur.*

In the midst of her joy, however, Jeanne the Bayonnaise felt a certain unease.

Although she had not ingested and narcotic, she had, at least, drunk wines that were a trifle heady, and no matter what efforts she made to stay awake, she felt her eyelids gradually becoming heavier.

Nevertheless, she was still struggling against sleep when a slight sound made her shiver.

Having been lazily stretched out on the ottoman, she suddenly sat up straight.

The sound persisted.

Someone was knocking, very discreetly, on her door.

She thought it was Madame Edwige and said: "Come in!"

But a voice that she did not recognize replied: "That's impossible! The door's locked."

Then Jeanne remembered that after the chambermaids had left, she had shot the bolt. She therefore got to her feet in order to open the door.

Before drawing back the bolt, however, she asked: "Who are you and what do you want?"

"Open up," said the voice, which lost its normal pitch and sonority in passing through the door. "I'm a friend..."

Taking a chance, Jeanne opened the door.

Scarcely was the door ajar, however, than the Bayonnaise uttered a scream. Standing before her was Sergeant Lafolie, her first lover.

XI

Meanwhile, Madame Edwige, an hour after having taken leave of the Bayonnaise, who already saw herself as the wife of the old Margrave and to whom she had been obliged to profess tenderness and devotion, had returned to the dining-room.

She had not, however, returned there alone. Conrad, her docile husband, was with her.

The fellow was trembling slightly, for he had no idea what was about to happen.

The Margrave, on one side, and the Chevalier, on the other, were still profoundly asleep under the table.

"Conrad," said Madame Edwige, in an authoritative tone, "go fetch me the case of mysterious bottles that we brought from Germany."

Conrad went out, leaving his wife—who fixed a stare full of scorn and hatred upon the Margrave.

A few seconds later, Conrad reappeared carrying the box that we have already seen at the hostelry in the Rue de l'Arbre-Sec, from which Edwige had taken a bottle, some of whose contents she had made the Margrave swallow.

"It doesn't seem to be necessary today," said Conrad, as he put the box on the table.

"Why is that?"

"Because the Margrave is sufficiently asleep already."

Madame Edwige shrugged her shoulders. "You're an idiot," she said.

Conrad inclined his head, like a man accustomed to similar compliments.

"Beside the poison," Madame Edwige continued, "the remedy is always to be found. There are days when we need the Prince to sleep..."

"Indeed!"

"Today, we need him to be awake."

"Ah!" said Conrad, who still did not understand.

Madame Edwige, who did not deign to explain further, took a different bottle from the one containing the narcotic out of the case. Then she said to Conrad: "Pick your master up and carry him to that sofa."

Conrad obeyed.

"Madame Edwige, directing him with gestures, got him to pile cushions beneath the Margrave's head in such a fashion that he was almost sitting up.

That done, she took a spoon from the table, poured a few drops of the bottle's contents into it, and spread it over his lips.

Immediately, the Prince uttered a sigh—but he did not wake up.

Madame Edwige then took a napkin and steeped it in the same liquid, after which she began rubbing the sleeper's temples.

The Prince uttered another sigh.

Then Madame Edwige said to Conrad: "He's waking up. Go away!"

Conrad would rather have stayed, but his terrible spouse had given an order, and it only remained for him to obey. He went out, therefore, while Madame Edwige delicately continued the friction, while placing the napkin impregnated with the mysterious liquid over the Margrave's nostrils.

The Prince uttered a few more sighs; then, all of a sudden, his eyes opened and the lethargy that gripped him suddenly ceased.

"Oh, it's you, hussy!" he said, recognizing Madame Edwige.

"It's me," she said, coldly.

She had dominated him for such a long time that fear gripped him again; nevertheless, he thought that he had an auxiliary, and exclaimed: "Where's the Chevalier?"

"There he is," said Madame Edwige.

She pushed back the table, and the Margrave saw the Gascon lying on the floor.

"Dead!" he exclaimed.

"No more than you," said Madame Edwige, "but his sleep will last longer than yours, and we have time to talk for a while, Monseigneur."

"Ah, rogue!" said the Prince, hiding his terror beneath a feigned anger. "You want to talk to me?"

"Yes, Monseigneur."

"Doubtless you want to tell me the story of that glass..."

"Perhaps." Madame Edwige remained impassive.

Suddenly, the Prince cried: "Where is she?"

"Who?"

"Jeanne...the princess..."

Madame Edwige stated laughing. "Well," she said, "I respected Your Highness' wishes."

"What do you mean?"

"I had her taken to the bridal chamber."

"Ah!"

"But she isn't alone there..."

The Margrave stated, and came to his feet, his eyes on fire.

"Monseigneur," Madame Edwige continued, taking him by the arm and forcing him to sit down again, "I told you that I wanted to have a little talk with you."

"What do you want, slut? Speak!"

"To prevent you from being duped."

"What?"

"And from falling into a trap."

"Explain yourself, wretch!"

"Yes, Monsieur—if you'll give me time."

"Well, speak!"

Madame Edwige kicked the foot of the Chevalier, who was still asleep. "Do you know," she said, "who this Gascon is?"

"He's Jeanne's brother."

"Jeanne has no brother."

"Ah!"

"But she's had lovers."

The Margrave was gripped by furious anger. "You're lying!" he said.

"Monseigneur," said Madame Edwige, tranquilly, "if I'm lying, I'm ready to leave Your Highness' service this very instant, and leave without taking an obol."

"Then give me proof of what you're saying," said the Prince, on whom the housekeeper's self-confidence was making a considerable impression.

"That's why I caused you to breathe smelling-salts in order to wake you up," she replied.

"Speak...speak..." he said. "The proof? Where's the proof?"

"If you'd like to follow me," said Madame Edwige, "I'll show you a man at Jeanne's feet."

The Prince stood up.

"Come on," she concluded. "Lean on my arm, for you're not very steady on your feet..."

And she drew the tottering old man out of the room.

XII

As one can imagine, the redoubtable housekeeper had taken full advantage of the hour that had gone by between the moment when she had taken her leave of Jeanne the Bayonnaise and the one when she had set about rousing the Margrave from his lethargy.

She had gone up to the room where she had left Sergeant Lafolie eating and drinking.

"Are you ready?" she had said to him.

"Ready to go with you," he said.

"Come with me, then."

She had opened a door and led him along a corridor, at the end of which was a staircase. The staircase and the corridor were illuminated by alabaster lamps that spread a muted light around them.

At the bottom of the staircase there as another corridor, and at the extremity of that corridor was a door with two battens.

"Your former mistress' bedroom is there," said Madame Edwige.

"And she's there?"

"Yes."

"Alone?"

"Yes."

"Well, what do you want me to do?"

"I want you to wait here. When the steward dressed in red who came to find you comes back, go knock on the door."

"All right. And it will be opened?"

"Yes, if you don't give your name and disguise your voice slightly."

"Perfect!"

"When Jeanne has opened the door, you'll go in, and you'll make sure that she recognizes you."

"But what shall I say?"

"Oh, anything you like. That's your business, not mine."

And Madame Edwige, who did not want to explain any further, went to extract the Margrave from his sleep, after having told Conrad what he had to do.

Let us now follow her, while she lent her arm to the old man.

"Where are you taking me, hussy?" said the Margrave.

"Come along, Monseigneur."

She took him through a number of rooms, arrived in the main vestibule of the house, and climbed the main staircase, supporting the Prince all the while.

"You're not taking me to Jeanne," he said, "since her room is on the ground floor."

"I'm taking you to a place from which you can see her as if you were beside her."

The Prince, still tottering, climbed the stairs and went along a corridor. Madame Edwige introduced him into the same room in which the sergeant had eaten.

"What's that?" he said, seeing the table still laden with the debris of the supper.

"One of Jeanne's lovers had a bite to eat here."

The Prince roared with ager. "Where is the wretch, then?"

"With her."

With these words, Madame Edwige raised the carpet in the corner opposite the one where she had displayed the glass floor to the sergeant. Bright light struck the Margrave in the face.

"Lean over and look," said Madame Edwige.

The Prince leaned over, and realized that he was above the bedroom in which Jeanne had just finished dressing for bed.

"Ah! Hussy! You can see that she's alone."

"Wait!" she replied.

Indeed, it was doubtless at that moment that the sergeant knocked on the door, for Jeanne got up to open it.

"Now, Monseigneur," said Madame Edwige, "if you'd like to promise me not to make any noise, I'll even enable you to hear what is being said and done down there."

"All right," said the Prince, "I promise."

Then Madame Edwige pressed a switch, and a leaf of the glass floor rose up, thus allowing sound to pass through.

A tenacious and furious curiosity had gripped the Margrave.

He watched, and he listened.

Jeanne the Bayonnaise had, therefore, gone to open the door and had uttered a scream on finding herself face to face with Sergeant Lafolie.

She was so overcome with emotion that she took several steps backwards—which permitted the sergeant to come in an close the door.

The latter had a conquering step and a loud voice.

"Well, Jeanne," he said, "do you remember me?"

"Yes," she stammered. Fear had taken possession of her, and she murmured: "Yes, I recognize you...but be quiet..."

"Oh, you want me to be quiet?"

"At least lower your voice..."

"Why?"

"Because someone might hear us..."

"Oh, that's true," he said, in a mocking tone. "You're on your way to becoming a princess."

"Shut up!"

"So be it—I'll speak quietly—but you recognize me?"

"I recognize you."

"I'm Lafolie."

"Yes."

"The man that you loved so much..."

"I don't deny it, but shhh!"

"You didn't expect to see me again..."

"No," she stammered. "But how did you get in here? Where have you come from?"

"I'll tell you later. Now..." And the soldier recovered his conquering stance and his victorious expression.

"Now what?" she said, still distressed.

"It's a matter of coming to an agreement."

"What?"

"Aren't you going to become a princess."

"Perhaps..."

"But I'm still a sergeant, and the role of son of Mars is beginning to bore me."

"What do you want me to do?"

"That's what I'm about to explain."

And the Sergeant stretched himself out on the ottoman where Jeanne had been lying a little while before.

"Well, Monseigneur," said Madame Edwige, in the Margrave's ear, "what do you think of all that?"

"Shut up!" said the Prince, impatiently. "I don't want to miss a word of the confidences of that ruffian and that whore."

Madame Edwige had triumphed!

XIII

They were good times, then; a soldier had his way with women and scarcely had to hide it. Sergeant Lafolie was so thoroughly imbued with those principles, imprinted with a pleasant philosophy, that he forgot how and why he came to be there, and, tempted by the princely luxury that surrounded him, started giving some thought to his future.

Then, lying voluptuously on the ottoman, soiling the silk with which it was covered with his greasy leather boots, he resumed speaking.

"So, as I was saying, the profession of soldier is boring me."

"All right," said Jeanne.

"I'd like to live contentedly, with money in my pockets."

"So?"

"And since you're going to be a princess, if you're a good girl, you can help me lead that life."

"I'd like nothing better."

"So I'd like you to do me the favor of giving me a few pistoles."

"As soon as I have some."

"Why not right away?"

"Well...because I don't have any yet."

"Is that true?"

"I swear to you..."

"All right, I believe you. Let's chat about the situation you're going to create for me, then."

"Well," she replied, naively, "when I'm a princess, I'll tell my husband that you're one of my relatives."

"All right."

"That you're unfortunate..."

"Very good."

"And he'll give you twenty or thirty thousand livres, with which you can live in our homeland."

"No, that's not what I want."

"What do you want, then?"

"I want to stay with you."

"That's madness!"

"You can pass me off as your brother if you like."

"But I already have one," said the Bayonnaise, thinking about the Chevalier.

"Oh yes...that Gascon."

"Exactly," she said.

"Well, as I don't like the Gascon, you'll have to get rid of him."

"But that's impossible!"

"Why?"

"Because...he's the one who brought me here..."

"Ha ha!" The soldier burst out laughing noisily.

"Shut up!" cried Jeanne alarmed. "Someone might come...and then I'm doomed..."

"If you want me to shut up, promise me you'll keep me with you."

"But since I'm offering you a fortune," she said, bewildered, "why don't you prefer to go away?"

The sergeant straightened up, and started fidgeting with his moustache. "Here's how it is," he said. "I've had a return of love..."

"What?"

"You've never been so beautiful..."

In spite of her distress and anguish, the Bayonnaise laughed in the sergeant's face. "Oh," she said, "you're mistaken, my dear."

"What?" he said, in his turn.

"When love has gone, it never comes back. I'd rather welcome the first lover who comes along..."

The sergeant's cheeks reddened. "Oh, it's like that!" he said. "You're mocking me?"

"No, but I don't love you anymore."

"You will love me!"

"Never!"

He was about to take her in his arms when, taking refuge behind a table, she said to him: "But tell me, wretch, before causing a scandal, before forcing me to shout for help, how did you get here?"

There was such a tone of authority In that question that the sergeant sobered up somewhat. "Oh, that's right," he said, "I forgot tell you…it was a good lady who had me come in."

"A lady?"

"Yes."

"Madame Edwige!"

"I believe that's her name."

"And she brought you here?"

"That is to say, she began by giving me supper, and then she lifted the carpet and showed me you, your future spouse and your pretended brother through a hole in the floor, having a joyful supper…."

The Bayonnaise uttered an exclamation. "And then she told you to knock on that door?"

"Of course."

"Then we're doomed!"

"What are you saying?"

"The truth," said the Bayonnaise. "That woman is an enemy, and while we're talking, there are doubtless people watching us…listening to us…"

"Well, so much the better!" said the sergeant. "While we wait for the sky to fall, give me a kiss."

He was drunk, and everything around him started spinning. He tried to catch up with her and grab her, but as he turned, the walls and the furniture seemed to turn in the opposite direction…

And suddenly, he fell,

He fell as if he had been thunderstruck, so suddenly did drunkenness take hold of him.

Jeanne had been saved by his drunkenness…

"Well, Monseigneur?" said Madame Edwige, then, looking at the Margrave.

"Well, then," he replied, "call Conrad."

Madame Edwige closed the transparent floor. Then she rang a bell.

Conrad appeared.

"Call my pages," said the Margrave, "and tell them to throw that ruffian and that whore out."

Conrad inclined his head.

As he was about to go out, though, Madame Edwige said: "What about the other one?"

"The Gascon?"

"Yes. What does Your Highness want done with him?"

The Margrave was a Prince, and Princes are ingrates. He immediately forgot that, thanks to the Chevalier de Castirac, he had defied Madame Edwige's anger for an hour.

"Well," he said, "carry the Gascon outside and put him in the gutter. He can finish sleeping off his wine in the open air."

And Conrad went out, to carry out his master's orders.

XIV

An hour later, on the orders of Madame Edwige, the Margrave was transported, with the greatest precaution, to his apartment.

As a consequence of what he had seen and heard, the old Margrave Prince of Lansbourg-Nassau had been afflicted by a nervous crisis and had soon lost consciousness. So many emotions in a few minutes were too much for a man whom the physicians tormented by rendering him an appearance of youth every two days. When Conrad had come back to tell him that the "whore," as he had called Jeanne the Bayonnaise, had gone without making any difficulty, and that the Chevalier de Castirac and Sergeant Lafolie had been carried out, both drunk, one to the gutter of the Rue Saint-Honoré and the other to the Rue des Bon-Enfants, the Margrave had immediately uttered a sigh of relief.

Then, turning to Madame Edwige, he had said: "My head seems to be reeling a little."

Madame Edwige had sat him down in an armchair.

The Margrave had uttered another sigh and closed his eyes, saying: "I believe I'm going."

And he had, indeed, fallen unconscious,

Madame Edwige had thought it unnecessary, however, to send for one of the Margrave's two physicians, who had gone to bed some time ago.

The box of mysterious bottles was there, and Madame Edwige was able to find a sufficiently energetic cordial therein to recall the Margrave to life. In the meantime, she called the pages and had the unconscious Prince carried to his bed.

Then she sent the pages away and remained alone with Conrad by the Margrave's beside.

For the first time in several hours, the two spouses finally had the time to breathe.

Conrad looked at his wife and said, naively: "I believe we've had a narrow escape."

"Pooh!" said Madame Edwige.

"I could see the moment when the accursed Gascon was about to have us both thrown out."

"That's because you lose your head too easily, Master Conrad," said the housekeeper, disdainfully. "But instead of congratulating ourselves, let's prepare for tomorrow—which is to say, carry through our plan."

"The Prince is unconscious," said Conrad, "and if you don't make him breathe salts, he'll stay that way for hours."

"That's what I'm counting on."

"Ah!"

"And we're going to take advantage of that time."

Conrad looked at his wife curiously. That came from the fact that Madame Edwige only ever made him party to her plans at the last minute, and only let him in on half of her plans.

"Everything we've been through this evening wouldn't have happened if the woman on whose behalf we're acting had been ready today."

"That's true," said Conrad.

"So we need to use the time profitably and go in search of her right away."

"In the middle of the night?"

"You know as well as I do that there's neither day nor night for her."

"That's true."

"Go, then—I'll wait for you to come back to take action."

And Conrad left Madame Edwige sitting at the beside of the still-unconscious Prince.

An hour later, Conrad came back.

"Well?" said the terrible housekeeper.

"She told me that everything will be ready tomorrow, as things have been agreed."

"Very well...you can go now; I don't need you anymore."

The docile Conrad went out.

Then Madame Edwige made use of the cordial contained in one of the bottles in the mysterious case for a second time.

She rubbed it on the Margrave's temples, nostrils and lips, and the latter began to sigh and stir; then, after a quarter of an hour, he opened his eyes.

The whole night had gone by, and the first rays of dawn were sliding through the curtains.

The Margrave looked at the housekeeper.

"Oh, it's you," he said.

"Yes, Monseigneur."

"Have I had a dream, or was it real?" the Prince went on. "Jeanne...the Chevalier...the soldier...?"

"Jeanne was a ruined girl and the two men were adventurers," said Madame Edwige.

"It was true, then?"

"Undoubtedly."

"So I wasn't dreaming?"

"Not in the least."

"And what's become of the wretches?"

"They've been thrown out, on your orders, Monseigneur."

The Margrave sighed. "Edwige," he said, "I'd still like to marry."

"Your Highness has come to Paris for that purpose."

"Alas, shall I ever find a woman as beautiful as that adventuress?"

"More beautiful, Monseigneur."

"Oh!"

Madame Edwige assumed a mysterious expression. "For some time," she said, "Your Highness has mistrusted me and no longer given me all his confidence, as he once did."

The words awoke in the still-troubled mind of the Margrave the memory of the mirror that the Chevalier de Castirac had broken with a blow of his fist.

"Ah, hussy!" he said. "If I don't trust you it's with good reason, damn it!"

"Monseigneur."

"And if you'd like to explain to me the story of that glass through which all the women seemed ugly..."

"Nothing is easier," said Madame Edwige.

"Go on, then!"

"There is in the world a woman so beautiful that Your Highness would only have to see her to fall at her feet."

"Ah!" said the Margrave, whose eyes were shining.

"That woman, who is coming from far away—from the Far East—with the sole aim of meeting Your Highness, was to have arrived in Paris yesterday."

"So?"

"She suffered a delay, and will only arrive this evening. In Your Highness' own interests, Conrad and I contrived that glass, in order that Your Highness would not make an imprudent choice."

"And you say," said the Prince, "that this woman is beautiful?"

"She can have no rival."

"And I shall see her?"

"This evening."

"That's a long time," sighed the Margrave.

"No," said Madame Edwige. "You're tired. You need rest. It's necessary that you don't seem too old to her; she might not want you."

"Oh!" said the Margrave, smiling. "I'm so rich!"

"She's richer than you are," said Madame Edwige.

Those words plunged the Margrave Prince into profound amazement, and he looked hard at Madame Edwige, to see whether she might be making fun of him.

XV

While these things were happening inside the house, our friend the Chevalier de Castirac was sleeping off his wine—or, rather, was still in the grip of the violent lethargy into which he had plunged at the same time as the Margrave.

Conrad, the scarlet-clad steward, had carried out the Margrave's orders punctiliously and had the Gascon carried into the gutter of the Rue Saint-Honoré. He had been laid down full horizontally with his head toward the wall and his feet toward the roadway, but as they went away, the two pages charged with the task had been kind enough to place a lantern on his belly in order that no belated carriage would run over him. This occurred about an hour after the watchmen had made their round, and, in consequence, the street was deserted.

At four o'clock in the morning, no one having passed that way as yet—or, at least, having paid any attention to the lantern that served the Gascon as a lighthouse—a litter emerged from the Rue des Bons-Enfants. The bearers of the litter seemed to be in a hurry, and were going at a rapid pace when the first of them collided with the Chevalier's inert legs.

"Hey!" he said. "What's this?" He stopped.

The other porter did the same, and they set the litter down on its four feet. The litter was doubtless empty, because no one protested.

The two porters, who were large and robust lackeys dressed in dark livery, leaned over the sleeper, and struck up a conversation.

"Do you think he's drunk?" said the first.

"One might think that he were dead," said the other.

"The dead aren't heirs," said the first.

The other looked at him.

"Don't you think," added the one who had emitted that singular opinion, "that we've had a bad day at work, eh?"

"Damn!" replied the other. "When one's hired by President Boisfleury, one shouldn't attend to anything else."

A brief explanation will suffice to clarify these words. In that epoch, one hired a litter in exactly the same way as a carriage, and, in the same way that there are people who have three, four or as many as ten numbered carriages for the use of lords and all those who do not have carriages of their own, so there were businessmen who hired out chairs and porters by the hour, for half a day or an evening.

Now, the two fellows who had just pronounced the name of President Boisfleury belonged to an enterprise of this sort, and they had no specific wages except for the tips that their generous clients gave them, the fee for hiring the portable chair being paid directly to its owner.

Now, President Boisfleury was not exactly a generous client. A member of the Parlement and the President of the Criminal Court, Maître Boisfleury was notorious in the Rue de la Vrillière, where he had lived for a quarter of a century, as the greatest pedant in France and Navarre. He was a short, middle-aged man, severe and bilious, with an olive complexion, possessed of an immoderate love of justice, and his redoubtable functions had accustomed him to seeing guilty parties everywhere. He was a bachelor, who lived meanly with an old serving-woman, spent little money and let the life of an anchorite. Evildoers trembled when the mounted the bench; the bourgeois of his neighborhood made a thousand jokes about his avarice but no one in the world would have dared to say that President Boisfleury was not the most honest and upright judge in France.

Now, that evening, the President had had a great many visits to make. He had called in one several of his colleagues who were wintering merrily and giving balls and feasts, and had only gone back home at about three o'clock in the morning. For that, he had hired a chair, and when he had dismissed his two porters he had given them, by way of a tip, a twelve-sou coin.

So, the two porters had put down their chair on the ground, and were contemplating, thanks to the lantern, the unconscious Chevalier de Castirac.

233

"You're right," said the second. "The dead aren't always heirs, but they can be..."

"Bah! The night's dark, the street's deserted..."

"Besides, how do you know he's dead?" The second porter put his hand on the Gascon's breast. "No—he's certainly not dead."

"Oh!"

"His heart's beating."

"But he's drunk, and one is so poorly paid by men of law that it makes one want to turn thief."

"Thieves are hanged."

"Yes, when they're caught."

"And then again," continued the second porter, more honest than his companion, "look at him."

"All right—I can see him..."

"He has an épée at his side, it's true, but his clothes are threadbare, and I'll wager that he hasn't got ten deniers in his purse, if he has a purse."

"Let's look anyway."

"No," said the other, "to become a thief for so little is utterly wretched."

"Let's go, then."

"I've got an idea."

"What?"

"You're cursing the President...so am I..."

"The miser!"

"Would you like to put one over on him?"

"I'd like nothing better."

"You know that he's always avid to render justice day and night."

"So?"

"Let's put this chap in the litter."

"And then?"

"We'll go back to the President's."

"He's in bed and asleep."

"That's the whole point."

"I don't get it."

"We knock so long and loud that the old witch of a maidservant will come to open up and he'll wake up."

"And then?"

"Then we dump this drunkard in the corridor, telling him that we thought he might be a criminal. He gave us twelve sous for carrying him around for six hours; he's capable of giving us an écu for having brought him a man to judge."

"Indeed," said the first porter, "it's a good trick to play on him to get him out of bed as soon as he's gone to sleep."

And the two of them picked the Chevalier up and put him in the litter.

The Chevalier was sleeping so profoundly that a cannon-shot would not have woken him up.

XVI

The first of the two porters had been correct; President Boisfleury was in bed and probably asleep, for the two jokers knocked vigorously on the old door or the old house without obtaining any response.

President Boisfleury had gone to bed when he got home and was doubtless sleeping the heavy slumber that is the reward of a tranquil conscience.

Finally, a window opened above the front door and the President, wearing a cotton night-cap, demanded what they wanted.

"It's us, Monsieur le Président," replied one of the porters.

The President recognized the chair of which he had recently made use. "What do you want, wretches?" he said. "Have you some complaint to make? Have I, perchance, paid you with a clipped écu?" The magistrate's voice was sharp, as befitted a man discontented to have been woken up with a start.

"No, Monsieur le Président," replied the other fellow, without being in the least disconcerted, "but we've discovered evidence of a crime, and we've come to alert you."

At the word *crime* the zealous President had jumped like a warhorse retired to the plough pricking up its ears at the sound of a trumpet.

The first porter completed his subjugation by adding: "And as we're aware of your great love of justice and your execration for malefactors, we didn't hesitate to wake you up."

"But what's the crime in question?" asked the President.

"We found a man in the street."

"Well?"

"A man who isn't dead, and yet can't succeed in waking up. We think there's something about the singular drunkenness with which he's afflicted that isn't natural."

"And where is this man?"

"We put him in the chair and brought him here."

The President disappeared from the window, saying: "Wait there—I'm coming down."

"Well," said he second porter, "what did I tell you? The fellow's capable of spending an entire night without sleep for the love of justice and hatred of thieves."

"That's true."

"Isn't it a good trick?"

"Oh, excellent!"

President Boisfleury's old housekeeper was deaf; she had, in consequence, not heard knocking, and her master, finally woken up, having not hesitated to get up himself, thought it unnecessary to disturb her slumber. He therefore went down himself to open the door in his undershirt and night-cap, holding a candlestick in his hand by way of a lamp.

Once the door was open, the two porters did not give the President time to set foot in the street. On the contrary; they picked up the chair and carried it into the vestibule.

Monsieur Boisfleury approached, candle in hand, parted the leather curtains of the chair and saw the Chevalier de Castirac, still plunged into a profound sleep.

"Hmm!" he said. "There's a face that I don't much like the look of."

"That's the effect it had on us," said the first porter.

"So we didn't hesitate," added the second.

"That's good, that's good," said the president Then he examined the Chevalier's threadbare garments. "Hmm," he repeated. "He's an adventurer, a mercenary...that's obvious." Then he added: "Pinch the fellow for me—wake him up so that I can interrogate him."

The two porters shook their heads.

"We've never been able to wake him up," they said.

"Pinch him anyway."

They obeyed conscientiously, but the Chevalier did not wake up.

"Take him out of the chair," ordered President Boisfleury.

The Chevalier was like an inert mass. The two porters laid him out on the floor of the vestibule.

"But he's dead!" said the President.

"We thought so too, Monsieur, but you can tell that his heart is beating."

The President, delighted, placed his hand on the Chevalier's heart, and felt the pulsation distinctly. Then he set about shaking him and pinching his arms, hard enough to inflict veritable bruises.

The Chevalier was still asleep.

"That's quite extraordinary!" the little man murmured, his eyes shining with a somber joy, for he was already glimpsing a magnificent investigation to be carried out. He opened a door in the hallway—that of a small room in which there was a bed.

"Pick the man up and bring him in here," the President instructed. He went in first, and stood beside the bed, candle in hand.

The Chevalier was laid down on the bed, and in response to a gesture from the President one of the porters set about unfastening his waistcoat and unbuttoning his chemise.

Neither the throat nor the breast bore any wound or any other trace of violence. The lethargic sleep into which the Chevalier was plunged seemed perfectly regular, and his breast was rising like that of a man sleeping naturally.

"This is truly quite extraordinary," murmured the President, increasingly joyful. He went to fetch some vinegar and dabbed it on the Chevalier's temples, lips and nostrils. It was a waste of effort.

"Where did you find him?" he asked.

"In the gutter of the Rue Saint-Honoré, at the corner of the Rue des Bons-Enfants."

"Ah!"

"He had a lantern on his belly."

A memory seemed to come to the President's mind. "Rue des Bons-Enfants, you say?"

"Yes, Monsieur le Président."

"Isn't there a house there in which a somewhat…unusual individual has taken up residence? A German prince?"

"Indeed."

"Hmm!" And President Boisfleury got an increasingly clear scent of a fine criminal investigation.

"Search the fellow for me," he said. "Perhaps he has some important papers on him."

The two porters obeyed again, and it was the one who had offered the opinion, a quarter of an hour before, that a man with such faded clothes could only have the devil in his purse who dug his hands into the Chevalier's pockets. To his companion's great amazement, he pulled out a purse—and that purse was round. When the President opened it, it proved to be full of gold.

The two porters looked at one another in consternation, and the one who had shown himself to be so honest sighed.

The President, by contrast, murmured: "A man so badly dressed who has his pockets full of gold—this is becoming less and less natural." And he put the purse on the mantelpiece adding: "That will be the starting-point of my investigation." At the same time, he looked at the two porters. "You're worthy fellows," he said. "You have, to all appearances, rendered a great serve to the law, and you deserve a reward.

So saying, he rummaged in his own pocket and pulled out another twelve-sou piece, which he offered to them majestically.

XVII

The joke was on the jokers. The threadbare sleeper had gold in his pockets, and the chair-porters had had no suspicion of it. When they could have robbed him in peace, they had preferred to transport him to President Boisfleury with the sole aim of disrobing the latter's sleep and avenging themselves for his meanness. Now they had another derisory gratification to make them repent their good conduct.

President Boisfleury paid no heed to their discomfiture, however. On the contrary; he continued to congratulate them on their good thinking, warning them that they might perhaps be obliged to make a sworn statement, while pushing them gently out of the room where the Gascon was asleep into the vestibule, and along the hallway toward the door.

The two porters were so crestfallen that they allowed themselves to be guided without resistance.

Then President Boisfleury went back to the sleeper.

He tried once again to make him breathe the vinegar and wake up, but he recognized that it was impossible. The sleeper was under the influence of a narcotic, the President realized, and the man of law did not know how to break the spell.

Nevertheless, the courageous magistrate stood guard over the strange prisoner. Instead of going back to his own room, he installed himself in an armchair beside the bed, left the candle alight, and waited.

While waiting for the Chevalier to wake up, the President went to sleep, and daylight was penetrating the room when he opened his eyes again.

The Gascon had not even changed position, and his lethargy continued.

The President ran to open the door and shouted: "Marianne! Marianne!" That was the name of his old housekeeper.

The good woman, who was busy with the usual occupations of an only servant, was sweeping the stairs at that moment, and came down in response to her master's summons.

The latter had gone back into the room where the Gascon was sleeping.

"Lord Jesus!" cried the old woman, upon going in behind the President. "What's this, Seigneur? A man, here! Some thief, perhaps..."

"Shh!" said the President. "Instead of uttering exclamations, listen to me, and get ready to carry out my instructions."

Marianne raised her arms and her eyes to the heavens.

"Do you know the barber Révol?" said the President.

"Yes, Monsieur," Marianne replied. "He's the one who came to bleed me last year."

"Precisely. He lives in the Rue Saint-Honoré, next door to an apothecary."

"That's right," said Marianne.

"Run to his house..."

"But the man...is he dead, then?"

The President thought it unnecessary to give his maidservant an explanation, and went on: "And tell him to come right away, and bring his lancet."

"And you're going to remain here alone...with...?"

"Go on, then!" said the President, impatiently.

The maidservant raised no further objection.

It is not far from the Rue de la Vrillière to the Rue Saint-Honoré, and Monsieur Boisfleury calculated that Marianne would be back within a quarter of an hour, accompanied by the barber-surgeon. What he wanted from the latter, as you will doubtless have guessed, was a means of waking the obstinate sleeper, in the person of whom the zealous magistrate persisted in seeing a great and mysterious evildoer.

For the thirty years that he had been a criminal judge, President Boisfleury had never trembled before villains. In consequence, he did not even give a thought to the fact that he was alone with a man he believed to be a bandit, that the man might wake up abruptly and make use of the épée he had at his side and at least reconquer his liberty, if he did no worse.

On the other hand, convinced that the barber would be able to extract the man from his lethargy, and that he would then be able to commence his investigation immediately, he went to put on his red robe and his square cap, and then came back to sit beside the bed in that imposing attire to await the arrival of the surgeon.

The barber Révol did not take long to get there.

Marianne, who was loquacious, had told him on the way that she had found hr master in the presence of a man so soundly asleep that one might have thought he was dead. How had the man come to be in the President's house? That was what the old maidservant did not know, and what the barber had to find out for himself after crossing the threshold of the President's abode.

In that epoch, as is well-known, surgeons were barbers; they bled the sick and shaved the healthy. They had consulting-rooms and shops in which clients in good health chatted at their ease while awaiting the moment to offer their cheeks to the soap. The barber was, therefore, a gossip, and he was already promising himself an extraordinary tale to tell his clients when he saw the President clad in his red robe, in the severe attitude of a judge in session.

President Boisfleury was a veritable legend. The entire quarter knew about his meanness, and the bourgeois who saw him pass by, walking on tiptoe so as not to get muddy, frequently laughed—but no one had ever laughed at him when he was on his bench, and his robe inspired a salutary terror. So Master Révol became tremulous, and, while looking at the sleeping man curiously, silently awaited Monsieur Boisfleury's orders.

"Look at that man," said the latter.

The barber leaned over the Gascon, examined him, and said: "He's asleep."

"Wake him up."

The barber shook the Gascon, who continued to snore.

"You can see," the President said, "that his sleep isn't natural."

"Certainly not," said the barber. "He's in lethargy."

"Is there a means of waking him up?"

"There are several."

"Then make use of the quickest and get to work."

"I'll bleed him."

And Master Révol picked up his lancet and rolled up the Chevalier's left sleeve.

President Boisfleury remained impassive.

When the lancet was applied, the Chevalier's blood suddenly began to flow, and the sleeper made an abrupt movement. His lips parted, and let out an exclamation.

Finally, he opened his eyes.

"Sandis!" he cried. "Where am I, then?"

He saw his blood running, and, uttering another exclamation, fell out of bed and reached for his épée, which was still at his side. Then he saw the President in his red robe.

In those days, as at any other time, the robe of a magistrate inspired more terror than a soldier's sword. Swordsmen are always afraid of men in robes, and the Chevalier left his épée in its sheath.

"Where am I, then?" he stammered.

"In the house of a man who judges criminals," replied President Boisfleury—and he made a sign to the barber, who set about trying to stop the blood flowing from the Chevalier de Castirac's arm.

XVIII

For more than thirty years, as we said, President Boisfleury had been rendering justice. He was not only thoroughly accustomed to his functions, therefore, but had an almost immediate ascendancy over the people he was interrogating.

The salutary fear that the law inspires had, therefore, taken possession of the Chevalier de Castirac. Confronted by that red robe, the Gascon's braggadocio had faltered; he scarcely remembered that he was a swordsman, and certainly had not the slightest desire to put his hand on the hilt of his innocent rapier.

The barber-surgeon, Master Révol, had stopped him bleeding and bandaged his arm in the blink of an eye.

The Chevalier gazed at the red-robed President and the black-clad barber fearfully.

"Master Révol," said President Boisfleury, finally, "sit down at that table, bring that piece of paper toward you, take up that quill and write to my dictation. You're going to serve as my clerk and transcribe this man's interrogation."

Then the Gascon found his tongue again. "But what crime have I committed?" he asked.

"Shut up—or, rather, confine yourself to answering my questions," replied President Boisfleury, severely.

The Gascon looked around in bewilderment.

"What is your name?" Boisfleury went on.

"Hector, Chevalier de Castirac."

"Where do you come from?"

"I don't know, any more than I know where I am," the Gascon replied.

"Don't try to deceive the law," said the President, fixing his little gray eyes on the Chevalier.

The quick wit that is the prerogative of the Gascon race, which it only abandons rarely, came to the poor Chevalier's rescue.

"Monseigneur," he said, "I not only have the greatest respect for the law, but an absolute confidence in it."

These words caused Boisfleury to quiver. Firstly, the Chevalier had addressed him as *Monseigneur*, which flattered him; secondly, a man who has confidence n the law can have nothing to fear from it.

However, as the good criminal judge he was, President Boisfleury continued: "Beware! Don't try to mislead the law with lies. You were found dead drunk in the street."

"Oh! Really?" said the Gascon.

"In lethargy, rather," said the barber.

That word was unknown to the Gascon, who was not very well-read. "I don't know what that is," he said.

"Let's pass on," said the President. "So, you were found in lethargy and it was necessary for this gentleman, who is a barber by trade, to apply a stroke of the lancet in order to wake you up."

"I still don't understand how I got here," said the Gascon, "and I should like the law, which protects the weak against the strong, to take up my case."

"What!" said President Boisfleury.

"I've fallen into a veritable trap," said the Chevalier de Castirac.

"What do you mean?"

"The Margrave Prince invited me to supper."

At the word *Prince*, President Boisfleury started violently. "The German Prince?" he said.

"Yes, Monsieur."

Bizarrely enough, President Boisfleury had been aggravated for two days by everything that he had heard about the Margrave—and as, after all, one criminal was sufficient for him, provided that he found one, he told himself that perhaps the man was right, and that instead of being the guilty party, he was a victim. He softened his voice slightly, therefore, and said: "Well, if, instead of having to punish you, the law owes you aid and protection, it will not fail in its duty. Tell me what had happened to you, and how you came to be found dead drunk in the street."

"In lethargy," the barber corrected.

Monsieur Boisfleury made a small gesture of impatience, but he did not deign to reply to Master Révol, and awaited the Gascon's response.

The Chevalier continued: "The Margrave Prince is an old fool who had otherworldly ideas. He's fabulously rich...richer than the King."

"Oh! Really?" said Boisfleury disdainfully.

"He's had a very strange idea, Monseigneur, as you shall see. He's made it known all over Paris that he wants to marry."

"How old is he?"

"Seventy."

Boisfleury surged his shoulders. "So?" he said.

"So, all the marriageable women were to present themselves to him; he would choose the most beautiful and marry her.

"That doesn't explain...."

"Patience, Monseigneur."

And the Chevalier, who was beginning to familiarize himself singularly with the law, thought that mingling a little romance with the story might not go amiss. He went on, therefore: "I ought to tell you, Monseigneur, that I have a sister who is very beautiful, as beautiful as she is virtuous, and would make a gallant man very happy."

"Aha!" said Boisfleury.

"The Gascons are not rich," the Chevalier continued, "and the idea occurred to me yesterday of introducing my sister to the Margrave, thinking that, if she became a princess, she would have enough gold and dignity to recover the fortunes of our family, which is contemporary with Noah, the first vine-grower."

A semblance of a smile played upon Boisfleury's lips. "So?" he said, again.

"So I introduced my sister to the Margrave yesterday evening.

"And he thought her beautiful?"

"So beautiful that he closed the doors of his house and swore to me that he wanted no other woman than her."

"And then?"

"And then he invited me to supper. Then, I remember that I drank a certain wine, which suddenly burned my breast; my ears began to buzz, my temples to throb, and I fell down."

"The wine doubtless contained a narcotic," the barber put in.

"What happened to you then?" asked Boisfleury.

"I don't remember any more."

"Did the Margrave give you any money?"

"No."

"In that case," said Boisfleury, resuming a severe expression, "how is it that, with clothes as wretched as those you're wearing, you have your pockets full of gold?" And the president went to the mantelpiece, to fetch the Chevalier's purse, from which gold coins were overflowing.

The Gascon was not disconcerted by so little, however. "That, Monseigneur, is another story."

"What?"

"A story even more curious than that of the Margrave."

"Beware!" repeated the President. "If you're try to mislead the law..."

"On the contrary, I'm serving it."

The Gascon had an expression of sincerity that seduced President Boisfleury, whose faced cleared, and he said: "Speak, then!"

My God! thought the Chevalier. *Here's a good opportunity get my own back in that boor Guillaume, half-bourgeois and half-swordsman, who maltreated me as if I were a small boy.*

"Get ready to write," said Boisfleury, looking at the barber.

The improvised clerk took up his pen again.

XIX

The Chevalier began his statement thus:

"I arrived in Paris a fortnight ago and was staying in a hostelry in the Latin quarter which bears the sign *Au Cheval Rouan.*"

"I know it," said Boisfleury

"The day after my arrival, I was in bed and asleep when a lot of noise coming from inside the hotel woke me up. I went downstairs half-dressed and saw a man stained with blood who had been brought into the hostelry and laid upon a table. The man had a large wound in his chest and he was unconscious. I was told that he was the Marquis de la Roche-Maubert.

"That name is not unknown to me," said President Boisfleury. "Continue."

"He'd been found at the door, bathed in his own blood, and carried to his room, where a surgeon, after examining him, shook his head and said that he wouldn't recover."

"Someone had doubtless tried to murder him?" said Boisfleury, who scented a fine criminal investigation.

"No, he'd been injured in a duel."

"With whom?"

"Nobody knew, although I found out subsequently."

"So?"

"The Marquis didn't die, though. The rumor of his misadventure caused quite a stir, for the next day, the Regent and Cardinal Dubois sent for news of him.

This time President Boisfleury uttered a veritable exclamation of joy. "Continue, continue," he said.

"After a week, the Marquis was out of danger, and he asked me to keep him company. When we were alone he told me that he was in love."

"How old is he, then?" asked Boisfleury.

"Nearly as old as the Margrave."

"A madman!"

"I don't deny it—but you'll see. 'I'm in love,' he said to me, 'with a woman who's trying to avoid me. Will you help me, and give me a hand to carry her off?' I had the devil in my purse, I'd come to Paris to seek my fortune and I had nothing better to do, so I accepted the Marquis' proposition and went with him, that same day, to lay siege to the house where, according to him, the unkind woman lodged."

The Gascon stopped to draw breath.

"You're still writing, aren't you?" said Boisfleury, addressing the barber.

"Still," replied Master Révol.

Castirac went on: "She was resident, the Marquis said, in the Rue de l'Hirondelle, which opens into the Rue Gît-le-Coeur."

"I know that."

"At the street-corner we met a gipsy woman, who told the Marquis' fortune."

"What did she predict?"

"That something bad would happen to him, if he went any further."

"But he went on."

"Naturally."

"In fact," said Boisfleury, who was not only a zealous magistrate but also a great philosopher, "that had to be the case; love is a far-reaching folly."

"When we reached the door of the house the Marquis stood aside and I was the one who knocked. A man opened the spy-hole, and debated momentarily, but finished up withdrawing the bolts and letting us in. Then the Marquis put the point of his sword o the man's face and said: 'Prepare to die of you don't show me the secret passage that leads to *her*.'

"Then the man seemed frightened. He begged us—not merely for his own life, but that of the Marquis, who was, he said, in danger. The Marquis was inflexible

Then the man forsook violence and, sighing, said to the Marquis: 'Since you insist, I'll show you the secret passage, but you won't come back.' At the same time, he pressed a switch that operated a slab in the fireplace, which, as it rotated, revealed a staircase that seemed to head underground.

"Then the Marquis said: 'If my life is in danger, so is yours.'—and he gave me orders to remain with the man and killed him if he—the Marquis—hadn't come back in two hours.

President Boisfleury frowned again. "So you accepted the mission of killing an unarmed man?" he said.

At this point, the Chevalier de Castirac thought that if he gave an accurate account of his misadventure with Master Guillaume, the bourgeois swordsman, it would not exactly be to his advantage, so he modified it slightly

"Certainly not, Monseigneur," he said. "I didn't accept such a mission seriously, for the simple reason that I didn't believe that the insane Marquis was in any danger."

"What happened, then?" demanded the President, impatiently.

"When Monsieur de la Roche-Maubert had disappeared into the depths of the stairway, the bourgeois started laughing. 'Look at me, Sir,' he said to me. 'I'm a placid and peaceable man, and I wouldn't hurt a fly, but, at the same time, I'm not a jealous husband, and it's my wife, who's young and beautiful, with whom he Marquis is in love; I defend my good fortune and my honor as best I can.'

"'But what will become of the Marquis?' I asked, slightly disturbed, in spite of myself, but the worthy man's naivety.

"The bourgeois laughed more loudly. 'That stairway,' he said, 'goes down into a cellar pierced by a corridor that descends a rapid slope. At the end of the corridor is the Seine. The Marquis, whom I know distantly, is a good swimmer. He'll slide down the slope, fall into the Seine, take a cold bath, which will calm him down, and swim to the bank. Instead of fidgeting with your rapier, would you like two hundred pistoles and a glass of old wine?'

"In truth, Monseigneur, I scarcely knew the Marquis, and the bourgeois defending his wife interested me. I emptied a glass of wine to his health, pocketed the two hundred pistoles and left."

"And have you seen the Marquis since then?"

"Never."

"And this was..."

"About a week ago."

Monsieur Boisfleury's frown deepened. "You were wrong to behave thus," he said, "for some abominable crime might have been committed in the depths of that stairway."

"It's possible."

"And I'll mount an investigation. Are you still writing, Master Révol?"

"Still, Monsieur le Président," the barber replied.

The Gascon assumed a piteous expression. "Monseigneur," he said, "I still have one more thing to tell you."

"Speak..."

"On leaving the house in the Rue de l'Hirondelle, I returned to the hostelry."

"Good."

"The next morning, the day after, and on the days after that, I waited for the Marquis, but he didn't come back. Then I thought about informing the law, all the more so when I knocked loudly on the bourgeois' door and the door didn't open."

"It will open to me!" declared the zealous President.

Then he put both hands to his forehead, and seemed to reflect.

XX

President Boisfleury's reflections were of short duration, and he appeared to have come to a decision.

"Master Révol," he said to the barber, "I thank you for your assistance. Leave what you have written there; I'll need it for the investigation."

The barber put down his pen.

"Pick up your lancet and go," Monsieur Boisfleury continued, "and keep quiet about everything you've just heard and seen, for if you impede the progress of the law, you might perhaps suffer misfortune. Don't forget."

The barber had a holy terror of President Boisfleury. He knew that the zealous magistrate would stop at nothing in his love of justice, and he left, having bowed to the ground at protested his absolute discretion.

Monsieur Boisfleury remained alone with the Gascon. "My friend," he said, "I have no evidence that what you've told me is not scrupulously true, but I also have no proof that what you've told me is not a pack of lies, with the sole aim of explaining how your pockets came to be filled with gold. In these conditions, I must keep you prisoner until I have fuller information."

The Chevalier de Castirac stifled an exclamation of surprise, but the President did not give him time to reply. He began shouting for Marianne, his old housekeeper, with all his might.

Marianne arrived. The President showed her the Gascon. The housekeeper made a gesture of astonishment, almost of fright. She had seen the Chevalier seemingly death, and now found him on his feet. In addition, she had never seen her master in his red robe at even o'clock in the morning.

After showing her the Gascon, Boisfleury said: "Monsieur is one of my friends."

Marianne's surprise increased

"Serve him breakfast."

Marianne raised her eyes to the heavens.

"And don't let him leave, on any pretext."

The Chevalier, listened, mouth agape. After having been terrified, he had a great desire to laugh, simply at the thought that the President in the red robe might think a wench like old Marianne capable of carry out his order. He was able to bite his lip, however, remain serious and reply: "I can ask for nothing better, Monseigneur, that to remain your prisoner until you have verified the veracity of my assertions."

The terrible magistrate Boisfleury had, as is evident, a singularly naïve side. In addition to the whim he had just had of holding court in his own home, he had no doubt that his sentence could not be carried out, and he had given old Marianne the order to watch his prisoner as seriously as if he had been addressing the governor of the Châtelet, or any other prison.

Privately, the Chevalier said to himself: *If I wanted to go, that old crone wouldn't stop me, but as I've been offered breakfast, I don't see why I should refuse.*

While Marianne continued to manifest her astonishment—an astonishment all the more forceful because the President, who had never offered a glass of water to anyone, had mentioned giving the Gascon breakfast—and the latter was deciding to wait until the fellow have had the pleasure of completing his investigation, Boisfleury underwent a minor metamorphosis before their eyes. He took off his robe, put on a black coat, a black waistcoat and shoes with silver buckles, stuffed the notes made by the barber into his pocket and, with his cane in hand and having saluted the Gascon with a amicable gesture, headed for the door.

"Let's get to work, straight away," he said to himself—and he went out, leaving the Chevalier de Castirac alone with old Marianne.

President Boisfleury was too thrifty a man to travel by carriage or litter except on any but great occasions. If he had adopted the latter mode of locomotion the previous evening, it was because he was making ceremonial visits. It was, in any case, not far from the Rue de la Vrillière to the Palais de Justice.

President Boisfleury started walking at a brisk and sprightly pace, went down to the river, followed the bank as far as the Pont Neuf and went into the Palais. Men of law get up early, and there were already, judges, advocates and solicitors in the main hall. The ushers, who were then known as runners, the clerks and the prosecutors were already at their posts.

President Boisfleury entered the registry of the great criminal court, handed the notes taken by the barber Révol to the clerk and said: "Make a neat copy of all that for me and await my instructions."

Then, as today, the Palais and the Châtelet were connected by corridors and doors guarded by soldiers. The Lieutenant of Police was lodged in the Châtelet.

Having given his order to the clerk, President Boisfleury headed for the Châtelet. Everyone at the Palais knew him and feared him. The soldiers presented arms as he approached, the doors opened in front of him, and he arrived at the Lieutenant of Police's abode shortly before eight o'clock in the morning.

The other magistrate, although watching over the security and rest of Parisians, did not have President Boisfleury's habit of rising early. He was still in bed and his staff raised some difficulties about going into his room and waking him up—but President Boisfleury threatened them squarely will all the thunder of the law, and they ended up obeying.

The Lieutenant of Police, snatched from his sleep, got up in a very bad mood. Nevertheless, he gave the orders to introduce the President into his study. Then he went to join him, and, after the usual salutations, still yawning and stretching, he asked the President whether someone had set fire to the four corners of Paris.

"No, Monsieur," replied Boisfleury, dryly, "but crimes have been committed here that you ought to have prevented." And without pausing for breath, he told the Lieutenant of Police the story of the Margrave who was staging a competition for his hand, got people drunk and had them carried unconscious into the street, and the story of the Marquis de la Roche-Maubert, who had disappeared."

The lieutenant listened until the end. When it was finished, he said: "I think, Monsieur le Président, that you have blithely taken some sticky business in hand."

"Ahem?" said the President.

"And that if you get mixed up in it, you'll run the risk of annoying a very important person."

"What?" said Boisfleury, amazed.

"That's all I can tell you," said the Lieutenant of Police, tranquilly. And he rose to his feet, as if he wanted Boisfleury to do likewise and not to take his questions any further.

The austere President remain in his seat, however. "Monsieur," he said, "I know of no one in France who is above the law, and I demand that you explain yourself."

XXI

President Boisfleury adopted such a high tone that the Lieutenant of Police decided to deny all responsibility immediately.

Monsieur le Président," he said, calmly. "I think you will deign to listen to me with the calm befitting those who, like you, represent the law."

"Certainly," said Boisfleury.

"Everything that you have just told me," said the Lieutenant, "or almost everything, I already knew."

"Ah!"

"Let talk about the Margrave first. He's an exceedingly rich German prince, very well connected, who enjoys great credit, and who has come to Paris to strew his gold around regally. None of that is any concern of the police and the law. If it pleases the fellow to make his house into a fairground, or, rather, a marketplace is which all dubious women or those of loose morals can expose their charms and seek the honor of being married by him, I do not see anything in it that ought to concern me."

"All right," said President Boisfleury. "But what about the man he put to sleep and had thrown into the street...?"

"The man is an adventurer, and perhaps he hasn't told you the whole truth—as, for instance, that his pretended sister was a whore and that he wanted to be the first to put one over on the Margrave."

"But the Marquis de la Roche-Maubert..."

"Oh that's different."

"You agree with that?"

"The Marquis, on whose account I can give you further information, has certainly disappeared, but he disappeared after refusing to follow the advice that was given to him."

"He must be found!"

"That's what I said at first. The hotelier of the Cheval Rouan came to see me.

"When?"

"A week ago. He told me almost all of what you've just told me, and I gave orders for a search to be mounted for the Marquis—or his murderers, if, by chance, he had been the victim of a crime."

"And your agents haven't found anything?"

A smile played upon the lips of the Lieutenant of Police. "You don't get it, Monsieur le Président. You ought to understand, though."

"What?"

"A whisper..."

"Once again, Monsieur," Boisfleury said, severely, "I demand that you explain."

"When I put my agents on campaign," said the Lieutenant of Police, coldly, "I was warned not to go any further."

"And who permitted himself..."

"That's what you ought to have deduced by now."

"I haven't deduced it, and I want to know."

The Lieutenant of Police made a gesture of impatience. "Oh, good God!" he said. "Go see Monseigneur Philippe d'Orléans, Regent of France, and he'll inform you more fully than I can."

That name made President Boisfleury pale slightly, but he was a man of rare tenacity and never admitted defeat. "Well, so be it," he said. "I'll go to see His Highness right away."

"Pardon me," said the Lieutenant of Police, with a mocking smile, "but in that case, I'll ask you for one small favor."

"What?"

"That of telling his Highness about this conversation."

"You can count on it!" said Boisfleury, beside himself—and he got up, and took his leave.

Another man might have given himself pause for thought. The Regent was the foremost person in France, and he would pay back anyone who defies his wishes—but Boisfleury was convinced that Parlement, which had judged and condemned the greatest lords in France, and stood up to kings in many circumstances, must be placed above the Regent and dictate its will to him if need be.

The fellow therefore returned to the Palais. There he put on his robe, collar and square cap, and commandeered four of the mace-bearers who accompanied members of the Parlement on ceremonial occasions.

The entire cohort of solicitors, judges and advocates stood there in amazement on seeing these preparations, and one might have thought it some great political event. Boisfleury's anger had cooled down, however, during the journey from the lieutenant's study to the great hall, and he had recovered the sphinx-like face before which even people with clear consciences trembled.

No one, except the clerk who had already made a fair copy of the notes taken by the barber knew what it was about.

Monsieur Boisfleury took the clerk's work, stuffed it under his robe and climbed into the fleur-de-lysed litter that was at the disposition of members of the Parlement, giving the order to be taken to the Palais-Royal.

That order convinced those who overheard it even more firmly in the opinion that it was a matter of a political event—such as, for instant, a conspiracy similar to that of Monsieur Cellamare, the ambassador of the King of Spain and the accomplice of legitimate Princes.

Three quarters of an hour later, President Boisfleury made his entrance to the Palais-Royal in great pomp and had himself announced to the Regent.

Philippe d'Orléans had always manifested great deference to the gentlemen of Parlement, who had set aside Louis XIV's testament and appointed him Regent. Although the Prince usually went to bed very late, he got up very early, and had been working with Dubois, his first minister, all morning. President Boisfleury was not made to wait in his antechamber, therefore, but was introduced into his study right away.

The criminal judge's instincts and keen faculties of observation permitted Monsieur Boisfleury to catch a gesture and an anxious glance that the Regent and the Cardinal exchanged on seeing him come in.

"Monseigneur," he said, "I have facts of the utmost gravity of which to inform Your Highness."

"Speak, Monsieur le Président," replied the Regent, with the affectionate dignity that never abandoned him. "God forbid that my government should ever be at odds with the law!"

These words disarmed Boisfleury's sudden irritation, who thought that the Lieutenant of Police had deflected the responsibility of his own conduct upon the Regent—and the stubborn magistrate started singing his anthem, making use of the barber's notes, and following his story with a diatribe against the Lieutenant of Police—who seemed, he said, to be misunderstanding the authority of Parlement.

The Regent listened until the end without interrupting, and without pronouncing a word.

Then Boisfleury waited.

"Monsieur le Président," said the Prince, then, calmly, "everything that the Lieutenant of Police told you is perfectly true."

Boisfleury took a step backwards.

"Permit me," added the Regent, "to take care of a little urgent business, and I will then give you an explanation of my conduct."

So saying, he took up a pen and wrote the flowing words, which he handed to the cardinal:

Find the Chevalier d'Esparron; I need to see him today.

Dubois took the note and went out.

XXII

The Regent was now alone with President Boisfleury.

In spite of his usual perspicacity, the latter had not been able to divine what the piece of paper contained that Monseigneur Philippe d'Orléans had just shown to Cardinal Dubois and the latter had taken away.

"Monsieur le Président," the Prince said, looking at Boisfleury, "I shall follow the example of my Lieutenant of Police and speak to you first about the Margrave of Lansbourg-Nassau. The Prince is a cousin of all the German sovereigns, beginning with the Emperor and extending all the way to the King of Prussia. To become mixed up in his affairs would expose us to disagreements with several powers, and if you don't mind, we shall not say any more about it."

Philippe d'Orléans was speaking in a tone that was courteous, but very firm, and which imposed itself on President Boisfleury.

The Regent continued: "Let's talk about the Marquis de la Riche-Maubert now, who has disappeared and, according to you, might have been murdered."

"I'm convinced of it," said Boisfleury.

"But not certain."

"And that's why I've come to beg Your Highness to give orders..."

The Regent stopped the President with a gesture. "Excuse me," he said. "I know more about this business than you do. The Marquis is a former servant of my father, and I am very fond of him."

"Then Your Highness will not let his death go unpunished."

"But the Marquis isn't dead," said the Regent.

Boisfleury took another step backwards.

"Apart from the fact that the Marquis is my friend," the Regent went on, "he is a close relative of Dubois, my prime minister, and you can imagine that if he had been murdered, we would not relieve anyone of the duty of searching for the murderers and bring them to justice."

"But the Marquis has disappeared?" said Boisfleury.

"Yes."

"Where is he?"

"I know that, but it is impossible for me to tell you.

Boisfleury made a gesture of astonishment.

"Monsieur le Président," said the Regent, coldly, "listen to me carefully. The law ought only to go into action when a crime has been committed. I give you my word as Prince and Regent that the Marquis is alive." He went on, in a tone of supreme authority: "At the same time, however, I order you to abandon completely this investigation, which, if pushed any further might compromise people highly-placed within the State, and perhaps a woman's honor."

So saying, the Regent rose to his feet with great dignity, thus making Boisfleury understand that the audience as at an end.

The latter, pale with chagrin and concentrated irritation, bowed deeply, and went out without saying a word.

Then the Regent lost the mask of impassivity that he had maintained until then, and his face expressed an extreme anxiety. "Poor d'Esparron!" he murmured. "Poor Janine!" And he supported his head in his hands, seemingly sinking into a profound and dolorous dream.

A few minutes afterwards, a curtain masking an emergency door was raised, and Dubois showed his ferrety face. "Monseigneur," he said, "d'Esparron's here."

"Send him in!" said the Regent, swiftly raising his head.

Dubois disappeared and d'Esparron immediately came in.

"My dear chap," said the Regent, "you'll do me the justice that until now, the police have left you and Janine alone."

"Yes, Monseigneur."

"But the police are not the Parlement, and now some old fool of a president of the criminal court wants to interfere in our affairs. If you and Janine haven't completed your work within a week, I can't guarantee anything."

"Everything will be concluded in a week, Monseigneur," the Chevalier replied, in a measured and grave voice.

"And you'll be gone?"

"We'll be out of the realm."

The Regent looked at Dubois. "Do you know Boisfleury too?" he asked.

"Certainly," the Cardinal replied. "He's the most obstinate man in France and Navarre."

"And don't think he'll admit defeat," said the Regent. "Do you know what he's going to do on leaving here?"

"No, Monseigneur."

"I have two enemies: Monsieur de Bourbon and Monsieur de Fripes,[20] not to mention Madame la Duchesse du Maine and her imbecile husband. He'll go in search of them. I've forbidden him to take his investigation any further, but he won't pay any heed to my prohibition, and in three days, all Paris will know that the Marquis de la Roche-Maubert has disappeared."

"That's probable, Monseigneur."

"It's necessary to make haste, therefore," added the Regent, addressing the Chevalier d'Esparron. "Not to mention that this accursed Gascon will make a din, and will be flattered to have a role to play."

"Monseigneur," said Dubois. "I've got a good idea."

"Let's hear it!"

"I was here just now and I didn't miss a word of that old fool Boisfleury's story."

"Good. So?"

"If I heard correctly, it's in his home that he subjected the Gascon to an interrogation."

"Yes."

"And it's in his home that he's keeping him prisoner."

---

[20] *Fripes* are old clothes, but the Regent is presumably making a punning reference to Philip of Spain.

"Indeed."

"Well," Dubois continued, "assuming that Boisfleury hasn't run straight to our enemies, he'll have returned to the Palais to take off his robe and dispose of the Parlement's litter."

"That's probable."

"From here to the Rue de la Vrillière it's only a few steps. Suppose Your Highness were to sign a *lettre de cachet* and hand it to the guards, with orders to seize the Chevalier de Castirac and take him to the Bastille?"

"You're right," said the Regent. He signed the *lettre de cachet* and the Dubois went out to give the order to the Captain of the Guard."

"That's that!" said the Regent, then, looking at Monsieur d'Esparron. "The Marquis really is alive, isn't he?"

"Yes, Monseigneur, but he's quite terrified..."

"Make sure he doesn't escape," said the Regent. "If you had that old fool and Boisfleury on your heels simultaneously, I'd be powerless to save you..."

And the Regent, having said that, fell back into his reverie.

XXIII

Let us return to the Gascon, the Chevalier de Castirac, whom President Boisfleury had left at home in the custody of his aged housekeeper, Marianne.

The President had taken one useful precaution to conserve his prisoner: he had instructed his housekeeper to give him breakfast, thinking that a man who is eating and drinking has no need of liberty. In that, President Boisfleury was mistaken, just as he was mistaken in having blind faith in Marianne.

Not that the worthy woman had not become attached to him in the thirty years she had been in his service, nor as she capable of cheating him out of an obol—but she was perhaps, justifying the proverb which says that no man is a hero to his *valet de chambre*, the only person who did not think much of her master's judiciary talents.

As stingy as he was, Marianne claimed that the President was consuming his wealth for love of justice, when he was old enough to retire and live in peace. Marianne had, therefore, shivered when President Boisfleury had mentioned serving breakfast to the Chevalier. She had the habit of obedience, however, and in spite of raising her eyes to the heavens, when the President had gone, she laid a table in the same room where the interrogation had taken place. And while fulfilling that duty, she lad looked at the Chevalier out of the corner of her eye.

He was tall, he was thin, and to complete the work of making him hungry, a pint of blood had been taken from him that very morning.

The man will eat us out of house and homme! the old housekeeper thought, fearfully.

Even so, she placed a chicken carcass on the table, bread and a small piece of cold boiled beef.

Castirac was hungry; he sat down at the table. At the third mouthful, however, he said to Marianne: "Are you losing your mind, my girl?"

"What?" said Marianne, sharply.

"Do you think I can eat like a donkey, with nothing to drink?" At the same time, he pushed away the pitcher of water that she had placed on the table.

Marianne was not disconcerted. "Perhaps," she said, with a hint of irony, "you'd like to drink wine?"

"Of course!"

"But that's impossible."

"Why is that?"

"First of all, Monsieur le Président doesn't drink. He only drinks water, and says that a judge should never expose himself to the risk of troubling his mind."

"Yes, but I'm not a judge."

"True—but you're a prisoner, and prisoners don't drink wine."

"Oh! A good joke!"

"You're a prisoner," Marianne repeated, "and as long as you're here, your fate won't be very unfortunate...but afterwards..."

"What do you mean, afterwards?"

"You don't know what fate awaits you, then?" said Marianne, who saw with increased alarm the Chevalier open an immeasurably large mouth with pointed teeth like those of carnivores. "But I'm the President's guest rather than his prisoner," said the Chevalier naively.

Marianne smiled—a smile of dolorous pity. "Poor young man!" she said.

""What do you mean, my good woman?"

"That you're young."

"Eh?"

"And that you don't know President Boisfleury. Once you fall into his hands, you never get out."

"But..."

"He treated you mildly, just, now—even affably—didn't he?"

"Indeed! He called me his dear friend."

"Well, that's to lull your suspicions to sleep."

"What?"

"Enough," Marianne continued, who had developed an obsession in a matter of five minutes. "Do you know that the President has never offered a glass of water to anyone?"

"Bah!"

"And that you're the first man to whom he's ever given a meal."

"Get away!"

"If he does such a thing, it's because he has a purpose."

"And what purpose is that?"

"To have time to run to the Palais, find sergeants, give them a *lettre de cachet* and bring them here, to take possession of your lordship and take him to the Bastille."

Castirac had been listening to Marianne with such interest that he was no longer thinking about demanding wine, and had bravely drunk water. While listening to the worthy woman, however, he had caused the chicken carcass, the piece of beef and the loaf of bread that had accompanied them to disappear.

Marianne felt her hair standing on end and pursued her obsession—that of scaring the Gascon in order to make him go away.

The word *Bastille* had brought a slight shiver from the Chevalier.

"You're young," Marianne continued, "and I like you, even though I'm seeing you for the first time."

"You're a thousand times too kind," replied the Gascon.

"You remind me of a poor young man, a cadet from Gascony like you..."

"Really?"

"Who was put in the Bastille twenty-five years ago and is still there."

"And what had he done?"

"Nothing, or almost nothing. He had not saluted a procession that was passing by—but President Boisfleury had seen him."

This time, the Chevalier pushed the table away—on which nothing any longer remained, in any case—and stood up swiftly, saying: "But I don't want to go to the Bastille!"

"You'll have to, when the sergeants come looking for you."

"Yes, but I won't wait for them."

"What will you do?"

"I'll leave right away." The Chevalier buckled his sword-belt and put his hat on his head.

"But you're my prisoner," said Marianne.

"Oh! That's true."

"And I'll have to answer to the President for you."

"That's all the same to me!" He tried to move Marianne aside.

"But my master will throw me out!" she said, in a lamentable tone, placing herself in front of him.

"I don't want to go to the Bastille."

"But if..."

She looked at him with an imploring expression.

"What?"

"If you were to find a rope in the house..."

"And?"

"And, having tied my hands and feet, you were to put that napkin in my mouth..."

"Right!" said that Chevalier. "That's an idea."

"When the President comes back with the sergeants, he'll find me bound and gagged, and will see that I did my duty in full."

"Well, where is there a rope?"

"I'll go fetch you one," replied the triumphant Marianne. And, indeed, she came back almost immediately, armed with a rope, allowed herself to be bound and gagged, and made a sign to the Chevalier that he had better make himself scarce as soon as possible.

The latter did not make her repeat the gesture; the word *Bastille* had planted a veritable terror in his mind.

Marianne had not realized that she had spoken so truly. A mere six minutes after the Chevalier de Castirac had launched himself out of the house, the captain of the guard of His Royal Highness the Duc d'Orléans arrived with four musketeers, looking for the Chevalier de Castirac, in order to take him to the terrible State prison from which people only emerged ten or fifteen years after having gone in, when they came out at all.

XXIV

Let us now return to the Margrave de Lansbourg-Nassau, over whose mind the terrible Madame Edwige had regained her empire.

The Prince had shown himself docile to all his house-keeper's desires. Without a murmur, he had taken the narcotic that would procure him a long and profound slumber, designed to repair his strength and bring back an appearance of youth to his aged body.

He had slept for thirty-six hours.

At the end of that time, perhaps subject to some new drug, skillfully administered, he had come round, opened his eyes and then leapt out of bed with a youthful vigor.

Madame Edwige was there, and the faithful steward Conrad was there too.

"Monseigneur," said Madame Edwige, "you can order us to call your pages to dress you; you're as fresh as a rose and as sprightly as an adolescent."

A connection was established in the Margrave's memory between the moment that he had gone to sleep and the one where he had woken up—which is to say that he remembered everything that had happened since his supper with the Bayonnaise woman and the Gascon, including the promise that Madame Edwige had made to show him a woman whose beauty would eclipse all those he had already seen. Thus, he hastened to say: "How long have I been asleep?"

"Thirty-six hours."

"Ah!" The Margrave's eyes shone, and he added: "*She* has arrived, then?"

"Yes, Monseigneur."

"How long ago?"

"This morning. She's waiting for you."

"Where?"

"In her house."

The Margrave's cheeks reddened. "What!" he said. "She only arrived this morning and she already has a house?"

"For three months, a legion of workers has been toiling to prepare a splendid dwelling for her, and that dwelling is intended for you, Monseigneur."

"She's beautiful, then?" said the Prince, in a tone of sensual avidity.

"The angels seem ugly by comparison with her."

"But is it certain that she will love me?"

A thin smile glided over Madame Edwige's lips.

"All the more so," said the Margrave, "as I'm no longer in the first flush of youth, and I have a certain scar on my forehead that doesn't embellish me."

"Monseigneur," Madame Edwige replied, "you are one of the great seducers of the world."

The Margrave coughed modestly. "Perhaps there's some truth in that," he said.

"Al the unguents and pomades with which you will be rubbed, combined with the reparative sleep that you've just enjoyed, make you a young man, at first glance."

"You think so!"

"I'm sure of it—and as for the language that you speak so well, and which turns the heads of all women, you can't have forgotten it."

"Certainly not!"

"Be full of confidence, then; she will love you."

The Margrave had a further frisson of joy." Well," he said, "summon my pages. I want to be dressed in the latest style of fashionable society."

Conrad rang a bell and the pages came in.

Then, while he was being dressed, the Prince bombarded Madame Edwige with questions.

"Didn't you tell me that she's rich?" he said, finally.

"Yes, Monseigneur."

"Richer than me?"

"I believe so."

"And I'm old, while she's young, and she wants to marry me?"

"Yes, Monseigneur."

"That's bizarre," the Margrave murmured.

"But simple to explain," said Madame Edwige, smiling.

"How?"

"She wants to be a princess, and put a crown on her head."

"Oh, that's true!" said the Margrave. "I forgot that I was a prince and a sovereign."

"And I won't hide it from you any longer, Monseigneur," Madame Edwige went on, ready to dare anything at present, "that I've been promised a bribe of a hundred thousand livres."

"Oh, you hussy!" said the Margrave. "I suspected that your services weren't disinterested. I'll wager that she's ugly."

"If Your Highness judges her so, there'll be nothing to be done about it, and I'll lose my hundred thousand livres," the housekeeper replied, with the calmness of a person sure of her facts.

The Prince's costume was almost complete and he had just put on a beautiful blue velvet coat with silver trimmings, which gave him the appearance of an aristocrat scarcely thirty years old, while he wore on his head—whose hair was as black as ebony, by virtue of a cosmetic—a braided tricorn hat.

"Is my carriage ready?" he asked, buckling on his little court épée, enriched with precious stones and fine pearls.

"Yes, Monsieur."

"And you say that she's waiting for me?"

"Impatiently."

"Let's go then, right away," said the Margrave, urgently—and he took Madame Edwige's arm, as was his habit.

They arrived thus in the courtyard of the house, in which a ceremonial carriage was waiting. Madame Edwige opened the door respectfully.

Then, before climbing into the vehicle, the Prince said to her: "Where is the house of my unknown beauty, then?"

"I don't know, Monseigneur."

"What?" said the Margrave, amazed.

"If Your Highness will look more closely, he will see that this is not his carriage, but one that has been sent by *her*."

"Well?"

"The coachman has his orders..."

The Prince hesitated to climb up.

"But Your Highness need have no fear," Madame Edwige concluded. "I can reassure him with a word."

"Ah!"

"I shall have the honor of accompanying him."

"To *her* house?"

"Yes. I have to collect my hundred thousand livres." As she spoke, Madame Edwige took her place in the carriage, beside the Margrave. Then she shouted to the coachman: "You can go!"

The coachman gave free rein to his horses, and the carriage drew away from the house at a rapid trot.

XXV

Madame Edwige's confidence was such that the Margrave, under her dominion, had raised no objection. The carriage rolled noisily along the Rue Saint-Honoré and appeared to be heading for the Place du Châtelet.

"I can guess where we're going," said the Margrave, then. "We're going to the Marais?"

"I don't know," Madame Edwige repeated.

"The Marais," the Prince continued, "especially the Place Royale, was the high society quarter forty years ago. This dear child, in her capacity as a foreigner, is some forty years behind the times in terms of fashion."

And so saying, the old man, having become young again, shook off a few grains of tobacco scattered on his ruff.

The carriage arrived in the Place du Châtelet—but there it made a right-angled turn, and instead of going into the Rue Saint-Antoine it went down toward the river.

"Oho!" said the Margrave. "Does she live in the other side of the river, then?"

"I don't know," repeated Madame Edwige, for the second time.

The Seine had its bridges then, but did not yet have its quays. Here and there, on the natural banks, poplars and elms grew between two bridges, and fishermen moored their boats to their trunks.

The Margrave's astonishment increased when he saw the carriage, instead of going on to the Pont du Change, take a road fringed by fishermen and mariners, who were hauling their boats with horses, and descend to the river bank.

"Where the devil are we going?" said the Margrave, again.

"I don't know." Madame Edwige was entrenched behind that negation.

Having reached the water's edge, the carriage stopped. The Margrave put his head through the window.

Night had fallen, calm, silent and rather somber, and a penetrating frost was separating out of the mist.[21] The ruddy light of a few sparse lanterns was reflected in the river, which was flowing soundlessly.

The hour, the deserted location and the singular journey then had the privilege of evoking in the Margrave's enfeebled mind a whole world of memories.

"My God!" he said. "Am I not the victim of a dream, Edwige?"

"You're wide awake," the housekeeper replied.

"This reminds me of Janine."

"Which Janine?"

"The witch who made gold."

"Was it here that she was burned, then?"

"No, but it was here that she arranged her rendezvous."

"Ah!"

"The men whose heads she had turned," the Margrave went on, "came here, on foot or by carriage."

"And they waited here for the witch?"

"No, for a boat that took them to her."

"Really?"

"There was a whistle, blast, and then..."

The Margrave interrupted himself then.

The coachman had just taken a whistle from his belt and had drawn a shrill blast from it.

At the same time, a similar sound was heard in the distance, from the other side of the river.

---

[21] The chronology of the story does not makes sense; although there was frost on d'Esparron's cloak when he first appeared and there is frost again now, it was "the Monday after Pentecost" a few chapters ago, which would usually refer to the day known as Whit Monday in England, although it could conceivably refer to Easter Monday—a spring date, either way. This detail in consonant with evidence shortly to be provided suggesting that it is the end of November, but the datum in question will only add to the confusion.

"Just as in Janine's time," said the Margrave, with a slight tremor in his voice.

"Yes," said Madame Edwige. "But Janine is dead?"

"Of course! I saw her reduced to ashes."

"Then it can't be her with whom you have a rendez-vous."

"No...and yet..." The Margrave stopped, and could not suppress a shudder.

"Well?" said Madame Edwige.

"Janine had the custom, while alive, of saying that she was immortal."

"Yes, Monseigneur," replied Madame Edwige, shrugging her shoulders, "but I assumed Your Highness to have an intelligence above such stupidities."

"Of course of course," said the Margrave, "but...this similarity...at a distance of forty years...is at least bizarre."

He was interrupted again.

After the whistle-blast, another sound became audible. This time, it was easy to recognize oars dipping into the water and striking the waves with monotonous regularity.

The Margrave began trembling. "Still as in Janine's time," he murmured. Seized by a sudden impatience, he leapt out of the carriage.

Madame Edwige followed him.

"Why have you brought me here" demanded the Margrave, addressing the coachman.

The coachman leaned toward him and addressed a few words to the German Prince in an unknown language.

The sound of oars became increasingly distinct, and something black could soon be seen gliding over the surface of the river. It was a boat. Madame Edwige was still beside the Margrave, but did not say a word.

The boat reached the shore. Then the Margrave saw two men, who exchanged mysterious signs with the carriage's coachman.

"Still as in Janine's time," he murmured.

"Monseigneur," said Madame Edwige, coldly. "I thought you were bolder."

"But..."

"If you're afraid, let's go back to the house."

"Pooh!" said the Margrave, placing his hand on the hilt of his sword.

"In that case," said Madame Edwige, "go on to the end. I tell you that a young woman, beautiful and rich, is waiting for you. Are you going to hesitate, then, because an old memory comes to mind? Is there only one woman in the world who makes use of a boat for amorous rendezvous?"

"This observation was full of justice, and the Margrave was ashamed of his weakness. "But are you still going with me?" he asked Madame Edwige.

"Still, Monseigneur."

"Well then, let's go."

And he headed for the boat.

The two oarsmen were masked.

"Oh!" exclaimed the Margrave. "Still as in Janine's time."

Madame Edwige made no reply. Seeing that, the Margrave climbed into the boat, and the housekeeper followed him.

The two oars dipped into the water again, and the boat glided over the river, heading for the opposite bank, passing under the black towers of the old Châtelet.

XXVI

While the Margrave was allowing himself to be drawn on by Madame Edwige—or, rather, shortly before—a cavalier enveloped in a cloak and walking at a rapid pace crossed the Seine by means of the Pont Neuf and went into the Latin quarter.

It was the Chevalier d'Esparron, who was coming back from the Palais-Royal and heading in a great hurry for the Rue de l'Hirondelle.

In spite of its sinister name,[22] the Rue Gît-le-Coeur, to which that of the Rue de l'Hirondelle is perpendicular, was a placid street populated by worthy people who minded their own business and went to bed early.

Ordinarily, when the Chevalier d'Esparron returned after ten o'clock at night, he did not meet anyone along the way.

So, that night, when it was nearly midnight, the Chevalier was astonished to see two men walking slowly ahead of him, stop at the corner of the Rue de l'Hirondelle. Like the Chevalier, they were wearing voluminous cloaks, which covered them from head to toe.

A vague anxiety took hold of Monsieur d'Esparron. He was brave to the point of temerity, but perhaps, at that moment, it was not himself for whom he was afraid. He paused momentarily, therefore, as the two men stopped, who were talking in whispers, and he was even tempted to retrace his steps to the river bank.

His hesitation did not last long, however; the Chevalier had never retreated—and beneath his cloak, he was wearing his sword, which was beating his calves. He resumed walking, and went past the two men.

At that moment, however, one of them took him by the arm and said, in a low voice: "Hey, comrade!"

---

[22] The word *gît* is most familiar in the phrase *ci-gît* [here lies] as used in epitaphs.

The Chevalier stopped, and although the night was dark, he was able to see when he looked at the two men that they were completely unknown to him.

"What do you want?" he asked.

"Oh!" replied the one who had taken his arm, in order to have a look at him. "Excuse me, Monsieur—I mistook you for Porion."

That name made the Chevalier shudder. Porion was not unknown to him. He was a very artful police agent, whom Cardinal Dubois often employed and who had played a significant role during the Cellamare conspiracy.

Monsieur d'Esparron had an inspiration then, and, guessing that the men had been posted there by Porion, replied: "I'm not Porion, my lads, but I outrank him, and if you have a police report to make, you can speak..."

The two men looked at one another.

"Do you know what this is?" said the Chevalier, then—and he took something out of his pocket, which he showed them, drawing them under the lantern placed at the entrance to the street. The object he showed them was a small key in the form of a Latin cross, made of solid gold. There were a dozen keys like that one abroad, if not in the world, at least in Paris, and there was a story attached to them.

When Monseigneur Philipp d'Orléans had become Regent of France, he had favorites like Nocé and the Marquis de Simiane, who had a rather bad reputation, and who roamed the streets at night, exposing themselves to disagreeable adventures, and sometimes running into trouble with the watch and the sergeants of the Lieutenant of Police.

The Regent, who took things very seriously and did not want his friends molested, summoned the Lieutenant of Police one day and said to him: "Monsieur, I've just had a dozen keys made, of which this is the model. These keys, which are not adapted to any lock, will nevertheless open all doors—which is to say that I want those who carry them to be respected, and not to have any difficulty with your agents."

For a good two or three years these keys, distributed by the Regent to his friends, had been in circulation, and not only could those who had them go wherever they wanted by night, but could even requisition the help of sergeants and policemen if necessary.

Monsieur d'Esparron had one of those keys.

The two police agents nodded their heads when they saw it, and the one that had addressed the Chevalier is comrade immediately changed his tune.

"Excuse us, Monseigneur," he said, "but the night's so dark that one can easily mistake a great lord for a fellow of our own sort."

"Yes, indeed," said the Chevalier, laughing. "It seems to me that you're absolutely right."

The two policemen were vile flatterers, and started laughing.

"So what are you doing here, lads?" asked the Chevalier.

"Waiting for Porion, Monseigneur."

"Aha! And what work has old Porion given you to do?"

The two men looked at one another again, and appeared reluctant to reply.

D'Esparron took two pistoles from his pocket and handed them over. "Here," he said, "drink to my health."

Gold is perennially irresistible.

The two rogues exchanged another glace; then the one who had spoken first replied: "Monseigneur, Porion told us to watch this street/"

"The Rue de l'Hirondelle?"

"Yes, and that house." He pointed at the bourgeois Guillaume's house.

D'Esparron did not blink. "Whose house is it?" he asked,

"We don't know."

"Ah!"

"He told us to watch the people coming in and out, and, if there was a woman among them, to grab hold of her and arrest her."

"Very good—is that all?"

"We don't know anything else."

"Well, my lads, if you'll take my advice, you'll go drink the two pistoles I just gave you."

"But Monseigneur..."

"There's a tavern on the river-bank a few steps away, where the wine is very good."

"But Monseigneur," said the other agent, "Porion's going to join us here."

"When?"

"At midnight."

"It's only eleven o'clock—you have time." And to prove to them that the advice he was giving them was an order, d'Esparron opened his cloak to allow the sight of the hilt of his sword, and said: "I have business here tonight as well, not in that house but another, and as I don't want to let you in on the secret of my amours...get lost, my lads!"

And the Chevalier drew his sword part-way out of its scabbard.

Porion's agents took flight.

Then the Chevalier headed for the house at a rapid pace, murmuring: "It's surely President Boisfleury who's set those fellows on our heels."

He had a key to the house; the door opened immediately, and closed again behind him.

The Chevalier, however, did not suspect that Porion's men, having retreated, had retraced their steps and, hidden beneath the dark porch of a door at the corner of the Rue Gît-le-Coeur, had just seen him go in.

XXVII

The Chevalier d'Esparron went into the house and through the unlit vestibule, guided solely by a thread of light filtering under a door.

When that door was opened, he was on the threshold of the room in which we have already seen the Marquis de la Roche-Maubert and his chance acquaintance the Gascon Castirac.

A singular spectacle, however, which caused him to shudder, was then offered to his sight.

The room was in utter disorder, and the overturned furniture testified that a violent struggle had recently taken place there.

There was a man lying on the ground in a corner, whom one might have thought dead or unconscious, so motionless was he. The man was the bourgeois, Guillaume.

The Chevalier ran to him.

Guillaume was no dead or unconscious; his eyes were wide open—but he had been bound and gagged so tightly that he could neither utter a sound nor make a movement.

D'Esparron drew his sword and used it to cut the ropes that were bruising his wrists and ankles; then, having removed his gag, he said to him, in a distressed tone: "Speak—my God, what's happened?"

The bourgeois got up. "Nothing bad, yet," he replied, "save for a misadventure."

"Who tied you up and gagged you, then?"

"Police agents under the orders of a wretch named Porion."

"Ah!" said d'Esparron. "I suspected as much. How did they get in?"

"It's the Gascon who's betrayed us."

"I know."

"Fortunately, since the day I sent him away, putting two hundred pistoles in his hand, we've blocked the entrance to the subterranean passages behind the fireplace, which thwarted those fellows."

"But how did they get in?"

"Wait a moment," said Guillaume, "While I catch my breath." There was water and a glass on a table. The bourgeois took a long draught. "Monsieur le Chevalier," he said, then, "not only has the Gascon betrayed us, but the Regent's protection is no longer covering us."

"Which is to say," d'Esparron replied, "that although the Regent is protecting us, an old madman, President Boisfleury, has taken it into his head to track us down like wild beasts."

"That's the one," said Guillaume. "I heard Porion pronounce his name."

"You still haven't told me how they got in."

"By saying to me through the spy-hole: 'We've come on behalf of the Regent, who wants to see the Chevalier d'Esparron right away.'"

"They knew my name?"

"Yes, Monseigneur."

"And you opened up to them?"

"That was my first mistake. When they were in the house, they jumped me. I defended myself for some time, vigorously, hoping that you might come back in time to help me, but I was finally knocked down, bound and gagged, as you found me. Then they started searching for the catch that caused the block in the fireplace to move, and when they didn't find it, they broke the slab."

Indeed, the Chevalier d'Esparron then perceived that the fire had been put out and the slab had been broken. Behind the slab, however, instead of the opening they had expected to find, Porion and his men had encountered a solid wall, which seemed to be as old as the rest of the house. That discovery had even drawn an exclamation from Porion: "Perhaps that accursed Gascon was making a fool of President Boisfleury."

"So," Guillaume continued, "they searched the house from top to bottom, from the attics to the cellar—but they didn't find anything, as you can imagine. Porion, half-discouraged, said to his companions: 'Let's go! We only know one thing, which is that the Chevalier d'Esparron is living here, and that he's not at home. Come on' And all three of them went out, leaving me in the state in which you found me. But my opinion is that things have gone sour for us here and that we need to clear out."

"That's my opinion too," said Monsieur d'Esparron, with a sigh, "but it's not up to me. Only *she* can decide. In the meantime, my friend, I'll take you to a safe place. You can follow me underground."

"So you're leaving the house empty?"

"Yes."

"It's true," said Guillaume, "that unless they demolish it, they won't find the other entrance, for the simple reason that they'll find a solid wall behind the fireplace, and the fireplace is the only place to which they'll direct their investigations."

"The essential thing," said the Chevalier, "is for us to remain undisturbed for two or three days. Come on, let's go."

As he said the final words, the Chevalier picked up one of the chairs that Porion's men had overturned, brought it to the fireplace and made a footstep of it.

The fireplace as very old, at least contemporary with King Louis XIII; it was sufficiently capacious to shelter twenty people, and an entire ox could have been set to roast on its cast-iron andirons. The bourgeois gentleman who had had it built had not forgotten his coat of arms, and had had them painted over the mantelpiece, on the left-hand side, on a panel framed by rich sculptures.

The Chevalier d'Esparron climbed on to the chair, ran his hand over the panel and touched a catch similar to the one that had previously caused the slab at the back of the fireplace to move. The panel swung like a door, opening outwards, and unmasked a second opening fitted into the thickness of the wall.

"Let's go, quickly," said Monsieur d'Esparron. And he stepped into that mysterious gap, and disappeared.

Guillaume followed him, and the panel closed again.

XXVIII

What no one, including the Marquis de la Roche-Maubert, had guessed, was that the subterranean workings to which the fireplace served as an entrance, did not extend under the bourgeois Guillaume's house, but the house next door. One could therefore dig indefinitely in the cellar of the former without discovering anything.

When the Gascon had left, Monsieur d'Esparron had thought that it was necessary to anticipate the circumstance that he would talk and tell someone about the secret door hidden behind the fireplace. Guillaume and he had not wasted any time; they had walled up that door, being careful to mix a little soot in with the mortar, which had immediately given the wall the appearance of antiquity that had deceived Porion and his acolytes.

Guillaume was correct, moreover, in saying that the fireplace was the only place to which any further search would be directed.

Once in the tunnel, the bourgeois swordsman and the Chevalier d'Esparron went down rapidly. The most profound darkness enveloped them, but the route they were following was evidently familiar, for neither of them gave any thought to procuring a light.

The two doors that we have seen the Marquis de la Roche-Maubert go through opened before them and closed again, and then a third—and then light succeeded darkness for them.

They were on the threshold of the verdant room in which the immortal woman had received the Regent a few days earlier. She was there now, and on seeing the Chevalier come in she uttered a sigh of relief.

"Ah!" she said. "I was beginning to despair of seeing you again." Then she perceived Guillaume. "Has something extraordinary happened up above?" she asked, anxiously.

"Janine," replied the Chevalier, in a sad and grave voice, "the people I mentioned yesterday have not followed his Highness' recommendations."

"What do you mean?"

"That accursed Parlement man has taken it into his head to find the Marquis de la Roche-Maubert."

"He won't find him," she said, coldly.

"But he might discover us, and we need to hurry."

"I need a week," said Janine.

"A week."

"Yes, and my work will begin this evening." She pronounced these words is a sad, grave and solemn tone. On might have thought it the voice of Destiny. Then she picked up a watch suspended from her waist. "I still have an hour before me, my beloved," she said. "The Margrave won't arrived before then."

"It's definitely this evening that he's coming, then?"

"Yes," she said, still looking at Guillaume.

The latter understood that she wanted to be alone with the Chevalier, and took a step backwards.

"Open that door," said Monsieur d'Esparron, "and go to join our servants down below."

Guillaume obeyed, and Janine remained alone with the Chevalier.

Then she took his hands in hers, sat him down beside her, looked at him lovingly, and said: "My dear beloved, you only know part of my story as yet, and the time has come when you need to know everything."

"I don't need to know anything," relied the Chevalier, kissing the young woman's swan-like neck. "I love you, and have made myself your slave."

"So be it," she said, "but I want you to know that I'm pursuing a sacred objective, that I'm carrying out a terrible but pious task. Listen to me, then, my friend."

"Very well—speak!" said the Chevalier, stealing another kiss.

Then Janine spoke.

"I am not, and there has never been, an immortal woman. I'm twenty-four years old, and I shall die when my time has come. A strange and striking resemblance to the woman whose name I bear has permitted me to take up the long and terrible task of our family.

"Janine, who loved the Margrave, and whom the Margrave sent to the pyre, was my aunt. She had a sister, my mother, who resembled her feature for feature, and my mother swore to avenge her—but my mother died before being able to fulfill her promise, and bequeathed that family heritage to me.

"You know now who I am, but what you don't know, is what we are, where we come from, and what the mysterious work is that three successive generations have sworn to accomplish."

Janine was speaking in a grave and melodious voice, to which a tone of sadness added a further charm, and the Chevalier was listening with a respectful avidity.

"We are of the Bohemia race," she went on, "and there is some truth in what that old fool de la Roche-Maubert related at the Regent's supper. My grandmother, Janine's mother, came to France, came to France in the retinue of the beautiful and unfortunate Leonora Galigai, who, under the name of the Maréchale d'Ancre, came to such a tragic end. She was not her maidservant, but rather her friend.

"My grandmother was a Bohemian, but of princely origin. Our ancestors had had palaces in Germany and Italy, and then they had been persecuted, ruined and betrayed.

"Leonora Galigai was twenty years old when, one evening, in the streets of Florence, she met a little girl who was singing, accompanying herself on the guitar. She took her in and brought her up.

"The child knew her family's past; she knew that her father had been betrayed by a man who had long enjoyed his confidence and his friendship. That man was Prince Peter of Lansbourg-Nassau, the father of the Margrave who, in his turn, caused Janine's death. The wretch had hatched a plot against the life of his sovereign, the Emperor, and had drawn a

286

Bohemian lord into it—my ancestor. Then he had sold his accomplices and, as the price of his treason, had been given the wealth confiscated from his friend, who lost his head on the block.

"The little girl taken in by Leonora Galigai knew all that. The woman who was to call herself the Maréchale d'Ancre brought her to France and married her to an Italian lord in her retinue."

At that point in her story, Janine stopped.

"All that's very confused, isn't it?" she said, looking at the Chevalier d'Esparron. "But you'll soon see a luminous clarity emerging from those confused events, and you'll understand that the duty I'm charged with accomplishing is sacred."

And Janine resumed her story, abandoning her hands to the Chevalier d'Esparron, who kissed them ecstatically.

XXIX

"You shall see," Janine went on, "What that accursed race of Lansbourg-Nassaus was. The man that had ruined my ancestor was soon ruined himself. He was a drunkard and a gambler. When the wine took hold of him, he demanded a cup and dice, and with the cup and dice in hand, he wagered, with one of the châteaux that he had stolen from my family as a stake. One morning, he woke up poor and in debt.

"Then, as now, those betrayed by fortune who hope that it might yet return, come to Paris in the hope of finding it.

"Ruined, forgotten by his master the Emperor, the Margrave turn his eyes toward Paris. At that moment, Leonora Galigai was at the height of her power, and her husband governed the kingdom. My grandmother as I told you, had been married by her to an Italian lord whom she had placed in the French court. The Italian lord, my grandfather, was named Mattéo; the family documents left to me do not bear any other name. He was charged with a message for the Emperor's court by the Maréchal d'Ancre, then prime minister, and it was while returning from that journey through the mountains of Tyrol that he met the Chevalier de Flavicourt."

That name, which Janine was pronouncing for the first time, drew a gesture of surprise from d'Esparron.

Janine smiled. "The Chevalier de Flavicourt and the Margrave of Lansbourg-Nassau are one and the same," she said. "It was the name he had adopted in order to come to Paris and hide from the pursuit of the Jews from whom he had borrowed considerable sums when they thought he was still rich, although he was already ruined.

"The wretch was a man with a golden tongue and seductive manners; he was endowed with a kind of fascination, which had been the original cause of the doom of the great Bohemian lord, my grandmother's father. Mattéo and he became friends.

"The Chevalier de Flavicourt—for I shall not call him by any other name henceforth—came to Paris with Mattéo, and the latter introduced him to the Maréchal d'Ancre, on which mind he exercised the same fascination. Mattéo's wife—my grandmother, Janine's mother—experienced by contrast, a profound repulsion or the man as soon as she saw him.

"She knew that the ruin and tragic death of the Bohemian lord, her father, was the work of the Margrave of Lansbourg-Nassau, but she had never seen that wretch, and could not, in consequence recognize him in the Chevalier de Flavincourt. However, she immediately experienced a kind of horror of that man—a sentiment very different from those that the Margrave inspired in Mattéo, for the latter had become his intimate friend, and hence his damned soul.

"The Chevalier de Flavicourt made his way to the court in a matter of weeks; he was given a lucrative employment, and became one of the Maréchal's favorites. Although he was over fifty, he looked scarcely thirty-five, so well-preserved was he, and that appearance of youth had banished any thought on my mother's part that he might be her father's murderer, for the latter's death had occurred twenty years before.

"Heaped with the benefits of the Maréchal d'Ancre and those of Leonora Galigai, leading a life of pleasure and debauchery, the man was still not satisfied. Only one person did not participate in the general infatuation, and treated him with a disdainful coldness, although all the other women adored him. That person was my grandmother, the wife of Mattéo, his first friend at court, to whom he owed his second fortune. The wretch was not stopped by that consideration; my grandmother hated him, but he fell madly in love with her and dared to tell her.

"She tried to get rid of him, threatening to tell Mattéo everything. She rejected him; he tried to use violence. Fortunately for her, Mattéo came in at that moment and found his friend at Janine's feet. Any explanation would have been futile. The two men were wearing épées; they went down to the street, placed themselves under the light of a lantern and crossed swords.

"The duel was long and hard-fought, and Mattéo was victorious. His adversary fell, struck by a thrust that seemed mortal, and Mattéo went back upstairs, leaving his former friend, now his enemy, bathed in his own blood.

"The next day, the body of the Chevalier de Flavicourt had disappeared.

"Mattéo, jealous of his honor, did not mention the sinister adventure to anyone, even the Maréchal. When he was asked what had become of the Chevalier, he replied that, having become infatuated with a beautiful woman with a powerful husband, he had run away with her. That singular story was believed at the French court, and no one had any suspicion of the terrible duel that had taken place between him and Mattéo.

"Six months went by. On a cold winter night, Mattéo, who lived in the Place Royale, like all the noblemen of that era, was attacked by a gang of thieves and cutthroats a short distance from his house. He defended himself valiantly but they were ten against one, and he ended up falling, mortally stabbed. Because the murderers had robbed him, the crime was not attributed to any other motive than theft. The archers of the watch arrived too late to save Mattéo or to capture his killers , who had run away with his jewels and purse.

"My grandmother was thus left a widow at thirty-five, with two daughters, one of whom as already ten years old, and was to be the Janine whose tragic end you know, and the other still in the cradle, who was to become my mother.

"People forget quickly in Paris, and meteors disappear as rapidly as they have arisen. It was nearly a year since any mention had been heard of the Chevalier de Flavicourt when he suddenly reappeared. He had come back from the Orient, he said, and he had ceased to love the woman for whom he had left the court.

"My grandmother, who was still mourning Mattéo, was with the Maréchale one evening when the Chevalier came in. She felt a chill in her heart, and a secret voice cried out to hr: "There is Mattéo's murderer!" But she shivered from head to toe when he said: "Now that the Jews who were my creditors are dead, I can resume my own name. I am the Margrave Prince of Lansbourg-Nassau."

"Mattéo's murderer was, therefore, the murderer of the great Bohemian lord—and my grandmother uttered a cry and fainted in the Maréchale's arms."

XXX

"The next day," the young woman continued, "my grandmother, at the Maréchal's feet, demanded vengeance—but the Chevalier had got in ahead of her. He had seen the Maréchal and had made up a story—a veritable tissue of lies—that established his innocence, not only of having had anything to do with Mattéo's murder, but also the tragic end of the Bohemian lord.

"The man exercised such an empire over anyone to whom he got close, that the Maréchal took him at his word and returned him all his favor. The unequaled and almost unprecedented favor that the Maréchal had enjoyed had made him powerful and ardent enemies. They had succeeded in taking possession of the mind of the young king and that of the queen mother. The storm that was brewing around him was still some way off, but liable to burst suddenly.

"The Chevalier de Flavicourt divined the situation, and as treason was in his blood, he turned abruptly to his benefactor's enemies. He was the one who stole the Maréchal's secret correspondence, who organized the first conspiracy against him and finally took charge of leading the gang of murderers who broke into the prime minister's palace and massacred him, his wife and his servants.

"Janine was ten years old then; she witnessed the massacre, and only owed her salvation to the devotion of an old Bohemian maidservant who carried her away in her arms, having put her young sister in a safe place. As for my unfortunate grandmother, she fell, like the Maréchale, under the murderers' daggers, and was able to see, as she died, the impassive Chevalier de Flavicourt, his lips twisted in a cruel smile, nourishing himself on her death-throes.

But Janine's mother had rendered her last sigh bequeathing to her daughter the duty of avenging her and her benefactors, the Maréchal and Maréchale d'Ancre. The old Bohemian maidservant hid the two children, brought them up in shadow and mystery, and when Janine was sixteen, she gave her a piece of paper covered with bizarre symbols, but which had meaning for her, for my grandmother had taught her older daughter the Czech language that was her mother tongue.

"That piece of paper ordered the young woman to pursue the Chevalier de Flavicourt—or, rather, the Margrave Prince of Lansbourg-Nassau, wherever he might be. It also included a recipe for making gold.

"The latter secret had been given to her by an old woman who said that she was a centenarian and claimed to have found a means of prolonging human life and maintaining eternal youth. If she had renounced profiting from it herself, she said, it was because she had no relatives or friends, and was weary of life.

"My grandmother had not had any great faith in that marvelous recipe. Rich and laden with favors, she had had no need of gold; widowed and still mourning Mattéo, what did wrinkles and old age matter to her? Nevertheless, she had written, under the dictation of the old woman, the magic words that were supposed to produce gold and conserve beauty. Did she not have a legacy of vengeance to bequeath to her daughters? When Janine became a woman, therefore, the Bohemian maidservant gave her the document written in the Czech language.

"Janine began to study it. In order for vengeance to bear fruit, it is necessary that its seeds must be sown with a golden plough, and Janine, who was poor, dreamed of becoming rich. Then again, it was not only for her project of vengeance that Janine wanted treasures. The Maréchal d'Ancre and his wife, Leonora Galigai, had left a child. That child, like Janine, had escaped the massacre, saved by an old maidservant, and was living in a remote corner of Italy, poor and deprived of bread. Janine had sworn to revive the splendor of her mother's benefactors. She therefore tried to make gold.

"At first, her attempts remained fruitless; a few words on the mysterious document had been partly erased, and it was doubtless the impossibility of deciphering those words that was paralyzing her efforts.

"One evening, she had the idea of rubbing the paper with oil and exposing it to the light of a candle. Suddenly, through the paper, which had become translucent, the uncomprehended words appeared clear and distinct—but she shuddered with terror and threw the paper away. She had read the words *human blood*. 'Never!' she cried. 'Never!'

"The following night, as she was sleeping fitfully, she had a vision. Her mother, bloody, with a severe expression, clad in the dress she had worn on the day of her death, was sitting by her bedside, and said to her: 'Avenge me!' And Janine woke up, having resolved to obey her mother.

"She only wanted the death of one man—the Chevalier de Flavicourt—but she needed human blood. Then she joined forces with a surgeon to whom she promised a share of the gold she hope to make—without, however, surrendering her entire secret to him. The surgeon found the means of procuring human blood without killing anyone. One or other of them would go out into the streets and taverns of Old Paris, collecting poor devil who, for one or two pistoles, would consent to allow half a pint of their blood to be taken.

"The problem was solved; Janine manufactured gold. Then she set out in search of the Margrave.

"Many years had gone by since the death of the Galigais, however, and God had taken responsibility for their vengeance. The Margrave was dead.

"Jeanne was thirty years old then, but she was so beautiful, and seemed so young, that she scarcely looked twenty. She was already rich; she thought about undertaking a journey to Italy to search for the Maréchal's son in order to offer to marry him. On the night before her intended departure however, her mother appeared to her again, and said: 'I am not avenged.'

"'But the Margrave is dead!' Janine exclaimed.

"'He had left a son in the world. Seek him, and continue to make gold, for you are not yet rich enough.'

"As Janine nodded her head submissively, the phantom added: 'It is not you who ought to marry the son of Leonora Galigai but your young sister. Send her to Italy and stay here.'

"And after giving that final order, the phantom vanished, and her daughter woke up, bathed in cold sweat, with her eyes full of tears."

XXXI

"So Janine resumed making gold," the young woman went on, after a pause, "and she sent her sister to Italy, accompanied by the old maidservant.

"Two years went by. One morning, she received news of her sister. She had found Leonora Galigai's son, and he had been smitten by her beauty. They were married, and they loved one another.

"Then Janine thought that she had enough gold, and again she thought of traveling the world in order to search, not for the Margrave, who was dead, but for his son.

"She made all her preparations for departure, exchanged her ingots, which were found to be of high quality by the goldsmiths, for gold coins, and was due to set out the following day when, in the middle of the night, her mother appeared to her once again.

"Janine woke up with a start—but it was not a dream, and her mother really was at the foot of her bed, looking at her, no longer with severity, but with sadness. All her wounds were bleeding, and her eyes were filled with tears.

"Janine held out her arms toward her; but the dead woman put a finger upon her hips and said to her: 'Limit yourself to replying to my questions. Where are you going?'

"'To search for the Margrave's son.'

"'Alas,' said the dead woman, 'you have no need to leave Paris for that,'

"'He's here, then!'

"'He will come..'

"'Where shall I find him?'

"'You will encounter him in your path.'

"'Without looking for him?'

"'Without looking for him. Wait.'

"But the dead woman was still weeping.

"Then Janine said to her: 'Have I disobeyed you, then, Mother, or have I offended you?'

"'Not yet,' said the dead woman.

"'Shall I disobey you, then?'

"'Perhaps!'

"'Oh, that's impossible!'

"The dead woman uttered a sigh. 'Although I am no longer anything but a pure spirit,' she said, 'I can only see the future imperfectly—but what I see there frightens me.'

"'What do you see, then, Mother?'

"'Your heart betraying your reason.'

"'Oh!' said Janine, fearfully,

"'You will forget the work with which I have charged you.'

"'Mother!'

"'And you will come to a miserable end, because you will have loved...'

"Janine uttered a scream. She wanted to question the phantom further—but the phantom said no more. The blood-stained dress faded away gradually, and soon, at the foot of the bed, Janine could no longer see anything but a faint cloud, a mist that vanished as the first ray of sunlight entered the room.

"Janine did not leave; but, a slave to her work, she went back to it, pursued by the dead woman's sinister prediction.

"Time went by, and several more years elapsed, but they passed over her head thanks to the old woman's mysterious cosmetics, without hollowing out a wrinkle on her forehead or tarnishing the brightness of her eyes. She was still young and beautiful.

"One evening, when she was searching in a tavern for an honest man who wanted to sell her a pint of blood, she met a young and handsome cavalier whose gaze burned her. The cavalier had drunk his last pistole, exhausted all his credit; he no longer had a hearth or home, and he consented to sell his blood. And she took him home.

"Then he said to her: 'I'm noble, and very well-born; I'm the Prince of Lansbourg-Nassau.'

And when he said that, Janine felt all her blood flow away from her heart. She had before her the Margrave's son, the man she had to strike. For a moment, the lancet trembled in her hand and she thought, instead of using it to puncture a vein, of plunging it into his heart—but the man's gaze burned her, and she threw the lancet away with a gesture of horror.

"The next day, Janine was mad! She was mad with love and had forgotten everything: vengeance, her mother's predictions and the frightful origins of the man whose lips kissed hers."

The young woman interrupted herself. "I've already told you what happened after that."

"That's true," replied d'Esparron.

"From that moment on," she continued, "Janine was no longer in communication with her mother's spirit. The wrathful dead woman withdrew her protective hand. But on the day when Janine was arrested, on the denunciation of the Marquis de la Roche-Maubert, and plunged into a dungeon as a witch, something strange happened.

"Janine's sister, who was living happily in Italy with her husband and who had never heard mention of her mother, saw the latter appear to her. 'Your sister is mad,' she said. 'Your sister has forgotten her duty. She has given her heart and soul to the son of my murderer; it is up to you to continue the work of vengeance that she has abandoned.'

"And Janine's sister meekly asked the phantom what she had to do. 'Go to Paris,' her mother ordered. And Janine's sister set forth, in the company of the old Bohemian maidservant. She hardly paused by day or night, only sleeping for a few hours when fatigue triumphed over her mental energy.

"On the last night of her journey, she stayed in a poor inn in Villejuif; during the night, she saw her mother again.

"The dead woman said to her: 'Tomorrow Janine will be burned in the Place de Grève, but it is necessary that Janine should not die. Janine is the immortal woman.' And, as she did not understand, the dead woman dropped a medallion on to her bed. That medallion bore a portrait of Jeanne. 'Get up,' said the dead woman, 'go to that mirror and look at yourself, after having looked at the medallion.'

"There was no light in the room but the dead woman was luminous and spread a bright glow around her. Janine's sister went to the mirror, looked alternately at the medallion and her own face, and then understood the phantom's words.

"The two sisters resembled one another as two drops of water resemble one another..."

XXXII

The young woman paused again.

"Be patient," she said to the Chevalier, who was, so to speak, hanging on her every word. "I shall soon reach the end of my strange story."

And she continued:

"The dead woman then gave Janine's sister detailed instructions as to what she had to do following her sister's death.

"The next day, she arrived in Paris.

"When Janine went up on to the pyre, her sister, her face hidden by a mask, was in the crowd at the foot of the scaffold. She raised her mask momentarily, and Janine, perceiving her, made a movement of joy. It was then that she looked at the Marquis de la Roche-Maubert and shouted to him: 'You know full well that I'm immortal!'

"In fact, Janine did not die entirely, since her sister resembled her feature for feature, and was to continue her work.

"And it is for that reason that one the night of the execution, lights were seen at the windows of Janine's house, and those who went into the house swore that they had seen her again.

"The Margrave had caused Janine's death, but he had not been able to steal her entire secret.

"The dead woman appeared to her sister again. 'Must I strike the Margrave?' she asked.

"'No,' the dead woman replied. 'It is not you who will accomplish that work.'

"'Who, then?' she asked, astonished.

"'Your daughter.'

"'But I have no daughter,' she replied. 'I've been married for more than ten years, but my union has remained sterile.'

"'It's necessary to return to the conjugal hearth.'

"Janine's sister continued to obey. She went back to her husband. A year later, she died bringing me into the world—

and, strangely, I resemble my mother as perfectly as she resembled Janine, whose name she gave me.

"My mother was dead, but the phantom of my grandmother had not abandoned us. When I was twenty years old, she appeared to me and gave me her instructions—and it is to carry out those instructions that I have come to Paris, and the hour of expiation will sound for the old man who is covered in Janine's blood, as his father was in that of my ancestors."

At that moment a muffled noise interrupted Janine. One might have thought it a bell resonating in the distance through the thickness of a wall.

"Finally!" said Janine, swiftly rising to her feet.

"It's him?"

"Yes—in a quarter of a hour he'll be here."

"He's coming by the route that I followed with the Regent, then?"

"Yes," Janine replied.

"One thing astonishes me," said d'Esparron.

"What?"

"Old as he is, the Margrave cannot have lost his memory."

"Certainly not."

"And the route that he has followed must have awoken his memories."

"No, for that route did not exist in Janine's time."

"Ah!"

"It's my mother who hollowed it out."

"But that boat...those two masked boatmen..."

"Will remind him vaguely of Janine."

"And when he sees her?"

"It will only be me that he sees."

"And who will then...?"

A smile came to the lips of the new Janine. "Listen, my beloved," she said. "It's necessary that you know everything now. Since we have loved one another, you have never gone down to the subterranean level that is below this one, and which was, like the channel by means of which the Regent came, excavated on my mother's orders.

"On that level, there is a bizarre palace, the work of Italian and Bohemian laborers, who were magicians of a sort. In that palace, I have accommodated a dozen servants brought by me from Italy, whom you have never seen. They are the characters in the comedy of death in which the Margrave will play the leading role, and that of victim. Among them, there is a woman. You think me beautiful, do you not?"

"Ah!" said the Chevalier, with admiration.

"Well, the woman of which I speak is more beautiful than me; she's a daughter of Naples; she's nineteen years old; she has turned the heads of many princes and one king, and that is the woman I've destined for the Margrave." In speaking thus, Janine wore a cruel smile.

"I don't understand yet," said d'Esparron.

"Edwige, the Margrave's housekeeper, and secretly my slave," the new Janine continued, is the granddaughter of one of my family's servants. She is, in consequence, devoted to me. In addition, she has a ferocious hatred for the Margrave, for her grandfather, like mine, lost his head on the scaffold.

"It was my grandmother's phantom, once again, who made me that revelation and put me in communication with her. Now, Edwige is accompanying the Margrave. She is the one who will introduce him into the mysterious palace, where everything is ready to receive him."

"But how do we know," said the Chevalier d'Esparron, again, "that the Margrave will find this woman to his liking?"

"She possesses an irresistible beauty."

"All right—but I don't see that one can take such a terrible vengeance on an old man by throwing him into the arms of a woman dazzling with youth and beauty."

"That's because I'm contriving the torture of Tantalus for him."

"What do you mean?"

"I've found a means of becoming as fluid as a specter."

The Chevalier made a further gesture of astonishment.

"And every time the Margrave makes a move toward her, my specter will come between them. That man, I predict, will die mad with rage and with live. I asked you for a week, my beloved, but I don't believe that he has the strength to live as long as that."

"I don't understand any of this," murmured the Chevalier, naively.

"Follow me, and you will understand."

She took him by the hand, lifted up a curtain that masked a door, and they both left the hall of foliage, and disappeared.

XXXIII

Let us return now to the Margrave Prince of Lansbourg-Nassau, who had not climbed into the boat rowed by the masked me without reluctance. Fortunately, Madame Edwige was with him.

For nearly twenty years he had been subject to that woman's iron yoke and obedient to her slightest caprice. For an hour he had hoped to escape that domination, and had had all the joys of a rebellious slave whose revolt is encouraged on seeing the Gascon Castirac mistreat Madame Edwige like a common mortal. As we have seen, however, the terrible housekeeper had not taken long to recover all her empire.

The Margrave had, therefore, climbed into the boat, and he justly reasoned as follows: *I'm rich, fabulously rich, but I'm only Edwige's slave and it's her who governs my immense fortune. She has, therefore, every interest in my being alive, and if I were running the slightest risk, she would not be with me.*

The boat made rapid progress.

The night was black and a light mist extended lazily along the banks of the river.

The house bordering the Seine appeared as confused masses through that mist, and the Margrave said to Edwige: "We're going so fast that we're certainly following the current."

"You're mistaken, Monseigneur."

"Oh!"

"We are, on the contrary, going upstream."

"In truth!"

"Look—there are the towers of Notre Dame; we're about to go past the terrace and reach the other arm of the Seine."

"And then?"

"Then we'll come back down again."

The Margrave uttered a sigh. "But that's the route that those whom Janine brought home once took."

Madame Edwige shrugged her shoulders. "Janine is dead," she said.

"Who knows?" said the Margrave. And he fell into a profound reverie.

The boat did, indeed, follow the route indicated by the housekeeper. It doubled the terrace of the Cité, went into the narrower arm of the Seine, and it progress then acquired a vertiginous rapidity.

"We're going to Janine's house," the Margrave repeated, with a hint of terror.

Madame Edwige made no reply, but she fixed her master with an authoritative stare that seemed to say: *We might be going to Hell, and it would still be necessary for you to follow me.*

The boat passed under the Pont Saint-Michel and suddenly made a singular maneuver. The two oarsmen had abruptly veered sideways, abandoning the current and heading straight for the bank.

The Margrave breathed out. "We're going to get out, I imagine?" he said.

"No," said Madame Edwige.

Indeed, the boat came to shave the walls of a damp, dark house, at the windows of which no light was visible, and the foundation of which plunged into the water. Then, suddenly, a kind of whirlpool formed beneath it, and the boat began to spin—and the Margrave, bewildered, closed his eyes.

When he opened them again, opaque darkness enveloped him, and the boat was going along a subterranean channel at an infernal speed.

Madame Edwige took his hand and said: "Don't be afraid."

"But where are we, then?" he demanded, his voice strangled by terror.

"We're in the home of the future Princess of Lansbourg-Nassau," Madame Edwige replied.

"We're going to death, more like," he replied, his voice full of anguish and fear.

The boat seemed to plunge down below the level of the stream, in which it made a kind of profound wake; then it ran in a straight line beneath somber vaults. One might have thought that it had gone into one of the subterranean channels that the aldermen of Paris were beginning to excavate under the city.

After that, the Margrave sensed that the boat was rising again, as if it were placed on top of a gigantic jet of water.

All of a sudden, it stopped, and collided with a resistant surface.

"We've arrived," said Madame Edwige.

They were still in darkness.

One of the masked boatmen undoubtedly pulled a bell-cord, for the Margrave heard the bell resonating in the distance. Shortly thereafter, the opaque darkness was succeeded by a faint light. One of the boatmen had just struck a flint and lighted a torch—and the Margrave, still terrified, was able to see where he was.

The boat was on a channel similar to a cul-de-sac, for it did not appear to extend any further. Above his head, at a height of six feet, the Margrave perceived a stone vault. In front of him was an iron door.

Less than five minutes after the bell shaken by the boatman had rung, the Margrave heard the grating of bolts and the turn of a key in a lock—and the iron door opened.

Then Madame Edwige said to him: "Let's get out. We're in your bride's house."

When the door was open, bright light struck the Margrave in the face, and he found himself on the threshold of a tunnel lit by alabaster lamps suspended from the ceiling.

Madame Edwige took him by the hand and enabled him to pass from the boat on to the firm ground of the tunnel.

The iron door closed again immediately, and the Margrave saw the boat and the two masked boatmen disappear.

The light succeeding the darkness had restored some of his courage.

Madame Edwige drew him along. The tunnel was about a hundred paces long and ended at another door, alongside which hung the cord of a small bell. As the housekeeper reached out to ring the bell, the Margrave stopped her. He was mortally pale, and his legs were giving way beneath him.

"Edwige," he said, "do you swear that we're not going into Janine's house?"

Edwige shrugged her shoulders. "Janine is dead," she said.

And she rang the bell.

XXXIV

A second chime was heard, and the second door immediately opened. Then the light became more dazzling.

The Margrave, drawn by Madame Edwige, had just entered a small round room illuminated by vast globes of different colors, the walls of which were hung with Oriental fabrics with bright and sparkling hues. Turkish divans, piles of cushions, and narghiles with long flexible pipes terminated by amber tips comprised all the furniture.

Two negro boys of microscopic stature, veritable redclad dwarves, were standing, motionless, to either side of the door. One might have thought them two ebony lamp-stands, for each of them was holding a candlestick.

A curtain lifted up at the back and an old man with a white beard dressed in a long brown robe came in. One might have thought that he was one of the respectable eunuchs serving in the seraglio of a great lord. He came forward slowly, with great majesty, to stand in front of the Margrave, folded himself in two in order to bow to him, and said: "Greetings to him for whom the celestial woman whose humble slave I am, and who is as superior to me as a star to an earthworm, is waiting."

This picturesque Oriental language reassured the Margrave slightly—but his heart as still beating forcefully, and his ears were still buzzing with the infernal splashing of the water in the subterranean channel.

"The celestial daughter who has crossed the seas to come to you," the old man went on, "Will soon dazzle your eyes with her incomparable beauty. But she desires that you should rest a little from the fatigues of your journey before then."

The Margrave was still so distressed that he let himself fall on to a divan.

Madame Edwige remained standing beside him.

The old man went to a silver bell next to which there was an ebony rod, picked up the road and struck it twice.

At that sound, the curtain lifted again, and two more dwarfs, as black as the first, came in varying a tray on which the Margrave saw Oriental preserves, sorbets and pastes.

At a sign from the old man, they came to offer the tray to the Margrave.

The latter hesitated. Was he not in Janine's house—who, to avenge herself, might want to poison him?

But Madame Edwige aid to him in German: "Go on, Monseigneur."

And to set him an example, she took a sorbet and drank it in a single draught.

The Margrave imitated her.

Suddenly, the disorderly beating of his heart eased, and a sovereign wellbeing took possession of his entire body. He sensed his sweat-bathed brow suddenly cool, and as if a new vigor were circulating in his veins.

The negro children placed the tray in front of him and when to fetch a narghile, which they brought.

"Smoke!" ordered the terrible Madame Edwige then.

And the Margrave took the pipe that was offered to him, and meekly raised it to his lips.

Then he was gripped by the incomparable intoxication and plunged into the celestial bliss that takes possession of smokers of hashish at the third puff, and he exclaimed: "Where is she? Where is she?"

"Here I am," said a voice as harmonious as the sigh of the breeze in the pine trees bordering the Mediterranean shores. And, the curtain having lifted for the third time, a woman came in.

But the woman was masked.

Only her curvaceous figure, her long black hair falling in scattered curls over her white half-bare shoulders and her ardent and voluptuous gaze, shining through the mask, declared, eloquently, that she was beautiful.

The sight of the mask, however, immediately drew the Margrave out of the ecstatic state into which he had begun to plunge; his memories assailed him and he cried: "Janine! It's Janine!"

"Janine?" said the unknown woman, in a tone full of astonishment. "Who is Janine?"

"A woman I...loved..."

"Ah!" she said—and smiled through her mask.

"Janine!" the Margrave repeated, his teeth chattering.

"But that's not me," she said.

"She was masked...always masked...like you..."

"Then you never saw her face?" she said, coming to sit down beside him.

"Oh! Yes!"

"And...you would recognize her..."

"Would I recognize her?" said the Margrave, his fear increasing.

"Well, look!"

And the black velvet mask fell.

The Margrave uttered an exclamation—not a cry of fright, but a cry of joy and admiration.

It was not Janine.

It was a young woman of dazzling beauty and youth, who took the Margrave's hands and said to him: "Do you know that I have come from the depths of the Orient expressly to see you? Do you at least find me beautiful, and do you think that I am worthy to be called the Princess of Lansbourg-Nassau?"

"You're not a woman," he stammered, inebriated by lust, "you're an angel." And he took the beautiful, perfumed hands of the young woman in his own hands, as thin and desiccated as parchment, and raised them to his lips.

"But tell me," she said, intoxicating him with her smile, "who was this Janine? Do you know that I'm horribly jealous?"

And the Margrave, fascinated, contemplated her ecstatically, and did not perceive that Madame Edwige was no longer beside him, and that the old man with the white beard and the four negro boys had discreetly withdrawn.

XXXV

"But who is this Janine?" the young woman repeated, fascinating the Margrave—who was already three-quarters inebriated by opium vapors—with a smile.

"A woman I loved," he said.

"Was she more beautiful than me?"

"Oh, no..."

"And it was a long time ago, wasn't it?"

"Yes...yes...a very long time."

Her radiant face suddenly darkened. "I'm jealous," she said.

He made a gesture of protest. "It's you that I love," he said. "And then, Janine is dead..."

"Really?"

"I can assure you of it."

"Then why...just now...did you think that I was that same Janine?"

Forgive me...your mask...a hallucination..."

She removed the tube of the narghile from his lips.

"You've smoked enough," she said. "Come on, let's talk. So you find me beautiful?"

"As the angels cannot be."

"And you will make me a princess?"

"Oh, certainly..."

"When?"

"As soon as possible...tomorrow...today...if you wish," babbled the amorous old man. "It's necessary to summon a priest..."

"But I'm not a Christian," she said. "I'm a daughter of Mahomet."

"It's all the same to me," replied the Margrave. "I'm not much of a Christian myself."

"Ah!"

"I only believe seriously in the Devil. But how, then, are we going to be married?"

"I've brought a priest of my own religion."

"A muezzin?"[23]

"Yes—and tomorrow morning, if you wish..."

"Certainly, certainly," stammered the Margrave, increasingly gripped by the intoxication of opium.

She was close beside him, and the luxuriant curls of her hair were brushing his face.

Inebriated by lust and opium, the Margrave experienced a bizarre sensation at that moment. It seemed to him that his feet were no longer touching the ground and that he was gradually rising in a cloud toward the ethereal regions.

"What is your name, queen of my heart?" he asked, finally.

"Fatma," she replied. She put her arm around the old man's neck. "So," she said, "you want me for a wife, and I shall be a princess?"

"Yes, yes," he repeated, drunkenly.

"And when we're married," she went on, "where shall we go?"

"Wherever you wish. But why don't we stay in Paris? It's the land of pleasure and love."

"No," she said, "we'll return to the Orient, beneath my palms and sycamores, in the vast estates that my forefathers left me." She added, in a sly tone: "And then again, I don't want to stay in Paris."

"Why?"

"Because you would still be thinking about Janine."

That name seemed to extract the Margrave from his blissful torpor.

"Janine!" he said. "Again Janine!" And he made a gesture of fright..

"What do you have to fear, since she's dead?" said Fatma, smiling.

---

[23] The Margrave's knowledge of Islam is evidently limited—a muezzin, who calls the faithful to prayer—is not a cleric—but it is hardly surprising that the Italian masquerader does not bother to correct his misapprehension.

But fear had taken hold of the Margrave, and he repeated, through clenched teeth: "I know full well that she's dead, but I also remember that she claimed to be immortal."

And as he said that, something strange occurred.

The negroes, as they left, had extinguished some of the candles illuminating the Oriental boudoir; the alabaster lamps hanging from the ceiling had gradually dimmed, and the room was in semi-darkness. Aided by the opium, the Margrave, whose gaze was concentrated on the divine Fatma, had not noticed that transition.

Now, all of a sudden, the wall facing him lit up, while the rest of the room remained in shadow. One might have thought that, with the aid of some powerful optical instrument similar to a magic lantern, an artificial light was being projected on to that wall.

"What's that?" asked the Margrave, dazzled by the light.

"What?" said the young woman.

"That light..."

"What light are you talking about?" she asked, ingenuously.

"There...there..." said the Margrave. And he extended his hand toward the wall.

"I don't see anything," she said.

Suddenly, however, the Margrave uttered a terrible scream.

The double intoxication of opium and the charm that the beautiful creature spread around her had just dissipated abruptly. The Margrave stood up, pale and trembling; he extended his hands toward the wall. His entire body was prey to a convulsive tremor, while his taut lips let slip a name.

"Janine!"

Indeed, in front of that wall, dazzlingly bright, a specter, a phantom, had suddenly loomed up.

It was the specter of a woman, and that woman, the Margrave could not doubt, was Janine.

Janine extended her hand toward him, as if to mark his forehead with a fatal sign.

Janine looked at him, as she had looked at him from the height of her pyre at the moment when the flames began to rise.

Janine seemed to be saying to him: *No, this creature of ideal beauty is not for you.*

And the Margrave was seized by a sudden fir of fury and courage, and he drew the épée that he had at his side, saying: "I'll find out for sure whether you're living or dead!"

"What are you doing?" Fatma exclaimed.

"I'm going to kill Janine," he replied. "Can't you see her there?"

"I can't see anything," she replied.

There...that light...in front of that wall. Do you see her?"

"I can't see anyone."

"Well, I can see her!" cried the Margrave.

And, sword in hand, he rushed at the phantom.

Janine did not budge.

The Margrave's épée seemed to go all the way through the body, ran into the wall, and snapped.

At the same time, mocking laughter resounded in the Margrave's crazed ears, and darkness closed in around him.

XXXVI

The sentiment of anger that had taken possession of the Margrave was then succeeded by a sentiment of inexpressible horror.

Plunged into darkness, no longer having anything in his hand but the stub of his épée, doubtless surrounded by invisible enemies, he experienced a kind of memory of his sinister and criminal past, and in the profound darkness that enveloped him, it seemed to him that he saw all the evil actions of his life passing before him, as a repulsive phantasmagoria.

He dared not move.

Cold sweat inundated his temples; his sparse hair bristled; his legs could scarcely sustain him and his tongue, stuck to his palate, dared not proffer a word.

After a few moments, however, he made a supreme effort. And, remembering the beautiful young woman who had intoxicated him with her gaze and her smile a little while before, he called: "Fatma! Fatma!"

But no one replied.

His voice faded away into the void, and his fear then knew no limits. He dared not take a step forward, doubtless for fear that some unfathomable abyss might open up beneath his feet.

How much time did he remain thus?

Neither he nor anyone else could say.

But the fumes of opium, momentarily dissipated by terror and anger, could not have taken long to resume their empire.

A hardened smoker, a man who makes quotidian use of hashish, passes almost without transition, and hence without dolor, from a wakeful state to ecstasy. A novice smoker—and the Margrave, although he was a man who had abused everything, was making his debut—does not arrive without dolor and an incomprehensible malaise in a blissful dream.

The Margrave suddenly felt a circle of fire grip his head; his ears were buzzing; and infernal heat was circulating in his veins, and it seemed to him that he was being carried away by a fantastic whirlwind.

Then, the fire that was devouring him was succeeded by an opposite sensation.

He was cold; the blood froze in his veins; a gradual annihilation took possession of him, and he ended up collapsing inwardly under the influence of a leaden slumber,

Then the dream began.

The Margrave was no longer in darkness.

On the contrary, he found himself in a vast room illuminated by a discreet glow.

Where did that glow come from? The Margrave could not have said, for he could not perceive any lamp or candle. However, the fantastic light permitted him to see the surrounding objects with perfect clarity.

The chamber in which he found himself was, like Fatma's boudoir, furnished in the Oriental style, but the wall-hangings were different, and the Margrave felt his gaze suddenly fascinated by the subjects the hangings represented.

In fact, there were landscapes, interiors and people to be seen there; it was all divided into panels, each of the panels representing a different scene. The mysterious light that reigned in the room was sufficient for the eye not to lose any detail.

The Margrave then perceived that he was lying fully dressed, on a bed placed in the middle of the room. He tried to get up, but an unknown force—or, rather, an extreme weakness—would not permit it.

All his life and all his energy seemed to have taken refuge in his gaze, and that gaze was fixed on the bizarre pictures on the tapestries that covered the walls.

He set about examining the panels one by one.

The first represented a boat gliding along a river. It contained two men and a woman; all three were masked. The boat was moving between two banks bordered with houses, and the Margrave recognized the Seine.

The two unknown men and the woman all wore velvet masks over their faces. Was that not Janine going in search of a man who wanted to sell a pint of his blood for a little gold?

On the second panel the scene changed. It was the interior of a tavern. The landlord was immobile at his counter; two men were whispering in a corner, and a third was drinking silently to one side—and in the latter, the Margrave recognized himself.

It was himself.

He tried to turn his head away, but a sharp curiosity took hold of him and forced him to look at the third panel.

That one represented Janine's laboratory. The crucible was simmering. Gold fell, limpid and rutilant, into bronze basins—and he, the Margrave, was at the witch's feet, contemplating her amorously.

The Margrave turned his head away again—but the mysterious force constrained him to turn on the bed and contemplate the fourth panel.

That one represented Janine's execution.

The witch, calm and smiling, was standing on her pyre.

The crowd was flooding the Place de Grève, and among that crowd, the Margrave saw himself again, and recognized himself perfectly. He was at the very foot of the scaffold, insulting the woman who was about to die with his eyes and his smile.

Terrified, beside himself, the Margrave tried to turn his head away, but the invincible spell kept him motionless and his eyes pen before the flamboyant picture. Every head seemed to be alive, and the flames of the pyre were genuine flames. Janine, beautiful and disdainful, seemed to be braving death, and the Margrave thought he heard he cry to him, as she had forty years before: "You know full well that I'm immortal."

And the wretch, bewildered, fought against the paralysis that was constraining him, and was striving to triumph over that frightful hallucination—for he had the conviction that he was asleep and that everything he could see as the result of a dream—when it seemed to him that the heads moved, that the crowd undulated around the scaffold, that Janine stirred on her pyre, and that an immense murmur reached him.

Then the flames rose up, enveloping the witch, who disappeared momentarily.

Then the Margrave made a supreme effort, and closed his eyes.

Almost immediately, however, the mysterious will to which he was obedient forced him to open them again.

Then—O stupor!—he saw Janine descend from her pyre, come through the crowd, which parted, approach the bed on which the Margrave was lying, come to sit down beside him, smiling…and he heard her say to him, in her grave, sad voice:

"You committed a futile crime there, Prince, since I'm immortal!"

And as he attempted to scream, as he made a futile effort to throw himself out of the bed and take flight, she added:

"For a long time, Prince, I've wanted to have a word with you. Let's talk, Prince…"

And she took him by the hand.

And the bewildered Margrave felt his hand in a hand of flesh and bone, a soft and perfumed hand, a dainty and charming hand, which he had once covered with burning kisses.

The magic lantern was now concentrated around the bed and the panels of the tapestry had retreated into the shadows, with their bizarre pictures.

XXXVII

The Margrave's terror was indescribable.

Janine was there. Janine was holding his hand. Janine did not have the wrathful and disdainful expression that she had worn a little while ago.

On the contrary: she was smiling at him sadly.

"Fritz," she said to him, finally, making use of the pet name that the witch had once given him, when they were in love, "Fritz, you have been ungrateful to me, and if I had not been immortal, you would have my death for which to reproach yourself. And yet I loved you, Fritz...and I love you still!"

The bewildered Margrave looked at her, and felt a shiver run through his entire body, and an emotion that he had perhaps never known before overwhelmed him.

Janine was radiant with youth and beauty, and almost effaced the radiant image of Fatma, the daughter of the Orient.

"I loved you," she went on, in her softest and mot harmonious voice, and I would have made you even more rich and powerful if you had wanted that. But you believed that with me dead, you would inherit my secret of making gold—but you were only able, poor fool, to steal the gold that I had already made.

Sweat inundated the Margrave's forehead. Several times he had tried to pull his hand away, but she held on to it gently.

"Listen," she continued. "I have traversed seas for you. I have come back from the other hemisphere believing, in my immortal naivety, that you had remained young and beautiful. For I love you still, ingrate!"

She bathed him with the magnetic effluvia of her gaze; she pressed the stiff and wrinkled hand of the old man in her own beautiful hand.

"Alas," she said, then, "I was mistaken. You're no longer anything but an old man leaning over the grave, and death will soon take you, unless I order it to retreat."

319

Those last words had a magical effect on the Margrave. They triumphed over his fear and his anguish; they broke the paralysis that gripped his entire body. He made an abrupt movement; the tongue stuck to his palate was loosened, and clearly articulated these words:

"You could make me young?"

"And immortal, like me, if I wanted to."

"Oh!"

A sad smiled brushed Janine's lips.

"But I don't want to," she said. And as he uttered a cry, she said: "It's not me, though; it's you who doesn't want it—for I can only use this new power, the fruit of further research and long alchemical labor, in favor of a man who loves me."

The Margrave's eyes shone.

"Well, I love you," he said.

But she shook her head. "No," she said, "you don't love me. You never loved me. You're a blackguard and an evil man, Fritz...and if you love someone, it isn't me...it's Fatma, the daughter of the Orient...the beautiful infidel, at whose feet you were just now."

"Yes," replied the Margrave, "I found her beautiful—but not as beautiful as you, Janine."

"If you saw us one beside the other, you wouldn't say that."

"Well then, summon her and you'll see..."

Janine shook her head for a second time. "Fatma is here in my house, and yet she doesn't know me, she has never seen me, she doesn't even know that I exist—but I have the power to evoke a phantom that resembles her feature for feature, and since you want to make the test, be satisfied."

Then Janine clapped her hands.

Suddenly, the blinding light that had covered the wall of Fatma's boudoir a few hours earlier, allowing Janine to appear, bathed one of the walls of the room, and in the midst of that light the Margrave saw Fatma loom up, calm and smiling.

It was certainly the daughter of the Orient, of whom he had promised to make a princess.

"Look," said Janine, then. "Don't you find her more beautiful than me?"

"No," said the Margrave.

As if that word were a condemnation without appeal, the light went out and Fatma disappeared.

But Janine was not convinced by that.

"No," she said, "I don't believe you, Fritz. When I've made you young again, you'll play some infamous trick on me, for, as I told you, you're a blackguard!"

"Janine," said the Margrave, putting his hands together, "I love you—I swear it." As he put his hand together he had adopted an imploring attitude on his bed.

Janine remained pensive for a while.

Finally, she looked at the Margrave and said to him: "You can be certain that I can only make you young if your words are sincere. If you're lying, the power I possess won't have the necessary virtue. Now, I'll try."

So saying, she took a golden pin from her hair.

"What are you going to do?" asked the Margrave, with a fearful movement.

"You can see," she said, "that you don't love me, for if you loved me, you wouldn't be afraid of anything."

"I'm not afraid of anything," said the Margrave, making his voice firm. "Tell me—what are you going to do?"

"In order to rejuvenate you," Janine went on, "it's necessary that your old and impoverished blood be drained, to the last drop."

"Oh!" The Margrave shuddered.

"Then I'll infuse your veins with a young and generous blood. For that, it will be sufficient for me to give you a kiss every night."

"But if my blood abandons me, I shall die," said the Margrave.

"No, because I shan't take it all at once."

Was the Margrave sincere at that moment? Did the ardent desire to become young and handsome again allow him to believe that he still loved Janine?

It seems probable, for he said: "Well, then, do as you say."

Then Janine got up and went to fetch a silver ewer from a side-table. Then she rolled up the Margrave's left sleeve and laid his arm bare.

"Remember," she said to him, then, "that if you don't love me, my kisses will be powerless to return you to life."

"I love you," he repeated.

Then, with the golden pin, Janine pricked a vein in the Margrave's arm—and the blood flowered in a little jet, more pink than red, into the silver bowl.

The old man was overtaken by a sudden weakness, and fell into a long faint.

XXXVIII

When the Margrave opened his eyes again, he was alone.

Instead of lying down fully dressed, he was undressed and in an excellent bed—but he did not recognize the room with the wall-hangings representing Janine's story, and thought that he had been transported into another.

What had happened?

The Margrave was so weak that he only had a confused idea.

However, Janine's name came to his lips—and as he pronounced it, a door opened and someone that the Margrave Prince of Lansbourg-Nassau had completely forgotten came in.

That person was Madame Edwige.

"Ah!" she said, approaching the Prince, in a slightly disrespectful tone. "When you go to sleep, you sleep well..."

"Edwige!" murmured the Prince. "You here?"

"Well, of course. Are you surprised?"

"But..."

"Didn't I come with you, yesterday evening?"

"That's true, but...where's Janine?"

Madame Edwige shrugged her shoulders. "Now you're losing your mind," she said.

"Oh, certainly not!" protested the Margrave, whose memories were becoming clearer.

"Janine is dead."

"You're mistaken."

"Get away!"

"I've seen her...last night...she spoke to me...she still loves me."

"In truth?" sniggered Madame Edwige, in a mocking tone.

"She promised to make me young again, and immortal, like her."

"Monseigneur," said the housekeeper, coldly, "I fear that you might be mentally deranged. I'll summon your physician in order that he can bleed you without delay."

The word *bleed* caused the Margrave to start.

"She's already taken blood like that," he said.

"Who?"

"Her—Janine."

"He's mad!" murmured Madame Edwige, raising her eyes to the heavens.

The Margrave felt a surge of anger. "Listen to me, hussy," he said, "and you'll see whether I'm mad."

Madame Edwige sat down in the large armchair that was beside the bed of His Highness the Margrave Prince of Lansbourg-Nassau.

"Speak, Monseigneur, since that's your desire," she said, in a resigned tone.

The Margrave said: "Where did you leave me?"

"At the feet of Fatma, that miracle of beauty who will suffer an old fool like you," Madame Edwige replied, bad-temperedly.

"That's precisely what I wanted to tell you."

"Well?"

"While I was at Fatma's feet," the Margrave continued, "as I was kissing her hands and intoxicating myself with her smile, the room was suddenly filled with a bright light."

"Oh!"

"And Janine appeared to me."

"And then?" said Madame Edwige, in a tone of utter incredulity.

"Then I couldn't see anything but Janine, and, as I thought that she was calling me to account for her death, I drew my sword and charged the phantom."

"Good!"

"My épée broke."

"Go on," said the skeptical housekeeper.

"Then I found myself in darkness; then the darkness was succeeded by a new light, and I found myself in an unknown room whose walls represented my story and Janine's in flamboyant pictures."

"Very well," said Madame Edwige, with a mocking laugh.

"I saw Janine on her pyre."

"Naturally."

"And when the flames had enveloped her, she came down."

"Without being burned?" sniggered the housekeeper.

"She came to me, sat down at the foot of my bed..."

"So you were lying down?"

"Yes, and I can't explain how that came about."

"Go on, Monseigneur."

"Then Janine told me that she still loved me, and that if I wanted to love her, she would make me young again."

"A nice gift, Monseigneur!"

"And she would give me immortality."

"Damn!"

"You're mocking, but I'm telling the truth," said the Margrave, in a tone of profound conviction.

"And what means will she employ for that?" asked Madame Edwige.

"She's begun..."

"Oh, has she?"

"She went to fetch a ewer, and laid my arm bare."

"And then?"

"Then she pricked me with a golden pin and my blood flowed."

"Into the ewer?"

"Yes, of course—and I fainted."

"And then what?"

"I don't know what happened then."

"Well," Madame Edwige said, coldly, "I'll tell you."

"You?"

"Yes, me. You smoked opium yesterday evening, and everything you've recounted to me was a dream."

"Oh, really?"

"Ask the future Princess of Lansbourg-Nassau," added Madame Edwige.

As she spoke, the door opened again, and Fatma, even more beautiful than the day before, appeared on the threshold.

"Prince," she said, "What Madame Edwige says is the simple truth: you went to sleep on the divan where you were sitting with me. It was a treason of the hashish."

"And I didn't see Janine?"

"No," said the beautiful Turk, laughing, "since she's been dead for forty years and more. The dead only come back in our imagination."

"And did I also dream this?" exclaimed the Margrave.

He pulled his left arm out of the bed. His arm bore a small puncture-wound.

Fatma, however, continue smiling. "Look," she said. "there's the guilty party." And she took the Margrave's épée from beneath the bolster on the bed.

The Prince uttered a cry.

His épée, which he had broken against the wall after passing it through Janine's fluid body, was whole and quite intact.

He could not believe that a new épée had been substituted for the one that he claimed to have broken. It was definitely the one that he had always carried; he recognized the hilt enriched with precious stones and the blade, which had a few patches of rust.

"And I'll wager," said Madame Edwige, "that that prick isn't the only one."

With those words, she opened the Margrave's chemise, and showed him three more puncture-wounds spaced out on his breast.

"So I was dreaming!" he cried, crestfallen.

"Yes," replied Madame Edwige, "and I made the mistake of placing that épée under your bolster, as usual, which has played the role of Janine's golden pin, although I knew that hashish produces such hallucinations."

"It's enough to drive one mad!" murmured the Margrave, looking alternately at the terrible Madame Edwige and the beautiful Fatma, who had crossed the seas to offer him her hand.

XXXIX

For the Margrave, only one thing could confirm the reality of the night's events. That was the extreme weakness he felt—but he attributed that to the hashish.

Then again, Madame Edwige gave him a restorative beverage, and insisted that he get up and get dressed.

Madame Edwige was the only member of his household who had gone with him to Fatma's mysterious retreat, so the old man with the white beard and the little negroes who comprised the domestic staff of the beautiful Turk came to put themselves at his orders.

With their help, the Margrave became amorous of Fatma again, while sighing and telling himself that it was a pity that he had not really seen Janine, and that the promised immortality and youth had only been a dream...and, with their help, he got dressed.

First he was given a bath; he was washed with embalmed essences; his hair and beard were tinted, as usual; his stooped body was imprisoned in a corset; the wrinkles on his forehead disappeared beneath flesh-colored ointments; and finally, he was clad in a splendid ceremonial costume that had arrived by courtesy of Madame Edwige.

When he was thus transformed, the Prince saw Fatma and Madame Edwige reappear.

The beautiful Turk was dazzling with youth, and her rich Oriental costume, her heavy gold bracelets enriched with pearls and gems, the diamonds as large as pigeons' eggs that she wore on her ears, and the monstrous sapphire attached to the plume of her small blue velvet fez attested to her opulence and the treasures of which Madame Edwige had boasted.

"Well," she said to the Prince, "do you still want to marry me?"

"Can you doubt it?" he said, flexing a knee before her and kissing her hand.

"Do you love me?"

"With all my heart," he replied, ardently.

"And you won't mention Janine to me again?"

"Never."

"Well," said Fatma, "today is our wedding day and the priest who will consecrate our union is waiting in the mosque."

"What!" said the Margrave. "There's a mosque in Paris?"

"In this very house." And Fatma rang a bell.

Then the Margrave thought that the bizarre fevers of hashish were recommencing.

At the chime of the bell, the wall opened, separating in two, and the two pieces withdrew to the right and the left, like the scenery of a theater moving back into the wings when that modern enchanter, the technician, waves his magic wand—and the mosque appeared: a mosque in miniature.

The Margrave saw a kind of oval temple, with walls covered in arabesques and inscriptions taken from the Koran.

In the middle was a kind of supportive column covered in red cloth with gold fringes. On that column a book was open: the Koran. Beside it stood a tall old man with a long beard. That was the muezzin.

Take your shoes off," said Fatma, "for one must enter Allah's temple barefoot."

Two negroes took charge of removing the Margrave's boots while he reflected: *A Turkish marriage is not binding on a Christian. This beautiful girl is as naïve as it is possible to be. If I weary of her, I can repudiate hr like a chorus-girl.*

Then he offered her his hand gallantly and led her to the altar, barefoot.

The muezzin read them two or three pages from the Koran in Arabic, threw a linen veil over them, extended his hands, for toward the Orient and then toward the Occident, and made them a sign indicating that they could retire.

The Margrave was married, and the beautiful Fatma had become the Princess of Lansbourg-Nassau.

Then the walls closed again on one side, to open on the other.

While the mosque disappeared, another room appeared, and the sound of bizarre instruments was heard.

Fatma led her aged husband to a throne, where she sat down next to him, and immediately, a flood of almas and bayaderes came in, dancing. It was the ballet that follows an act in a drama.

Then the almas disappeared; there was a new change of scene, and the Margrave found himself in a voluptuous semi-obscurity.

Only one person was with him now: Madame Edwige.

"Is it really you?" the Margrave said to her.

"Yes, Monseigneur."

"I'm not dreaming?"

"You're wide awake."

"And I'm married?"

"Yes, Monseigneur."

"Where's my wife, then?"

"In the bridal chamber."

"Ah!"

"And she's waiting for you."

An amorous frisson passed through the old man's body.

"Come on," said Madame Edwige. "Lean on my arm; I'll take you."

They took two steps forward, but the Margrave suddenly uttered a cry and stopped.

"What's the matter?" said Madame Edwige.

"Janine!" stammered the Margrave, whose teeth were chattering—and he extended his hand toward the wall. The wall was resplendent with the light from the unknown source that the Margrave had seen the day before—and bathed in that light, Janine, pale and sad, was looking at him.

"There! There!" stammered the bewildered Margrave.

"I can't see anything," Madame Edwige replied. She tried to draw him away—but as the Margrave took a step forward, Janine took a step toward him.

He uttered another cry.

"Monseigneur," said Madame Edwige, "You're mad...I'm going to fetch the physician." And she went out, leaving the Margrave with his forehead bathed in cold sweat and his hair standing on end.

Then the phantom took another step.

"Fritz," said Janine's voice, "you can see that you're a blackguard, and that you don't love me..."

And certainly, she was so beautiful at that moment that the Margrave's terror gave way to admiration.

He fell to his knees, put his hands together and murmured: "Oh, forgive me, Janine...but I feel that my mind's wandering...all these people have convinced me that I was dreaming last night."

She smiled bitterly. "And it's for that reason," she said, "that you married the Turk?"

"Forgive me."

"Ingrate," she said. "When I had thought of rendering you young and immortal!"

"Janine! Janine!" babbled the distraught Margrave. "I love you!"

"I don't believe it," she replied.

And she made way for him, saying: "Go—your wife is waiting for you."

The Margrave remained on his knees. "I love you," he repeated. "I love no one but you."

XL

The Margrave remained on his knees.

Janine, silent and sad, looked at him.

"Forgive me," he repeated. "I love you."

"I don't believe you," she said, again.

"What do you want me to do to prove it?"

She seemed to reflect again. Then, suddenly, she said: "Get up and come with me."

The tremulous Margrave obeyed.

Then Janine took him by the hand and let him to the other side of the room. There she clapped her hand twice.

Immediately, a door opened and the two negroes the Margrave had seen on his arrival in the enchanted house appeared, each carrying a candlestick.

The raised curtain allowed him to see a corridor that seemed to follow a slope, and was vaulted like the subterranean passages of some feudal dungeon. At a sign from Janine the two negroes started walking, in order to light the way—and the immortal woman, still holding the Margrave by the hand, followed them.

"Where are you taking me?" asked the Margrave.

"Come on," she replied. "You'll see."

As they walked, distant memories arose in the troubled mind of the Prince of Lansbourg-Nassau.

"It seems to me," he stammered, finally, "that I've been this way before."

A muffled sound was audible in the distance, as if above their heads. "It's the Seine," he said.

Janine made no reply.

Finally, the negroes stopped. They were in front of a closed door.

Janine took a key from her belt and opened the door.

Then the Margrave exclaimed: "I recognize it now—this is the laboratory in which we worked together for such a long time."

"And where you betrayed me," replied the immortal woman.

The Margrave lowered his head.

They were, in fact, on the threshold of a bizarre room with no windows, and without any other apparent exit than the door that had just opened.

Crucibles, retorts and flasks of every size cluttered the room, a veritable laboratory of an alchemist in search of the philosopher's stone.

In one corner there was an immense iron chest, whose steel fittings, carved into diamond shapes, were sparkling in the light of the candles that the negroes were carrying.

"There," said Janine, "is the strong-box in which my riches were stored, and which you stole."

"I repent," said the Margrave, humbly.

Janine took a second key from her belt and opened the chest, having turned they key in the inverse direction several times.

When the chest was open, the Margrave saw that it was empty.

"Fritz," said Janine, then, "you robbed me; you must return what you stole."

The Margrave shivered, and the sordid voice of avarice rose up in his vile soul.

"But," he stammered, "If you're going to marry me…what's the point?"

"No," said Janine. "I can render you young, I can make you immortal, like me, but that is on the condition that you prove to me by means of a sacrifice the love that you claim to have for me."

"Alas," said the Margrave, "I've dissipated the gold that I took."

"You're mistaken—or, rather, you're trying in vain to deceive me. You're a miser, Fritz, and far from being poor, like your father, you've doubled the fortune of which theft was the primary source. You've bought back your vast estates, your châteaux, your principality. You're the richest lord in Germany. You need to return all that to me, Fritz."

"But I can only return it by marrying you," said the Margrave.

"No, you're mistaken, Fritz. "For one thing, you can't marry me. I'm immortal, and those who are above death are above human laws."

"But I love you!" the Margrave repeated.

"Then give back what you took from me."

"But how?"

"Listen," said Janine, then. "You're old, broken, almost infirm, and you only came to Paris, wanting to get married, in order to have an heir to whom you could leave your vast wealth and treasures. Isn't that so?"

"Yes," said the Margrave.

"Well," Janine went on, "suppose that I give you back your youth, that instead of being seventy, you're no more than twenty-five."

"Well?" said the Margrave.

"And that you leave Paris and return to your principality."

The Margrave did not know yet where she was heading, and he looked at her with a curiosity full of suspicion.

"And then?" he said.

"The most intimate of your servants will fail to recognize you. 'I'm your master, the Prince of Lansbourg-Nassau,' you'll say. Everyone will reply: 'You're an impostor!'"

"Oh!" said the Margrave, alarmed.

"The best thing that can happen then," Janine continued, "is that you'll simply be expelled from your estates—unless you're locked up as a madman. But as it will also be the case that the old Margrave can't be found, you might well be accused of being his murderer. You might be hanged in your fine city of Lansbourg, by virtue of laws that you have promulgated yourself."

A frisson ran through the Margrave's body.

"Now, listen to me again," Janine went on. "Suppose that you're in Paris, in your house in the Rue Saint-Honoré."

"Good!"

"The rumor spreads that you're very ill; then, it's said that you're dead. Your servants, your vassals and your subjects don mourning-dress, waiting for the opening of your testament designating your successor. In the meantime, I return your youth and beauty; I make you immortal—and you present yourself one day as your own heir."

"That would be possible!" exclaimed the Margrave.

"Yes, if you do as I say."

"Speak, then," said the Margrave.

Janine led him to the table that was cluttered with flasks and retorts. On one of its corners there was a sheet of parchment, wax and a seal, which the stupefied Margrave recognized as his own.

"Sit down there, pick up that quill," Janine continued, "and wrote to my dictation. You're going to make your will."

"In favor of whom?" the Margrave asked.

"In favor of yourself," she replied. "Except that you'll have to change your name, and I've found you a new identity."

As she spoke, Janine took a portfolio from her bosom, which she opened, and from which a few pieces of paper escaped, which fell on to the table.

XLI

"What's all this?" asked the Margrave.

"The papers that establish who you are."

"But where did they come from?"

"I'll tell you. As I was coming back to Paris, proud of my new discovery, nursing the hope that you might still love me and that I might be able to render you the youth and beauty that once turned my head and were nearly so deadly for me, when I was only a few leagues from the great city, my carriage stopped at an inn situated on the edge of the road that passes through the heart of the Forest of Sénart.

"Travelers who stop there are rare. That evening, there was only one petty gentleman from the provinces, who was coming to Paris to seek his fortune. He was twenty years old; he was a handsome lad; and his dark eyes fixed themselves on me with a sudden enthusiasm. At his age, love comes quickly. He solicited the favor of supping at my table. Before the meal was over he was at my feet, telling me that he loved me.

"I was insensible; I could only think about you. The next day, however, I allowed him to go with me. That evening, we entered Paris, and we came straight here—which means that no one has seen him."

"Ah!" said the Margrave."

"The poor fellow hasn't left this house, which will become his tomb."

"What! He's dead?"

"Yes. He ran himself through with his épée in a fit of amorous despair, and left for his unique heritage these papers, which are, firstly, his birth certificate, as authentic as a document can be; secondly, a letter of recommendation from the governor of his province to the captain of His Majesty's guards—for his only ambition was to enter the Red House; and finally, a letter from his sister, who is married to a poor gentleman of his region."

"And he's dead?" said the Margrave.

"Yes."

"Has his death been certified, then?"

"No. I had him thrown into the Seine by night. In consequence, on the day when, having become young, you present yourself to the captain of the guards, you'll obtain the musketeer's cape of which the poor boy dreamed without any difficulty."

A disdainful smile came to the Margrave's lips.

"The following day," Janine went on, "the testament of the late Margrave Prince of Lansbourg-Nassau will be opened, and, becoming your own heir, to will renounce being a musketeer in order to go take possession of your principality."

"That's all very well," said the Margrave, looking at Janine with a clear and investigative gaze, "but..."

"But what?"

"How do I know you're not deceiving me?"

The immortal woman laughed disdainfully.

"Oh, you don't trust me!" she said. "Well, go away, then—be old and worn-out, and die."

"Janine..."

"Oh, blackguard," she went on, "Triple traitor, you want me to return your youth, and give you immortality in order to sell me once again to judges who will put me on the pyre again. Get out! Get out!"

The anger shining in her gaze burned the Margrave.

Then a new fear took hold of him, and he threw himself to his knees again. "Mercy!" he said.

"No—get out!" she said. She had made a sign to the two negro boys, who stepped backwards as if to light the way for the Margrave and take him back the way he had come—but the Margrave did not move.

The man, who was only old in body, whose mind had retained all its penetrating activity and his soul all of its infernal inspiration, had reasoned as follows: *Janine is as young and beautiful as she was forty years ago; why should she not really be immortal? And if she promises me youth, it's because she still loves me, and I'm therefore risking nothing by robbing myself—for if I don't become young; if I continue to live, bowed down and worn out, I won't owe anything to this imaginary heir.*

And the Margrave believed, once again, that he had deceived Janine, his calculations resting on the basis that it really was the witch burned forty years before with whom he was dealing.

Then he was able to feign the most violent despair. He rediscovered the most passionate tones of youth; he spoke of love like an adolescent, and, precipitating himself toward the table, wrote breathlessly, without even raising his head, the singular testament that the immortal woman demanded of him, signed it, and added his seal.

Janine, leaning over his shoulder, had read as he wrote, and a smile of satisfaction spread over her lips. When he handed her the testament he took it, slipped it into her bosom, and said: "Well, now I believe you, Fritz, and I'll continue the treatment that will render you young and make you immortal."

He had one last surge of suspicion, however.

"Truly?" he said.

"Follow me—let's go back to the room we were in a little while ago."

They left the laboratory, which Janine locked carefully, and set out.

In the middle of the corridor that they had followed before, however, the Margrave suddenly came to a halt.

"What's wrong?" said Janine.

"It seemed to me that I heard a sound."

"It's that of the river, which is flowing overhead."

"No, it's not that..."

"What did you hear, then?" She was smiling mysteriously.

"Some kind of howling."

"Oh," said Janine, "that's my prisoner."

"What prisoner?" The Margrave trembled at the word.

"I have a prisoner in chains," said Janine. "He's an acquaintance of yours."

"What?"

"His name is the Marquis de la Roche-Maubert."

"But I saw him a fortnight ago!" exclaimed the Margrave.

"I don't say otherwise."

"How did he become your prisoner."

"He wanted to meddle in my affairs."

"Ah!"

"Would you like to see him?" Janine asked. "It will only take five minutes."

"Indeed," said the Margrave.

Then Janine took a key from the bunch she had at her belt and made a sign to the two negroes. They stopped at a door set in a recess, which the Margrave had not noticed on the way.

XLII

Janine opened the door.

"A fine lock!" murmured the Margrave, who was able to hear metal grating as the little key moved and enormous bolts moving in their slots.

Janine made no reply.

When the door was open the Margrave saw a staircase plunging downwards, spiraling like the shell of a snail. How deep did it go, beginning from the already-incalculable depth at which Janine and the Margrave were standing? There was no way to be sure—but the moans, plaints and occasional howls of the prisoner, while arriving more distinctly in the Margrave's ears, still seemed to him to be coming from the depths of Hell.

Janine made another sign to the two negroes.

One placed his foot on the first step and began to descend solely. Then Janine, still holding the Margrave by the hand, went down after him. Finally, the second negro boy, holding his candle above their heads, brought up the rear.

As they went down, the prisoner's howls and imprecations became more violent and more clearly articulated.

"But after all," the Margrave said to Janine. "Explain..."

"How the Marquis comes to be in my power?"

"Yes—for I saw him a fortnight ago."

"I know that."

"Ah! Really?"

"Now that you've given me proof of love," Janine went on, "I don't want to return to the past—but I ought to tell you that the Marquis, then aged twenty, was your accomplice when you sent me to the pyre."

"He was the one who denounced you, treacherously."

"Yes, but you drove him to it."

The Margrave did not reply.

"Two days before my death," Janine continued, "for, so far as he and you were concerned, I was about to die, I no longer loved you; I detested you, and I loved the Marquis.

When I went up on to the pyre, my heart underwent a change. I saw you both I the crowd, and I resumed loving you with all the wild frenzy of which I am now giving you striking proof, and I swore to punish the Marquis."

Janine smiled sadly, and in a melancholy voice she went on: "Then again, forty years have passed, and I haven't taken my vengeance; I'm a loving woman, not a hateful one. I loved you, and on the day when I was on the track of the discovery that would return your youth and make you immortal, I no longer more than one goal, one thought and one ardent desire: to reconquer you entirely, my adored Fritz."

The doddering old man with the sparse hair and vanished teeth, was so conceited that he did not blink at Janine's ardent words.

The immortal woman continued: "But the Marquis got it into his head to find me, to see me again—he believed in my immortality. He made a great deal of noise, and almost compromised my plans concerning you—so I set a trap for him, and he fell into it."

The howling was continuing.

Soon, the Margrave, who was still going down, was able to hear these words, clearly articulated: "Janine, I will cause you to perish by the executioner's ax, and when your head is detached from your body, we'll see whether you really are immortal!"

"Here we are," said Janine to the Margrave.

The latter then perceived an enormous grille, which closed a kind of cell hollowed out in the stairwell—which continued to descend into the earth.

The two black boys placed themselves in front of the grille, projecting into the singular prison the light of their two candles. The Margrave saw the Marquis, half-dressed, his hair unkempt, his shirt torn, pale and haggard, grinding his teeth and clinging to the bars of his cage with his clenched fists.

"Ah, there you are, Janine!" he cried, waving his fist at her. "I loved you once, but I hate you now, and I'll see that you die by the executioner's hand."

Janine shrugged her shoulders imperceptibly and drew aside to let the prisoner see the Margrave.

That sight led to a redoubling of rage, and he shook his fist at his rival.

"Marquis," Janine said to him, "the hour of your liberation is approaching."

He cackled furiously. "If you free me, hell-witch," he said, "you'll hasten your punishment."

"I'm going to make the Margrave, my beloved Fritz, young again," she continued. "Then we'll marry and leave France. From then on, Marquis, I'll brave your anger, and you'll obtain your release—for which I'll furnish the instrument right away."

So saying, she took a small file from her bosom and threw it through the bars to him. "Assuming that you make use of it night and day," she told him, "it will take you two weeks to break these bars, and in a fortnight, we'll be far away from France."

The exasperation of the Marquis increased instead of easing.

"Even if you go to the ends of the earth," he cried, "I'll catch up with you!"

"Let me tell you one last thing, Marquis," Janine said. "When your bars are broken, go down this staircase. It ends at another corridor that rises up again to the level of the Seine. You're a good swimmer, as you've proved."

And she turned her back on him.

"Come, my beloved," she said to the margrave. "Now I shall work to render you young again."

Ten minutes later, the Margrave was lying on the bed where Janine had already taken several pints of blood from him. One of the negro boys held the silver ewer; the other illuminated the bizarre scene.

Janine had not yet pricked the vein from which the blood would flow, however.

A suspicion dawned in the Margrave's mind as she approached the golden pin to his bare arm.

"Stop!" he exclaimed.

XLIII

The suspicion that had just traversed the Margrave's mind was this: *Janine has imprisoned the Marquis de la Roche-Maubert; she's avenging herself on him. Who can tell whether she might not avenge herself on me too?*

"Well?" said the immortal woman, leaving the golden pin suspended above he arm.

"You're not deceiving me, are you?" said the Margrave.

"Deceiving you? Why?"

"If my blood flows out to the last drop, you'll let me die!"

Janine shrugged her shoulders.—but instead of protesting, she was content to go to the fireplace, beside which hung a bell-cord, which she pulled.

"What are you doing?" asked the astonished Margrave.

Janine did not reply. After a few seconds, however, the door opened and someone came in, the sight of whom the Margrave was far from expecting. That person was Madame Edwige.

The terrible housekeeper was like the point of connection between real life and the fantastic existence that the Margrave had been leading for twenty-four hours.

Madame Edwige smiled.

"Madame," Janine said to her, coldly, "I can't keep the promise that I made to you/ Poor Fritz is mad. You alone know how much I loved him—you who have written to me every day to tell me what he was doing."

"That's true," said Madame Edwige.

"What!" stammered the Margrave. "You knew?"

"I know everything," said Madame Edwige, fixing the Margrave with her dominating stare, "and I went to a great deal of trouble to get you here."

"Well, take him away," said Janine. "He's unworthy of my love."

"Janine!" cried the Margrave, confused. "Forgive me, once more. Here...let my blood flow...I trust you..." And he held out his arm.

But Janine had replaced the golden pin in her hair.

"No," she said. "not now."

"Why?"

"I told you that if you didn't love me, I would be powerless to return your youth."

"But I do love you!"

"I'd like to forgive you again," she said, "but on condition that you submit to a final proof."

"Speak."

This time, Janine made a sign to Madame Edwige.

The housekeeper went to fetch a silver goblet and a bottle that were on a dresser.

"Your nerves are agitated," said Janine, "and you need to calm down. Drink that."

Madame Edwige had poured a part of the contents of the bottle into the goblet and she presented it to the Margrave.

The latter, who had become as docile as a child, took the goblet and emptied it in one draught.

The effect was rapid, almost lightning-fast. The Margrave uttered a cry, started on the bed, and fell back again. His eyes had closed abruptly and a paralysis took possession of his entire body.

Then Madame Edwige looked at Janine. "He's dead," she said.

"No," Janine replied, "but all his senses are paralyzed with the exception of one."

"Which?"

"Hearing."

"He can hear what we're saying?"

"Yes, and his punishment is about to begin."

And Janine, who had suddenly struck the solemn attitude of a judge delivering sentence, looked at the man, who had the appearance of a corpse, and said: "Fritz, Margrave Prince of Lansbourg-Nassau, I am not Janine the witch, Janine the woman who made gold. She died on the pyre you set for her—but Janine, in dying, bequeathed her vengeance to her heir; that was my mother, and God, who punishes murderers and traitors, has permitted me to bear a resemblance to her that would be your doom."

The Margrave did not budge; his eyes did not open, but a few muscles in his face twitched. That was the only visible trace of the terrible and profound emotion he was experiencing at that moment, for Janine had told the truth; although his entire body was plunged into a profound lethargy, his hearing remained unimpaired.

Janine went on: "Fritz, Margrave Prince of Lansbourg-Nassau, your last hour is near, and I have condemned you to death, but your death will be slow; your blood will drain away drop by drop, and you will be able to hear the doors of eternity opening for you.

"Every night I shall take a few pints of your blood, until your veins are empty and your infamous heart has ceased beating.

"Listen again, Margrave Prince: just now, insensate man, you made a testament and indicated your heir. That heir is alive and I love him. Here—if you cannot see, at least you can hear the sound of my kisses on his cheek."

And Janine rang for a second time.

Then a man came in. It was the Chevalier d'Esparron.

The Chevalier undoubtedly knew nothing about what had just happened, for he looked at Janine in astonishment.

"Margrave Prince of Lansbourg-Nassau, I salute you," she said. And as he took a step backwards, she extracted from her bosom the testament bearing the Margrave's arms.

"Here," she said. "The wretch has done well; he had restored to us the treasures stolen from my aunt, and named you his heir." And Janine explained to the Chevalier d'Esparron by what graceful trickery she had led the Margrave to release his wealth.

"He's not dead, though?" asked the Chevalier.

"He'll live for another five days."

The Chevalier frowned. "That's four days too many," he said.

"Why?" asked Janine, astonished.

"Because our enemies are on our track," said the Chevalier.

"Yes, but the Regent will protect us," Janine replied.

And she pricked the Margrave's arm with her pin, and a jet of blood fell into the ewer that the negro boy was still holding.

PART TWO

I

Let us return now to our friend President Boisfleury, who was going to so much trouble and doing so much harm for the sake of the most striking triumph of justice, of which he believed that he was the purest representative on earth.

President Boisfleury had done a great deal of harm in a matter of days.

We know how the Regent and Cardinal Dubois had received him—but such a welcome could not deter the indefatigable magistrate.

All his life, President Boisfleury had sought the guilty, and it was not at the end of his career that he was going to set aside his principles by seeing no one around him but innocents.

Send away from the Regent's study, he had gone to see the Duchesse du Maine.

The Grand Mistress of the Ordre de la Mouche à Miel had said to him: "The Regent is a wretch who protects good-for-nothings, murderers and thieves—but he's omnipotent. As you can see, I'm exiled to my estate in Sceaux and can't be of any assistance to you."

From the Duchesse, the President had gone to the Duc de Bourbon, and then Madame de Prie, his mistress. They had had all given him the same reply.

The obstacles, however, instead of deterring the dogged President, excited him.

Anyone else would have renounced finding the Marquis de la Roche-Maubert and getting mixed up in the Margrave's affairs, but the President exclaimed: "Even if I have to be a police agent myself, I shall go on to the end.

The Gascon Castirac had run away, but the President did not give up on finding him. Besides which, he had learned that a captain of the guard had arrived to arrest the Gascon five minutes after the latter's departure. People were, therefore, afraid of Castirac!

If I can get my hands on him again, Boisfleury said to himself, *he'll be the best trump card in my hand*. And far from renouncing the task he had set himself, the President had summoned the police agent Porion.

Porion, who was later to play an important role, under the name of Père Cannelle,[24] in the arrest of the regicide Damiens, was not only a clever man but am ambitious one. He wanted to be the Lieutenant of Police—him, a man of no account!—and was only waiting for an opportunity to bring himself to the attention of the people who held the reins of power. Had the Lieutenant of Police perceived his ambitious ideas? It seems probable, because he had no longer been employed for some time.

Policemen in those days did not have fixed salaries, but were paid according to the importance of each case.

So, Boisfleury sent for Porion. He did not mention the Regent to him, but told him that the Lieutenant of Police had refused to involve himself in the affair. Porion saw it as an excellent opportunity, not only to distinguish himself, but to mount an open rebellion against his chief, assuring himself of the support of Parlement.

Three days after setting out on campaign, he came back to see Boisfleury one morning.

"Monseigneur," he said. "I hold all of the threads of a vast intrigue."

"Ah!" said Boisfleury. "Let's see!"

---

[24] Père Cannelle is a character in Ponson's novel *L'Auberge de la Rue des Enfants Rouges* (1876), which, like *La Femme immortelle*, opens with tales of vampirism. I hope to translate it within the next two years.

This was taking place in the chamber of criminal instructions; the President had put on his red robe and given orders to his usher not to let anyone in.

"Monseigneur," Porion went on, "the Margrave and the Marquis de la Roche-Maubert are in love with the same woman."

"Ah!"

"I don't believe that the Marquis is dead, but I don't yet have positive evidence as to his fate. As or the Margrave, he left his house yesterday evening."

"Where did he go?"

"To the river-bank near the Pont du Change, by carriage."

"And then?"

"There he got into a boat with his housekeeper. The boat went upstream. My agents followed it along the banks, and saw it disappear at the level of a house in the Rue de l'Hirondelle, downstream of the Pont Saint-Michel."

"Did it capsize?"

"No, it was engulfed in a subterranean channel. In the meantime, I was having the Rue de l'Hirondelle watched. My agents had gone into the house I had pointed out to them and searched it from top to bottom, after having bound and gagged the bourgeois gentleman."

"And they found the subterranean issue indicated by the Gascon?" said he President, his eyes gleaming.

"No."

"What!"

"The slab in the fireplace covered a solid wall. Then, having found nothing, they set up a kind of mouse-trap in the street. A gentleman went past and they wanted to arrest him, but he showed them one of the famous keys that Monseigneur le Régent gives to his favorites. They pretended to leave but saw the gentleman go into the suspect house."

"Very good."

"And we know his name."

"Ah!"

"He's the Chevalier d'Esparron, and I assume that he's the witch's lover."

While Porion was speaking, Boisfleury took notes.

Porion continued: "The house is being watched from the street. Two of my men, hidden in a laundrywoman's boat, are standing sentinel on the river."

"Excellent!" said the President.

"Finally, yesterday evening I had the husband of the Margrave's housekeeper arrested. He's a German named Conrad. The man claims that he doesn't know anything, but if Your Lordship orders that he be put to the question, he might tell us a great deal."

"Nothing easier," said President Boisfleury, coldly. And he wrote down the following:

The Chambre Criminelle des Mises orders that Sieur Conrad be put to torture.

And he signed it.

Porion took the order and said: "Now, Monseigneur, everything will go smoothly."

II

While President Boisfleury was making every effort to find the Marquis de la Roche-Maubert, the latter strongly resembled those wild animals that circle their cages relentlessly, always hoping to find an exit.

In fact, as we have seen, the Marquis was indeed in a cage.

But how had he got there?

In a very simple fashion, if we go back to the moment when the Marquis was pursuing Janine through a narrow corridor and, drunk with love and fury, trying to catch up with her. You will recall that the ground had suddenly disappeared beneath his feet. Then he had uttered a terrible cry, and the Chevalier d'Esparron and Janine had heard nothing more.

This is what had happened.

At a certain point in the corridor the floor gave way to a rotating slab like those which cover oubliettes. The slab had given way beneath the Marquis' feet, and the Marquis had felt himself falling into an unknown abyss. That had only lasted for a quarter of a second, during which the Marquis, falling into darkness, had thought that he was doomed.

Instead of falling on to sharp rocks, pikes or sword-blades, however—the usual furniture of oubliettes—and instead of encountering hard ground on which he might break like glass, the Marquis had fallen into water.

The sensation of cold succeeding that terrible anguish had been welcomed by him as an inexpressible beneficence. Not only had he not been killed, but the freshness of the water calmed his excitement.

He started to swim.

The most profound darkness enveloped him, and he thought that he had fallen into a cistern or a well. In fact, having tried to go straight ahead, he had bumped into a wall; then, going backwards, he had encountered another; finally, he had rapidly acquired the conviction that he really was in a cistern.

But how could he get out of it?

For about an hour, he sustained himself in the water, sometimes swimming vigorously, feeling the walls and searching for a door, sometimes floating on his back, trusting to luck for his salvation.

Suddenly, something strange happened.

The Marquis thought he could feel the water disappearing beneath him, and that its level was dropping. The cistern slowly emptied through some suddenly-opened outlet.

It emptied slowly, to be sure, and that might have lasted long enough for the exhausted Marquis to have drowned, but the instinct of self-preservation and perhaps the thirst for vengeance gave him new vigor. He kept on swimming, for a long time, until, exhausted, he closed his eyes and lost consciousness—but his feet had finally touched the bottom of the cistern, and he only remained under water for three minutes, for the water ran out, to the last drop, leaving him inanimate but alive.

And when Monsieur de la Roche-Maubert came round, he was in the cell looking out on a subterranean staircase, from which he was separated by a trellis of iron bars as thick as a man's arm, interleaved with one another.

He had been put in different clothes and was not wet, to the extent that he might have been able to believe that he had had a bad dream.

On the other side of the cage, a man was sitting on the steps of the staircase, with a candle-tray beside him. Monsieur de la Roche-Maubert had looked at him fearfully. Then he had recognized him—and, gripped by a sudden furry, had rushed at the bars of his prison.

But the Chevalier had started laughing, and had said: "Monsieur le Marquis, do me the justice of granting that I have put up all sorts of resistance to your reckless projects, and that if you have almost drowned, it's your fault—absolutely your own—and not mine."

"Ah" Wretch!" the Marquis howled.

The Chevalier shrugged his shoulders. "Instead of insulting me," he said, "listen to me."

Either the Marquis' rage was exhausted, or the curiosity to know what would be done with him was sufficiently powerful to calm him down momentarily. Either way, he shut up.

"Marquis," said the Chevalier, then, "you've disobeyed the Regent, you've disdained the advice of the Abbé Dubois, your relative, and everything that has befallen you is your own doing. The immortal woman does not love you; she will never love you, for two reasons: the first is that you've long passed the age of amours; the second is that Janine loves me, and her heart isn't vast enough to lodge us both."

The Marquis clenched his fists, but he did not breathe a word and continued to look at the Chevalier. The latter continued:

"In addition, Janine and I have important work to do, in the accomplishment of which we didn't want to be disturbed, and as, if we set you free, you'd make a great deal of fuss and noise again, allow us to keep you until we have nothing more to fear. Reassure yourself, however—it's a matter of a few days."

And the Chevalier had gone away, taking the candle.

The Monsieur de la Roche-Maubert, the intractable old man had fallen prey to a further fit of fury. He had banged his head against the walls of his prison, bruised his fingers on the iron bars, shouted and howled unrelentingly for several hours.

Finally, exhausted, foaming at the mouth, he had fallen on the ground and had not given voice to anything else but words devoid of meaning and inarticulate sounds.

Then a light had reappeared on the stairway.

The Chevalier had come back carrying a basket of provisions. Stopping in front of the bars, he had said: "Marquis, I don't want you to die of hunger!"

III

Nearly a week had gone by.

Captivity had changed into ferocious hatred all the other sentiments that had once divided the prisoner's heart and soul.

The Marquis de la Roche-Maubert no longer loved Janine. The Marquis had conceived a savage and mortal hatred for her.

Instead of abating, his fury had been overexcited by that isolation.

For a week, the Marquis had howled and blasphemed unrelentingly, swearing at the Chevalier d'Esparron, who visited him every evening and passed provisions through the bars of his cage.

Then, one night, he had seen two other visions, as you will recall: Janine and the Margrave. And Janine had said to him in a mocking voice: "The hour of your liberation is approaching, Marquis, and I want you to do the work yourself."

And with those words, you will recall, she had thrown him a small file, saying: "That's for your bars; but, even by working relentlessly, you won't secure your freedom for a fortnight."

After Janine disappeared, about three hours had gone by. The Marquis had not even picked up the file, and had continued to vociferate. At the end of that time the light had reappeared on the stairway. It was the Chevalier d'Esparron again.

The Chevalier was carrying an enormous basket this time, which had to contain provisions for several days.

"Marquis," he said, "I shall be very busy from now on, and I don't know whether I'll have time to visit you regularly, so I've brought you enough food for a week. She has told me that she has given you a file, of which you can make good use."

With these words, the Chevalier passed bread cut into small pieces and cold meat through the bars, then threw a packet of candles inside the cage and left one lit next to the bars, saying: "Since you're going to work, it's as well that you can see!"

And the Chevalier left.

The Marquis had not even picked up the file. The tool was so small and the bars of the cage so stout that his first thought had been that Janine and the Chevalier d'Esparron were mocking him.

However, the light succeeding the darkness that had enveloped him since his captivity returned a little clam to his mind. He stopped howling and blaspheming. Then he picked up the files and set about examining it.

It was small, but made of well-tempered steel, and when he tried it on the bars he felt its teeth biting well.

Then he remembered a host of stories of prisoners who had pierced bars with a nail and sawed through their chains with a watch-spring—and the hope of liberation rose in his brain like an intoxication, and he set to work.

For about half a day the Marquis filed and filed, relentlessly, only stopping to replace a burned-out candle by another, and even forgetting to eat.

After several hours, the Marquis, breathless, his brown bathed in sweat, recognized the truth of what Janine had said. Working unceasingly, it would take him a fortnight. The file bit, but how thick the bars were! Then again, the bars were so close to one another that it would be necessary to saw through at least four vertically and as many horizontally to contrive an opening large enough for him to be able to get through.

He had a fit of discouragement and, abandoning his work momentarily, went to sit on the camp-bed at the back of the cage on which he slept. The candle, set on the ground, illuminated the cell from bottom to top.

The Marquis' distracted eyes went from the grille to the ceiling, formed by enormous joists. As the ceiling was quite low, when he stood upright, his head was almost touching it.

Suddenly, it was as if the Marquis' gaze was riveted on two of the beams. He had spotted a leak—and that leak told him that there was a gap. He got up, picked up the candle and lifted it up to the ceiling.

The beams had been daubed with a coating, but the damp had gradually caused the rough-casting—to make use of a mason's expression—to crumble. The Marquis recognized in two of the beams the existence of a covered trap-door.

How had it once been opened?

The Marquis did not know, and the people previously locked in the cage had probably never suspected its existence, for it would have been masked by the plaster.

Then, with the point of his file, Monsieur de la Roche-Maubert set about gradually pulling away the plaster-and in less than half an hour, he had freed the grooves and uncovered two hinges, on which it must once have turned.

The hinges were iron, but of an ordinary thickness.

Monsieur de la Roche-Maubert dragged his camp-bed directly underneath it, stood on it, and, abandoning the bars of the cage, set about attacking one of the hinges with the file.

The iron was rusted, and the file bit easily.

It only took an hour for the Marquis to break the first hinge.

Then he started on the second, and, less than an hour later, the trapdoor was only held to the ceiling by an invisible bolt that must open it from above.

Just as it is easy to force a way through a door once the hinges have been broken, however, by introducing an implement into the groove that had supported the hinges, it would be easy to force the trap-door.

Unfortunately, the file was too small, and the implement the Marquis needed he did not have to hand. He looked around, made a tour of his cell, searching but not finding anything.

Suddenly, his eyes fell upon a large stone in one corner, which sometimes served him as a seat. The stone was heavy, weighing more than forty pounds—but the Marquis, in spite of his sixty-six years, was robust.

He took the stone in both hands, raised it above his head, and then, using it like a battering-ram, began hammering the trap-door violently.

IV

At first, the trap-door resisted. Then it oscillated slightly. Then a further, more vigorous attack lifted it up about three inches, and it fell back.

Then Monsieur de la Roche-Maubert was afraid of his success.

Who could tell whether all that racket might not have been overheard, and whether, just as he believed that he had found a means of escape, the Chevalier d'Esparron would appear, followed by two or three lackeys, who would throw themselves on him, tie him up and put him in another cell?

Love of liberty gives a man the instinct and cunning of certain wild beasts caught in traps.

The Marquis now knew one thing, which was that the trap-door would lift entirely when he made one more great and supreme effort.

He put the stone back in the place from which he had taken it, went to lie down on his bed, and waited. There were two possibilities. Either the blows struck on the trap-door had been heard, or they had not reached his jailers; in the former case, they would not take long to come down; in the latter, the Marquis would still have time to recommence his escape attempt. He waited, therefore—and although his heart was beating violently, he spent nearly two hours lying on his bed, listening for the slightest sound.

A deathly silence reigned in the cage and on the stairway.

The Marquis thought that Janine and the Chevalier might perhaps have left the house. That seemed probable, given that they had brought him provisions for several days and a file that would eventually serve to set him free.

Having made these reflections, Monsieur de la Roche-Maubert did not hesitate any longer.

As we have said, the ceiling of the cell was so low that the Marquis could almost touch it with his head when he stood up. Then he had another idea. Instead of picking up the stone with both hands and making use of it to batter a breach in the trap-door, he dragged it directly underneath. Then, making used of it as a footstep and bending over, he braced his shoulders against the trap-door.

The Marquis was, as we know, robust. He was one of those tall, broad-shouldered Normans with muscular arms, descended from the companions of William the Conqueror, who seem to be born for the eternal battle. The Marquis also had a thirst for liberty and vengeance, and hated Janine all the more because she loved the young and brave Chevalier d'Esparron.

Like Samson, who, feeling his hair grow back, used a thrust of his shoulders to topple the pillars of the hall filled with Philistines, the Marquis made a gigantic effort—and the trap-door did not fall back, remaining open.

The Marquis bent down and picked up the candle that he had left on the ground. Then he raised it above his head, in order to explore the cavity that he had just exposed.

He recognized a kind of corridor, whose extremity was lost in darkness.

The Marquis could no longer hesitate. He left the candle on the edge of the trap-door, put the file in his pocket, suspended himself with his hands like a gymnast from his bar, and hoisted himself up on to the upper floor.

He now found himself in the corridor whose extremity the candle was impotent to illuminate—but once he was standing in the corridor, the Marquis enjoyed a relative freedom.

Where was he? It hardly mattered. He was no longer in the cage where he had spent long hours of rage and despair—that was the essential thing.

As one can imagine, he no longer had his sword or pistols, and his only weapon was the little file that Janine had thrown to him through the bars—but he had enormous fists at the ends of his robust arms, and he counted on making use of them to knock down any one who barred his way.

He therefore picked up the candle and started walking straight ahead.

The corridor followed a slope, and was also slightly curved. As it had a certain sonority, the Marquis walked on tiptoe.

Suddenly, there was an abrupt bend in the corridor, and the Marquis fund himself at the entrance to a staircase. The staircase went downwards. The Marquis took it, and, having reached the bottom step, realized that it connected with another—doubtless the one that went past the cage.

Now, Janine had said to him: "When you've sawn through your bars and are on the stairway, go down. It ends at the Seine, and as you're a good swimmer, you'll get out of trouble easily.

Monsieur de la Roche-Maubert thought it necessary, therefore, to make sure that it really was the staircase that went past the cage, and instead of going downwards he started to climb. On the thirtieth step he found a landing, and on that landing was the grille with the enormous bars forming the prison in which he had been abandoned.

From then on, he knew his way—and yet he was tempted to carry on going upwards, in order to reach the place where Janine and the Chevalier d'Esparron might be. He had no weapon, though, and prudence was speaking more loudly, for the moment, than the violent hatred in his heart.

He went back down the steps.

He went down for a long time; the steps went on and on, and it seemed that the stairway was Jacob's ladder.

Finally, a muffled sound reached his ears. The Marquis listened, and soon recognized the splash of water.

Janine had told the truth.

The Marquis continued going down

Suddenly, a gust of moist air blew out the candle. That accident did not stop the Marquis in his tracks, however, and a few minutes later, his feet dipped into the water. He was at the level of the Seine.[25]

---

[25] The author appears to have forgotten that the corridors and rooms in which much of the recent action took place were

The Marquis went down another two steps and found himself waist-deep in water. At the same time, his foot trod on muddy ground and, raising his arms, he realized that he was in a kind of subterranean tunnel invaded by water.

He walked straight ahead, and soon lost his footing—but he was a good swimmer, as we know, and he began to cleave through the water in the darkness.

Sometimes, his head bumped into the stones of the vault.

The Marquis kept swimming...and suddenly, a pale ray of light struck his gaze.

---

below the level of the Seine's bed, and that Janine had told the Marquis that the descending staircase led to an ascending passage that would take him back up to the river. The topography of the house has never made much sense, though.

V

The light that had had just struck the Marquis in the face was a moonbeam.

He swam for a few seconds more, and suddenly found himself outside the subterranean channel and in the Seine. Then he started taking deep breaths. He was free.

It was night; the moon was shining on the houses of Old Paris, and the two banks of the river were deserted.

The Marquis tried momentarily to get his bearings.

Should he cross the river, or should he try to cling on to one of the boats moored on the left bank?

As he was deliberating over which way to go, however, a boat left the shore and came straight toward him. It contained three men.

The Marquis heard one of them say: "Finally, we've got one!"

Two of the three men were plying the oars and rowing vigorously; the third was standing at the rear.

Meanwhile, the Marquis, thinking that he was dealing with Janine's people, or the Chevalier d'Esparron's, tried to escape the pursuit.

Good swimmer as he was however, he could not stay ahead of his pursuers for long. The boat gained speed, and he soon heard a dry click that dominated the sound of the oars dipping into the water. It was the sound of a pistol being cocked.

At the same time, the man standing in the boat shouted: "If you don't stop, you're dead!"

The Marquis took no notice of the injunction, and continued swimming.

There was a flash of light and a detonation, and the whistle of a bullet.

The Marquis suddenly disappeared under the water—but only to reappear a few meters further on. He had dived deliberately, and the bullet had passed over his head without hitting him.

"Stop! Stop!" cried the irritated voice.

Then the Marquis half-turned and replied: "By God! As true as my name's the Marquis de la Roche-Maubert, you won't take me alive!"

A triple exclamation replied to him: an exclamation of astonishment, and almost of joy. And the voice that had been angry a moment ago suddenly softened, and said: "But Monsieur le Marquis, we're your friends, and we've been searching for you for a fortnight."

There was such a tone of sincerity in those words that Monsieur de la Roche-Maubert, instead of fleeing, began instead to swim toward the boat. Two minutes later, he was clinging to an oar that was held out to him.

Then he looked at the men who said that they were his friends.

All three were completely unknown to him. However, the one who was standing up, and appeared to be the leader said: "Truly? You're the Marquis de la Roche-Maubert?"

"Since you're my friends, you ought to know that," replied the Marquis—and he hoisted himself into the boat.

"We aren't exactly your friends," said the man who was standing, "But we've been paid by your friends to find you, and we've been surrounding that mysterious house for three nights..."

"Say that infernal house!" cried the Marquis, all his anger returning.

"So," the man went on, "we thought at first that it was one of the witch's henchmen escaping."

Then the Marquis told the three men, who were Porion himself and two of his agent, how he had succeeded in escaping. When he had finished, he added: "Oh! What protection Monseigneur le Régent is granting them..."

"Monseigneur le Régent won't be protecting anyone any longer," Porion replied.

"What!" said the Marquis. "What are you saying?"

"The truth."

"What! The Regent has resigned his power?"

"The Regent died last night, as he emerged from supper in Madame de Phalaris' boudoir," Porion replied.[26]

Monsieur de la Roche-Maubert uttered an exclamation.

"And Monsieur le Duc de Bourbon, Regent of France since this morning," Porion added, "has given orders for the witch and her accomplices to be arrested."

The Marquis was shivering, and the emotions through which he had passed in a matter of hours had developed into a kind of nervous fever.

"Where should we take you, Monsieur le Marquis?" asked Porion.

"Wherever you wish," he replied, "provided that I can get warm and change my clothes."

Porion gave an order, and the boat, moving rapidly upstream, passed under the Pont Saint-Michel and alongside the city, and stopped at the so-called terrace. There was a tavern there well-known to fishermen and mariners, which bore the sign *À la pomme d'or*. As the Marquis was rigid with cold, Porion and his men lent him the support of their arms and they went to knock on the door of the tavern.

Half an hour later, the Marquis as lying in a warm bed, and Porion said to him: "You'd do well, Monsieur le Marquis,

---

[26] Philippe d'Orléans died on 2 December 1723, after having supper with Madame de Phalaris at Versailles. This detail however, results in the story's factual background becoming badly confused. Cardinal Dubois was already dead by then, having died on 10 August 1723, and Philippe had stepped down as Regent when the king had been declared to have reached his majority in February 1723—at which point he had become First Minister. In order for the events to have taken place at all, therefore, they must have occurred prior to February 1723, at a date more in keeping with the one cited in the prologue. If the impossibility of this belated revision was pointed out to Ponson, it might help to explain the reasoning behind the abrupt and distinctly peculiar ending that he attached to the story.

to sleep for a few hours. Tomorrow, at daybreak, President Boisfleury will come to take your deposition."

"Who is President Boisfleury?" asked Monsieur de la Roche-Maubert.

"He's the magistrate who made it his mission to find you, without whose zeal your enemies might perhaps have escaped the punishment that awaits them."

"Ah!" said the Marquis. Then, looking at Porion, he said: "But instead of surrounding the house, why didn't you mount an assault on it?"

"Because we were afraid that the witch might have you murdered."

"That's true," said the Marquis. "I was a hostage."

"But now," Porion said, "I can promise you that within an hour, the witch and her accomplices, whom the Regent can no longer protect, will be in the hands of the law."

And Porion left, to put his promise into action.

VI

Porion had told the Marquis de la Roche-Maubert the truth. The Regent was dead.

That fact, which all of Paris had known since morning, was unknown the residents of the mysterious house in the Rue de l'Hirondelle.

How could that be? We shall explain briefly.

As you will recall, President Boisfleury, rebuffed by the Lieutenant of Police and then by the Regent had made a great fuss—but the Regent, whom Janine had taken into her confidence, and who was very fond of his friend the Chevalier d'Esparron, had sworn to protect them. He had, therefore, said to d'Esparron some time before: "I'll give you another week, and during that week, with the aid of the Lieutenant of Police, I promise you that no one will get into the house in the Rue de l'Hirondelle—but after that time, I can no longer guarantee anything. Make arrangements, therefore, to complete your work by then, and Janine and you can escape."

For his part, the Lieutenant of Police had summoned Porion.

Porion, who had committed himself body and soul to the service of the President, presented himself with an insolent attitude.

"Clown," the Lieutenant of Police had said to him, "listen carefully to what I have to say to you. You're making use of Parlement against us, but we have the Bastille at our disposal, and here's a *lettre de cachet* prepared for you."

"Monseigneur," Porion had relied, "I'm under the protection of Parlement."

"Outside of here, that's possible—but you'll see that I can have you arrested."

So saying, the Lieutenant of Police had called two runners, who had come to place themselves at Porion's sides.

"I'm caught," the police agent had murmured, resentfully.

"Unless you want to come to an arrangement with me. You serve whoever pays, don't you?"

"Yes," Porion replied, "and if Your Lordship had given me work, I wouldn't have gone to look for it elsewhere."

Then the Lieutenant of Police had proposed as singular transaction to Porion. He would promise that neither he nor his men would go into the house in the Rue de l'Hirondelle for a week, and to distract President Boisfleury with insignificant reports. After a week, he could do whatever he wanted. In exchange for that concession, he would receive the sum of two hundred pistols at the end of the week.

Porion, however, had what is known as a policeman's temperament. Although working for the money, he loved his work, and he had sworn to capture the pretended with and her accomplice, to find out what had become of the Marquis de la Roche-Maubert and what was to become of the Margrave, and he would not have renounced is mission for anything in the world. So, before agreeing to the lieutenant's conditions, he had made one restriction. He would not go into the house, but he would have it surrounded and arrest anyone who tried to go in or out.

The Lieutenant of Police had agreed to that clause.

The reason for that concession was quite simple. The lieutenant was sure that he could save Janine and the Chevalier d'Esparron on the last day. How? In the most natural fashion in the world, as we shall see.

The Lieutenant of Police knew, via the Regent, that a subterranean passage excavated under the house in the Rue de l'Hirondelle led to the Seine. Neither President Boisfleury nor Porion had any suspicion of that. It was, therefore, only necessary to do two things: firstly, to agree with the Chevalier d'Esparron that he would not leave the house, and secondly, to fix in advance the hour at which he and Janine would escape via the subterranean channel in a boat.

In that era, the police had established a security patrol on the Seine. A heavy boat manned by a troop of sergeants and archers, made a round by night to keep watch on the numerous vessels moored on the two banks. The boat would be ordered took take up a position at the agreed time at the entrance to the channel, and thus pick up the two fugitives, under the noses of Porion and his men, who would not have sufficient numbers to attempt their arrest.

As one can appreciate, it had all been well-planned. Unfortunately, the Chevalier d'Esparron, whom the Regent had informed of the Lieutenant's plan, replied that he needed to confer with Janine. It had then been agreed that a man would be sent to receive his orders, and that the man would enter by means of the channel rather than going to the door in the Rue de l'Hirondelle. In fact, a few hours after the Chevalier had gone in and freed Guillaume, whom he had found tied up, the man had presented himself. He was a vigorous fellow who could swim like a fish, and of whom the Lieutenant of Police was sure.

The man had come into the channel, and the Chevalier d'Esparron, who was waiting at the bottom of the stairway by means of which the Marquis de Roche-Maubert had escaped had said to him: "We'll be ready on Saturday, at midnight."

The man had started swimming again, but the moon was shining, and Porion, who was on watch at the Pont Saint-Michael, had seen him. Then Porion had understood that the house had another exit, to the river. Faithful to his agreement with the Lieutenant of Police, however, he had limited himself to placing a boat and two men at the entrance to the channel saying: "Monsieur le Lieutenant de Police will be disappointed when the week is up."

No one, therefore, had come out of the house since.

The following night, the Regent died suddenly as he emerged from supper.

Then Porion had found himself liberated, all the more so as the first concern of the Duc de Bourbon, having been proclaimed first minister, had been to sack the Lieutenant of Police.

However, the whole day had gone by without him daring to invade the house in the Rue de l'Hirondelle. As he had told the Marquis de la Riche-Maubert, he had been inhibited until then by the fear of what might befall the Marquis.

With the Marquis safe, Porion had no further need for hesitation, and he went into action, as we shall see.

VII

The Margrave had been unconscious for forty-eight hours.

His body had the rigidity of a corpse and his eyes were closed, but he was still alive. Not only was he alive, but he could hear. While paralyzing his other senses, the mysterious beverage that Janine had made him drink had left intact the sense of hearing, and had even sharpened it.

He was lying on his bed, and every two hours Janine pricked his arm with her golden pin, and he could hear his blood running noisily into the ewer that one of the negro children held.

And while his blood ran out, Janine said to him: "I want you to watch yourself die, wretch. I want your life to ebb away slowly, and for you to feel your last breath rising from your heart to your lips.

"Then, listen carefully to what will happen to us—to the Chevalier I adore and to me. When you're entirely dead, you'll be transported to your house, and physicians will affirm that you've succumbed to a malady from which you've been suffering for a long time. You'll be given a fine funeral, and you'll be regally buried.

"Then the testament will be opened by which you have established the Chevalier d'Esparron as your heir. Then the Chevalier and I will be married, and we shall go to live in Germany, in the principality that has become our domain, and we'll have masses said for you—futile masses, for your soul belongs to Satan, and he won't give it back!"

And Janine laughed as she spoke thus.

At the same time, she placed an apparatus on the Margrave's arm to interrupt the flow of blood.

The Chevalier shook his head sadly. "Janine, Janine," he said, "the man has been punished enough.—better to finish it off right away."

"No, no," she replied. "We still have five days ahead of us. The Regent is protecting us."

"Janine," said the Chevalier, again, "I have somber presentiments."

"What folly!"

"The Regent is protecting us but President Boisfleury has sworn to defeat us, and the house is surrounded."

"You know that when the police agents come in, we'll have gone," Jeanne replied.

But as she said that, there was a noise outside; the door of the room opened precipitately, and Guillaume came in, terrified.

"What is it?" said Janine.

"What's wrong?" asked the Chevalier.

"We're doomed!" Guillaume replied.

"Doomed!"

"Yes—the Marquis has escaped."

"That's impossible!" cried Janine.

"It's true—he's no longer in the cage. Come and see..."

Guillaume had a candlestick in his hand, and he had opened a door that led to the subterranean stairway. Janine and the Chevalier followed him into it.

Guillaume had told the truth; the Marquis was no longer in the cage, and it was easy to see which way he had gone.

"Well," said Janine, what does it matter? The Regent has promised us not to let anyone come in before the agreed date." And she went back up to the room where the Margrave was still lying.

There were two other people there, however, no less distressed: Madame Edwige and the young woman who had played the role of the Oriental princess.

"Someone's in the house," said Madame Edwige. "Can you hear them?"

Indeed, muffled noises were resounding above their heads, and it was easy to deduce that the upper floors of the house had been invaded by a troop of men who, not having found the secret passage in the fireplace, had started attacking the floorboards with axes.[27]

D'Esparron had drawn his sword and placed himself in front of Janine—but Janine, entirely intent on her vengeance, cried: "At least they won't take the Margrave alive!"

She tore away the bandage, and the blood began to flow again. At the same time, she pricked two other veins with her pin.

The sound of ax-blows became more distinct. Madame Edwige and the young woman, mad with terror had fallen to their knees.

The Chevalier and Guillaume had placed themselves in front of Janine in order to defend her.

As for the immortal woman, she watched the Margrave's blood running with a somber joy.

Suddenly, the ceiling of the room trembled, and a large piece of woodwork flew into splinters. At the same time, a troop of armed men irrupted into the room.

Porion was marching at their head.

"In the name of the King," he said, "arrest all these wretches!"

A man with small eyes sparkling with joy was at the side of Porion, the vile police agent. That man, as you can guess, was President Boisfleury.

"This will be a fine criminal case," he said.

The Chevalier charged the assailants, épée in hand, but he received ten dagger-thrusts and fell, crying: "The Regent will avenge me!"

"The Regent is dead," Porion replied, "and we're here on the orders of Monseigneur le Duc de Bourbon, the First Minister!"

---

[27] The author also seems to have forgotten that the subterranean working are not underneath the house in which Guillaume was as resident but the one next door, and hence inaccessible by this means.

VIII

The Chevalier d'Esparron had fallen, pierced with stab-wounds, but none of his wounds was mortal. Confided to the care of skillful surgeons, he was in a fit condition, three weeks later, to appear before the judges in company with Janine.

It was a criminal trial that impassioned the city and the court.

Conrad, Madame Edwige, the young Italian woman were accused of complicity in murder—for, as one can imagine, the Margrave was dead.

The Marquis de Roche-Maubert and President Boisfleury distinguished themselves by their ardor against Janine and the Chevalier.

The Marquis told the story of his torture and captivity with a savage eloquence; he maintained that Janine was a witch and a vampire, that she drank human blood and that she had found a means to live forever. He even permitted himself to give some advice to the members of the Parlement.

"Forty years ago," he said, "all possible precautions were taken to ensure that the witch would not escape her fate; however, she was burned in vain, since you have her before you. My advice, therefore, is to have her decapitated before burning her, for fire belongs to Satan, and Satan is this woman's friend."

The Parlement paid no heed to the hateful old man's advice.

The Chevalier d'Esparron did not deign to defend himself. He loved Janine and wanted to share her fate.

The Parlement returned a verdict that condemned the steward Conrad and Madame Edwige to life imprisonment. The young Italian woman, the negro children and the old man who had played the role of Mufti were acquitted. The Chevalier d'Esparron and Janine were sentenced to be burned alive.

On the eve of the execution, however, something strange happened.

Madame Edwige and Conrad were found to have vanished from their cell.

How had they escaped? No one could determine that.

The next day, the Chevalier and Janine were led to execution, barefoot, clad in chemises, with candles in their hands.

The sky was laden with thick black clouds, torn repeatedly by hectic lightning-flashes.,

When the condemned couple had been tied to the same stake, the executioner threw a flaming torch on to the pyre. The flames crackled, and thick smoke rose up and enveloped the two lovers.

Suddenly, however, the clouds burst. A bolt of lightning killed the executioner and dispersed the crowd. The rain that began to fall in torrents extinguished the fire, and it was claimed that Satan had shown himself, standing over the pyre with an ax in his hand, and had cut the bonds of Janine and the Chevalier, who descended tranquilly from their scaffold, holding hands, without the archers or the curious watchers, paralyzed by the thunderbolt, thinking of barring their passage.

EPILOGUE

Such is the denouement of this absurd story, which I found in its entirety in a book printed in The Hague in 1760.

The d'Esparron family in one of the best-known families in Provence, and the Marquis of that name lives in a small village in the Basses-Alpes.

I sent him the volume, asking for an explanation. This is his response:

Monsieur,

I have consulted my family papers, interrogated my childhood memories and the tales of my forefathers. No Chevalier d'Esparron was ever condemned to the pyre.

Yours very humbly,

Marquis d'Esparron

The archives of the Parlement make not the slightest mention of the trial of the immortal woman, and the custody records of the Châtelet do not mention it either.

However, according to the little book printed in The Hague, the affair impassioned the court and the city—and I was going over and over my two volumes, searching for the key to the mystery, when a few words written by hand inside the front cover caught my attention:

This book belongs to the library of the House of the Fathers of Saint Jean de Dieu at Charenton. They were signed *Decoulmier.*[28]

---

[28] The French order of the Frères de Saint Jean de Dieu, named for a sixteenth century Portugueuse hospital-founder, were also known as the Frères de la Charité. They founded Charenton lunatic asylum in 1645. Abbé François de Coulmier

Abbé Decoulmier had been the first director of the House at Charenton when it was reconstituted and passed from the hands of the Brothers of Saint Jean de Dieu to the civil administration.

Charenton has conserved its archives, and it is thanks to the kindness of a senior functionary that I obtained the key to the enigma.

In 1734,[29] by order of the King and by virtue of a *lettre de cachet*, a poor devil of a junior clerk named Boisfleury was interned at Charenton. The madness of that worthy man consisted of believing himself to be the President of the Criminal Court, charged with finding conspirators and called to render great services to the State.

He even wore a red robe at home, and the people of the Rue de la Vrillière, where he lived, took a malign pleasure in calling him "Monsieur le Président."

The said Boisfleury had a maidservant whose robust feminine charms had succeeded in tempting an unfortunate Gascon cadet named Castirac.

In order to introduce himself into the house, this Castirac had come to an understanding with two scoundrels and, taking Boisfleury seriously, had told him a story of witchcraft and vampirism, which, he said, was preoccupying all of Paris.

Boisfleury lost his mind completely. He went out in his red robe, went to see several lords, who threw him out, then had himself thrown out of the Palais, and, in the end, was imprisoned at Charenton, confided to the Brothers of Saint Jean de Dieu.

There he wrote a memoir, which was nothing other than the Gascon Castirac's story, embellished by the numerous resources of his crazed imagination.

---

became director of the institution in the early 19th century, under Napoléon I.

[29] This date is, of course, blatantly inconsistent with either of those given earlier in the story, but that might be deliberate, in order to emphasize Boisfleury's supposed insanity.

Boisfleury died in 1752; his madness had lasted eighteen years.

A prisoner at Charenton who was not mad, but had displeased Madame de Pompadour, succeeded in escaping. He took away Boisfleury's manuscript, which had fallen into his possession, had it printed in The Hague, and sent a copy to the Brothers of Saint Jean de Dieu at their House at Charenton.

And that, my dear readers, is how I came to relate to you, with the best will in the world, a story in which there is not a word of truth.

Forgive a trickster, for he has been tricked himself.

SF & FANTASY

Henri Allorge. *The Great Cataclysm*
Guy d'Armen. *Doc Ardan: The City of Gold and Lepers*
G.-J. Arnaud. *The Ice Company*
Charles Asselineau. *The Double Life*
Cyprien Bérard. *The Vampire Lord Ruthwen*
Aloysius Bertrand. *Gaspard de la Nuit*
Richard Bessière. *The Gardens of the Apocalypse*
Albert Bleunard. *Ever Smaller*
Félix Bodin. *The Novel of the Future*
Louis Boussenard. *Monsieur Synthesis*
Alphonse Brown. *City of Glass; The Conquest of the Air*
André Caroff. *The Terror of Madame Atomos; Miss Atomos; The Return of Madame Atomos; The Mistake of Madame Atomos; The Monsters of Madame Atomos; The Revenge of Madame Atomos; The Resurrection of Madame Atomos*
Félicien Champsaur. *The Human Arrow; Ouha, King of the Apes; Pharaoh's Wife*
Didier de Chousy. *Ignis*
Captain Danrit. *Undersea Odyssey*
C. I. Defontenay. *Star (Psi Cassiopeia)*
Charles Derennes. *The People of the Pole*
Georges Dodds (anthologist). *The Missing Link*
Harry Dickson. *The Heir of Dracula*
Jules Dornay. *Lord Ruthven Begins*
Alfred Driou. *The Adventures of a Parisian Aeronaut*
Sâr Dubnotal *vs. Jack the Ripper*
Alexandre Dumas. *The Return of Lord Ruthven*
Renée Dunan. *Baal*
J.-C. Dunyach. *The Night Orchid; The Thieves of Silence*
Henri Duvernois. *The Man Who Found Himself*
Achille Eyraud. *Voyage to Venus*
Henri Falk. *The Age of Lead*
Paul Féval. *Anne of the Isles; Knightshade; Revenants; Vampire City; The Vampire Countess; The Wandering Jew's Daughter*
Paul Féval, *fils. Felifax, the Tiger-Man*
Charles de Fieux. *Lamékis*
Arnould Galopin. *Doctor Omega*; *Doctor Omega and the Shadowmen*

Judith Gautier. *Isoline and the Serpent-Flower*
Léon Gozlan. *The Vampire of the Val-de-Grâce*
G.L. Gick. *Harry Dickson and the Werewolf of Rutherford Grange*
Edmond Haraucourt. *Illusions of Immortality*
Nathalie Henneberg. *The Green Gods*
V. Hugo, P. Foucher & P. Meurice. *The Hunchback of Notre-Dame*
Romain d'Huissier. *Hexagon: Dark Matter*
Michel Jeury. *Chronolysis*
Gustave Kahn. *The Tale of Gold and Silence*
Gérard Klein. *The Mote in Time's Eye*
Fernand Kolney. *Love in 5000 Years*
Louis-Guillaume de La Follie. *The Unpretentious Philosopher*
Jean de La Hire. *Enter the Nyctalope; The Nyctalope on Mars; The Nyctalope vs. Lucifer; The Nyctalope Steps In; Night of the Nyctalope*
Etienne-Léon de Lamothe-Langon. *The Virgin Vampire*
André Laurie. *Spiridon*
Gabriel de Lautrec. *The Vengeance of the Oval Portrait*
Alain le Drimeur. *The Future City*
Georges Le Faure & Henri de Graffigny. *The Extraordinary Adventures of a Russian Scientist Across the Solar System* (2 vols.)
Gustave Le Rouge. *The Vampires of Mars; The Dominion of the World* (w/Gustave Guitton) (4 vols.)
Jules Lermina. *Mysteryville; Panic in Paris; To-Ho and the Gold Destroyers; The Secret of Zippelius*
Jean-Marc & Randy Lofficier. *Edgar Allan Poe on Mars; The Katrina Protocol; Pacifica; Robonocchio; Tales of the Shadowmen 1-9*
Xavier Mauméjean. *The League of Heroes*
Joseph Méry. *The Tower of Destiny*
Hippolyte Mettais. *The Year 5865*
Louise Michel. *The Human Microbes; The New World*
Tony Moilin. *Paris in the Year 2000*
José Moselli. *Illa's End*
John-Antoine Nau. *Enemy Force*
Marie Nizet. *Captain Vampire*
C. Nodier, A. Beraud & Toussaint-Merle. *Frankenstein*
Henri de Parville. *An Inhabitant of the Planet Mars*
Gaston de Pawlowski. *Journey to the Land of the 4th Dimension*
Georges Pellerin. *The World in 2000 Years*
Ernest Pérochon. *The Frenetic People*
Pierre Pelot. *The Child Who Walked on the Sky*
J. Polidori, C. Nodier, E. Scribe. *Lord Ruthven the Vampire*

P.-A. Ponson du Terrail. *The Vampire and the Devil's Son; The Immortal Woman*

Henri de Régnier. *A Surfeit of Mirrors*

Maurice Renard. *The Blue Peril; Doctor Lerne; The Doctored Man; A Man Among the Microbes; The Master of Light*

Jean Richepin. *The Wing; The Crazy Corner*

Albert Robida. *The Adventures of Saturnin Farandoul; The Clock of the Centuries; Chalet in the Sky*

J.-H. Rosny Aîné. *Helgvor of the Blue River; The Givreuse Enigma; The Mysterious Force; The Navigators of Space; Vamireh; The World of the Variants; The Young Vampire*

Marcel Rouff. *Journey to the Inverted World*

Han Ryner. *The Superhumans*

Brian Stableford. *The New Faust at the Tragicomique;The Empire of the Necromancers (The Shadow of Frankenstein; Frankenstein and the Vampire Countess; Frankenstein in London); Sherlock Holmes & The Vampires of Eternity; The Stones of Camelot; The Wayward Muse.* (anthologist) *The Germans on Venus; News from the Moon; The Supreme Progress; The World Above the World; Nemoville; Investigations of the Future*

Jacques Spitz. *The Eye of Purgatory*

Kurt Steiner. *Ortog*

Eugène Thébault. *Radio-Terror*

C.-F. Tiphaigne de La Roche. *Amilec*

Théo Varlet. *The Golden Rock. The Xenobiotic Invasion; The Castaways of Eros; Timeslip Troopers* (w/André Blandin); *The Martian Epic* (w/Octave Joncquel)

Paul Vibert. *The Mysterious Fluid*

Villiers de l'Isle-Adam. *The Scaffold; The Vampire Soul*

Philippe Ward. *Artahe*

Philippe Ward & Sylvie Miller. *The Song of Montségur*

MYSTERIES & THRILLERS

M. Allain & P. Souvestre. *The Daughter of Fantômas*

A. Anicet-Bourgeois, Lucien Dabril. *Rocambole*

A. Bernède. *Belphegor; Judex* (w/Louis Feuillade); *The Return of Judex* (w/Louis Feuillade)

A. Bisson & G. Livet. *Nick Carter vs. Fantômas*

V. Darlay & H. de Gorsse. *Arsène Lupin vs. Sherlock Holmes: The Stage Play*

Séamas Duffy. *Sherlock Holmes in Paris*

Paul Féval. *Gentlemen of the Night; John Devil; The Black Coats ('Salem Street; The Invisible Weapon; The Parisian Jungle; The Companions of the Treasure; Heart of Steel; The Cadet Gang; The Sword-Swallower)*

Emile Gaboriau. *Monsieur Lecoq*

Goron & Emile Gautier. *Spawn of the Penitentiary*

Steve Leadley. *Sherlock Holmes: The Circle of Blood*

Maurice Leblanc. *Arsène Lupin vs. Countess Cagliostro; Arsène Lupin vs. Sherlock Holmes (The Blonde Phantom; The Hollow Needle); The Many Faces of Arsène Lupin*

Gaston Leroux. *Chéri-Bibi; The Phantom of the Opera; Rouletabille & the Mystery of the Yellow Room; Rouletabille at Krupp's*

Richard Marsh. *The Complete Adventures of Judith Lee*

William Patrick Maynard. *The Terror of Fu Manchu; The Destiny of Fu Manchu*

Frank J. Morlock. *Sherlock Holmes: The Grand Horizontals; Sherlock Holmes vs Jack the Ripper*

Antonin Reschal. *The Adventures of Miss Boston*

P. de Wattyne & Y. Walter. *Sherlock Holmes vs. Fantômas*

David White. *Fantômas in America*

SCREENPLAYS

Mike Baron. *The Iron Triangle*

Emma Bull & Will Shetterly. *Nightspeeder; War for the Oaks*

Gerry Conway & Roy Thomas. *Doc Dynamo*

Steve Englehart. *Majorca*

James Hudnall. *The Devastator*

Jean-Marc & Randy Lofficier. *Royal Flush*

J.-M. & R. Lofficier & Marc Agapit. *Despair*

J.-M. & R. Lofficier & Joël Houssin. *City*

Andrew Paquette. *Peripheral Vision*

Robert L. Robinson, Jr. *Judex*

R. Thomas, J. Hendler & L. Sprague de Camp. *Rivers of Time*